More Praise for *Friends and Lovers* . 09/2020

"Recommended. . . . Dickey uses humor, poignancy and a fresh, creative writing style . . . connects the story line to believable real-life issues."   —*USA Today*

"What distinguishes Dickey from the pack is his hip prose, which crackles with wit and all the rhythm of an intoxicatingly funky rap."   —*Cincinnati Enquirer*

"Engaging, dynamic, skillful."   —*Publishers Weekly*

"Real characters and invigorating, believable dialogue."
—*Kirkus Reviews*

"Written with wit and sarcasm . . . ultimately produces both laughter and tears."   —*Cleveland Plain Dealer*

"With his trademark sharp wit, genuine characters, and real-life issues, Dickey delivers a sexy, searing novel of betrayal, love, and friendship."   —*Inland Valley News*, CA

"Dickey has crafted another fine novel of love and friendship."
—*Library Journal*

"Dickey has done a remarkable job of being not only perceptive but also witty and moving in his portrayal of relationships."   —*Booklist*

(continued on next page . . .)

Praise for *Cheaters* . . .

"This is a book about dawgs. Not dogs, but d-a-w-g-s. Cheatin', lyin', no-good, no-'count, dirty lowdown mendawgs and womendawgs. . . . You can't read *Cheaters* without becoming an active participant. You easily find yourself turning a page, shaking your head, and tsk-tsking."
—*Los Angeles Times*

"What gives the book a compelling edge is the characters' self-discovery. . . . Thankfully, Dickey often goes beyond the 'men are dogs and women are victims' stereotype." —*USA Today*

"Wonderfully written. . . . Each character's voice [is] smooth, unique and genuine." —*Washington Post Book World*

"Hot, sexy and funny. . . . *Cheaters* not only makes readers examine their own behavior but keeps them laughing while doing so." —*Library Journal*

"Dickey's prose is poetic and sings with fluency."
—*Detroit Free Press*

"Captivating . . . plenty of sin, sex, and steam."
—*Durham Herald-Sun*

"A deftly crafted tale about the games people play and the lies they tell on their search for love." —*Ebony*

"A generous helping of humor and a distinctly male viewpoint." —*Atlanta Journal & Constitution*

"Sprinkles raw, street-savvy humor on almost every page."
—*Publishers Weekly*

(continued on next page . . .)

Praise for *Sister, Sister* . . .

"Dickey imagines [his characters] with affection and sympathy. . . . His novel achieves genuine emotional depth."
—*Boston Globe*

"Vibrant . . . marks the debut of a true talent."
—*Atlanta Journal & Constitution*

"A hip, sexy, wisecracking tale."   —*New York Beacon*

"Bold and sassy . . . brims with humor, outrageousness and . . . affection."   —*Publishers Weekly*

"Dickey is able both to create believable female characters and to explore the 'sister-sister' relationship with genuine insight."
—*Booklist*

"A good summer read you won't be able to put down. . . . Depicts a hard-edged reality in which women sometimes have their dreams shattered, yet never stop embracing tomorrow."
—*St. Louis Post-Dispatch*

"Spirited, successful. . . . Dickey is a witty observant cousin to such writers as Terry McMillan and Connie Briscoe."
—*Kirkus Reviews*

"Will captivate your fancy . . . an engaging read."
—*Cincinnati Herald*

"One of the most intuitive and hilarious voices in African-American fiction."   —*St. Louis American*

"There's a little sumthin', sumthin' in this book we can all relate to. Buy the novel, read it. Relate. Relax. Release."
—*Crusader Urban News*

Also by Eric Jerome Dickey

Liar's Game
Cheaters
Milk in My Coffee
Sister, Sister

ERIC JEROME DICKEY

FRIENDS

AND

LOVERS

 NEW AMERICAN LIBRARY

New American Library
Published by New American Library, a division of Penguin Group (USA) Inc.,
375 Hudson Street, New York, New York 10014, USA
Penguin Group (Canada), 90 Eglinton Avenue East, Suite 700, Toronto,
Ontario, Canada M4P 2Y3 (a division of Pearson Penguin Canada Inc.)
Penguin Books Ltd., 80 Strand, London WC2R 0RL, England
Penguin Ireland, 25 St. Stephen's Green, Dublin 2,
Ireland (a division of Penguin Books Ltd.)
Penguin Group (Australia), 250 Camberwell Road, Camberwell, Victoria 3124,
Australia (a division of Pearson Australia Group Pty. Ltd.)
Penguin Books India Pvt. Ltd., 11 Community Centre, Panchsheel Park,
New Delhi – 110 017, India
Penguin Group (NZ), 67 Apollo Drive, Rosedale, North Shore 0632,
New Zealand (a division of Pearson New Zealand Ltd.)
Penguin Books (South Africa) (Pty.) Ltd., 24 Sturdee Avenue,
Rosebank, Johannesburg 2196, South Africa

Penguin Books Ltd., Registered Offices: 80 Strand, London WC2R 0RL, England

Published by New American Library, a division of Penguin Group (USA) Inc. Previously
published in Dutton and Signet editions.

First New American Library Printing, May 2000
20   19   18

Copyright © Eric Jerome Dickey, 1997
All rights reserved

REGISTERED TRADEMARK—MARCA REGISTRADA

New American Library Trade Paperback ISBN: 978-0-451-20102-7

The Library of Congress has cataloged the hardcover edition of this title as follows:

Dickey, Eric Jerome.
Friends and lovers / Eric Jerome Dickey.
   p.   cm.
ISBN 0-525-94127-4
I. Title
PS3554.I319 F75   1997
813'.54—dc21   97-23040

Printed in the United States of America

For Karla with a K

beautiful woman with dignified hair
a face that blushes like an intelligent schoolgirl

see ya at the top of Valley Ridge

ACKNOWLEDGMENTS

I want to thank everybody who helped me out along the way.

My friends who are better than sunshine on a cloudy day—Brenda Denise Stinson, Chiquita, Gina, April, Danielle, Tiffany Royster.

My family—Mrs. Virgina Jerry, Keith and Monica Pigues, Kevin Pigues, and the rest of the crew.

Dwayne and the running crew. "All right, all right."

And to my editor, Audrey LaFehr. Thanks for the faith.

Thanks to Sara Camilli, my agent.

Tyrone, Delia, Taylor, Devin. Hugs and kisses.

Thanks to Robert "Bobby" Laird for your support.

Special thanks to Shirley "The poetry lady" Harris. Keep pen to paper at all times.

Special thanks to Audrey Cooper, a brother, a true friend.

Special, special thanks to Karla Denise Greene, Esq. You are truly an inspiration! (And thanks for the tuna!)

Okay, okay. If I accidentally forgot ya, fill it in below.

Thanks _____ for whatever you did to make this possible.

PART ONE

GOOD-BYES AND HELLOS

TYREL

1

If all I knew about how to treat a woman was based on what I learned from watching my daddy and the way he mistreated women, then I wouldn't know a damn thing worth knowing.

Daddy's first store was a little grocery store in South Central. He went there from sunup to sundown, every day of the week, took money, and made more money with money he took. That was where I inherited my business sense. Daddy provided for his family.

And others.

I'd see all of my daddy's girlfriends-of-the-week come and stand around and flirt and eat for free. He'd even take money out of the register and give them a scrap or two. I wouldn't speak to any of them. Neither would my twin sister, Mye. We call each other Twin. Momma never came over to the store from our house. Never. Not even the time one of the stores caught on fire. She had a look in the corner of her eye that said she wished the whole store had burned to the ground. I guess she knew what was going on before Mye told all. Momma had to know. No way a man could carry on like that for years and she wouldn't know.

By the time I graduated from Crenshaw High, Daddy had three stores. After school, me and Twin used to work

3

the stores. Me and Pops were at odds because I couldn't really handle the situation, but Mye knew how to put the women in check. Gave them all a hard time when they came by expecting something free. What I learned about women being good and strong, I learned from watching my own mother. She had serious resilience. Character and integrity. If it wasn't for the respect I have for Momma, the way she put me in check whenever I did something disrespectful, I'd be just like my daddy.

When me and Twin went to college and rented an apartment in Leimert Park—I went to CSULA with Leonard, and Twin went to UCLA—I guess Momma and Daddy figured we were grown, on our own, could handle the rent and the truth that we, the neighborhood, and the church already knew. After being married on paper for thirty years, they moved out of their separate bedrooms, packed up separate U-Hauls, and went their separate ways. Without a quarrel or a kiss good-bye. He sold the stores, the house, pretty much sold out of our lives, and went to Nashville. Momma bought a condo in Diamond Bar, but went to Chicago for a weekend and didn't come back. Twin fell in love with one of her law school professors—an older brother—and jumped the broom.

I'm still in Los Angeles. Wondering when I'll start my own family . . . When I'll do it right, like my twin has done.

That's what I was thinking about this morning when my financial planner said she could finally meet me for lunch. Only today she wasn't my financial planner. Lisa Nichols was the sister who had been avoiding me for the last two weeks. Which was fine. Because that two weeks had given me enough time to cool off. Enough time to play the message she'd left on my machine over and over. Gave reality a chance to waft in and thicken.

Hi, Tyrel. This is Lisa giving you a call. It's 12:38, Tuesday afternoon. Awkward moment last night, yes.

Ahem. Wanted to tell you, wanted to tell you, ahem, I wanted to tell you in person, that I was seeing Rick again and, ahem, didn't get the opportunity to because you didn't, well I guess I didn't get to page you because I had to go to a possible meeting and, well, plan a briefing, so, didn't get to talk to you and didn't think I was going to hear from you last night, so, kind of awkward with, ah, huh, my husband right beside me, so, anyway I did want to tell you and let you know and, you know, because you're a friend and sorry you had to find out that way, so, didn't mean to hang up on you. I dunno. I dunno what this does to our friendship. I mean not intimacy, but like friendship friendship. So, I dunno. If you don't want me to call you let me know. Just talk to you later. 'Bye.

I was at a Mandarin fast-food restaurant on Fairfax and Slauson. The place was crowded with blue-collar Mexicans and blacks and Asians ordering the three-dollar lunch special. Most people stuck their food in a bag and left. The booth I was in gave me a view of Home Base, LA Hot Wings, and a 76 gas station. I had been waiting since eleven fifteen. Lisa pulled up in her Volvo wagon a few minutes after twelve. Her first time being late. She parked facing me. We were eye to eye. I nodded. She nodded. She opened her door, sat there a moment like she was contemplating coming inside; then at last she eased out. Took a hard breath, shivered despite the heat, had a let's-get-this-over-with attitude under her hard expression.

She stood next to her car like she was some sort of diva de jour, her back to the gas station and oil fields, dark shades hiding what I could already see. Uneasiness in her breathing. Mahogany skin, slender, pageboy haircut, blue pinstripe pantsuit, dark Ferragamos, diamond earrings, wedding ring.

I nodded. No smile. Just a nod.

She adjusted her jacket, moved her hair from her face, adjusted her purse on her shoulder, took a fidgety step in my direction.

Inside my head I heard her voice, echoes from the message she had left on my machine the morning after the incident. She didn't have the nerve to call me at home. And I've never missed a day of work since I was old enough to work.

She had chopped her hair off since last we freaked and fled, had traded the Miata and bought a family Volvo wagon, changed her hair and the color of her nails. Lisa sat down at the table and smiled at me like I was a customer at the DMV. The smell of her perfume sweetened the bitter taste in my mouth.

She said, "You order?"

"Yeah. Broccoli and chicken. I ordered you the usual."

"I'm not really hungry enough to eat a combo."

"Take it with you."

She opened her purse and slid me a five-dollar bill. I opened my wallet and handed her a dollar.

Her eyes darted left to right. "Would you mind if we moved to a table not facing Slauson?"

"Why?"

"Because."

"Where?"

"Back over in the corner."

We moved where we couldn't be seen from the streets. When we were settled, I said, "How are the kids?"

She cleared her throat. "Malik and Jasmine are fine."

I didn't know why I asked about her children, especially since I'd never met them. I knew that question, that dose of reality would make her uneasy. She acted like her children were her shame. They were with her husband. When she left him six months ago, he kept the kids and the house in View Park. Their place was right next to the Ray

Charles mansion. She moved into the condo overlooking the Pacific in Hermosa Beach.

The Asian man who ran the business brought our trays to us.

He gave a brief bow and said, "How are you, Tyrel and Lisa? Nice to see you."

We spoke. He left. Smiling, rushing to the next customer.

Like me, the food was silently steaming. Lisa grabbed her chopsticks and started eating at a hundred miles an hour. Head down, shoulders square and forward. Kept her eyes on her plate.

I said, "Thought you weren't hungry."

"Nerves."

Neither one of us said anything for a while. Ate and thought. Made me wonder if everything to say had already been said. Or if what needed to be said wasn't really worth saying.

The first thing Lisa said when she finished was, "It's best for my children."

I nodded. That was a tired line. Damn tired.

She said, "I hate it when you shut down like that."

"Hard to talk in a fucked-up situation."

"How do you feel about it? Don't shut me out, Tyrel."

"Oh, now you want to be a therapist?"

"I've never been in a situation like this."

"Ball's in your court. What do you feel?"

She shifted. "Lonely. I have to make this decision myself."

I said, "Actually, since you've got your husband in your bed, you're already out the door. I just want to know what happened so I don't make the same mistake twice."

Her tone was lean when she repeated, "Mistake."

"What would you call it? Or was I just Mr. T?"

"Mr. T?"

"Mr. Transitional. The transitional man."

"No. It wasn't like that. Everything was going fine until we had that scary incident two weeks ago last Monday."

"When I left work early and met you at the Hilton?"

"Yeah, when I rented the room. When your damn condom came off."

"And you freaked out."

"I didn't freak out. Reality of what I was doing hit home."

"You screamed, fell on the floor, kicked the wall, ran around the room, locked yourself in the bathroom, and cried 'Why me?' for a while."

"Okay, I freaked out. I was upset. I mean, you're nice and I care about you, but I could've gotten pregnant."

"Would that have been so bad? You know I want to have kids."

"And I don't want to have any more kids."

"You're only twenty-nine."

"Twenty-nine, with two children, and I'm done having babies. And I don't want to have a house filled with babies by different daddies. That's ghetto. I don't want to have to explain to my five- and seven-year-olds why their mother is having another child by a man other than their father, a man I'm not married to. Shit, I have a daughter. That could change her value system."

"What about your son's value system?"

She blinked. Mouth was halfway open. She swallowed. Tapped the table with the tips of her nails. A don't-do-this-to-me gaze was in her eyes. She said, "It's already hard enough explaining to them why their father and I aren't together."

"How did you end up back with your husband?"

"It wasn't planned."

"But it wasn't as out of the question as you made it sound."

"I was mad then."

"Uh-huh."

"He'd fucked me over with seeing the kids. He'd tell me I could see them on the weekend, and when I got there, he'd be gone all day, then say he forgot I was coming to get them."

"I'm talking about you and him re-consummating the night after you were consummating with me."

"You know how I feel about him. I don't need a man who feels threatened every time I do a little bit better for myself."

"But you're going back."

"You know how it is."

"I wouldn't know. Monday you're telling me how you despise him because of custody. Tuesday you're hanging up on me."

"That moment the condom came off put things in perspective. I have a family, and I don't think it's right for me to not give it a second try."

"A third try."

"Okay, a third try."

"Do you love your husband?"

"He's my husband. I don't have to love him."

I laughed.

Lisa asked, "What's funny?"

"That put things in perspective for me."

All I needed was closure. And this relationship that never was a relationship was closed. If she never wanted to have any more kids, then this was a dead end. Now I needed to move on to single, sane, and stable sisters.

She said, "How's your friend Leonard doing?"

"He's fine."

"I think I heard his name on KJLH. He's supposed to be at the Color of Comedy or something."

I shrugged. "Haven't talked to him in a couple of weeks."

"I saw him on some sitcom. He's still on the road?"

"Yeah. Comedy is keeping him busy. He's back from D.C. and doing a show on Sunset this weekend." I paused. "You know I had already bought tickets for me and you to go to the Playboy Jazz Festival this week."

"I know."

"And I had bought us box seats. One hundred a ticket."

She rubbed her neck and let out a weak, nervous laugh. "This means we won't be going. Not together anyway."

"You're going?"

"Yeah. Me and my husband are going."

"Oh. You two have tickets already?"

"Uh, yeah. We're taking the children. You still going?"

I shrugged. "If I can hook up with Leonard. Maybe I'll get him to go so I won't be throwing my money away."

"I could reimburse you."

"You've done enough already."

Before she could adjust her tense mood, or reach for her tan-colored Coach handbag, I flipped to a business tone and talked about who was going to handle my finances.

She said, "I can still handle your portfolio. I have no problem dealing on a professional level. That's how we started out. It could work. We wouldn't have that much contact."

"I'm not comfortable with trusting you right now."

"Business is business."

"And the rest is bullshit."

"Right. I handle my business. I've never mishandled yours."

I took the trays to the trash, emptied them. We headed for the door. Outside in the heat, she put her shades on. I put mine on too. L.A. felt small today.

I said, "I want you to know, I don't have a problem with your being responsible and putting your children's welfare in front of your social life. I just don't like being the last to know what's going on. I don't like decisions being made without me."

"What you're saying is you like to maintain your control."

I didn't answer. The underlying accusation pierced and stung. Looking at my watch gave me a moment to ease my mood.

She touched my hand and asked, "You want to get a room?"

"One for the road?"

"No. I mean, we can go on seeing each other off and on. When it's convenient for the both of us. When we can get away."

"Sounds like you're trying to maintain your control."

"Not control. I'm not controlling. Just me missing you."

"Asking for a sperm donation?"

"That a yes or a no? We're good together like that."

"Jury's still out on the booty call."

She licked her upper lips, glanced at her shoes. Looked like she was about to go into a *PleaseBabyPleaseBaby-PleaseBabyBabyPlease* routine. She said, "You seeing somebody already?"

"Not your business."

"Are you?"

I didn't answer. I just said, "What about your kids?"

She shifted, pursed her lips. "Can I have an hour today?"

"I've gotta get back to work."

"Meeting?"

"Yeah. Another corporate tryst."

"Think about my offer. I'm free after six."

I moved my hand from her life. "Thanks for the offer."

"You're right. I don't know why I did that."

The pissed-off mood I had held back the entire lunch meeting seeped out as soon as I left. Coolness changed to fire. All around me were carloads of women. I drove like a demon, top down, shades on, necktie swinging in the winds. My charge to some kind of resented freedom was slowed by a red light by Pepperdine University and the 90 expressway.

A Range Rover stopped next to me. I peeped and saw a bucktoothed sister with a crooked weave, smiling like she was in nirvana. I pushed a button and let my convertible top up.

It was almost one. Leonard should be awake. I flipped open my cellular and called my buddy.

The first thing Leonard said was, "How did it go?"

We've been ace-coon since elementary. Outside of Twin, Leonard was the only person who knew me so well he could pick up my true mood from the first tone. I gave him the details.

He said, "You should've known that shit when she didn't call you back. How you feel about it?"

"I'm cool."

"Ty."

"Serious." I chuckled. "I'm cool."

"You know I'll snatch that weave out of her head and break both of her knees for you. She'll come crawling back."

We laughed. His phone beeped. It was the brother who books the Color of Comedy calling him about a show next Friday.

I said, "What are you doing later?"

"Speaking for a few minutes at one of those survivor of drug-abuse programs, hitting the Comedy Store to try and get on. The usual. Got time for the gym this eve?"

"Cool. Handle your business. See you at six."

Leonard said, "I'll check back with you in a couple of hours to make sure you ain't gone postal and hurt nobody."

"Do that."

"Learn to vent."

"I'm cool."

"See ya later, alligator."

"After a while, crocodile."

I hung up. My smile dropped; brotherly laughter faded in the winds the way smog did after a sweet summer rain.

SHELBY

2

I didn't want to go home because of the man who was sleeping in my bed. But Bryce should be sound asleep. Maybe I could crash without him putting his hands on me. Damn shame when a sister hated to go get in her own bought-and-paid-for bed.

The last leg of my flight was delayed big-time because of thunderstorms back east. It was about two in the morning in L.A.

So when the L1011 screeched and bounced on the runway, I gave all the passengers one generic bye-bye and kicked them out before the plane came to a complete stop. I grabbed my luggage-on-wheels, sprinted through the airport with my low heels *click-clopping* with each of my impatient strides. All I wanted to do was yank off this blue monkey suit they called a uniform, let my hair down, and kick my heels into a corner. Couldn't wait to get into my four-year-old 300ZX with the T-top, zoom home, crawl into *my* bed and crash on *my* brand-new mattress.

But like I said, there was a man sleeping in my bed. A

man I wasn't too fond of. I could tell Bryce the same thing thrice and he wouldn't remember when I had told him the first time. A few months back we started off as platonic roommates, but we slipped and crossed the line known as physical attraction.

Trust me, physical attraction and a couple of wine coolers at midnight is the perfect formula for regret. Once he was privileged with a sample of the juicy, it was obvious that was all he wanted. Juicy had him crazy. I never thought I was in love with him, but he told me he was falling in love with me. I know the only thing he was in love with was the act.

I should've cruised over to Debra's crib, but it was late and she went to sleep around eleven and woke up at five to do whatever people do that damn early in the morning. She was one of those people who woke up happy for no damn reason, reading the Bible, reading *Don't Block the Blessings*, music on, listening to social issues on *Front Page* on KJLH, bouncing around all chipper and sipping on hazelnut coffee. That's why I stopped rooming with her. Eight years of living with Ms. Happy-Go-Lucky had worked my nerves.

So the home I had for the moment was the only place I had to go. Back to Bryce's apartment on the other side of Fox Hills, right off the 405 and La Tijera. It's a nice gated damn-near-all African-American community of about five hundred about ten minutes from LAX with built-ins, high walls, a couple of eight-foot-deep swimming pools, Jacuzzi, beaucoup stuff that made the place cost an arm and a leg.

When I passed by the guard shack, the security sister in the booth was knocked out, sitting up, her peanut-shaped head tilted to the side, deep-deep-deep in her twelfth dream. I could have used my passcard and been through the automatic gate without her knowing it, but I stopped, tooted my horn, let my window down, belted out "Hey, girlfriend" a time or two. She didn't wake up.

I sighed, cussed to myself, and went over and tapped on the window. She still didn't move. So I grabbed the door handle and shook it as hard as I could. Kicked the base of the wooden door so hard the metal ID REQUIRED FOR ALL RESIDENTS: ALL VISITORS MUST SIGN IN AND OUT sign on the glass fell off and danced a jig on the floor. That scared her ass good. Sister-girl screamed so hard her braids went side to side and upside her head. Her eyes popped wide open, and she slipped off the stool and staggered left and right, like she'd woke up in the middle of an earthquake.

I said, "All right now."

She caught her breath. Held her jacket where her heart was. Talk about a drama queen in training.

Sister had to be all of twenty. She was under five feet, brown-skinned, with a thin nose that turned up. She adjusted her blue security jacket and looked around. Her petite size made me wonder what the hell her frail butt could do in case of emergency.

She said, "You scared me."

"Better me than somebody else. You know people are complaining about you guys falling asleep."

"I don't know when I nodded off."

"Most people don't. That's why it's called nodding off."

She let out a few nervous laughs. "It's boring down here."

"Don't you have a radio or something?"

"Nope. The one we had broke. I was reading *Essence*, and I guess I nodded off."

"Be careful."

Sister waved, looked embarrassed, yawned, rubbed her right eye, sat back on her barstool. I hopped in my Z, bounced over a couple of speed bumps, headed down into the garage. You know what? I love the way my tires *screech* when I make a sharp turn. Loved it so much, I backed up and *screech*ed again.

Bryce's Toyota truck was parked in our double space, but he hadn't pulled his truck all the way to the wall. We parked bumper to bumper facing the storage bins on the cinder block walls. That meant I had to get out of my car in the musty and dusty garage, and move his car up about three feet so nobody would clip the end of my car when they passed by. I've told him about parking like that over and over. Another one of life's inconveniences brought on by the inconsiderate.

I touched his truck's hood before I took out the extra keys and started it up. It was cold. He'd been home for a while.

Bryce is about five-nine and works at Northwest, loading planes, and part-time at the gym. LAX Family Fitness. He's a trainer-in-training, has an exciting body, but is boring as hell. I've given this living together thing three months—which was three months too long. It's almost like we don't live together because I'm flying city to city to city most of the time. So we only see each other a couple of times a week, less if I can help it. The bottom line? He ain't the one, the two, the three, the four, or the five.

When I walked in, Bryce was sitting up in his plaid boxer shorts, scratching his genitals, with the television on ESPN. His ass would probably be up half the night with the TV blasting. I was gonna say something to him about his car, but he always made me feel like I was making a big deal out of nothing.

I said, "You been home all evening?"

"Yeah."

"Anybody call?"

He was in the front room sitting in the leather lounge chair with his size-twelve feet stretched out on the ottoman. I didn't get a decent hello. He didn't bother to get up to give a sister a hug. I know he saw me struggling and didn't help me with my luggage. Guess that would be too much like right.

I repeated myself, "Anybody call?"

Bryce said, "Didn't you call and check the messages a few minutes ago?"

"Yeah."

"Then you know who called."

I heard one of my nerves *snap*. But like I always did when I was upset, I ran my fingers through my hair, twisted the mane on my neck by the roots like I was trying to pull tension out of my body, and counted backward from ten.

I said, "Bryce?"

He stood and strutted over to me. "Yeah?"

"I think it's time for me to move."

"When you leaving? You still have to pay for next month."

"Damn. That wasn't exactly the response I was expecting. Not at all. I thought you might at least ask how I was doing."

"You're the one who keeps saying that this isn't working."

"It isn't."

"Then when you leaving?"

"Bryce. Can I ask you something?"

"You're gonna anyway. Why you always ask if you can ask me a question?"

"Because when I do, you get that what-the-hell-does-she-want-now? look on your face. Like the one you have now."

"It's how you say it. Ask the stupid question."

I cringed when he said the s-word. That subtle insult had become part of his abusive vocabulary a bit too often. I have a degree in secondary education from USC, and this community-college-going bastard called me *stupid*? It took me two seconds to swallow my attitude and not go off. Part of my face smiled, but most of it didn't when I said a nasty, but not loud, "Why do my questions have to be stupid?"

"If you would think before you asked, then they wouldn't be."

"Never mind."

I went into the bathroom, took a quick shower, washed my face with Noxema, put on some Ambi, tied my hair back. Felt pressure in my temples. Closed my eyes for a few and held onto the edge of the counter. Counted backward from one hundred. Tapped my nails on the counter a few times. Tapped and thought and tapped.

When I went into the bedroom and clicked on the lights, I saw the bed was made up, but not the way I had made it up. I made a better bed than they did at the Hilton. Bryce would straighten out the green paisley sheets, pull the red-flowered comforter up so you couldn't tell how messed up the sheets really were. That was some improvement from what he used to do—nothing.

Then I checked the alarm, made sure it was set, and crawled in bed on my side. Closed my eyes. Took a deep breath. Inhaled like a bloodhound, over and over and over. Didn't believe I smelled what I smelled. Opened my eyes so wide it hurt my head. Took another deep breath and madness took over. All of the stuff that I was pissed off about didn't compare to what I was about to get pissed off about.

I smelled my pillow. Then I sniffed another pillow. The one I was on, the one on my side of the bed, reeked like some damn perfume. And the shit wasn't mine.

I hopped up and went back to the living room.

Bryce looked up from the television. He said, "What?"

"You're wrong, Bryce. Damn. I don't believe this."

"You want me to come to bed and hook you up, boo?"

"Boo?"

"You my boo, right?"

I stared at him for a few, then I went back into the bathroom. All of my brushes were in the same drawer, and I looked through each one of them. Found one with strands of hair that didn't match anybody's who lived in this house. Long hair. I plucked out a strand of mine, put them side by side. Not as dark or as thick as mine. And it felt like it had been disconnected from a weave. Either that or it wasn't from a sister.

I looked up.

You know how hair floats and gets stuck to the walls and ceiling and shower? Some of the same long black hair I had yanked out of my brush was on the ceiling.

Bryce was standing behind me. I kindly put four or five strands of the stray hair into his palm.

All I said was, "Not my hair, Bryce."

I turned the bedroom light on and yanked my comforter back. There was a dried up crusty patch of leftover love smack-dab in the middle of the sheets.

Bryce said, "It's not what you think—"

By then I had walked by him. I wasn't storming or being rude; my stride had a gentle stroll, kind of the way my girlfriend Debra always walked. I went to the kitchen, microwaved some hot water, mixed it with vanilla coffee, put it in a thermos, went to the closet and pulled out the CD boom box Bryce had given me a while ago. I had on boxers and a ribbed CK T-shirt. No shoes. My body was warm from the inside. The back of my neck was cranking up sweat. I grabbed my keys and headed for the door.

Bryce said, "Where you going in your pajamas with coffee and a radio?"

"To do some research."

I shuffled down three flights of stairs, across the complex, and went back to the guard's shack. The security sister was awake, but struggling with her eyelids. I tapped on the door; she jumped. She was scared as hell, probably because it was dark and I had crept up on her blind side. When she saw it was me she turned into bubbling brown sugar and opened the door.

She yawned and said, "I wasn't sleep—"

"Yeah, right."

She stretched and laughed.

I said, "Brought you something."

"Oh, girl, thank you so much."

"Can I step in for a few?"

"Yeah. Girl, what are you doing half-dressed like that? You could get raped walking around here like that."

"I've already been raped. Most of us have."

"Me, too. When I was twelve my uncle—"

"Not like that. What I'm talking about is that if you're sleeping with a man who is deceiving you, you're being raped. If a man misrepresents himself to get inside your shit, it's rape."

She was too busy with the thermos and plugging the radio in. I was too busy flipping through her log book, looking to see who had been let in the gate to come visit apartment E313—my unit.

The security sister said, "What you doing?"

I winked. "I didn't see you sleeping then, and you don't see me peeping now."

"Okay."

She turned her back and sipped coffee while she bobbed her head to rap coming from 92.3.

My fingers walked down every column. Date. Time. Name. I had left three days ago at noon. Nancy Zi had signed in around two p.m. the same afternoon. Signed out at nine p.m. tonight. See, that's what my butt gets for taping my work schedule to the front of the fridge. If a brother knows where you are and when, he will take advantage of it.

Nancy taught hip-hop, step aerobics up at the gym. Me

and Debra had been to her class a time or two. I flipped back to the last few times I was working. Nancy Zi had been signing in and out for a while. At least a month.

Ten minutes later, I was walking back into my apartment, gritting my teeth and thinking up new ways to kill a man. Bryce was hanging up the phone when I walked in. More like hung up midsentence when I slammed the door. I know that noise had to wake up a neighbor or two.

I said, "Who were you talking to this late?"

He said, "I was calling Debra to see if you went over there."

"Sure that wasn't Nancy from up at the gym?"

Bryce didn't say anything.

I breezed by him and picked up the phone.

Bryce said, "Who are you calling this late?"

I said, "Debra." I lied and pushed redial. When a wide-awake female answered I said, "Hello, Nancy."

She said, "Who is this?"

"Shelby. From the gym. From Bryce's bedroom. The one you popped your coochie in all week. Why didn't you at least change the sheets?"

I could imagine her little Asian-American butt freaking out when she shrieked, "Oh, my God! How did you get my number?"

"Oh, my God! Miracle of technology." I counted backward from five, exhaled and said, "Why did you screw in my bed? I'm not mad because you screwed Bryce. I just don't appreciate you doing it in my bed. You could've at least took him to your place."

When Nancy started talking like she was crazy, I handed Bryce the phone. By the time he hung up with her I had packed some clothes and taken my work uniforms out. Bryce stood over me while I gathered up a few pairs of shoes and stuffed my gym bag with Reeboks and T-shirts and spandex.

Bryce said, "This isn't all my fault."

"Of course it isn't. I had the remote for your dick and accidentally programmed it for the wrong vaginal channel."

"You haven't been the most affectionate sister I know."

I said, "Asian either, for that matter."

"If you took care of my needs, then that wouldn't have happened. You're always with Debra, don't have time for me."

"You know what? It don't matter. Because if we take fucking out of this relationship, which I already did, you see it ain't about shit. And I can't be in a relationship based on how much sex I give up."

"You ain't took care of my needs in over a month."

"And?"

"All I'm saying is compromise."

"Compromise?"

"Maybe we could do it on Monday and Wednesday and on the weekend."

I didn't believe what I was hearing. And he had the audacity to say it like it was the most logical thing in the world. You know, if I wanted to deal with children, I would've kept on being a teacher.

Bryce said, "Where are you going at four in the morning?"

"Debra's."

"Sure?"

"Don't even play the jealous role. I'm going to my friend."

"Figures. Why don't you stay? We can talk this out."

"Already stayed too long."

"Are you mad?"

"Nope, just disappointed."

"I didn't mean to disappoint you."

"You didn't. I disappointed myself. You don't have the power to disappoint me."

Bryce picked up the heavy stuff. I carried the rest. Brother was moving so fast I couldn't tell if I was leaving or if I was being kicked out. Let me tell you, I crammed as much in the hatchback as I could, barely managed to get it closed. There was so much stuff I'd hardly be able to shift gears.

Bryce asked, "Anything else you need?"

"I want you to pay me for my bed."

He looked at me like I was Queen of the Stupids. He asked, "How you gonna get your stuff?"

"I'll come back with Debra. And if you're going to be fucking one of your bitches on my mattress, please put something down, maybe a towel, so I don't have stains."

I *screech*ed my Z out of the parking lot. *Screech*ed so hard it sounded like a demon screaming. I don't think I had ever been so glad to leave a man in my life. Didn't feel bad in the least. That's one good thing about me. Give me half a reason and I'll leave a brother in a heartbeat. Will leave and won't look back. Because there ain't but three things a man can do for a woman—I'll tell you about that later.

Debra was dead asleep. She didn't hear me when I tiptoed into her rented condo and dumped my stuff between the sofa and love seat, right below all of the pictures of me and her family. Her cousin Bobby is our age, twenty-eight, and a photographer. Thanks to him, Debra had family pictures for days. She had a bunch of shots of me and her. Pictures from middle school to the ones we took last month in the Bahamas.

Debra didn't stir when I went into the bedroom and turned off the little television on her dresser. Robin's egg–colored night lights were on all through the place. Debra is afraid of the dark. She was on her back, glowing like she was sixteen.

Debra is the same age as me, only I'm a Cancer and she's Leo. We're almost the same size, only my butt is bigger and her hips are wider. My booty's not too much bigger than hers; it's definitely just higher and fuller and rings out *Africa!* with every sway of my sashay. I do a bunch of squats to keep my assets tight; do beaucoup abdominals to keep my waist looking small. Debra does the same. But I got the butt. In two shakes of my tail I could hypnotize a brother and any other.

Debra's skin is light brown, but next to me she looks like a stick of butter with light-brown hair. I'm dark brown. And I could stand to be two or three shades darker if you asked me. Would love it. Debra feeds my ego and tells me I'm beyond gorgeous and have the prettiest skin she's ever seen in her life. And I do. I haven't owned a blemish since high school graduation. Rarely had a monthly pimple. My high cheekbones give me a naturally smiling mouth that makes me always look happier than hell, even when I'm as pissed off as I am now. That's why I get away with being snappy and sarcastic. My cynical mood was one part character, one part defense mechanism. So it would take a special kind of man to calm me. And right now I don't know any men of that caliber.

When I did a creep-creep-creep into the bedroom, I stumbled over Debra's sit-up thingamajig she bought at Target. Hurt my damn toe. I limped and moved it between the pine dresser and the two fifteen-pound weights she had on the floor. Debra jumped when I plopped down on the bed, but she didn't sit up or open her eyes. This wasn't my first time doing this. And the way my life has been going, probably wouldn't be my last.

I said, "It's me."

"I know."

"For all you know I could've been a pillowcase rapist."

"With a door key?"

"True."

"How was your trip?"

"Same old. I worked with a new sister named Chiquita."

"Happy for you. Dag. What're you doing now?"

"Putting on my spandex and a T-shirt. I'm going running around the college and down to Crenshaw and back."

"What's your problem?"

"Gonna put in about ten miles and get rid of some stress."

"No you're not. It's dark outside. All those psychos are out and about looking for some free coochie."

"Can't fuck what you can't catch."

"Shelby. Get in the bed *now*. We can run later."

I huffed, kicked my shoes off, sat on the bed, yawned. And if the truth be told, I *loved* the attention. Loved it when a man begged. Loved it when a sister cared enough about my well-being to mother me for a minute or two. I crawled into her bed. The safest place this side of my mother's heaven. Somewhere inside, I was hurt, but I've never known how to let that much hurt come up and come out. Still, I played the role: grunted, groaned, mumbled, until Debra cracked open one of her eyes.

Debra said, "Everything okay?"

I hesitated. Then told her what had happened.

She said, "Good for you. About time you broke up."

I hit her with a pillow. "Thanks for the sympathy. I'm homeless. Bryce was screwing somebody in my bed."

"On your new mattress?"

"Ain't that disrespectful?"

Without explanation, Debra understood where I was coming from. When I grew up, I didn't have my own bed, didn't have my own mattress. It might sound trivial, but that was important to me. I spent most of my nights bundled up in covers on a floor. If the apartment floor was carpeted, that was a bonus. I slept in the twin bed with my momma sometimes, but only if it was real cold and she wasn't being a bed warmer for her boyfriend. Most of the time I made a pallet and slept on a hard floor by myself. Isolated. We had a sofa, but *nobody* slept on the sofa.

Debra said, "He's never been respectful."

"At least act surprised."

"Not surprised. He's always looking at other women. I hate that shit. Never date a man who doesn't like your friends."

"What does that mean?"

"That means you deserve better for yourself. You always date men who are beneath you. Upgrade to first class and stop flying coach. Are you scared of professional brothers or something?"

"Why didn't you say something before now?"

"I told you to keep me out of that shit. I don't meddle."

"Until after the fact." I popped her upside the head.

Debra chuckled and said, "Maybe you'll meet somebody nice at Playboy. Somebody professional."

"Don't be out there trying to hook me up when I just got disconnected."

"You never were connected. Not on the right level anyway."

"Debra?"

"What?"

"Go to sleep."

Debra said, "Keep putting those extra miles on your vagina. It's going to look as worn out as Pico Boulevard."

I kicked her ass. A real kick. Reflex action that time. What she said hurt my feelings down to the bone. Friends can do that to you. But I wouldn't let her know how bad she made me feel. Bad choices don't make me a ho. I really should've left right then and gone for a long run. Running always took away whatever was messing with me.

"Shelby?"

I snapped, "What?"

"You crying?"

"Yeah."

"Come here. Let me hold you, girl."

"Don't put your hands on me."

"What's wrong?"

"I didn't appreciate what you said about my coochie looking tore down like Pico Boulevard."

"I was joking."

"That shit wasn't funny."

"I'm sorry."

"It's okay. Guess I was kinda feeling that way and you said what I was thinking. I wish I was stuck-up and celibate and lonely and living by my damn self with a dried up and rusty coochie like you."

"Get out."

"Go to sleep."

My girlfriend kicked me and moved to the far side of the bed so I couldn't kick her back. I was asleep when my head hit the pillow. Not the most peaceful sleep I had ever had, but it was sleep. I could still smell another sleazy woman's cheap perfume left over in my nostrils.

DEBRA

3 *Positive* *Positive* *Positive*

"Debra—" Faith said my name three or four times. Each time a little louder, a little stronger. I heard her each time, but didn't answer. Then she said, "It came back positive three times. Each urine test had a high HCG. Hormones don't lie. There is no doubt in my mind, shouldn't be any in yours."

I trembled for a few seconds. Then I felt this knot in the pit of my stomach. My hands were working on their own, the tips of my French-manicured nails were scraping, smoothing out the wrinkles in my peach-colored nurse's uniform. My eyes didn't water up, but I wished they had, so that way I would be crying on the outside. Faith put her arms around me and led me to a chair. But I didn't sit down. The knot in my stomach loosened and became bearable. I snapped out of my disbelief.

I said, "I'm okay. I'm just shocked."

"Why *would* you be? It's not your problem."

My eyes wandered around the examination room. All the fluorescent lighting and mauve walls were so clean. Cotton balls. Rubber gloves. Smell of alcohol. So sterile and pure. Inside my head, the place spun a little. Maybe because I hadn't eaten anything except for a few orange slices, a bran muffin, and apple tea. I ran my tongue around the inside of my mouth and tasted muffin crumbs. Then I took a few deep breaths and felt okay. I smiled at Faith. Not a real smile, just one that let her know I was back to being professional. Personal feelings had been packed up and thrown into my closet.

I said, "I don't want to believe it."

"Neither does she. Anytime somebody takes this many

pregnancy tests, they're in some serious denial. You fuck, you get preg. Plain and simple."

Faith sounded as insensitive as an urban middle school teacher. That bothered me. Made me wonder how long it would take for me to become like her.

I said, "Faith, doctors shouldn't talk like that."

"This isn't about any code of ethics, sweetheart. If you have intercourse, knock boots, or whatever kids are calling it nowadays, just like yesterday you will get impregnated, fertilized, or whatever *you* want to call it."

Faith adjusted her kente-patterned doctor's smock. I picked up the patient's file. Read her name. Ericka Stockwell. It said Mrs. Stockwell was a social studies teacher at Rincon Intermediate in Culver City. Mr. Stockwell was in aerospace at Hughes in El Segundo. Faith adjusted her stethoscope. I did the same to mine. Faith's short graying Afro and her glasses made her look more like a chunky African studies professor than an OB-GYN.

I said, "Sorry for getting involved."

"You're only human. Remember what I told you when you were in college?"

"Leave my personal feelings at the door."

"Right. Otherwise you'll get eaten up with other people's problems."

"I'm a nurse. I'm supposed to have a higher level of responsibility."

"So you say."

Faith and I went into the adjacent examination room, which was being used as a private consultation room at the moment. When we knocked on the door, Mrs. Stockwell— that was what she wanted us to call her, even though every one else in Los Angeles was on a first-name basis—replied with a stiff "Come in, please."

She said it like we were intruding in her home. There was irritation, anger, disappointment mixing in her voice.

Mrs. Stockwell was around Faith's age, early forties, and dressed in a below-the-knee flowered skirt that hugged her kangaroo pooch a little too tight. She had been coming here for her yearly pelvic for the last ten years. I've only been working at Faith's clinic for the last four years, and have had the displeasure of looking up inside Mrs. Stockwell's vagina once every year. Some people you just don't want to know *that* well.

Faith and I stood side by side. Faith towers over me at six-foot-one, making my five-six-and-a-half seem insignificant. Mrs. Stockwell is an itty-bitty woman at five-three—and that height included her two-inch heels.

Her thirteen-year-old daughter was sitting on the table behind her mother. At first she was nervously toying with the stirrups, trying not to look up when we came back in. Her leg was bouncing up and down, thumbs making circles around each other. Ericka was already six inches taller than her mother; three inches taller than I'd ever be. She wore baggy jeans and a big cotton blouse with green and red sunflowers blooming happy faces. Her hair was parted down the center—a zigzag part—that gave her two shining ponytails which hung down both sides of her face. Sad, heavy ponytails of grief. Her middle school *Elements of Literature* textbook rested at her side. It looked like she had been trying to occupy herself with homework while she waited for the test results. Her mother was so strong-minded, so adamant, so much in disbelief, she'd made the poor child take a preg test three times this morning.

Mrs. Stockwell said, "*Well?*"

And she was so abrupt. But it saved us from an awkward moment. The one where Faith usually gave a Miss Black America smile and said, "Congratulations." I wish I could count the number of times Faith has said "Congratulations" and the women of whatever race, creed, or color broke into tears, screams, or simply plastered sardonic smiles over their trembling lips. I guess part of our job was to pretend that life stirring in a belly was always a good thing. It should be. Wish it always was. But I've witnessed so few smiles of joy. I've heard sisters cry "*But I don't know who the father is*," or clutch their crosses, start pacing and chanting "*Oh God oh God oh God.*" One sister fainted like the judge had slammed down the gavel and announced she was sentenced to death by lethal injection.

All that to say I didn't know what Mrs. Stockwell was going to do. I didn't know how her daughter was going to react. A teenager with child. Ericka's thirteen, so that meant she would be a teenager with pimples when her baby started preschool.

Faith said, "Maybe I should tell Ericka myself. Ericka?"

The girl stopped twirling her thumbs long enough to raise her face high enough for eyes to meet eyes. Her ponytails moved back and forth like they were measuring time. Then they stopped swaying, like her time was up. So many eyes were on her. Adult eyes. She looked so alone. I wondered what the world looked like to her right now. With nobody in her corner.

Faith said, "It came back positive again, Ericka."

"You sure?" Her voice was squeaky, still undeveloped, contradicting her overdeveloped body.

"Yes. I was sure the first time. You're about four months."

Mrs. Stockwell's hand gripped around her purse tight enough to make the leather creak. Her chest rose, slowly went back to normal, but her face never changed. She was calm about it. Pretty calm compared to what I have seen.

We were living in that moment. Decision time.

Then Ericka's eyes stayed with me. Lived on my face. Her eyes with mine. Maybe because both of us shared the same complexion, same light-brown hair color. I had an oval face and pouty lips. My hair was always pulled back from my face and ponytailed at work. What had shocked me about her being preg was she didn't look like the type. Didn't fit the mold or the build of the ghetto child gone wild.

Mrs. Stockwell snapped, "Ericka. My child. Ericka, the fruit of me. How?"

Ericka shrugged. A slow unsure shrug. Shuddered and shrugged a second time.

Faith said, "Would you like to discuss your options?"

Faith said that so businesslike. Too methodical with no compassion.

Mrs. Stockwell said, "May I have a dear moment with my sweet little child so we may decide? We had decided this morning, but there seems to be a change of heart on Ericka's behalf."

Faith walked out. I followed and headed toward another examining room, to another patient in waiting. Once in the hallway, we gave each other *looks*, those subtle girlfriend expressions exchanged in silence that told us we'd be gossiping about this one over Chinese food at noontime. By next week a new incident would have happened and this one would be unimportant.

Faith said, "Debra? What are you thinking that's got you looking so serious?"

I broke the awkward moment when I said, "Damn shame when a thirteen-year-old is having sex more often than you are."

Faith said, "Speak for yourself."

"I was."

That made me try to remember the last time I'd experienced the scent of a man's body next to mine, had hardness inside me, heard a man ring out my name in a tune of ecstasy, me feeling so good I wanted to cry and moan moan moan. I know I could capture a penis in a heartbeat.

They're everywhere. And you don't have to really know the owner to borrow it for a few. All I'd have to do was wink and they'd offer. But that's not what I'm about.

I was between lovers, wasn't dating much, so that meant nothing was getting between me. So I didn't have to deal with emotional pain and guilt, or pleasure and satisfaction. I didn't know if that was a curse or a blessing. Not that it mattered; it was just that whether or not you were in a relationship, had a steady supplier or maintenance man or whatever, the midnight urges kept on coming. No pun intended. Sometimes they came all day long. Instead of lying on my back with an old lover, I tried to get on my knees and pray the wanting away, but that didn't work. So over the last seventeen months, I had been getting extremely horny and having dreams about faceless men in unknown places doing some pretty kinky things to my aching body.

slap SLAP slap

The noise brought my wandering mind back to the here and now.

slap SLAP slap thud

That flesh-meeting-flesh sound was loud. Was getting louder.

slap SLAP slap

Muffled yells. Whimpers carried down the hall.

I about-faced without a word and sprinted back toward the examination room we had just left. Faith dropped what she was holding and did the same.

When we shoved the door open, Mrs. Stockwell was wide-eyed, breathing like she was in labor, foaming at the mouth, body stiff, arms straight up in the air, holding a King James version of the Bible like it was a hatchet. She was about to guillotine her whimpering child with the Word.

Ericka was on her back sprawled out on the floor, kicking her feet, one arm shielding her face, trying to get away.

Faith's big frame bumped me out of the way, made me
stumble into the doorjamb. She grabbed Mrs. Stockwell.
Threw her own body in the way. As I stumbled, I used my
body to shield Ericka. Faith must have caught Mrs. Stockwell's arm on its way down because the Bible flew across
the room and hit me in my eye, struck me at a blunt angle,
right below my left eyebrow. I was more shocked than hurt.

I pulled Ericka to the side. She held onto me tight. She
touched me where I was struck by the Bible and asked, "Are
you all right, Miss Mitchell?"

"What?"

She looked at my face and said, "Your eye okay? If
you put some ice on, it won't swell too much. Nobody'll
notice."

I was shocked by her words. By her knowledge.

Mrs. Stockwell was in the far corner by then, over by
the blood pressure cuff. Bottom lip thrust out three feet,
cheeks puffed out like a blowfish. She was straightening her
hair, redoing makeup, Bible tucked under her arm. All the
while she was calling her daughter *tramp whore Jezebel slut
bitch* and quoting Bible verses about *fornication* in between
vulgarity.

Faith snapped, "*Mrs. Stockwell.*"

Before Faith could say another word, a man the color
of a ripe banana was in the doorway. He was a little taller
than Ericka, but very wide—not fat, just wide. Receding
wavy hair, with a full beard. He had on dark pants and his
blue tie was loosened. Like he was overworked and up to
his neck in strife.

Faith said, "Mr. Stockwell, we have a situation."

He hesitated, then said, "She is pregnant, then?"

Mrs. Stockwell snapped, "Without a doubt."

I interjected, "Mrs. Stockwell assaulted Ericka:"

He said, "And?"

Mrs. Stockwell waved her Bible and rambled, "And *if*

I choose to discipline *my* child, I can do what I damn well want. Ericka is *my* child, came from me—"

Mr. Stockwell said, "Betty. Shut up."

The tiny woman folded her arms across her chest. Huffed. Ericka was still behind me, her big body using my little frame as a shield. A hiding place. I felt her breasts against my back when I stepped back into her. I was scared myself, but more angry than scared. Much more angry than scared.

I said, "Mrs. Stockwell, I understand how you feel—"

She said, "Are you married, *Miss* Mitchell?"

"No, but—"

"Do you have children, *Miss* Mitchell?"

"I don't have—"

"Then how in the *hell* do you know how I feel? My *child* just got her first period six months ago; already she's pregnant. *Four* months. Do you understand the position that leaves *me* in?"

Faith said, "Mrs. Stockwell."

"I'm the one who will have to buy Pampers, bottles, baby clothes, have to deal with shitty diapers, baby crying all the time. All of that will be on me."

"*Mrs. Stockwell.*" That was Faith in a tone I'd never heard.

It quieted.

Then Faith said a few things. Professional things. Things that calmed the room. She reminded Mrs. Stockwell who she was, who we were, told her what behavior was appropriate, what would be tolerated from this moment on, and said she would call Social Services and the police if needed. Then everyone fell back into their roles the best they could. I did the best I could.

Mr. Stockwell took out his keys, jingled them, rubbed his face, turned around, left without a good-bye. No words for his daughter. He abandoned Ericka to her stern-faced mother.

I remembered something I had heard my mother say once: "Men don't cry, they deny."

Then Mrs. Stockwell cursed and left.

Silence. Except for the hum of the air conditioner and the building's radio system playing jazz from 94.7. Sounds I hadn't noticed at first because I was used to hearing them. Toni Braxton sang a sweet song of sadness while Kenny G played his sax. That made me think of the jazz concert coming up at the Hollywood Bowl. Don't know why I thought about that now. I needed to escape madness and find tranquility. Had to find a safe thought in a moment yet to be.

Ericka looked at me. "What should I do, Miss Mitchell?"

I said a flustered "What?"

"I wanna know, what do you think I should do?"

I made myself sound professional, put a lifetime of distance between us, and said, "What do you want to do?"

Then her teenage eyes went to Faith.

Faith's face became less professional; her expressions raced through about a million subtle emotions and many thoughts. And I knew one of them was definitely about calling Social Services.

Her final expression said: another lose-lose situation.

I asked, "Ericka, did your mother strike you?"

"I fell by myself." She said that before I finished asking.

"Looks like you fell by yourself five or six times."

Mrs. Stockwell appeared in the door.

"Ericka," Mrs. Stockwell said. "Don't keep us waiting."

Faith nodded at me. I stepped to the side. Moved slowly, eased away and gave her back to her mother. As she moved toward that world, Ericka seemed void, looked as if she owned no essence. Mrs. Stockwell was smiling like it was Sunday morning in heaven. Smiling so hard it disturbed me.

Ericka went to her mother. Mrs. Stockwell took her child's hand, ran her other hand across Ericka's mane, smoothed it out.

Faith said, "Ericka, you need to get checked for STDs, blood tests, et cetera. Should I advise and prescribe prenatal vitamins and iron pills?"

"That will not be necessary," Mrs. Stockwell said. She adjusted her daughter's clothing, but addressed Faith, "Has RU 486 been legalized?"

Faith said, "No, Mrs. Stockwell, mifepristone hasn't been approved. And if the FDA had approved it, RU 486 could only be used in the first seven weeks to discharge the embryo."

There was silence again. Ericka's eyes held water. Confusion and fear. She was thirteen, but right now she looked all of nine. I couldn't imagine her with sex in her life. I couldn't imagine life growing inside her. But it was true. I had to burn away my own clouds of disbelief.

Mrs. Stockwell said, "Do you have outside connections for RU 486? I am willing to pay. Cash."

There was silence again. Very hard, very rigid silence.

I said, "I don't know if you were paying attention, Mrs. Stockwell, but Ericka is already in her second trimester."

Ericka chewed her bottom lip; her eyes were puffing up. More water. Dripping. She had no idea what we were talking about.

Faith said, "I recommend that your daughter receive counseling before going any further."

Mrs. Stockwell said, "Good day. I will contact your office in the next day or so for recommendations for late termination. You can at least do that for me, can't you?"

With clenched teeth Faith nodded.

TYREL

4

Mye said, "Damn shame when a married woman leaves you for her husband."

"Makes me wonder what this world's coming to."

"Next we'll have peace in the Middle East."

I was at work, with my office door closed, feet up on my glass-top desk, on the phone, talking to my sister in Atlanta. My office in Culver City faces east, toward Pepperdine University and a cemetery nobody ever noticed. I could almost see the condo I was leasing by the mall, had a view of endless palm trees, gray skyline, bumper-to-bumper traffic heading north into the Sepulveda Pass and south toward LAX. I promised myself that was the last time I'd speak Lisa's name. Outside of professional dealings—which we won't have much of, because I've already called to switch my portfolio over to another financial planner. Right now she had no integrity in my eyes. Wasn't worth another noun or a verb.

I said, "How's the dynamic duo?"

"Driving me crazy. I wish I'd had twin girls. Boys are ridiculous. Biting each other, pulling hair, flushing toys down the toilet. As soon as one calms down, the other one starts. And if I try to close my eyes for a moment, one of them screams for no reason. I know they're doing it on purpose too. Can't you hear them tearing up the house in the background?"

"Yep. You need to IV them to some Ritalin."

"Arsenic would be better."

"True that."

"To top it off, they saw Leonard on some stupid comedy show, and now in between playing they're running around the house telling his jokes—their four-year-old versions anyway. They were laughing and you know they don't bit mo' understand what Leonard is talking about. 'Mommy, Mommy, buy us a joke book so we can tell Uncle Leonard a joke when he call us.' Last thing I need to hear is a joke."

I said, "Twin."

"What?"

"You said *bit mo'*."

"Did I?"

"Yes, you did. With a touch of a twang."

"I've been in the South too long. I'm turning into one of them. Twin, they are so narrow-minded down here. Talk about countrified with a slave mentality. I expect to see us picking cotton by the middle of next week. And this humidity and these damn mosquitoes. And the white people—don't get me started. I bow down to *nobody*. I don't know what I was thinking when I followed Danny down here. I told him I'd give him two years to get his law practice going here. If it's not working, I'm going back to L.A., with or without him."

"You said L.A. isn't a good place to raise your kids."

"I'll have to move to Westchester or something."

"You love that man too much to leave 'im."

"Love has limits." She laughed. "Hell, I miss the beach, miss it always being good weather, miss the Beverly Center, miss my friends from law school, and I miss you."

"Miss you too."

"This marriage and kid thing seemed like a good idea at the time. Hell, I want to be trying cases, not changing diapers. I don't see how Momma did this shit and didn't go crazy."

I knew what Mye was thinking. In the two seconds of silence I knew. We were fraternal, but part of us was identical.

At the same time we said, "Did you—"

Then we both laughed. Apprehensive laughs in harmony.

I said, "Go ahead, Twin."

"You haven't talked to your daddy?"

"Nope. Your daddy hasn't called me. You gonna call?"

"I've been thinking—"

I said, "You've been thinking since I'm the man why don't I call and have a man-to-man?"

"Yeah. You call. Have a man-to-bastard conversation. You know I can't stand that bastard and the air he breathes."

I said, "He knows it too."

"I hope him and all of his bitches go to hell. Check to make sure he's alive, and if he needs anything, I'll send it to you and you can send it to him."

"Sure you don't want to talk to him? I could do it on a three-way."

"I don't do three-ways. That's why I broke up with Raheim."

"Anything you want me to tell your daddy *if* I call?"

"Not a goddamn thing *when* you call. If your daddy asks where I am, tell him I turned lesbian, married an African priestess, and I'm in Zimbabwe. And it's against tribal custom for deceitful grandparents ever to lay eyes on their grandchildren."

I laughed. "That your phone beeping?"

"Probably my hubby."

"Take your call. I'm going back to work."

She said, "Call your daddy."

After I sat and thought for a few seconds, I opened my digital diary and keyed in B-A-S-T-A-R-D. My daddy's name and number popped up. I picked up the phone, dialed the area code for Nashville, then changed my mind. Some other time.

A few minutes later I was in a meeting, talking about our latest plan to conquer the computer world, snatch Internet, and become kings of the information age. I shook hands with men and never saw their faces. Didn't hear their words about making Dan L. Steel the key to personal computing for this and all generations to follow. I took a seat at the round table. Became one of the knights. Nothing they said about being in a battle with Microsoft and Netscape mattered. There was nothing they could say to hold me here.

Two hours later, I was back in my office, tie loosened, sipping bottled water, shuffling papers in between throwing silver darts at a rainbow hued dartboard with Bill Gates' picture taped to the center.

There was a knock at my door. It was a few minutes before six. Minutes before everybody went home. Hated when people stopped by this late in the day. I sat up, moved a few things around my desk, wheeled my chair to the front of my computer workstation. Even though I frowned, I said a lively "Come in."

Before me stood a brother in a dark blue suit and Steeple Gate shoes. Thick as a tree stump. About fifty. His stomach spilled over his belt. Deep red patterned tie. Thin mustache.

He said, "Tyrel Williams?"

I stood and extended my hand. "Yeah."

"Joshua Cooper."

He was the one man I'd been avoiding for weeks on end. I gave my firmest handshake and best corporate smile and said, "Nice to meet you. I've heard good things about you. Plenty of praise for you in the company newsletter. You're here from San Francisco to talk strategy?"

"Actually, no."

He took a seat in one of the two chairs facing my desk. I moved my Far Side calendar so I could see his face.

He said, "We're familiar with your work. We know you've been here two years, did your undergraduate study at Cal State, did your master's at Pepperdine."

I nodded. "Yes, I did. And you're out of Cornell, pledged the black and gold, mastered at NYU, been with the company twenty-five years, worked the Paris office for two years."

"Closer to thirty, and I was in Paris for four. You sound like a man who has done his research."

"Likewise."

"So much buzz is circulating about you that I feel like I've known you for weeks. We want you to come to San Francisco."

That undesired offer was why I'd been avoiding his E-mail, faxes, and nonstop messages for the last six months. I'd already told his peons I wasn't interested. I told them no, but sometimes a simple word wasn't easy to understand.

I said, "This conversation may not be appropriate. Before you go any further, have you spoken to my superior?"

"The chain of command has been thoroughly respected. You can feel free to verify."

He went into the benefits, the substantial salary increase I'd get, a tax-free bonus, my new title, how the company would relocate me. About thirty other perks.

I said, "With our new assault on Microsoft, I'm in the middle of something here."

He smiled. "Bring her with you."

"Nothing like that. I don't make decisions like that."

He chuckled. "Take your time. Don't give the thought up. Mull it over. Either way, don't rush to judgment. Keep in contact. Let me know how the career is going. I'll always have room for you."

"I'll keep that in mind."

He lowered his voice and spoke with passion, "One black man to another, I've been all over this country, and it makes me proud to see somebody like you. You're highly regarded in this company."

Those few words carried weight. Had real meaning to me. I opened my middle desk drawer and dropped his card in with fifty or sixty others I'd collected.

Joshua's footsteps faded. Then I heard a new commotion stirring in the hallway. Sounded like everybody was leaving at the same time. Most of the women went to Evelyn's aerobics class at the Hilton—part of the company's effort at keeping employees well through fitness. I pulled my bag from underneath my desk. There was another knock at my door. Fast, playful taps. It opened before I said come in. It was Leonard, dressed in a jean shirt, beat-down 501s, and baseball cap. A red gym bag was over his shoulders.

Everybody always got excited when he showed up. After he had the hallway laughing, he sighed when he stepped in and closed the door. I knew the man beyond the wall of jokes. He knew me beyond the smile I had on my face.

I said, "You don't look like you in the mood to work out."

"Not really."

"But we have to."

"Yep. Give me a minute."

Leonard dropped his gym bag next to my desk and went over to the window. He did a brief pacing thing, kept stroking his mustache, then stared out the window. Leonard had faded. Lost in thought. He didn't blink for long moments. Then he came back to life and smoothed out his jean shirt, adjusted his clothes. He sat down and tapped his foot to an unheard rhythm.

I said, "Guess what?"

"What's that?"

I tossed my Gold's Gym bag to the side, opened my top

drawer and took out a jar of jelly beans. Leonard smiled. I slid the jar toward him.

He said, "Oh, shit. The gourmet kind?"

"Damn right. I don't buy lower end."

He poured himself a handful and put his feet up on my desk. I poured myself a handful and kicked back too.

I read the uneasiness in his face. "What's wrong?"

He bobbed his head and replied, "Scared."

"Of?"

"I need to make a decision about whether or not I'm gonna quit my part-time and do comedy full-time. I could, but you know how flaky the business is. Clubs book you, then close down, movies get postponed, TV shows get canceled, agents and managers rip you off. Not exactly a guaranteed paycheck every Friday."

"You know I got your back. I could take a loan against my 401 to float you for a while."

"Man, hang on to your security. I'm not struggling."

I told him, "Just say the word, and the cash is yours."

He waved me off, then vented a little more, saying, "Then there's Hollywood."

"What you mean?"

"It don't take but one person to like you and you're set. But on the other hand, it only takes one person to hate you and you're a has-been before you've ever been. What if I make a movie and screw up? I mean, it would be on a ninety-foot screen looking jacked up. Or even worse, it might get edited out."

"Kevin Costner was edited out of his first film, and look at him. Mega-star writing his own meal ticket."

"Even though he freaked him some Whitney Houston in that movie, he ain't exactly a brother in the business. You know they let us in one at a time. Then they pit us against each other."

"Your scenario is different. You've got talent."

"How you know?"

"You ever have to fuck somebody or let somebody fuck you to get an audition or a part in something?"

"Nope."

"I rest my case."

He smiled like a kid at Disneyland. "Thanks, bro."

I adjusted my tie, slipped on my size ten-and-a-half Steeple Gates and picked up my gym bag. We headed for the door, chomping on gourmet jelly beans.

If it would help, I'd liquidate my assets to get him where he wanted to be. He'd do the same for me. On many a summer night we've sat around 5th Street Dick's in hardback chairs, sipped Kenyan coffee, played chess, and talked about the future, envisioned the warm days and brisk evenings we'd kick back and watch our wives do the things that women do. And while we held on to the women of our dreams, we'd watch our children romp around together. Smile while they played some of the same games we did, see them grow up together, bond down to the soul, and become the best of friends for the rest of their lives.

We can do a lot for each other. But even true friendship has its limitations. I think about that from time to time. No matter how good of friends we were, no matter how much brotherly love we shared, only one of us would be able to be a pallbearer at the other's funeral.

DEBRA

5

I said, "Slow down before you kill me."

It was almost midnight and I was in a mood. Shelby drove like she was flying an airplane. Telling her to slow down made her speed up. She hit her high beams, made people screech out of the way. We had the T-tops off, 94.7 jazz, jean jackets on, living in a cool breeze that had traces of ocean air, underneath a full moon and a gray sky filled with twinkle-twinkle little stars. We'd just left the Playboy Jazz Festival and were so tanned that when I took my glasses off, I had raccoon eyes.

I said, "I want to go to Roscoe's in Hollywood."

"Denny's by the crib. Take it or leave it."

"You are such a bitch."

"Bet your bloated ass'll drive next time."

"You'll be bloated next week. We'll see who's tripping."

We stopped at a red light in Culver City, on Jefferson, right underneath the 405 freeway overpass. I glanced up at the concrete and hoped we didn't have a freeway-shattering earthquake right about now. To make it worse, we were trapped behind somebody's loud music. Another rude-ass loud-ass. Music so nerve-racking I forgot what I was fussing about in the first place.

I snapped, "There goes another stupid brother who thinks everybody wants to hear what he's listening to."

Shelby slapped the steering wheel. "*Damn*, quit complaining."

I shook my head. "My day is going every way but the right way. My stupid Unocal card got denied. Hell, I pay my bills on time. I'm calling their service center as soon as I get back home. But right now *I am hungry*."

Some older white people were in the next lane in an Infiniti, windows closed tighter than Ericka should have kept her little legs, and the way their faces were turned up, I knew they didn't appreciate the brother's misogynistic noise either. That public display of ignorance and disrespect made me feel ashamed.

Shelby blew her horn and got their attention. When they looked our way, Shelby shouted, "We don't know him."

They cringed and eased their car up a foot.

The light changed and Shelby had to blow the horn to get the fool to drive through the intersection. The Celica pulled into the same parking lot we did. Drove in a circle, flashed his damn headlights right in my face. Parked two spaces down toward the Unocal and Lucky's grocery store. Damn Unocal. They rejected my card for no reason.

Noisy's car cut off, but his headlights were still on. I glimpsed his way. He peeped my way. I shivered and looked the other way. Late night and broad daylight brought out some of the rudest people in L.A.

I grabbed Shelby's steering wheel Club from the floor. I pulled it loose and handed her one side of the metal.

Shelby said, "What are you doing?"

"In case that brother steps to us acting crazy. You use that side as a club, I'll use this half as a bat. Do like we did when we played softball and knock the living—"

"Give me that."

She clicked it back together and put it on the steering wheel. Snoop Doggy Dogg music thumped from the brother's car. Hearing gangsta rap was not a good sign.

I said, "Shelby, let's cancel this."

"Hell, no." Shelby adjusted her Old Navy baseball cap. She snapped, "After the way you've been bitching about how hungry you are. You will get out and you will eat."

"I'm not hungry."

"Yes, you are."

"No, I'm not."

"Yes, you are."

The moment we opened our doors, the brother stepped out of the Celica. Like he timed it. Then a crunching noise scared me more. He had stepped on an empty Ruffles bag. My legs felt awkward. My eyes went to him, then darted to Shelby. I sort of rushed, but didn't make it look like I was being hasty, pretended I was busy with my handbag and went to her side of the car. Two screams would be louder than one.

Then his soft-spoken voice came out of the darkness, its tone pleasant and cheery. Positive. But like I said, that didn't mean a thing. Ted Bundy sounded pleasant before death row.

The brother said, "How are my sistuhs doing tonight?"

He moved into the light. Dark skin with Asian eyes. Broad shoulders, which could've been an illusion caused by his short leather jacket. Neat hair, cut short on the sides, longer on the top, sideburns that stopped at the bottom of his ear. Thin mustache over a nicely shaped goatee. Circular earrings in both ears, which I hated to see on a man.

We made eye contact. For a moment. A moment that felt like an eternity.

He said a light "Oh, can't speak? See, that's what's wrong with the black woman. Brother says hi, sisters walk on by."

Shelby said, "What's up?"

I cleared my throat and released a slow "Hello."

He said, "Hello."

The next thing I knew, I sucked my stomach in and hoped my breasts didn't look lopsided in my bra. Prayed my jean jacket covered it all, including whatever bad smells sitting in the sun had roasted into my body. I ran my tongue around the inside of my mouth, over the film on my teeth. I needed to brush and floss.

He smiled at me and said, "You okay?"

I said, "I'm fine. You caught me off guard."

"Both of y'all wearing new jazz festival T-shirts," he said. His smile and his eyes were glued to me. I unglued mine from him, chewed my bottom lip, wished I had makeup on and didn't have raccoon eyes, got shoulder to shoulder with Shelby, and kept moving toward the door. He was right behind us. I felt his aura. Following. My reflection was rough. Smelled like a day of dried-up sweaty perfume. Felt a lump in my throat. Adjusted my jacket to make my hands busy. The brother stepped closer to us. I gripped my purse a little tighter. Fixed my mouth to scream. He stepped around us, held the door open, and let us in.

Then we were all at the counter, waiting for the waitress to find seats. Denny's was crowded. It looked like a busload of brothers had dropped by here to flirt with the vixens and vice versa. Most of their eyes drifted toward us when we came in. Seeing them notice made me take notice. I'd have to admit, the better lighting gave him some serious appeal. Maybe I felt safer about being out of the dark parking lot and in a crowd.

He asked, "How was the concert this year?"

I said, "What was that?"

He repeated himself.

"It was nice," I said. "Real nice. Beautiful. Everette Harp and Wayne Shorter were slamming. Bill Cosby's group was the bomb. Gladys Knight turned the show out."

"Yeah? Now I *really* hate I missed it. I wanted to check out Stanley Clarke and Hugh Masekela. But I had to work."

I said, "There's still Pasadena and L.A. and Long Beach."

He went over the list. He knew the line-up for JVC,

knew about the Creole Festival in Lancaster. Knew more
than I did.

I said, "Not many young brothers like jazz."

"I'm not that young. But that depends on how old you
are."

"Okay. How old are you, if you don't mind me
asking?"

"Twenty-nine. What about you?"

"You're not supposed to ask a sister her age. Strike
one."

"Didn't know I was up to bat. How old are you?"

I shifted, smiled some. "Twenty-eight. Strike two."

Shelby said, "Y'all need to quit."

We laughed. Mine was nervous. Didn't last long.

Shelby stayed in the background with this asinine grin
on her face, and without another word, knucklehead excused herself to the ladies' room. She waited for me to tag
along. That was my chance to break away, go into the bathroom with my girl, stay awhile, then ease back out and get
a table in whatever section of the restaurant he wasn't sitting in. Maybe even come out of the bathroom and leave.

I didn't move. Stayed put. Shelby raised a brow. I held
on to my growing conversation with the brother. Don't
even know why I did, but I did. Think it was his eyes,
maybe that combined with his schoolboy smile. He had a
gentle demeanor. Had crept into our space without intruding. Smooth. Smooth wasn't always good, but he made me
laugh. He had manners. And he was flirting with me. Flirting hard, but not aggressively. I knew I could walk away
without hassle. Might even make it back to the car without
being called a bitch. I just wasn't sure if I was reciprocating
and flirting with him or not.

Maybe I was having fun and just trying to see if I could
intimidate him like I did every other brother. Most of the
time when I told a brother what I did, said that I was con-

sidering going back to become a doctor myself, they digressed from the conversation one way or the other. Showed their shallow sides. Brothers who were weak in the mind and just chasing the behind.

I said, "I'm Debra."

He said, "I'm Leonard DuBois."

By the time Shelby came back from the ladies' room, Leonard and I were in a booth, sitting across from each other, talking about the concerts of the season. He was enchanting. Totally.

Shelby waltzed back with a *Times* in her hand, reading while she strolled. Probably doing that so she wouldn't make any eye contact. Straight posture. Leading with her chest, loads of feminine power in each stride. I saw other brothers' attention sway from whatever woman they were talking to and glance at Shelby from the waist down, smile that oh-my-god smile. When they looked up to see her face was just as gorgeous as the rest, a dreamy-eyed gaze said more than they could ever put to words.

Leonard took off his short, yellow-black-gold leather jacket and excused himself to the men's room to wash his hands. I surprised myself and damn near fell out of my seat trying to look at his mystical skin. That open staring was so unlike me. I'm subtle. His Wings cologne fragrance had tickled my fancy.

Shelby handed me a napkin.

I said, "What's that for?"

"Wipe your mouth before you drown in your drool."

"I'm not staring."

"And Popeye's not a sailor."

"Shush your face and stop blocking my view. Nice booty."

"Don't matter. You'll never see it butt-naked on payday."

"You're jealous because he's nice and a gentleman."

"Give him five minutes to show his true colors. The last thing you need is to have that stupid look in your eyes."

"What look?"

"That forty-ounce gaze that makes you look higher than a kite." She yawned. "Let's raise up before he gets back."

"We're staying."

"If we stay, you pay."

"I'll pay."

When Leonard came back, before he could sit, Shelby dabbed her mouth with her napkin and asked, "All right brother-man, since you all up in our booth taking up space, where do you work that made you miss the festival all day on a Sunday?"

"I work part-time for an itty-bitty, don't blink when you drive down 103rd, software company over by the Watts Tower."

"Doing?"

"Installations, upgrades, simple database stuff. Tutoring the kids in basic computer ops most Saturday mornings."

"That's yesterday. What had you wrapped up till midnight?"

"I do a little stand-up comedy. I was on Sunset tonight."

Shelby gave me that *please*-not-another-entertainer look.

Part of me felt the same. Brought back an instant memory of an angry waitress pulling me to the side and telling me that she was sleeping with the man who was up on stage, the man I thought I was falling in love with, the man I loaned a few hundred to get his car fixed and never received even a thank-you.

My voice lowered along with my shy smile. My brain

wanted this man to get the hell away from my table. Out of my light. But I guess I've never listened to my brain.

I said, "No wonder you're so funny."

Shelby said, "He ain't that damn funny. You're the one tee-heeing and ha-haing and whooping over every stupid thing he says. You a kitchen comedian or you get *paid*?"

He shrugged. "I get a dime every now and then."

Shelby said, "Every brother in L.A. think he's funny. I watch *Def Comedy Jam* and *Comic View*, and I ain't *never* seen or heard of you."

"I was on *Evening at the Improv*. Did MTV comedy half-hour back when I was starting out. *Caroline's Comedy Show*."

"Sorry, my brotha." Shelby shook her head. "White-folks jokes don't count. They fall out laughing at anything."

I batted my eyes at Shelby, then eased back into the conversation and said, "She's right. You white funny or funny funny?"

Leonard winked at me. "Give me your number. I'll invite you to a show, and you and Miss Pundit can tell me what you think."

I owned no expression. Felt boxed in by the inevitable.

Shelby high-fived me and laughed out her words, "Damn, that was smooth! See how he tried to sneak up on the digits? My brother got it going on. Her name is Debra Mitchell. She's single. Hasn't been on a decent date since God was born. And *if* she goes out with you, I'll chaperone her to the club just in case you one of those psycho brothers and get to trippin'."

Leonard said, "It's cool if you and your man tag along."

Shelby said, "Don't have no man, don't want no man, don't need no man."

Leonard said, "But you do like men, right?"

Shelby said, "They are a necessary nuisance."

He repeated, "Necessary nuisance?"

"Cheaper than batteries."

I interjected, "Tell Leonard the three things you always say about men."

Shelby said, "Men can't do nothing but get you pregnant, give you a disease, and leave you for another woman."

"Ouch." Leonard cringed. "You need to exhale. You give a good guy a bad reputation before you know what he's about. What you're catching depends on what you're using for bait."

I said, "Shelby gets crass when she's sleepy."

Shelby snapped, "Forget you. Was that polite enough for your ass? You're just acting all nice and shit because he's here."

Leonard laughed.

I said, "Shelby? Wait in the car. Do you mind?"

"Hell, yeah." She tapped her watch. "Wrap this shit up."

"Five minutes."

Shelby waved her hand in a f-u fashion, scooted away. Her eyes were puffed. Bloodshot. She opened her paper to the classified. She was checking out apartments. Then she unfolded the sales pages. That changed her mood. Made her mumble a few curses and frown her worst frown.

I said, "What's wrong?"

"My damn mattress is on sale, that's what's wrong. Thirty percent off. What's thirty percent of five hundred?"

I said, "Let me get my calculator."

Before I opened my purse, Leonard said, "One hundred fifty."

Shelby was about to explode. She snapped, "I could've bought a new outfit from Macy's."

Leonard said, "You could've invested in an IRA."

She hopped up and moved like a gale toward the pay phone.

Leonard said, "She looks upset."

I said, "She is. She's emotional and spontaneous."

"That's a tough combination."

"Yep. Ask anybody who's gone out with her more than once."

When we finished, Leonard offered to treat us, but I declined. Maybe that was what he expected me to want him to do, be typical and become opportunistic at the drop of a hat. The conversation was nice; that was a reward in itself, and I didn't know him. I pay my own way. I'm not the kind who'll spend any man's money just because he snapped out his wallet. Plus, if he did treat, I didn't think he should pay for me *and* Shelby. Leonard gave me enough to cover the apple pie and herbal tea he had, and I gave the waitress my charge card.

Then came the second embarrassment of the day.

My Visa was denied. Just like my Unocal was earlier. Leonard was with me when the exasperated waitress brought the card back, but Shelby hadn't come back from her rampage. I had spent my cash on T-shirts at the jazz festival. Visa was the only card I had with me. I tried to play it off with some humor. "Guess I'll be washing dishes tonight."

Leonard pulled the bill to his side and said, "I got it."

"I'll owe you."

"No problem. Don't need you back there busting suds."

My nervous laugh surfaced. "This is embarrassing."

"Don't be. It's happened to me a time or two before."

"I just mailed them a check a week or so ago."

"Maybe it hasn't cleared yet."

Leonard would no doubt think that either I did it on purpose, or I was a sister who couldn't handle her basic finances. This would be a serious demerit. *If* I was interested in him. But I wasn't, so it didn't matter. This was all about principle. Perception of self.

I said, "Shit. Excuse my French."

"I speak French myself, so French excused. What's wrong?"

"My cousin Bobby gave me a personal check and . . . never mind."

Minutes later, my shame had died down. We were loitering and laughing in the parking lot. I was next to Leonard's car. Shelby was in the passenger side of her Z, seat reclined, back to the window, arms folded, shifting around, nodding off.

I said, "You've mentioned your friend Tyrel several times."

"He's my best friend. More like a brother."

I asked him if he went to church. Asked him that because he wore a golden cross. He said he went to Faithful Central, mostly Bible study. I told him I went to FAME a few times a month.

He said, "Why don't you go to church with me next Sunday."

"You're asking me on a date to church?"

"Yeah."

"Hmmm."

"What?"

"That's, I don't know, most brothers shy away from church. Say two words out of the Bible and they run for the door."

"Sisters do too. Take off running like Flo Jo."

"True. Well, speaking of running, we're in a group and we run early on Sunday mornings."

"How far?"

"Six to ten. Sometimes we do a half-marathon. Depends."

He smiled. "Impressive."

"So if we do church, it'll have to be late service. Have to get my workout on and keep my thighs tamed."

"No problem. He understands."

We stood and stared. Then I felt a tingle from head to curling toes. One of those heart shivers I hid with a smile.

I exhaled, then asked a firm, "Okay. What's up?"

"What do you mean?"

"Are you married, going through a divorce, living with your wife but not getting along, hiding from the FBI, have six kids by seven different women in eight different cities, that's what I mean what's up? Brothers always have something up."

He laughed.

I said, "What's funny?"

"You. What you said."

"I was serious."

"That's why it's funny."

"Well?"

"Single as I was on the day I was born. What's up with you?"

"Not much."

"Not much ain't the same as nothing."

I blew air. "Not much. Nothing at all."

"Why you hesitate?"

"Hard for me to admit it because most guys think if you look a certain way you've got wolves howling at your door."

Police cars with lights flashing and sirens on sped up Jefferson toward Westchester. Typical nighttime in L.A.

I said, "Call me when you get in. Let me know you made it."

"If you get in before me, do the same."

Then we stood face-to-face and had a moment of silence.

He said, "I'm glad I missed the concert."

"Why?"

"Then I wouldn't have met you."

He leaned toward me. My mouth opened like a rose in bloom.

Leonard walked me to the car, opened my door, went back to his Celica, waved, made sure we got started, smiled, then drove away. His music was louded-up. I turned the radio to the same hip-hop station. Louded-up the radio until Shelby screamed.

He turned right and headed toward Leimert Park. I turned left and went deeper into Culver City. Smiling. Not believing the last few minutes of my life. Then my smile went away. I couldn't believe what I had just done.

Shelby huffed.

I said, "What's wrong with you?"

"You had me sit in the damn car by myself, that's what's wrong. If I had've done some shit like that to you, your ass would've been going off on me from January to December."

"Stop acting stupid. You need a time-out."

"You just remember that."

"You and your damn mouth."

"What about *your* mouth? Did you have to kiss him?"

I blushed. "I didn't kiss him. We hugged good-bye."

"I saw the whole damn thing. Did you have to kiss him?"

I smiled a little bit more. "Yep."

"Like *that*? You were busting slob all over the lot."

"Yes, yes. I was weak, yes."

Shelby kept on chastising me, sounding like she was somebody's mother, but my mind was on a mental trip with that Asian-eyed, mystical-complected brother. The one I kept trying not to think about because I was mad at myself. Forget about the charge card. I needed to concentrate on the road. This was L.A. and nighttime is crime time. But I put my mind on Leonard.

Then it floated further back to the others. To the memories I wanted to deny ever happened. I thought about the times I'd given my body to a man because I thought that would make a difference in a relationship. I found out that after sex, the relationship hit the wall and they hit the door.

Only moments had whisked by since me and Leonard stood there shaking hands good-bye, then holding hands for at least a minute like neither one of us wanted to let go of what the night had brought us. All of my feelings were mixed up, and I knew he could tell that. I moved my tongue around to see if I could taste anything he had left behind. It's hard to taste a memory. But I tried. All I tasted was film on my teeth. Made me wonder if my breath was funky when he put his mouth on mine.

It was quiet. Too quiet. I glanced over and saw that Shelby was asleep, one arm behind her head, mouth halfway open.

Soon as I got home I'd call and cancel my Friday night date with Leonard. Sunday's church excursion too. Tonight I'd toss and turn and be mad at myself for letting a man I didn't know, and didn't intend to know, kiss me before the third date he'd never get to have.

SHELBY

6

Sweating my ass off. I was so wet my jade and magenta sorority T-shirt clung to my back. Perspiration dripped from my forehead over my Nikes to the plastic part of the StairMaster. Fluids hopped off me and my black spandex shorts with every grunt and pant. Body heat, musty aromas, and cheap perfume stenches jammed the hallway. The stationary bikes were packed with people who finally hit the gym a little bit too late to do any good, because they had more jiggle than a bowl of Jell-O.

Bryce's big-breasted woman, Nancy, was up in the gym, teaching advanced step to about thirty people, mostly brothers and sisters, fools working on wearing out the cartilage in their knees. She had on blue tights with white stars and looked like she was one color away from being Wonder Woman. I know that bitch saw me because I intentionally got on the machine positioned right outside her class. And she had to pass by me to get in there. While she warmed up the class, I glared at her no-ass reflection and shot her a scowl or two. She was just a-smiling and a-stepping, calling out for them to turn-step, do the freeway routine, whatever, while her breasts were just a-bouncing and colliding like a pair of click-clacks.

First my pager went off. The Motorola vibrated in my fanny pack. It was the number at Faith's clinic. Debra was calling. I checked my ironman triathlon watch. Almost noon. Lunchtime was on the way. We were supposed to hook up at one o'clock.

Then I heard, *Umph-umph-UUUUMUPH* come from behind me.

There are some straight up nasty-ass Peeping Tom

brothers up at the gym. Strutting around gawking like they were at the Pussycat Lounge. Booty watching and crotch staring like big dogs. Makes a sister leery about opening her legs to get on the inner-thigh machine. I turned to check this mess out. A brother was back there drooling and licking his fat lips, his eyes going *way* up the crack of my butt. Made me wish I had gas. Smiling and grunting his way to whiplash. *Grunt, grunt, moan, grunt.*

I said, "Why don't you take a laxative for that."

"You work out this hard all the time?"

I didn't answer. Went right back to minding my own business.

He said, "What's your name?"

"Does it look like I came up here to socialize?"

I stopped long enough to give him a what-the-hell-are-you-looking-at? glower. I said, "Pervert."

He said, "I could be the man of your dreams. I could give you multiple organisms."

I said, "*Organisms?*"

"Yeah. When was the last time you had an organism?"

"Buy a vowel and watch *Sesame Street* when you get a chance."

He put his water bottle to his mouth and moved on, frowned back at me like I was crazy not to give him some play. Now my rhythm was messed up because I was trying to figure which *organisms* he had in mind.

I'd done thirty minutes on the bike; now I was at an hour-ten on the StairMaster. I gripped the handle like I had my fingers around a couple of necks. Every time my feet slammed down I imagined I was stepping on Bryce's groin. Every time I raised my foot, I imagined I was kicking Nancy up the butt for sexing on my damn mattress. That's called motivation by irritation.

Bryce walked in the glass doors by the counselors' desks. All cocky with his chest stuck out. I had hoped to get my workout in and be gone before he showed up. Too late now. He had on zebra-striped pants, sleeveless T-shirt, and was lugging his purple gym bag. I got off the machine, wiped it down, then went downstairs where the trainer's office was. Tried to get there before he started training somebody. He saw me following and kept on moving. Had the nerve to speed up. I shifted gears and caught up by the weigh-in station. People were all around, so a sister had to be cool and not clown a brother on his j-o-b.

I wiped my face, dabbed my neck with a towel, and said a casual, "Why haven't you returned my call?"

"For what?"

"So we can make arrangements for me to get my stuff."

"You got your part of the rent?"

"I'm not giving you any money."

"Why not?"

"Why you think?"

"You can't walk out when you get ready and leave me hanging."

"I want my mattress."

"Soon as you pay rent and give up a thirty-day notice."

I reminded Bryce the Bastard who had been fucking around on who on whose brand-new, five-hundred-dollar mattress. Who had stained whose paisley sheets for nights on end. He walked off while I was talking. I went in the other direction and finished the conversation by my damn self. A new direction was something I should've dashed in a long time ago. The first time I saw him.

I let it go, for the moment, and got on the stomach machines. Worked obliques. Lower abs. I was working hard, crunching and cussing, and cussing and crunching, grunting like a bear, slinging my sweat all across the room. Then I saw Nancy pass by upstairs, heading toward the ladies' locker room. She had the nerve to stare down on me like I was the Stupid of the Week. Then she stalled, tilted her head and watched me in a weird kind of way. Weird enough to make me stop cussing while I was crunching. I told myself I wasn't going to say anything to her. Let it ride; let it ride; let it ride. Told myself this issue was between me and Bryce. It wasn't like she had the remote control to his dick either. I was sure she'd find that out sooner or later when it strayed to another vaginal channel.

Debra was probably getting antsy because I hadn't called her back yet, but the phones were inside the locker room. Where Nancy had just gone. The only other phones were upstairs in the lobby of the hotel. I might've had my head high, shoulders back, might've looked okay and had much attitude, but right below the surface, I was uncomfortable. Very. Made me feel like a rabbit in lioness clothing. I didn't want to see Nancy face-to-face, mainly because I felt like I had lost whatever I had to lose, so far as Bryce was concerned. These feelings had no point.

I waited a few minutes, stalled by working on the back machines, waited long enough for my pager to go off again and let me know I was long overdue for lunch, long enough to give Nancy time to get the hell out of *my* gym. I figured I would pack up my stuff, catch the sauna for about ten minutes, shower, dress, throw on my sandals, Levi's, and white T-shirt, then hook up with Debra and Faith for lunch.

The locker room was practically empty. No sign of Nancy. Less stress. I stripped down to my chocolate delight, grabbed a towel, grabbed a razor so I could do my legs and underarms, and went to the sauna to center myself and recoup some Zen before I went to my friends.

Nancy was in the back corner of the sauna on the wooden bench. Naked with her yellow towel under her golden butt. One itty-bitty foot up on the bench. Showing me what she had spread out on my damn mattress. She saw me when I stepped inside into the heat. I wanted to turn around and leave, but I couldn't let the bitch chase me out of my own gym. Hell, I paid fifteen dollars a month for this crap. Had been paying my dues for the last five years. Always paying my dues. So this is *my* gym. I wished Debra was with me because then I could be a lot stronger, a lot bitchier. Intimate situations tend to leave a sister exposed.

Her eyes were on me. Mine on her. Then we both shifted our focuses. Made me glad this didn't turn into a sauna stare-down. I went to the opposite side of the room. Took my towel off. Put it under my butt. A real butt. Showed her what she couldn't compete with even if she tried. Showed her what only a *real* black man would appreciate.

Before five minutes had passed—five minutes of my inhaling the funky aroma of the nameless perfume that had violated my pillowcases—the sauna had me suffocating. Dizzy or not, I'd be damned if I left first. Five more minutes passed. Me and Nancy made eye contact again. More like I raised my head to get a sip of my bottled water and she was watching me. So I watched her back. Then she lowered her head. So did I. She looked comfortable, like she was used to living in this kind of hell. She had that weird gaze again. The one she had when she passed by and stared down on me in the gym.

She said, "Shelby?"

I raised my head. Tsked. Gave her the same kind of scowl I'd passed to the brother when I was on the Stair-Master.

She said, "I'm moving in with Bryce. He asked me to."

I chewed the inside of my lip. Rocked a bit.

She said, "Bryce told me a few things about you."

I said, "I just want you to know, I don't have anything against you. Me and Bryce have some unresolved business. The sooner we handle it, the better for everybody involved."

Nancy said, "You are a beautiful woman."

"*What?*"

"I said you are a beautiful woman. I've never seen anyone like you in my life. Would you like to go out sometime?"

"Go out with you? You asking me out on a date with you?"

"No. With me and Bryce. Maybe we could all get together."

I blinked a few times. Heard her say something about wine. Then I blinked a few more times. Swallowed twice. Heard her say something about it not being that unusual and she could look at me and tell we had something in common. Between each blink, it seemed like the heifer had scooted closer to me. I know she did because when I stopped blinking, she was next to me, right up on me, with her hand on my damn leg. Rubbing my sweat up and down.

I knocked her hand off me and hopped to my feet.

Nancy looked scared as hell.

The door opened and a couple of sisters stepped inside tittering, tee-heeing, and lollygagging. They stopped laughing and yacking when they saw me and Nancy the Nympho standing in front of the hot coals. The sisters' mouths gaped open, eyes bugged out with expressions of discovery, like they had stumbled across a couple of invisible lives.

I snapped, "It ain't that kind of party."

I was naked and angry as angry could be. I stuck my finger in Nancy the Nympho's face, said something, but it was so fast and had so many curse words it sounded like gibberish.

I couldn't get out of that sauna fast enough. Couldn't shower fast enough. Couldn't scrub where she had touched me hard enough. Couldn't dress fast enough. Couldn't leave fast enough.

TYREL

7

Six p.m. Friday. Leonard was on my sofa, reading the entertainment part of today's *Times*, laughing at the review he'd gotten from a show he had done at the Improv days ago.

He trudged around, sang along with a Keb Mo' blues song while he stopped in front of the pine bookcase, looked at the pictures of my twin sister and her husband and their twins, picked the photos up like he hadn't seen them a thousand times already. He did the same act with an old picture of my parents, when they were young and still together.

I said, "You nervous, bro-man?"

"Thinking about this girl Debra, bro-man. That's all."

"Feel free to clean up something."

"Ain't nothing here dirty."

"Cleaning lady came by yesterday."

Leonard rambled around and looked at the new tri-matted cultural print I had picked up down in Leimert Park Village. For six years I've tried to buy one piece of original art a year. A little something-something to pass on to my children, if I ever hooked up with a decent sister and had any. My main man eyed and touched it like he was a critic in an African-American museum.

I stepped into the bathroom and trimmed my goatee. Massaged a dab of Nexxus Humectress in my short hair so it would stay soft. Rubbed some Aveda over that so it would shine, but not be greasy.

Leonard asked, "How's the j-o-b?"

I told him about the pressure we were feeling from Bill Gates and Microsoft sucking up Dan L. Steel's business. Shareholders were getting shaky and stocks had dropped a few bucks today. Told him the San Francisco office had

contacted me five times in the last five days. They were trying to get me back up there on loan to their inept marketing
department.

"By the way," Leonard said. "I need about six computers."

"What happened?"

"Somebody broke in."

"How they do it this time?"

"Used an acetylene torch, cut the locks, stole all of the
computers. Didn't take one book."

"Books are too heavy with khowledge."

"What can you do for me?"

"I might be able to snag some ancient 386s from sur-
plus. IBM compatible at best. That's not guaranteed. Dan
L. Steel would rather donate to Beverly Hills than to a
South Central program."

"Tell your boss if the kids are busy in the center all day
learning how to work a computer and get a job, then they
won't be breaking into his mansion, stealing recipes for
quiche."

"I'll put that in a memo first thing Monday."

Leonard asked, "How's your mom?"

"She's dating a brother from her church. Met him at
singles' bible study. He's forty-three. Ten years younger
than she is. Mom's got it going on in Chicago. Getting her
groove back."

I didn't mention anything about Daddy and his new
bimbo wife. Leonard didn't talk about his mom and stepdad. Some things went without saying.

He asked, "Whose picture is this? The beat-up snapshot of the two bowlegged brothers with the dimples and
processed hair?"

"My granddaddy and his twin sister."

"Her hair is short."

"That's back in the forties when they were in a jazz or

blues band or something. Her hair is pulled back on her neck. She had on pants, so that was a real big deal. She was before her time."

"Look almost like you and Mye. Dents in the face and crooked legs. Damn birth defects."

I've never thought Leonard was super funny, just crazy and stupid. Playful, and he knew enough "yo' momma" jokes to keep him in detention back in high school. We've known each other for what seems like all our lives. Everybody else sees him as the comic or actor or whatever he's doing at the moment. To me he's the brother who grew up as a snotty-nose roughneck and kept bugging my daddy to let him work for some pocket change, and asked me to help him with calculus in our senior year.

Leonard was talking about the girl he met. If she was as fine as he claimed, her buddy had to be Quasimodo with a 'fro. Fine sisters always traveled with butt-ugly ones so there wouldn't be any competition.

I said, "What's wrong with her friend?"

"Attitude."

"Major?"

"Like a pit bull with cramps."

"And you want me to run interference?"

"Like a big dawg. If they show up."

"If?"

"You know how flaky sisters are. They get a brother's phone number, then play the wait-three-days-before-you-call game."

"Say no more. Ever since that stupid rule book came out."

"Sisters don't need rules. They got voodoo. They'll sprinkle something in your food to make brothers follow them around. How you think ugly sisters get good-looking men—voodoo."

I laughed. I said, "What's this Debra talking about?"

"I've been ringing her phone off the hook, and she just called this morning. After we had positive conversation, talked half the night when we met. Now she's in the 'maybe' zone."

At first I put on my usual after-work dress—jeans and leather boots—but Leonard had on earth-tone slacks, collarless shirt, and a vest, smelling like the cologne counter at Macy's. I felt obligated to suit up—basic tan slacks, olive three-button jacket, tan collarless shirt. I was in the bedroom wiping down my shoes when I heard him jump off my leather sofa.

He said, "Ty, you're slower than any sister I've dated."

"And I look better too."

Sounded like he was gobbling up all of the jelly beans in the glass jar on the coffee table facing the entertainment center. My refrigerator door opened. Heard him put my glass juice holder on top of the glass table hard enough to crack one of them.

I yelled, "Take it easy with my stuff, fool."

"Told you about shopping at the swap meet, fool."

"What this girl do for a living?"

"The one you're in charge of is an airline stewardess."

"You mean flight attendant."

"Yeah, right. I meant flight attendant," Leonard said. "Quick, pencil, and paper! I just thought of a joke."

The women were supposed to meet us at The Color of Comedy. Back in the *Shaft* and *Superfly* days, it was a strip club with a small dance stage. It had changed ownership and intentions and had been renovated. The small dancehall soapbox was now a wooden stage with a booming sound system and plenty of room for comics to bounce around.

When I walked inside the double oak doors and crossed the black-gray tile, I saw they had added life-size murals of Dick Gregory, Bill Cosby, and Robin Harris. Those carica-

tures were opposite a floor-to-ceiling mural of three pyra-
mids in the swirling sands of Africa and the Sphinx, his
wide pug nose intact.

We were early so I hung out by the green room. Already comics were bitching about the lineup. Nobody
wanted to go up first because the audience would be cold;
nobody wanted to go up last because the audience would
be tired and irritable.

A brother named Kwamaine went over and patted Leonard on the back. Kwamaine had on a black T-shirt with
90220 on the front—Compton's zip code. He unfolded a
Times and said, "Congrats on making the paper. Making
the paper means you might start making paper pretty
soon."

Somebody said, "And he wasn't gonna tell nobody?"

Leonard read it out loud. "They said I'm a 'new, successful, fast-rising, earthy, young African-American comedian on the Los Angeles scene. Catch his act at the Color of
Comedy.' Whoopty-whoop-whoop and stuff like that. Ain't
that a bitch? I've been on stage for five years and they just
now notice me."

Somebody said, "The flavor of the weekend."

"Better than not being a flavor at all."

Almost everybody congratulated him. A comic named
Jackson stepped over to Leonard holding a copy of the same
newspaper crumpled in his fist. The brother was around
thirty-five, some said he was fifty, and had some build, always wore a dark scarf on his head. Too much attitude.
He dressed in Kani boots, big Tommy Hilfiger T-shirt, and
oversized jeans that hung down to his hipbone.

He said, "Nigga, you thank you all that because a
white-ass newspaper said you was. How you get this shit
wrote on you?"

"If you can't stand the white man, why you want to
know?"

"You dissing me?"

Leonard said, "You all right, my brother? You walking in looking all mad, messing up the room's positive vibe."

I tensed. Thought I might have to yank off my coat. But Leonard wasn't shaken. He didn't acknowledge the anger.

Jackson said, "You ain't got shit but that tired-ass routine that you close with. And you stole that from Robin. Take that shit away and you ain't got no act."

"I know your joke-stealing ass ain't talking about me."

"I don't steal jokes. Say that shit again. Go 'head."

"You steal everybody's damn jokes. You do old Leroy and Skillets, and Pigmeat Markum, and Moms Mabley stuff you think nobody knows. But hey, I know my comedy. That's why nobody wants to go up when you're in the room. We see you hiding in the back with your tape recorder running, then the next week you switch a couple of verbs and swear you wrote the joke yourself."

He glowered around the room, then rested his eyes and words on Leonard. "Don't step to me talking no bullshit."

"I'm just telling the truth."

"You thank you know everything."

"I don't think I know everything. I don't even know half the shit I think I know."

A few people laughed. Jackson had a vein or two pop up in his neck. One of his nerves pumped up and down in his forehead.

Jackson said, "Oh, since you got your funky picture in the white man's paper, you think you a comedy god now, huh?"

"Man, chill. Why everything gotta be about the white man?"

"Like I said, you ain't funny."

Leonard smiled. "See you on stage."

"You up after me. Let's see you follow my act, *brother*."

"Give me something to follow. Something original."

Jackson adjusted his baggy jeans and pimped out of the room. Other comics stayed quiet; tried to blink the tension out of their eyes.

Then Leonard said, "His momma so stupid, she glued food stamps on the phone bill and tried to mail it."

Everybody busted up chuckling, then talked about the brother like he was a dog. I relaxed, let my fists turn into open hands, wiped my damp palms together until the moisture evaporated.

Somebody said, "You gonna let him punk you like that?"

Leonard smiled. "Who's up right before him?"

"I am." That was one of the female comics. Dark skin, in Halloween orange. Her legs were thin, her top heavy, her back length hair bleached to about three colors not found in nature.

Leonard smiled and said, "Switch spots with me."

We heard music coming from outside. Bumping some serious Blackstreet, thumping out *No Diggity*. The mood was being set; the show had begun. Some comics held hands with Leonard in a circle of prayer. I stood by his right side. He led the prayer. Others kept to themselves. Some paced, talked their acts out loud.

Jackson came back after the last amen. Paced the room with evil eyes, face so rigid it looked like it had been cast in concrete. I looked at Leonard. Gave him a what-you-wanna-do? shrug. He nodded. Returned a subtle gesture that said it was cool. He was always subtle. Silence said he could handle it alone.

A few minutes later I was seated at a round table with a blue candle, a reserved sign, and three empty seats. Up front, Kwamaine was anorexia-thin and did jokes about how bad he used to want crack, what he'd do to get crack, like work for the CIA "'cause they has the good shit."

My pulse quickened; Lisa and her husband came in. She was in a cinnamon pantsuit; he was in jeans, shirt open so the gold chain around his neck got the attention it deserved. Holding hands like they were afraid they'd lose each other again, squinting like they had been hit by an LAPD searchlight. My chest tightened, and I shifted about a hundred times. Moved side to side like I had the itchy booty disease.

They sat at the table to my left. Lisa saw me. Her mouth dropped into an O, like one of those plastic clown's mouths at the circus that you aimed and shot water inside. Then she swallowed and forced her lips up into a smile. All business.

Her husband, a mulatto brother who had a receding hairline and was tall enough to play center for the Lakers, saw her watching me a little too long. He glanced. We made eye contact. I nodded. So did he. Lisa leaned her mouth to his ear. He glanced again. Grinned. Nodded. I was pretty sure she told him I was one of her clients. Made me wonder how many she had had.

I adjusted my seat a bit so I wouldn't have to stare at Lisa. Sat voiceless in a tsunami of laughter. It was after nine-thirty; Leonard had been stood up. I'd hold for a minute, then give up my table and move to the back of the room. Maybe leave and catch up with Leonard later. Leaving on my own terms.

Somebody tapped my shoulder. Small fingers. Feminine. I winced. A sister stooped her face close to mine. I thought it was the waitress coming to harass me about the two drink minimum—because the sisters down here worked you until you ordered—but the help never looked that articulate.

She whispered, "Are you Leonard's friend?"

Her breath was baking-soda fresh.

I said, "Yeah. Denise?"

"I'm Debra."

"Sorry about that, Debra. We had given up on you."

She made a forgive-me face. "I'm a little bit late. Me and my friend had to fight over the bathroom."

Cream colored with wavy hair. Leonard's type. Usually those were the overrated and overpriced women who were drawn to brothers with darker skin. The reverse was true too. Her voice was soft, but came across as strong; her demeanor was definite.

Lisa was laughing at the comedy, but her eyes frowned on me. Then they were on Debra. Lisa's husband glanced again.

I introduced myself, then told Debra that Leonard had reserved the table. I said, "For you and whoever you brought."

She said, "I just wanted to stop by and reimburse him for the money, from the night at Denny's. I hadn't planned on staying."

"Stay for a few. At least watch his act."

"He hasn't gone up yet?"

"He's next. He's said a lot of positive things about you."

"He said good things about you too." She smiled, then read the pink sign on the table. "Madam C. J. Walker."

I said, "First sister millionaire. Born in 1867."

"You knew that?"

"Read it on the card."

She laughed, but looked antsy. "Girlfriend made a fortune off black beauty products. And Leonard saved this for us?"

"For you especially."

Her hand patted her leg. "That was sweet of him."

"Thank him later. Have a seat before the comics see you standing, hit you with the spotlight, and make you their act."

She checked her watch, glimpsed back, hand-signaled. Seconds later, another woman bumped around the tables. I was relieved; she wasn't butt-ugly. Last thing I wanted Lisa to see me lounging with was a mud duck.

Debra and her friend were different as night and day, but tit-for-tat in the Department of Fine. Debra waited for her friend to sit. Her friend hemmed and hawed, sat next to me. Scooted her chair a few inches away from me as soon as her butt touched down. Debra sat in the chair to the right of her friend.

They were dressed in jeans and busy cotton blouses. The other girl's radiated with the colors of Africa. Debra's hair was down in a shoulder-length bob; her friend's in a ponytail with a golden pin in it. And her friend's jeans were ripped at each knee, exposing fresh chocolate flesh.

Debra leaned forward. "Shelby, this is Tyrone."

"Tyrel," I corrected. "Tyrel Williams."

"I'm sorry, Tyrel," Debra said. "Tyrel, Shelby Daniels."

Shelby smiled. We shook hands. Shelby had smooth dark skin and a small, cute nose. Obvious African-American features. Swan neck. Fine eyebrows. Lustrous eyes. Righteous. An authentic black woman. Not too diluted or watered down. I caught myself watching what she'd brought to the table, then staring at Lisa's table of leftovers. Lisa had no appeal. Trust was gone and had stolen her gentle radiance. Made her harsh.

Shelby looked as beautiful as a sunrise on the beach. I told my eyes that I'd seen many a sunrise, that she was just another sister, and made my peepers stare at something else. My attention wandered back to Shelby. Wandered and wondered. Shelby caught my curious gaze grazing over her face.

I waved down the thin waitress with the super-weave. We all ordered overpriced drinks. Debra had a mimosa.

Shelby, white wine. Me, Coke with no ice. They laughed at my order.

"If you pay four dollars for a drink in an itty-bitty plastic cup, you might as well get some alcohol," Debra insisted.

Shelby said, "He can drink what he wants. Leave him alone."

Shelby walked her eyes over me.

I nodded.

She turned her face away and glanced around the room.

The comic left the stage. The M.C. did Leonard's intro.

Leonard was in command from the moment he walked into the spotlight. He came out dancing a spoof of the macarena. First he did it the corny off-rhythm way white people did it; then he did it the freaky way hoochie mamas did it. The crowd howled.

He did bits about how black people knew Tupac's catalogue lyric for lyric, but didn't know the black national anthem, couldn't sing it if freedom depended on it. He acted out how brothers and sisters looked baffled when the song came on, showed how most made up words and hummed it instead of singing.

The room had been rocking like we were in a quake for about fifteen minutes when . . .

". . . I was on a plane and I said, 'Excuse me, *airline stewardess*.' The bitch got an attitude."

The crowd laughed. Leonard acted like an SWA, sister-with-an-attitude—bugged out his eyes, snaked his neck, took his voice up an octave, enhanced it with a hip-hop ghetto flare, all while he wagged his pointing finger.

"I'm not an *airline stewardess*. I'm a *flight attendant*. *Stewardess* sounds like waitress, and I ain't no waitress."

Leonard held the attitude, poked out his lips, made the SWA mumble. Much laughter from the crowd. Then he switched and imitated the other side of the attendant, acted effeminate, *too* polite, with a very sexy gay voice as he batted his eyes. . . .

"Now, what can I get for you? Chicken or fish? Something to drink? Maybe a pillow?"

The crowd laughed and howled in a powerful wave.

"Ain't that a bitch?" Leonard said that to a young, amorous couple sitting on the front row. The guy nodded in agreement and his date elbowed him, real hard. More laughter.

Leonard continued, "And I hate flying; aw, man, I hate it. All of a sudden the plane started shaking like this . . ."

He dipped, swayed his body, vibrated hard enough to make his lips slap, held a look of confusion on his face. More laughter.

Leonard went on, "I said, 'What the hell is that?' She says, 'Air pockets.' I said, 'Bitch, air ain't got no pockets.'

"Then she says to assume the crash position. So I walked over and stuck my head between her legs."

The room filled with naughty oohs and shouts of "Hey now." Shelby sent a smirk to Debra, and Debra blushed.

Leonard had the room in the palm of his hand: "She yelled, 'I said crash position!' I said, 'This is crash position. 'Cause if I'm gonna crash, *this* is the position I wanna be in.' "

The laughter was contagious. It echoed and rebuilt itself. Women screamed. Sisters did high-fives across their tables.

"What flavor's that?" Leonard asked. He licked his full lips. "That gotta be strawberry. That's strawberry, right?"

Shelby nearly spat out her drink trying to hold back her laughter. She elbowed me in my ribs; I choked up my soda. Debra belly-laughed, lost control, slapped Shelby's leg hard enough to make her jump out of the way.

Leonard grinned that grin of success and said a heartfelt "Good night, take care of the babies, and take care of our future" to a cheering crowd that didn't want him to leave. He bowed, threw a peace sign, and exited the stage to the sounds of rap music and thunderous applause.

"He is crazy!" Debra howled. "Your friend is so stupid!"

She did the neck, pointed her finger at me, crossed her eyes, mocked Leonard's characterization. At first her prima donna face made me think she was another stuck up Ladera Heights sister who didn't know she was black because she didn't get the memo.

Shelby shook her head. "He was so serious when we met."

Debra smiled. "I didn't know he'd be all that."

Moments later, Leonard joined us. Debra rose from the table, hugged him. She pulled her chair closer to his.

Leonard leaned and shook Shelby's hand. That was when he saw Lisa watching us. Some of the grin seeped from the corners of his lips. Lisa's eyes weren't hawking our way anymore. Leonard's eyes met mine for a second. I gave a nod that let him know it was no big deal. His eyes went back to Debra.

He said, "I'm glad you made it. I didn't see you good-looking, foxy, intelligent black African, now living in America, Negro-colored, intelligent, Nubian, sassy, foxy sistuhs come in. I thought you had stood a brother up."

They both laughed and waved off his comments.

Shelby said, "Brother, I got a bone to pick with you."

Leonard asked, "What's up, Miss Pundit?"

Shelby flipped her hand. "I'm through with you. The *airine stewardess* had to be a bitch, huh?"

We laughed. I was glad both women had senses of humor.

Debra told Leonard, "Remind me to give you your money before the night's over."

"Money?"

"From Denny's. When my charge card was denied." Debra looked ashamed, but she went on, "You're very funny, Mr. DuBois."

"Thank you, Miss Mitchell."

"*But.*"

Leonard said, "But what?"

"Why don't you take the b-word out of your act? Just the part when you call a woman one. It's not too bad when you say a situation is a b-word, but it stings when you call a black woman a b-word. That's just my opinion. A few sisters around the room cringed too. They laughed, but they looked uncomfortable. Hope you don't mind me saying that."

"Done deal. And thanks for the honesty."

I imitated Leonard, "Ain't that a bitch?"

We laughed.

Jackson stepped on stage. Leonard watched. Two minutes into his act, people were yawning, talking, going to potty.

When he started doing another comic's material, the comics gathered in the back and shouted out the punch lines, messed up his already messed-up flow.

Somebody yelled, "C'mon, man, get your ass off the stage."

We eased out a minute after that. Bumped by Lisa's table and did a Soul Train line toward the front door. Lisa gazed up at me with a bold, call-me look. I gave her a fuck-you glower. I moved on with the party of new and improved women. We strolled out into the side parking lot and stood by Debra's Hyundai.

Shelby said, "Well, Leonard, it's a good thing you were funny, 'cause I don't think me and Debra could handle any more tribulation in one day."

Leonard replied, "Bad day?"

Debra nodded. "Laughter was just what I needed."

Leonard said, "Can't laugh and be upset at the same time."

I co-signed with, "True that."

Shelby said, "At least y'all didn't have lesbians trying to feel you up."

I hoped we were about to part and go our separate ways, but Leonard asked them if they wanted to go by a reggae club down near the Venice waterfront. Offered that to Debra as a way to dance off a little more of her stress. That invitation was the opposite of my mood. Shelby shifted around a bit. Looked about as irritated as I felt. I checked my watch. Almost eleven. Early and late at the same time. But not too late. I had a cold, black book at home, one with some hot numbers.

Debra said, "Shelby has to work early in the a.m."

"Debra!" Shelby said, then made her eyebrows dance.

Debra said, "My bad. I must've misunderstood you earlier."

"Must have."

Debra had parked right in front of the club. Before Leonard and I made it across the street, a chunky white guy in a UCLA sweatshirt bolted out of the club. He caught his breath, pulled Leonard to the side. I waited.

That was when I noticed that Lisa had parked next to my car. About as close as we had been over the last few months. I spat on her car. Over and over I spat. A few bricks were on the asphalt, rocks knocked loose from the last few earthquakes we had experienced. I was tempted to create my own natural disaster.

Leonard and the man talked. The white man was smiling, gesturing and chuckling. He gave a strong handshake, patted Leonard on the back, handed him a card, left with an eager stride.

Leonard was unfazed. Straight-faced. He said, "Stop spitting on that girl's car."

"I spat on the ground but the car kept jumping in the way."

"Stop. You wrong. You still knocking that off?"

"She's back with her man. She made the offer. Then had the nerve to bring him down here."

"And? You gonna get with her or what?"

"Thinking about it. Should fuck her just to be spiteful."

"Don't go out like that. She'll get you caught up in some mess. Next thing you know her husband will be kicking down the door and shooting you in the head."

I spat one last time, then said, "Who was that white guy?"

"He's from CBS. Talking about an audition."

"Time to celebrate."

He flipped the man's business card into the street. "Talk ain't nothing but talk. A promise ain't nothing until it's fulfilled. Brothers get stepped to like that every night."

I picked the card up and said, "What's wrong?"

He nodded at the club. "I was supposed to get paid a hundred for the night, but boss woman only paid me twenty-five. Said she was a little short and had to cut everybody's pay."

"Plenty of people paid to get in and bought drinks."

"Same shit happened last time I worked here. Had me down here working, then don't want to pay what they promised."

I said, "Leonard. Whoa, slow down. Take a breath."

He straightened his clothes. Glanced to see if Debra was pulling up yet. The light inside her car was on, but they hadn't moved. Probably doing the girl-talk thing.

I said, "You've got a fine woman on the way over. Chill."

"Right, right."

For a moment he looked old. Old like his own father, Big Leonard, did when he got back from Vietnam. Worn as shoes with holes in the soles. This wasn't my first time seeing Leonard step on a stage, have a bomb show, step off, then doubt himself and his life. Wondering when his funny gene would end. I think he needed to dance away some stress like the rest of us.

I felt immortal, but Leonard was solemn, like he was carrying the burden of life, looked like he wouldn't live forever.

Jackson stormed out the club. Pushed the door open so hard it slapped the stucco wall. He crossed into the lot. Stopped his military-style strut ten yards away. He stared at Leonard. Looked like he was ready to open a can of kick-ass.

Car headlights flashed over us. I moved between Leonard and Jackson. Blocked their view of each other. Killed Jackson's mad-dog act. I spat on Lisa's car again. Wondered how much damage one brick could do.

Debra and Shelby pulled up in Debra's Hyundai. Debra was smiling a big one. Shelby was putting on lip liner. I was close enough to their car to smell two kinds of sweetness when Debra let her window down. Shelby glanced my way again. Then put her eyes to Debra's face, like she was waiting to see what was up. I thought, Bees make honey, but they also sting you when you get too close.

Leonard was getting his mack on: "Debra, why don't I ride with you and Shelby ride with Tyrel?"

Shelby jumped into his conversation, "I don't think so."

Debra said, "Quit acting silly."

Leonard got into Debra's car. Shelby complained her way into mine. After I closed her door, she didn't say a word. Sat in silence and leaned her body away. I ignored her. Tuned my radio to KACE and played some soft oldies, *Mercy, Mercy, Me*.

I took a last look at Lisa's car when I backed out. Watched my puddles of spit slide down her windows.

A while later we were in an after-hours reggae club in Marina Del Rey. A din area lined with car lots, beach-motif storefronts, and mini-malls. Leonard and Debra were on the crowded dance floor, in a bump and grind, moving like freaks in heat, sexy-dancing each other into hysteria. I was stuck babysitting a chocolate-covered shrew. Dancing record after record.

We were in an easy zone, smooth dancing, swaying hips. She was an untamed woman who had some serious rhythm. When we first got here, I was left holding the wall because Shelby kept going to the phone. Probably trying to set up a booty call. But the glower in her face said no booty would be getting called tonight.

I said, "You don't seem like you want to be here."

"So you noticed. What gave it away?"

"The frown. Let's take a walk."

We shuffled through the crowd and stepped outside to Lincoln Boulevard. The air was cool, fresh. Shelby fanned her blouse. I leaned against the concrete wall and wiped sweat from my face with a paper napkin. She glanced at her watch, then saw I was watching her.

I said, "Hope you don't mind me staring."

"Look," she made a rough sound, "I'm keeping you company so Debra won't think I'm trying to be a CB with her and Leonard."

"Same here. I was ready to go home after the show."

"Likewise. And I'm just getting out of some bullshit myself. I just want you to know that before you, you know."

"I'm not trying to get in your space. Trust me."

"And you've got the nerve to have a cocky walk. You think you're a black Cary Grant or somebody?"

"That was corny. Can I get a black reference?"

"Nope. Can I touch your dimples?"

"First you insult me, now you want to touch me?"

"Just that dimple. Keep it above the neck."

"Sure. You have a nice eloquent walk yourself."

"And you call me corny. Chill with the compliments."

Shelby poked her fingers inside my dimples, turned her fingers left and right. She said, "It's like a cove on the beach."

We talked awhile. Talked to make time go by. First she said she was glad Debra got out the house because she had been stressed. I asked if she and Debra were roommates. Asked that because Shelby had said both of them being stressed in a one-bedroom apartment wasn't the best for the country.

She said, "Nope. I'm crashing at her crib until I get my situation straightened out."

She didn't speak on it anymore. Shelby tapped her fingers on her hips, kept an easy beat with the Bob Marley groove, brightened her disposition. She asked me about my marketing job at Dan L. Steel Computer Inc. I didn't talk about me too much. Women hated that. They asked you about yourself, and if you told them, they called you egotistical.

Shelby said, "You're a pretty impressive brother."

"Feelings are magnified and reciprocated."

"This is awkward."

"What?"

"I'm choosing my words and questions before I ask them because I don't want you to think I'm asking stupid questions."

"Questions are part of communication."

"Answers too. Brothers question a sister to death, but

don't give up answers. When a sister asks one damn question it's called stupid." She paused. "What do you look for in a woman?"

"You changed channels. So is this an interview?"

"Just making conversation. What do you look for?"

"Character. Integrity."

"Good answer. Definitely a good answer." Shelby put her frustration on pause long enough to twist part of her hair. She'd been doing that off and on since we'd been alone together. She said, "Want to exchange numbers?"

"That came out of nowhere."

"I said what you were thinking."

"Really? Thanks for letting me know what was on my mind."

"Tell me you weren't thinking that."

"Last thing on my mind."

"Good. Mine too. It's not a good idea anyway."

"Sure?"

"Give me a business card. We might could do lunch one day or something. If not, we'll run into each other again."

"Sooner or later."

"The way Debra and your friend are tee-heeing and ha-haing and whooping all over each other, it'll be sooner than later."

We stood in the light Pacific winds with sweaty faces and looked at each other. Some sort of discovery with no words.

I sucked up a little of the fresh air. Tried to clear my head. Wanted to kick myself for flirting with Shelby. For wanting to bed her arrogant mystery and tame her wicked attitude.

I thought about Lisa. Her face wasn't clear in my mind. Couldn't see her making that I'm-about-to-come face; couldn't hear her panting in my ear; couldn't feel her nails raking my back; couldn't feel her tongue lagging up and down my groin. Everything she had given was clouded with displeasure.

"Do you buy CDs?" Shelby's voice broke me out of my trance.

"Yeah. I get most of mine through BMG or at Block-buster."

"Tower has an outlet off the 101 up in Sherman Oaks. Kind of like the Nordstrom's Rack out in Chino. Only it's all CDs and you get a bunch of stuff dirt cheap. New music too. I ran across it when I was up that way. Buying my mattress. Spent ten dollars and got about eight CDs."

"Thanks for telling me."

"I'm telling everybody. Not just you."

"That's the kind of hookup I need. You got the address?"

"I could call and give it to you. Or pass it to Debra and she could pass it to Leonard and he could give it to you. Let me know if you go up there. I want to go back myself."

"I'll tell Leonard to tell Debra to tell you."

I thought that was funny, but she didn't laugh. So I didn't smile. Shelby glanced toward the club, with impatient eyes. I did the same.

The beat trembled the windows. Party was going on strong. Leonard and Debra were near a wall. She was in front of him, closer than close. Shelby yawned, raised her watch, tapped it at Debra. Debra raised five fingers, then her attention and unending smile went back to Leonard.

Shelby yawned, then said, "Debra looks happy for a change."

"Same for Leonard."

"Debra said your friend told her you have a twin sister."

I said, "Yep. She has twins too."

"Two rug rats?"

"Twins run in my family."

"I'm an only child. Wish I had a brother or sister."

She yawned, moved closer and put her fingers in my dimple again. Touched and twisted. Acted like a kid with a new toy. She didn't smile. Held a serious curiosity in her face.

She said, "What do you call it?"

"Call what?"

"Your dimple."

"Nothing."

"Can I name it?"

"Use your imagination."

"Shelby's Cavern."

DEBRA

8

After we ran six miles this morning, Shelby said she was going to lounge around all day, have herself a lazy Saturday, but it was a sunscreen and sunglasses day, and I was in the mood for some fun. I had to get outdoors and breathe. Besides, I needed some space from the Queen Bee.

Then Leonard called and invited me to lunch at the California Pizza Kitchen in the Beverly Center. We'd go there after his audition. He was trying out for a part on a show at CBS.

I changed shoes four times, couldn't decide on how to wear my hair, decided to let it flow, then ended up putting on my Guess jeans, roman sandals, and a deep purple blouse.

After I bought some gas and ran my car through the

Mobil car wash on the corner, I headed toward Leonard's apartment on Stocker and Degnan. If I was going to date anybody, I had to see how they were living first.

In Leimert Park, the area has beautiful one- and two-level homes built in the sixties and earlier, back before individuality played out. Almost all had well-manicured lawns and were old houses that showed good architecture is a thing of the past. God is in the details. But almost every house had wrought-iron prison bars on the window. A sign of the times. A reality check.

Leonard had a nice one bedroom in a U-shaped, reddish-brown, Spanish-style complex of twelve units: beige walls, arched doorways, high ceilings, earth-tone furniture, a ceiling-high bookcase across one wall of his living room, and more books than I'd ever seen in one man's home. His variety made me feel limited. He smiled when he saw me. Blushed. Gave me an easy two-arm hug. Kissed me at the door. Told me I looked good. I smiled. Then he kissed me again, like he did the night I met him. Not aggressive or wanting, just a nice kiss of welcome. Just enough of a kiss to mess up my lipstick. That threw me in an awkward moment. I was alone in the apartment of a man I'd just kissed. Had kissed too soon. The demise of a relationship.

I said, "Your apartment is nice. You sure have plenty of books."

"Yeah. That's my fetish. Books and bookstores."

"Knowledge and power."

"Knowledge is power."

I smiled. "You must spend a grip at Eso Won."

"That's my hangout. Sometimes I stand around so long reading books, I think they're going to charge me rent."

"What are the trophies for?"

"Baseball and boxing."

"You boxed?"

"Did golden gloves for a minute."

His two hooped earrings looked good, but I still would've preferred it if he only wore one. Actually none would be the best.

Pictures were on a wall. All in black frames.

I said, "Who are these people?"

He said, "My family. That's my dad in the army suit."

"You look just like him."

"Thanks. That's my mom in the blue dress. The rest of them are my brothers and my sister."

There were four brothers and a sister. Most of the pictures looked a few years old. I said, "You're the youngest?"

"Next to. I've got a brother two years under me. My oldest brother is forty-plus."

I said, "I've got two older sisters and a younger brother."

He said, "Ready to go?"

"Actually, may I use your bathroom before we leave?"

"Down the hall on the right."

A Miles Davis photo was matted and framed in the hallway. Sprinkles of hair were in the bathroom sink from where he had shaved his mustache and goatee. I smiled. Sort of wished I could've watched him shower, shave, and get dressed, wished I could've been a spectator to the things men do.

I didn't have to use the bathroom. Because of what had happened to Shelby, after the trick bag Bryce had put her in, I peeped at Leonard's shower walls. Did the same to the floor. Even looked in the trash to make sure there weren't any panty-liner packages. Looked up at the ceiling. Spied around the toilet seat. I didn't find any leftover female hair.

I realized my anxiety, saw my paranoid expression in the mirror. I ran my fingers through my hair and peeped inside his medicine cabinet. I didn't see anything but Magic Shave, deodorant, Colgate toothpaste, Wings cologne, and green alcohol for aching muscles. No prescription for any-

thing that would make me scamper for the door. I flushed
the toilet to make him think I had used it, then put more
lipstick on and went back into the living room, waited by
the CD rack.

I heard him in the bedroom, but I wasn't that curious.
I wasn't a mouse in search of cheese. But it took him a moment, so I did peep from the living room and try to see what
he was doing. I had one friend who went to visit a brother
she'd just met, and he came out of the bedroom butt-naked.
I exhaled and felt silly when I saw Leonard was making sure
all of his windows were locked, and shades were drawn.

I said, "Mind if I help myself to some water?"

"Go ahead."

There were seven or eight glasses in the sink. There
wasn't any lipstick on the rims of the glasses. His bottled
water was next to the microwave. I poured half a glass and
tried to wash this madness out of my system. It has been a
long time since I felt anything for a man. Too long. And that
was making me too scared. Oh great. Now I had to put
more lipstick on.

I said, "You should leave your radio on an all talk station."

"Why?"

"That way there'll be a steady stream of voices inside.
It makes it sound like someone's here."

"Good idea. Hadn't thought about doing that."

"Leave a hallway light on too."

He chuckled. "Am I going to be gone that long? Sounds
like you're kidnapping a brother."

I blushed. Sort of wanted another short kiss.

We hopped in his Celica and went through the urban
part of La Brea and cut across the Jewish section of San
Vincente. That led us up to Fairfax and the Ethiopian dis-
trict. Cuisine from the motherland was in the air of the
upper-middle-class area.

Leonard said, "Ever eat Ethiopian?"

I glanced at the African shops on the other side of Carl's Jr. I sipped some Evian and said, "Haven't had the pleasure."

"Maybe we could do that sometime. They have live bands at a couple of the restaurants on weekends."

"Sounds like a plan." I smiled at his plans for the future. "I'm curious about what you guys do on an audition."

"We get looked over and prodded like cattle, spend thirty seconds in a room with somebody who has your future in their hands, hope they'll pick you to get branded in the next roundup."

"That's power."

"Tell me about it."

We walked into the offices on Fairfax and Melrose, and I swear, there were a hundred medium- to dark-skinned casually dressed black men looking like they had missed the bus for the Million Man March. I recognized a few from TV or movies. A room waiting for others to look them over and decide their ebony fate. My nerves were on edge, and I wasn't the one who had to audition.

Leonard said, "We're definitely gonna be late for lunch."

I patted his hand and said, "No problem. TCB first."

Leonard nodded at a brother coming inside. The brother saw him, but didn't respond. That bit of rudeness caught my attention.

I said, "Who was that?"

"Jackson. Another comic."

"Oh, yeah. He was booed off the stage."

He had on the same outfit: boots, T-shirt, baggy jeans.

I asked, "What's his problem?"

"He started tripping when he got beat out at the audition on a show kinda like *In Living Color*."

"That show's canceled. That was a long time ago."

"Some people never get over stuff."

That reminded me of the bitter black women who never let go of their pain. Walking wounded. "Who beat him out?"

"He got beat out by a brother kinda like Tommy Davidson."

"What happened?"

"Jackson got mad because the producers and casting people didn't laugh, and took his Mr. Happy out. Tried to urinate on the brother who was kinda like Keenan Wayans."

"*What?*"

"He's crazier than a postal worker on crack."

Leonard found us a little space and was going over the script. He'd become so focused and intense, so intelligent. And for me intelligence was a definite turn on.

A white man in jeans and a T-shirt, who looked like a young Danny DeVito, stepped out and stared. Smiled at me. I moved closer to Leonard. The short-short man came right to me.

His whiny voice almost made me giggle. "What're you doing here?"

I said, "I'm with him."

"I was talking to him."

I saw he wasn't looking at me. He was cross-eyed. When he was looking at nobody, he was looking at everybody.

Leonard raised his face up from his script, said, "Hey."

The man repeated, "What're you doing out here?"

"Waiting."

"For the *Brother, Brother* pilot?"

"Yeah. That's what you told me to come down for, right?"

He lowered his voice to a whisper, but the murmur was

louder than his regular voice, "These schmucks are for five-or-under. You're down for a real part."

Leonard smiled. "All right."

The man motioned for Leonard to follow him through the crowd. I leaned against the wall. Leonard smiled back at me. He imitated the white man's pigeon-toed walk and made playful cross-eyes. I giggled, blushed, gave him a thumb-up and cross-eyes. Jackson stood up in time to bump Leonard. Bumped Leonard hard enough to make him lose his smile. That rudeness made me ache; nasty words brewed inside me. My nails felt like claws. I didn't know I felt so strongly for Leonard. Little old me was ready to protect him from a man bigger than the both of us.

Leonard chuckled, "Sorry, my brother. Didn't mean to bump into you. Please accept my deepest apology."

Leonard extended his hand. Jackson didn't. Jackson had his script, went to the other side of the room with the people reading for a five-or-under, whatever that meant. Lines of desperation were engraved in almost every face.

I found some space, sat down on the floor, and relaxed powwow style. Closed my eyes to say a silent prayer for my family, included Leonard and his dream, Shelby, even remembered Tyrel, and while I prayed, somebody sat down by me. I scooted down without stopping my grace. I was so deep in supplication, so busy asking for someone to watch over Ericka, that I had floated away; no one else existed. They scooted closer. Bumped into me. I raised my head. It was Jackson. He smelled like old tobacco and aftershave with too much alcohol in its formula.

I scooted down a little more.

He did the same.

I said, "Is there a problem?"

He said, "I wanna eat you out."

"*What?*"

"I know that punk you with cain't do nothing for you.

You need a *real* man. Let's go outside. You got some nice lips."

I felt naked. My hand wanted to strike his face, but it was stuck over my mouth.

A few others heard him. They said nothing and did less. One ignorant ass laughed. And that chuckle added to the violation. Others didn't care, were self-involved, went back to reading the stupid scripts in front of their faces.

I stood and hurried down the hallway toward the water fountain. All the way I tried to imitate Shelby's don't-mess-with-me sashay, but all I managed were awkward, jittery steps that I struggled to keep smooth. I gritted my teeth and wished I was Shelby, wished I owned an ounce of her toughness. Wished I had her four-letter vocabulary.

I sipped water, but couldn't wash away the feelings, couldn't rinse the violation out of my mouth. Wiped the anger that had manifested itself as sweat off my upper lip. Rubbed the wetness from my hands onto my jeans. Massaged the frustration in my hands so hard I felt heat on my hips.

And he was looking at me. Smiling as if he'd achieved some victory. Wagging his tongue like it was a flag.

I put my back to that world and made myself busy toying with the cuticles on my left hand. I didn't raise my head or speak to a few people on the far end who said a friendly hi, but in my restlessness I kept moving. I didn't know I was moving, but I was. My body took me outside into the sunlight. Trembling.

SHELBY

9

Yep. I called Tyrel. Right after Debra left to go hang out with Leonard, soon as the door clicked closed behind her, I yanked the covers off my head, picked up the phone, and said, "What's up, Tyrel?" We chatted a bit, and since he wasn't catching the hint, I asked those bowlegs and double-dimples if he would like to sneak out with a sister and catch a movie or ride the smog-free coast. As friends. I made that perfectly clear. If he expected more than my company and shallow conversation for a little while, it would be a gross misunderstanding.

When he picked me up, Tyrel had on a black nylon hooded warmup suit and Nike X-trainers, looking like a weekend warrior. His Nike cap had the slogan JUST DO IT on the front. I had on jean shorts, big-big pink-green sweatshirt. Looking funky, feminine, and fashionable. Without asking a brother if he'd mind a whiff of my toes, I took my hiking boots and socks off and slapped my feet on his dash. Then I tossed my NOC IT DOWN cap in the backseat, let my hair bounce with the beautiful beach breeze, nibbled on strawberry yogurt, inhaled Marvin Gaye, enjoyed life on PCH.

Tyrel said, "Where you wanna go?"

"Drive until you're tired."

"Did Debra want to tag along?"

"She left to kick it with Leonard."

We had the radio on KACE, jamming the oldies, but clicked it off because we never stopped running our mouths. Communication was strong. His eyes were on my legs a time or two. His eyes brushed mine in a gentle, curious way. I wanted to know what he saw when he glanced at me. I pulled down the visor and checked the mirror and made sure I didn't have a present swinging out of my nose. I slid my hand up and down my skin. Then I laughed.

He said, "What's funny?"

"I used to put bleach in my bath water, back when I was in first or second grade. Used to rub it on my skin."

"Why?"

"Thought I was too dark." We passed by Santa Barbara. I said, "What kind of sisters do you go out with?"

He chuckled. "All flash and no foundation."

"I always meet brothers that are dreamers and not doers. Brothers who befriend then betray. No true character."

Two hours passed, and soon Tyrel knew all about my family and I knew all about his. His mother was in Chicago; mine was in heaven. His father was a ho and mine was a no-show. Talking about parents made me deliberate. Made me think and count.

I asked, "How many kids did you know when you were growing up had both a mother and a father in the house? I mean the original parents and not a stepmomma, or a man stopping by to satisfy momma until the next stepdaddy came along."

"That's a tough one. My parents were together."

"Don't count. Infidelity is grounds for disqualification."

"Qualify."

"Okay. I'll qualify. How many of those parents were still sexually active with each other and only with each other?"

"Monogamous?"

"Yeah."

"That's harder than a differential equation."

"I don't know what a differential equation is."

"Okay. Harder than the final question on *Jeopardy.*"

"I can work with that. What about Leonard's folks?"

"His dad was shot up in Vietnam."

"Sorry to hear that."

"They put him on some kind of drugs for the pain, then put him on another kind to try to un-addict, if that's a word—"

"It is now."

"To un-addict him from the first one. Long story short, he overdosed."

"What was Leonard's daddy like?"

"Before the war his daddy was a boxer."

"What about his momma?"

"She would disappear. Sometimes Leonard would call me in the middle of the night and we had to go up and down Western."

"Nothing on Western but motels and bars."

"Right. That's where we'd find Leonard's mom in the middle of the night."

"What about his brothers?"

"They didn't care one way or the other. So it would be me, Leonard, and my sister Mye. We would pile in a car and search and search. She would be so drunk it was scary."

"She living?"

"Yeah. His momma's straight now, pretty much anyway. But they don't really have a relationship. Him or any of his brothers either for that matter."

"Why?"

"Victim mentalities and GED attitudes."

"My momma was always there. But she worked two jobs, so I hardly saw her. She worked evenings, so she never came to many of the school functions like Debra's momma did. Didn't make it to my graduation or anything. Had to pay them bills."

"You were a latchkey kid."

"Like everybody else I knew." I smiled, let my high

cheekbones give the appearance of joy, and pretended I
didn't want to cry. Tyrel had reached a place other brothers
had never even asked about. I'd lived with Bryce for
months, and he'd never asked me anything about me. Not
many had. Guess nobody cared enough to share a moment
of realness, to stop long enough to experience me from the
inside. Nobody gave up a concerned tone like the sexy black
man that was turning me on from the other side of this car.
I said, "I had to raise myself. I was at Debra's house all the
time. Most of the time."

I didn't say I was at Debra's a lot because when
Momma didn't work, she would have company and I got
tired of hearing them carrying on at night. Got tired of half-
naked strangers sitting at our breakfast table in the morning. I remember all of their faces. None of them ever came
around for long. None of them ever stayed. I used to wish
one of them would marry my momma so I could call one of
them Daddy, so on the stuff I filled out at school, I wouldn't
have to leave the information about "Father" null and void.
I'd never tell that. I'd never tell how I didn't feel like I belonged anywhere until I met Debra. Never tell all to a brotha. And I'd never say anything to make Momma look bad.

My mind was still with my childhood wishes when I
said, "What's your relationship like with your daddy?"

"Strained."

"You communicate with him?"

"Nope. Haven't talked to him in quite a few seasons."

I made a sound.

Tyrel said, "What?"

"Nothing. I was just wishing I had a daddy to call
sometimes when it got rough. That male point-of-view. You
should call."

"Too much happened in the past."

"Can't be that bad."

"He was late coming home one night. One of those late

nights filled with gunshots and police sirens and helicopters."

"That's damn near every night."

"Yep. But for some reason Momma was worried on that night. Woke me up, sent me and Twin down to the store. Long story short, we walked in on him and another woman. They were in the back room on a cot, naked, getting it on, with Johnny Carson on TV and a fifth of Ripple at their sides."

"No shit? Your momma find out?"

"Not by my mouth. Mye told. Daddy begged her not to, offered to buy her a convertible Mustang, but she told him where to get off and told the whole family. Then she got mad at Momma because she wouldn't leave Daddy. Which put strain between me and my momma for a while. She thought I had chosen sides. I was trying to be neutral, but in situations like that, if you don't condemn, they assume you condone."

"Caught your daddy with another woman. That's jacked."

"Changes how you view your daddy."

"I guess. Still wouldn't keep me from talking to him." A moment later I asked, "You ever mess around on your girlfriends?"

"Had something on the side with most if not all of them."

"Sort of like your daddy."

"I wasn't married."

"Since it was about *your* momma, guess that makes it different."

A moment passed.

He asked me, "What was your childhood like?"

"Welfare and food stamps. Nothing unusual. Yours?"

"Pops took food stamps and welfare money at his store."

"See? We needed each other," I said. "I like you, Tyrel. As a friend. You're cool."

"Same here."

The next thing we knew we were four hours from home. San Luis Obispo. We had detoured off the 101 freeway in wine country, ridden the side roads, had been by three or four mom-and-pop wineries, did some quick touring, light sampling. Bought three bottles of the sweetest wine I had ever tasted in my life.

We ended up riding by Hearst Castle, then headed out about twenty more miles to Morrow Bay. A hidden ocean town that smelled like seafood and held the echo of seagulls flying overhead and waves crashing on the beach. Morrow Bay was so Gucci. A Mayberry on the beach that sold mostly surfing and biking equipment. Didn't sell a damn thing for black people. I mean *real* black people. The two black people we had seen were carrying surfboards and referred to Tyrel as "dude." Both of them were with skinny blondes. The brothers had too much saltwater in their sister-free diet.

But the place was European and peaceful. Romantic and serene. Made me want to hold Tyrel's hand, put my head on his shoulder for a while. Scenery was beautiful. Quiet. The main attraction was a mountain-sized rock on a part of the village that looked like a peninsula. We parked over there like most everybody else did.

I said, "Tyrel?"

"Yeah."

"When's your birthday?"

"July ninth."

"You're lying."

"No reason to lie."

"Mine is July seventh."

"Guess we're having a Cancer party."

A moment or two went by with us watching people and

staring at the big black mound in the ocean. I said, "Why do you think people flock to see this rock?"

"Because it looks like a big black breast."

"You are such a man."

He said, "Hey, you asked."

"That I did."

"What're you thinking?"

"I was wondering how big the nipple would be."

"Such a woman."

"Hey, you asked."

We had parked in front of one of those erect concrete poles. A vertical shaft three feet high, with two feet of girth. Some serious girth. Hard. Straight. My bosom had that come-nibble-and-suck-me feeling. Had been feeling that way most of the ride up the coast. Now it had resurfaced because of a stupid piece of lifeless concrete. Then I read the words on the front of Tyrel's cap—JUST DO IT. Heard a whisper. I caught myself licking my lips. Squeezed my thighs together a touch without thinking. I swallowed and shifted around in my seat.

Tyrel said, "You okay?"

"I'm fine. Let's get out and stretch our legs."

We walked over near the edge that faced the ocean. I stared back at the mountain. Gazed up to where it disappeared into the overcast skies. I must've been tripping. The low clouds that formed around its top looked like fluffy pubic hair. I craned my neck and wondered what was up there. I moaned a bit with my imagination. Tyrel was gawking at the mountain with as much intensity as I had. He cleared his throat, shifted around. His eyes glanced at mine again and again. His face was so serious.

I said, "What're you thinking about?"

"Nothing."

He looked away. Moved his thoughts.

I turned away. Moved my thoughts.

Gazed around.

Concentrated on the people driving by and walking near the seafood restaurants. Most wore windbreakers and shorts, stuff like dockers and deck shoes. All looked tanned and well-to-do.

Tyrel said, "How do you feel?"

"Fine. The wine we tasted has me craving."

"Craving wine?"

I smiled and gently whispered, "Craving."

Since he wasn't trying to get into my space, I leaned over and put my finger in his face, twisted it inside of Shelby's Cavern. He smiled. That made me tingle with comfort.

"Is there somewhere I can get sweats?" I asked.

"Cold?"

"Some. But I've been colder. I want some herbal tea too. I saw a mall back in Obispo."

"Back on Madonna Road."

"Whatever."

Tyrel stretched. "Okay. They should have a food court."

"You don't mind shopping with a woman?"

"Not as long as you keep it under two hours."

"That's a decent compromise." I smiled. "Well, friend. This has been a wonderful day. I want to thank you in advance."

"Anytime. Friend. Wonder how Leonard and Debra's day is going."

"Who cares? They're so lovey-dovey it's sickening."

"True that."

We walked around the mall and stopped at a place or two. I bought some plain gray sweats and a toothbrush. I picked up some Mentadent because my mouth was starting to get stale as hell, and I didn't want to funky up the place when I exhaled. Tyrel must've felt the same way because when I was trying on sweats, he jogged back into the drug-store and picked up a toothbrush too.

The mall was one of those nice structures connected to an Embassy Suites. That's where we stopped for tea, down-stairs in the open court amongst all the trees and skylight. The hotel doors faced outward toward the court. Upstairs people were coming in and out of rooms. A few had suit-cases so I guessed they were checking out and heading back to wherever they were from. Tyrel was staring at the same old white couple I had been watching struggle with their luggage as they came out of the room up and across from us.

I said, "Don't they look happy?"

Tyrel looked at me.

Smiled.

I looked at him.

Smiled.

I had ripped open a bag of honey to put in my tea. Some of the sweetness spilled on my finger and I licked it off. And I saw Tyrel was watching me suck on my finger. It was one of those things I had done without thinking and didn't realize the connotation. Sort of like catching myself with my mouth open and eating a banana. Even worse, sucking and licking on a popsicle in front of a man. Things Debra told me not to do in public.

But Debra wasn't here. I was two hundred miles from anybody I knew. From anybody who knew me.

I put more honey on my finger. Licked it off again. Then I poured more on my finger, much more, let it drip. Tyrel reached over, took my hand, licked it off. Sucked. I didn't resist. Pretended like it was no big deal. Neither one of us had any kind of expression whatsoever. Waiting to see. My breasts swelled until they felt like they were as big as that mountain we'd witnessed in the bay, and I clenched my teeth so I could hold on to the moan that was clogged inside my throat.

I reminded myself, "Breathe, girl, breathe." I felt my voice getting low and thick when I said, "What are you doing, friend?"

"You really want to be my friend?"

"Cut the bull."

"Bull cut."

"What's on your mind?"

"You really want to know?"

"Don't be shy."

"Might not be appropriate for friends."

"You never know until you ask."

He was still holding my sticky hand when we got up to go. I thought we were heading for the car, but we got on the elevator.

I said, "Where are we going?"

"Sightseeing. Let's check out the view from up top."

We leaned against the rail for a while. He put his arms around me. My palms were sweating like somebody had turned on a faucet. Damn mouth had dried up like San Bernardino. We watched people walk from the mall into the hotel and vice versa. One of the Hispanic maids pushed her cart by us and tapped on a door down the way. Then she rattled her keys and went inside. Tyrel took my hand and led me that way.

I said, "What are you doing?"

"Come along."

When we got to the room, the maid had gone inside. Tyrel took my hand and led me in. The lady was middle-aged, gray around the temples, short, plump. One of the double beds was tossed, the other was fresh. The maid smiled at us.

Tyrel said, "Oh, I'm sorry. We weren't finished with the room yet. Could you come back later?"

"How long?"

"About two hours. May we have some fresh towels?"

The maid nodded, gave us towels, and left. Just like that. The woman had bought Tyrel's lie without a second thought.

Tyrel put the Privacy Please! sign out and closed the door behind her. Damn, I was scared. How did I end up here? In San Luis Obispo. In a stolen hotel room. Trembling from my little toe to the dandruff in the back of my scalp.

I said, "So. What's up with this?"

He smiled and said, "Craving."

"What?"

"Just craving."

The brother held my face, kissed me. Sent me to somebody's heaven. Made me feel so good I tiptoed and floundered with the feeling. Kissed me for almost fifteen, maybe twenty minutes. Overwhelmed me with some serious passion. Rubbed my breasts like they were the best thing since sliced bread, teased his hand all up and down my body like he was Columbus searching for whatever the hell Columbus was searching for.

I said, "We could go to jail stealing a room like this."

He shut my ass up with kisses. Pressed his body all up against mine. Moved his crotch in the crevice where mine lived. Made small circles. He was hard enough to make me forget about any concrete pole I'd seen a little while ago.

I moaned, "Stop. Don't have any protection."

He had a pack of condoms in the bag with his toothbrush. While I was buying sweats, he had slipped into the drugstore and come out more prepared than a boy scout on a nature run.

He kissed me some more. Chewed my neck. Real soft bites that made me *Oooh*. Real nice *Mmmmm*. I was lost in the feeling. And since we were creeping, it made it that much better.

He said, "You still want to be my friend?"

I said, "Yeah. Homey. Lover. Friend. A whole lot more."

I pulled his jacket off him. Sat him down. Took his clothes off him. Took mine off. Slow. Easy. Took off my pink and green sweatshirt and dropped it on my feet. Made him watch me wiggle out of my French-cut panties. Came out of those hiking boots and socks with ease. His wand was straight up and down like six o'clock, pointing at me like I was the one, the two, the three, the four, and the five. My own love was praying for a piece of his rhythm. And the freaky side of me made me savor his wand for a while. Made me wish I had one of those bottles of wine we'd bought so I could pour it over him and taste and taste. Then I kissed him and shared the appetizer I'd savored from him. Lay him back on the bed. Sat on him. His mouth was on my breast before I could move up or down. And his warm tongue felt damn good. Tasting my nipples, sucking on me, squeezing and nibbling and sucking and *Mmmmmmm*.

I moved my body like sex was going out of style. Exercised my power and made him my fantasy. I had lost control, but like En Vogue sang, I had the right to lose control, and I was exercising that right. Rocked back and forth and forth and back and felt him swell inside me. I heard myself let out some sounds and wailed some words that told him how much I really admired him. Admired his faults. Admired what he represented.

He whispered in my ear, "What do you like?"

I held him, closed my eyes to the fantasy who wanted to fulfill mine, put tender kisses on his face. He lay me back, I stretched my arms to each side, welcomed him with my love, and he worked me like I was his fantasy.

Tyrel's loving was so good he should've put it on his résumé.

Worked me deep, worked me shallow, worked me deep, worked me.

Damn, I wanted to cry from the satisfaction.

And I did.

He licked my tears of nothing-but-pleasure from my eyes.

Tyrel grooved my body with character, sucked my breasts with integrity, pushed and pulled my love into ecstasy. During our feast, I wondered if he could fall deep in love with me like I knew I was gonna fall deep in love with him.

TYREL

10

"Hello. May I speak to Mr. Vardaman Williams?"

"This him. Who this? What done happened?"

"How are you doing?"

"I was trying to sleep till the phone rang. Good Lord, it's near midnight. Who calling my house this time of the night?"

"It's me."

"Who?"

"Tyrel Anthony Williams. Your oldest and youngest son."

"Tyrel? What you—Where you at, son? You in Nashville?"

"I'm still in California."

"You in jail?"

"No, I'm not in jail. You get the cards I sent you?"

"Yeah. You ain't sent one in a while. Everything all right?"

"We haven't heard from you in over a year."

"Been that long since I talked to you?"

"Yeah. That was the last time I called your house. Remember? You were busy and said you'd call me back."

"Been kinda busy. The new store takes up all my day."

"You didn't write back either."

"You know I ain't much on writing folks."

"I put my phone number on the Father's Day cards."

"Why you call here this late?"

"Me and Mye were worried about you."

"Where she at now?"

"She turned lesbian and went to Africa to marry a high priestess or something."

"Good for her."

"It was a joke."

"That why you call?"

"Part of the reason. I guess. Yeah."

"What you now, twenty-four or five?"

"Twenty-nine."

"You that old?"

"Yeah. I'm that old. I'm old."

"How's Leonard?"

"He's doing pretty good. He asked about you."

"He still telling jokes and what have you?"

"Yeah."

"Tell him I said hello."

"Will do."

"You married yet?"

"Nope."

"Wasn't you engaged last time I talked to you?"

"Nope. Mye was engaged five years ago."

"You got children?"

"Nope. Mye had the children four years ago."

"Well, we just added a room onto the house so I ain't got no extra money to send you and your sister. . . ."

"We don't want any money. But you could send your grandchildren something."

"Hold on."

"Daddy?"

"Uh, Tyrel."

"Yeah?"

"It's middle of the night here, and me and my wife have to get up early to feed the horses. Phone calls this late upset her and make it hard for her to get back to sleep. It's okay by me, but Phyllis don't want you, or anybody else for that matter, calling here late at night."

"Mrs. Williams don't want us calling there period."

"Can I call you one day next week?"

For a moment I was ten years old. Me and my daddy were out on the side of the house changing the oil in his Mustang. Then I was eleven and all of us were piled into his Lincoln Town Car and heading for Vegas and spending the weekend at Circus-Circus. Somewhere in my thoughts I was six and he was at the kitchen table helping me and Mye understand numbers and words. At fifteen he was trusting me with his first store, letting me open it up all by myself. And right now, no matter what, I felt like Little Tyrel. The child that used to sit on his knee, the child he would bounce up and down while I yelled, "Giddyap, horsey!"

I said, "Daddy?"

"What, Tyrel?"

"No matter who you're married to, you're still our daddy."

"Thanks, son."

Shelby was at my side. I looked at her. She smiled. Made hand motions that told me to keep on talking.

I said, "Daddy?"

"Yeah, son."

"Why don't you and Momma ever ask about each other?"

"Don't start with that."

We soaked in silence for a moment.

He said, "You talked to Virginia?"

"Every Sunday morning. Momma is doing fine."

More silence.

"Daddy?"

"Yeah, son."

"I think we should put the past to rest and let it be."

"It ain't that easy."

"All of us should get together. At least all talk on the phone."

"When the time's right."

"Okay. Remember that song, 'The cat's in the cradle.' Don't be distant like that, old man."

"Between the stores and the ranch, I stay busy."

"Don't get too busy for the original family."

"We'll talk, young buck."

"Stay blessed."

"You too. Tell Mye I send my love."

"I could give you her number. Tell her yourself."

Daddy said, "If she wanted me to have her number, she'd've called long before now."

"Call her and talk to your grandchildren."

"Let me know if she needs anything."

"Tell the new Mrs. Williams I said hi."

"Good night, young buck."

He put the receiver back in its cradle. I did the same at the pay phone I was on. Disconnected each other once again.

Shelby's hand massaged my shoulders through my sweat suit. She had strong fingers. Her fondness took the bite out of my fury. She made easy circles and ironed out tension. Then we headed toward the car. Shelby had put on the sweats she had bought. Other things were in the plastic bag I carried. My Nike cap was backward on her head. Her cap was in her hand.

After we left the borrowed room, we sat around the lobby, sipped orange juice, tried to get our energy back, and marveled at what we had done. And we talked. It was like the reverse-engineering of the relationship—we got the sex out of the way and waited to see where it took us from there. Right now I didn't know. Lisa was gone with the wind, but I knew she'd call. Especially since she'd seen me with a better brand of woman than she'd ever be. Shelby had talked me into calling my father.

Shelby said, "It didn't go too well, huh?"

"About the same as usual."

"It's late. Maybe next time your pops'll call you."

"No big deal. If he does, he does; if he don't, whatever."

"Don't say that. Family is always a big deal."

I held her hand tighter. Felt like little Tyrel for a few moments, then straightened my back, adjusted my sweat suit, took a breath, made myself feel like the man I was supposed to be.

We cruised down to Madonna Road and got on the 101 south.

She said, "You okay?"

"Yeah." I smiled, leaned over and kissed her lips.

"I've got to be on a plane at seven in the morning or I'll be homeless and out of a j-o-b."

"Okay. Let the seat back and sleep to L.A."

"Okay." She sighed, then patted my hand. "Tyrel?"

"What's up?"

"Today is just today."

"All right."

"We shouldn't make any more out of this than it is. Or was."

"What're you saying?"

"It's not gonna happen again."

"Okay."

She sighed again. Sad and regretful energy filled the car. I don't know if she went to sleep, but she didn't talk. All of that high spirit was put to rest. With every mile we got closer to reality. Shelby rubbed her nose and took her hand back. It didn't matter. I was ready to let it go anyway.

———

We made it back to L. A. about one thirty in the a.m. Debra was surprised to see us creep into the dimly lit living room. Shelby was still solemn and had a look in her light-brown eyes that said she had hoped Debra would be asleep. The way she had hopped out of my car before I cut the engine off, I don't think she really wanted me to walk her to the door.

Like I said, Debra was wide awake. But not alone. Leonard was on the floor. Debra's coffee table had two half empty glasses of Spumante and a game of Jenga set up. Shelby had this subtle attitude come over her body, like she thought she was interfering. With Kenny G's *The Moment* playing nothing-but-love tunes on Debra's CD player, and both of them with their shoes off and shirts loosened, I wondered what their game would've been an hour from now.

Debra glowed when she spoke to me, then gave a short grin to Shelby. A blush that spoke of bad timing. Shelby tsked. Her expression didn't change. She gave a shallow wave. No words.

I said, "What's up, boss man?"

Leonard concentrated on the game and said, "Right now everything's calm. We're tied at two games apiece."

Debra glanced at the clock on the wall then said, "I thought you might've been gone on a trip."

"Sort of," Shelby said. "We went for a ride up the coast."

"Must've been some ride."

They shared one of those girlfriend looks. Shelby made her eyes open and close real fast, flutter like butterfly wings. Debra did the same and didn't ask questions. She went back to focusing on the game. She was deep in the same world Leonard was in. Both looked intense and competitive. It looked more like a bonding-of-the-minds ritual than a board game.

On his next pull, everything toppled.

Debra cheered and kicked her feet. "Yes!"

While they boxed the game up, Shelby was quiet. She kicked her hiking boots off. Tossed her hat on the dining room table.

Debra sang, "Shelby."

"Sorry." Shelby grabbed her cap then picked her shoes up. When she bent over, her butt created the shape of a nice unreachable heart. I moved my eyes away. When Shelby turned, her eyes were dull, empty. Shelby's words were plastic and distant, "Well, Tyrel, thanks for the ride up the coast. Don't forget about the CD place in the valley. Take care."

I said, "Sure. Thanks. You want to go if I go up there?"

"Nah. I've got enough CDs and nowhere to put 'em. Debra, did anybody call me about my furniture?"

Debra shook her head.

Me and Shelby shook hands good-bye without eye contact. Not even a good handshake. She touched me quick and shallow, like I had the plague. She gave up a fake yawn then went down the hallway to the bedroom without looking back. Closed the door.

A minute later, me and Leonard left. We stood around visitors parking and talked for a while.

He was keyed up. "What do you think about Debra?"

I shrugged. "Question is, what do you think?"

"I think I really don't need a relationship—not right now."

"Scared you might lose focus?"

"Yeah. Sisters are a black hole for attention."

"Think Miss Café au Lait is a drive-thru?"

He shook his head. "Far from it. What was up with you and Miss Pundit?"

I looked back at the window of the woman who had dissed me like it wasn't about shit. I said, "Drive-thru all the way."

Leonard told me what Jackson did at the audition.

My hands heated up. I said, "What you wanna do about it?"

He kicked a rock on the ground. "Can't do nothing."

"Why?"

"Debra made me promise. She told me I'm bonded to my word."

I laughed. "That's bull. As much as women change their minds over shit. Women invented unilateral decisions."

He was pissed.

I shook my head. Remembered how we would kick ass or get our asses kicked back in high school. Now we were mental gladiators.

He grunted. "If I can't do nothing, you can't do nothing."

"I hear you."

He talked about how great Debra was. How she had tackled responsibility and handled the situation like a champ. I didn't hear a word. He wasn't focused enough to pick up my true mood. Either that or he didn't care. Leonard stared back at Debra's apartment like he was Romeo in search of Juliet.

We got in our cars. Went our separate ways.

On the way home, everything seemed like a farce. Hanging out with Shelby didn't bring anything real. All I did was burn a tank of gas and wear out the rubber on my tires. Tonight wouldn't even add up to a page in my memoirs. She had done just like Lisa. Same shit. I called to check my messages, the ones on my cellular service. Lisa had called ten times. I figured she would be ringing my phone after she saw me with Shelby. That was why I had turned my c-phone off all day. I dialed her number. Her husband answered. I was in a don't-care mood.

I said, "Is Lisa around?"

"May I ask who's calling?"

"This her husband?"

"Yeah. Who is this?"

"Must be your turn to spank that booty tonight."

"What?"

"Damn. Thought you was outta town."

I heard her voice in the background; imagined her panicking. I hung up. Laughed to myself. Got some pleasure from that.

At home, I stared at the pictures of my family when we were a family. Then I stood on my patio like a man in isolation. Waiting for another silent morning. I stared at the darkness in the sky. Gazed at the stars, the crescent moon. Glared at the same sky that covered me, my mother, my father, my sister, my nephews. The whole thing seemed so full, yet so empty. Every piece of beauty in the heavens looked like a distraction from the truth.

There was a feeling I was trying to shake. One I didn't want to sleep with. Something I'd never felt before. It had nothing to do with Lisa or Shelby or anybody else who had abandoned me. It had to do with Leonard. My best friend. My brother.

Tonight when he was talking to Debra with a wide smile and easy words, something about it reminded me that my daddy had asked about him. My daddy didn't ask about anybody in my family. Not my sister. Not his unseen and never-heard grandchildren. He only asked how Leonard was doing. I think that was why I didn't tell Leonard I had called my old man. So I guess my resentment came from hurt. A deep damage. Hurt that came when you expected something from somebody else and they didn't deliver it to your expectations. I wondered if I'd ever talk to my daddy again.

I went to bed. Slept in my sweatsuit. Tossed and turned.

My phone rang with the rising of the sun.

"Can I speak to Tyrel Anthony Williams?"

"Speaking. Who is this?"

"How are you doing?"

"I was trying to sleep. Who is this?"

"Guess."

"Shelby?"

"Yep."

I paused, then finally asked, "What's up?"

She was silent for a few moments.

I was irritated. "Did you leave something in my car?"

She cleared her throat. There was plenty of bustle in the background. Footsteps. Car horns. People were being paged. I heard the announcement that the white zone was for immediate loading and unloading of passengers only.

Again, I said, "What's up?"

"Can I call you this evening from New York?"

"Why do you have to ask if you can call? You just called."

"You're so damn difficult."

"And you're not."

"Don't act like a booty." She paused. "Tyrel?"

"Yeah?"

She blew air. Her voice was snappy, angry when she said, "I've *never* done anything like that shit we did yesterday. I want you to know that— that— that I don't do one-night shit."

"Yeah, I'll go out with you."

"What makes you think I want to see you?"

"I said what you were thinking."

"That's not funny."

"You hear me laugh?"

A moment later she said, "Wish me a safe trip."

"Safe trip."

Sounded like she blew me a kiss. Then hung up.

LET THE
RAIN FALL

PART TWO

LET THE
RAIN FALL

11

"Shelby's moving in with me."

"Debra told me."

"Is there anything she doesn't tell you?"

"How would I know?" Leonard checked the time on his watch against the time on the dash.

Shelby had moved into her own place for three months, but she was gone most of the time, and when she was around she spent most of the time at my crib. My kitchen was better, and her place only had a shower, no tub. I told Leonard all of that, then told him how Shelby likes to soak in the tub, play Erykah Badu and Eric Benét, burn candles, sip wine, stuff like that.

The last six months have flown by. Flown. She's living in my place. In my space. In my life.

I paused for dramatic effect. "I gave Shelby three keys."

Leonard sat up. "Three keys?"

I'd been doing goofy stuff I hadn't done since high school. I'd caught myself phasing out in the middle of presentations, scribbling acronyms with Shelby's name. Like *S* is for Sexy, *H* is for Headstrong, and so on, then mailing it with a card and a few corny poems I'd made up. I'd been sending her little gifts, little collectible African dolls.

Maybe Leonard already knew, because women don't keep things like that a secret. If Debra knew, Leonard knew.

"You dropped down the three keys?" He said that like I'd be in waist chains and leg irons by sunrise. "You serious?"

I smiled so hard that if the sun was out, my gums would've gotten a suntan. I chuckled, thought about Lisa Nichols for half a second, remembered how that romantic flight of forever didn't get off the ground. All for the best. I told Leonard that Shelby was picking up the slack on things like groceries, whatever.

I said, "We're trying to build a team. Teamwork toward a common vision."

"Ty?"

"What?"

"Don't get anal."

We laughed.

He said, "You got enough room for her stuff at the condo?"

Shelby had arranged her stuff in the second bedroom. Along with my computer. She had me move my computer and the television out of the master bedroom. There were things I had to get used to, things other than her being a grumpy sister in the a.m. Last night, she reorganized the living room because she bought a room full of new plants from Target. By the time I made it in from work, she was walking around in ragged panties scratching her butt, hair pinned up, face scrubbed dry. There were three or four pair of pumps scattered on the floor. Clothes in the corner in a pile. Shelby would step over her mess for days before she picked it up, but she'd wash a glass or a plate as soon as she used it. Our kitchen was cleaner than most folks' faces.

Leonard said, "Sisters do know how to take over."

"Without a doubt. Now the bathroom cabinet is filled with cotton balls, nail polish, and things-with-wings."

"You need to slow down."

"You think we're moving too fast?"

"I mean slow down the car. Cut back from eighty."

I slowed to sixty-five, checked the rearview. "What's up?"

"Highway Patrol getting on right behind us at Indian Hill."

The car we thought was a Highway Patrol zoomed by. It was one of those low-budget, rent-a-cop security cars with yellow lights across the top. I sped back up to eighty, hit cruise control, left him and the city of Montclair in the gusty Santa Ana breeze. The mentally deranged winds had been rough enough to flip small Cessnas and take down a few power lines, made some serious traffic jams on a few surface streets.

"So you and Shelby on hit," Leonard said. "A brother goes to New York for a week and all kinds of shit changes around here."

"You knew it was in motion."

"I didn't think it would actually happen."

"I'm surprised myself."

Damn. I'd been seeing Shelby for six intense months. It had started off as an excursion up PCH with oldies playing on my sound system, moved to moments of seized pleasure in a stolen room in Obispo, but we had connected along the way. She had a magnetism I wanted to repel but couldn't.

I didn't actually see her for two weeks after Obispo, not until all of us went out to celebrate my and Shelby's birthdays. Not seeing her for a few weeks wasn't a long time, but when you thought about somebody damn near every second of the day, that was an eternity. She was on trips; I had a few weeklong marketing seminars in Arizona and Utah.

Then the night came that Shelby and I had planned to go on a date to the Ebony Fashion Fair. I had bought the tickets before we met, had planned on taking Lisa, but life had changed. The winds were blowing in a whole new direction. When I picked Shelby up, I was wearing a tuxedo, holding a single red rose, and projecting a good attitude for what I hoped was a great woman.

I didn't know what to expect. Even though we'd talked, her attitude was hot and cold. Sometimes she was very happy to hear from me, sometimes she was too busy and wouldn't call back for two or three days. She was trying to play by the rules.

An enticing fragrance of sheer sweetness flowed from her frame as soon she opened the door, dressed in a sultry black, open-back evening dress that melted around her butt and made every stitch of that material scream with joy. The dress was classy to the last piece of thread, and it had to be glad to be gripping all of her hidden parts like a greedy lover. All of that was topped off by a slamming, fresh spiral hairstyle that let me know that she'd spent many hours in somebody's beauty shop. Either she was a queen or the Eighth Wonder, the type of woman that brothers and others prayed to the gods for. I released all of that flattery before I said hello. She tried not to smile and lost. She radiated over my continuous compliments and blushed her way to me with a big hug. After she put her lips close to my ear and whispered some things that made me feel like Zeus, Shelby held me and let out one of those deep breaths that said she was all mixed up inside. Then she stepped back with a solemn face. She put her finger in my dimple, inside of Shelby's Cavern, and gave me a healthy, lengthy kiss. She wiped her lipstick off my face, and smiled at me for a few seconds. The smile left her lips; she bit the edge of her mouth; her eyes went feline; then she eased me closer and whispered in my ear, "Let's go to your place after."

I nodded and said, "Pack a bag."

"Give me five minutes." Her words were sultry.

Friday night turned into Saturday, and Saturday went by too fast, and rapidly turned into Sunday afternoon with us still wrapped around each other, pulling, pawing, nibbling, sucking, me licking almost every inch of her sexy chocolate. We felt good with each other, so there were hardly any restrictions for our feasting as we talked and kissed and sweated and made each other our own personal playground.

Hard to believe I've given her the three keys. Nobody had ever received three keys from me.

Nobody.

After that impromptu ride up and down PCH, like I said, we reverse-engineered the relationship and got to know each other beyond the sex. Hit Tilly's Terrace and danced hip-hop, sweated up a funk at little J's, watched Leonard rock the house at the Townhouse, went out for late-night jazz at the Baked Potato.

Last month, Shelby had a rare domestic moment, invaded my kitchen, and made some orgasmic sweet potato pies, threw down dinner, and invited Debra and Leonard over to feast—shrimp over angel hair pasta with tomato wine sauce, a little garlic toast, Beringers white Zinfandel. While we were laughing and talking, I checked out how at ease Leonard was with Debra. How she was picking lint off his shirt, how he was playing with her hair, how they were grooming each other without a thought. My homeboy was what they called smitten by the redbone who held his hand every chance she could. Debra had the giggles and a serious glow that made her walk look like the first day of spring. They were gazing at each other like they had discovered sunshine and moonlight. He never took his hand from her grip. When they moved, they moved slowly. Like they owned time.

Leonard said, "So, you guys are taking it to the next level."

Warmth and goodness circulated through my veins

when I said, "Moving on up. Taking this from ground floor to penthouse."

"It's hard for me to spend much time with Debra. I'm out half the night, in and out of town so much, it's hard going a couple of weeks, maybe three, without hooking up."

"You've got HBO calling, you're doing student films at UCLA, auditions. Leonard, you don't have time to rest."

"Tell me about it." His tone told me he'd rather be with Debra. Leonard switched the radio from 94.7 to 92.3 to 100.3. He said, "Sure living together is what you wanna do?"

"What's your opinion?"

"If you're already sleeping together and now you're living together, what's there left to do?"

His words lingered while I thought. It was the kind of thing a father should've said to his son. It had that effect. Something about what he said made me uncomfortable.

Leonard changed the radio, then started back talking. He said, "I don't have to live with her. Don't see how you can handle it. All I'm asking is if you're sure that's what you wanna do."

"I'm sure."

"No pressure?"

"No pressure."

"Then congratulations."

We were an hour east of civilization, sailing straight out the 10 eastbound and deeper into the desert heat, into San Bernardino County. Even at eight p.m., it felt twenty degrees warmer than Los Angeles. Leonard was closing a show out in redneck-ville Redlands at a white-owned Mexican restaurant that had black comedy on Sunday nights. Chocolate Comedy Night drew black people out of their hiding places, brought them out of the truck stop cities and desiccated places like Rialto, Riverside, and Moreno Valley, and about fifteen other obscure cities on the Thomas Guide. Out in the boondocks it was a major event for somebody from L.A. to drive through, let alone stop long enough to tell jokes. Tonight I got to leave behind my white collar, throw on my jeans and soft-bottom Kenneth Cole shoes, and cruise the freeways and talk with my brother. It was fellas' night out.

Leonard was telling me how Debra wasn't crossing the carnal line and giving him the pleasure of a lifetime. He griped about that from time to time. While me and Shelby were cuddled in bed at night, Leonard and Debra were kissing good night at the front door and going to separate beds in separate corners of the city.

If they cared about each other, and if she loved the brother like she claimed, I don't see how they could pass up on the greatest, the ultimate expression of love.

I said, "You gonna let her make you celibate?"

"How is Debra *making* me celibate?"

"If your girl ain't gonna hook you up, and you're not gonna get your needs taken care of elsewhere, she's tying up your sex and *making* you celibate. Most celibacy is voluntary. Yours is forced."

Leonard's mouth twisted like he was thinking about it, like he hadn't thought about it from that angle.

I said, "She at least helping you out some kinda way?"

"Nope." I had to strain to hear that. He sighed.

"No kinda way?"

"Nothing. Just heavy petting every once in a while."

"Man, get real. That's high school."

"Compared to what we used to do, less than high school."

"You're grown. She's grown. What's the problem?"

He whined, "She won't gimme none."

We laughed.

I said, "If she's your woman, then that's part of the relationship, part of her responsibility."

Leonard was listening and chuckling like I was an idiot.

I said, "Just because she has hang-ups don't mean you should give up your pleasure."

"At Bible study all they talk about is *not* doing it before you get married. Every week we get a don't-give-it-up sermon."

"Then *don't* go to Bible study."

We laughed. He told me about how they had gone to singles Bible study, heard a message about fornication, and when it came time for people to come to the altar for prayer to get spiritual relief from their freaking-out-of-wedlock all week, eighty percent of the sisters trembled and cried their way down the red carpet to the front of the room, stood underneath the chandelier and faced the minister, wailing like sad fog horns.

I chuckled. "Those the women you should've hooked up with."

Leonard said, "Just because you're getting your freak on—"

"Every chance I get."

"—don't mean something's wrong with my program."

"You down with that program?"

Leonard made an unsure face. He said, "Ninety-seven percent of the people who freak before marriage end up not jumping the broom."

"Oh, shit. You quoting stats?"

We laughed again.

Leonard said, "I'm questioning the way I've been doing business. So far as relationships are concerned, that is."

I said, "You content?"

A moment passed. He spoke low, "I'm content."

"Bullshit."

"Content and horny as fuck."

More deep laughter, and I swerved over the lane reflectors.

He said, "Yeah, I'm content."

"Then congratulations."

"What irks me is now that I'm in a committed relationship and got a *good* woman, after damn near every show some *fine* sister is trying to slide me her number."

"You accepting the digits?"

"Huh-ell no. Where were they when I was single?"

"Probably at Bible study crying."

He changed the radio station for the umpteenth time. KACE and its R&B oldies was fading out and some whacked country station was taking over. The genres overlapped, sounded like Brandy and Kenny Rogers were doing a static filled duet.

He said, "San Francisco still riding your jock?"

"Joshua Cooper still riding like a big dog."

"What about Lisa?"

"Leaving messages left and right."

The lot in front of the club was packed so we parked next door, in front of *El Goto Goro*, underneath the line of Mexican palm trees. Leonard adjusted his mustard colored slacks, did the same with his cream short sleeve shirt as we headed toward the noise. We stopped laughing and walking. We couldn't believe what we heard over the sound system. Crisp. Loud. Clear. Heard enough to make smiles turn upside down.

"What the fuck." Leonard sounded the way a man would if he'd just walked in while his wife was sexing his best friend.

We looked at each other.

Then sped up.

The intent way Leonard strolled terrified me.

From the parking lot, we saw inside the club. Jackson was onstage doing Leonard's multiple-character routine.

The ghetto-hard bit about the "the cockeyed sister and her stut-stut-stuttering dog." Leonard's career had picked up and everybody from the Hollywood to the Apollo Theater knew his routine. That was because of the *Brother, Brother* pilot. Only two episodes aired, but Leonard was impressive enough for his name to get tossed around Hollywood. Impressive enough for HBO to tell him to keep in touch.

The bullheaded glare in Leonard's eyes and his unyielding pace said none of that adulation mattered. Right now Jackson was onstage doing his act, noun for noun, adjective for adjective, verb for verb. But Jackson couldn't buy a laugh.

Just as we hit the door, Jackson walked off the stage to weak applause—a tired ovation that said the room was damn happy he was leaving. Leonard waited for him to come out the front door before he called the brother to the side.

Leonard smiled and said, "I'm flattered at your ability to re-create an original piece of art without ever buying a paintbrush. But please, I'm asking you as a fellow comic, and as a supportive African-American, don't disrespect what I've worked day and night to perfect by doing my material anymore."

Jackson jerked like he was ready to jump out of his Tommy Hilfiger T-shirt. He barked, "What you punk-ass niggas gonna do, huh?"

Leonard almost lost it, his body was harsh, but his tone was reasoning when he said, "Look, we almost came to blows before. This time I'm giving you respect and asking for the same. That goes for me and for my friends. Especially my woman."

They were staring, mad-doggin' each other.

I stepped in between and said, "Leonard. Chill."

Jackson said, "You'd better listen to that bitch."

I stepped to the side and said, "Leonard, kick his ass."

We were all ego to ego, waiting for somebody to look away and be less than a man. Cans of kick-ass were *psst*ing open.

Leonard bobbed his head, lowered his eyes. Stepped away. That pissed me off. I'd never seen Leonard back down.

He said, "Let it be, Tyrel. Let's go. I got a show to do."

Jackson said, "Go tell them jokes, *boy*."

Leonard paused for a moment. He said, "Assholes tell jokes; real comics relive experiences. Have a good night, asshole."

Jackson and his woman left, her following.

Leonard had his hands in his pockets, rocking side to side.

I said, "You cool?"

He closed his eyes, shook his head, said, "Gimme a minute."

He went out into the wind and darkness, stood on the other side of the lot by himself. Lowered his head. Hands folded.

When he came back he wasn't smiling. But he wasn't frowning. Some serious positive energy was pumping from his body.

Leonard went on stage, cool and calm. Focused. The first thing he did was look around the crowd, smirk, then say, "Sounds like my jokes got here before I did."

The crowd howled.

He said, "I didn't know I was a ventriloquist, but I had his dumb ass talking."

They howled again, loud enough to make the earth tremble.

He dogged out the brother for having such a weak show and jocking his act, gave him a verbal ass-kicking, then got a standing ovation for doing his routine the right way.

Leonard took the wheel on the way back. We talked about what had gone down in the lot. I thought we should've kicked that thief's ass. We argued, then agreed to disagree. Leonard sounded like he felt sorry for the brother.

Leonard said, "It ain't worth coming to blows over. If I fought every time somebody stole a joke, I'd be battling the rest of my life."

Rationality came back into my life, cruised my veins, reminded me I wasn't in high school anymore. "He'll end up either being judged by twelve or getting carried by six."

I put my mind back on Shelby Janine Daniels. Hanging out with my buddy was fun, but I couldn't wait to get home to my woman. The woman who was living in my space, jingling the three keys I'd given her every chance she got.

Two more miles of freeway were behind us before Leonard made a pent-up sound. A noise that made him sound old.

I asked, "What wrong, bro-man?"

He made a face, puffed, and said, "I'll just have to write two more routines for every one they snatch."

"Three more."

"Yeah, three."

DEBRA

12

Days turned into weeks. Those weeks into months. And it was a new March in the blink of an eye. Another colorful spring was on the way. For the last nine months I've held Leonard's hand and enjoyed more live jazz concerts and movies and comedy than one sister ever thought she could in a lifetime.

Some of it with Tyrel and Shelby at my side, most of it with Leonard.

I didn't get to see him as much as I would've liked, because he worked days in Watts doing the computer thing, and kept late nights doing the comedy thing. I didn't want to have the kind of relationship where a brother grew used to coming by in the middle of the night, crawling in between my sheets, and leaving before the sun came up.

Which was part of the reason I hadn't shared myself with Leonard. I had promised myself I wasn't going to have premarital sex ever again. If Leonard wasn't in my life, my promise wouldn't seem so much like torture.

Leonard had been busy the last week. He was blessed with a part in an Al Pacino movie and was in Alberta, Canada, for three days. He called each day, whenever he took a break in his fourteen-hour-day schedule. We had to miss the George Benson concert at Universal because of that. Leonard was supposed to open the show at the Amphitheater but had the opportunity to do the movie. He was only supposed to be there one day, but the director loved him and expanded Leonard's part, let him improvise most of his lines. Then he had audition after audition. And a show in Ventura, and another one in Barstow. Not much time to spend with me. I was wondering where I fit into his life. If I fit in his life in any major kind of way. Or if I was just a convenience.

"Why do you keep doing the small shows in the boondocks?"

"To work on my new stuff and polish my old stuff. There's no pressure when you leave Hollywood. Not like you feel on Sunset."

My hand was on his hand as he moved the stick shift from gear to gear. He was so sincere when he was with me. I liked that.

He asked, "You have any more gum?"

"Yeah."

I took out a piece of Care Free, licked it, teased it around his lips, then put it in his mouth. He liked it when I did that.

I said, "Where are we going?"

"Just looking at some houses. You said you liked looking at houses, right?"

I smiled. "You remember everything I tell you?"

"That's my job."

"It's the little things that impress a woman like me."

Leonard parked his Celica in front of a beige stucco house on Don Diego. We were on a narrow street that had no lane markings, and the tracts were intimately close. The house was at the end of a cul de sac, situated at what felt like the highest point of Baldwin Hills. I could see downtown L.A. and the mountains behind the Hollywood sign. In the sunset, African-Americans were coming in and out of their homes. Palm trees and evergreen trees and shrubbery in about thirty different variations and shades of greens blended in with outdoor plant life. Heaven on earth.

We sat in the car for a while, enjoyed the view, soaked up the unmistakable enchantment brought on by each other's presence, windows partway down, a Joshua Redman tape playing old-style instrumental jazz. We got out and stood at a spot that let us look down on La Brea toward Hollywood and see glittering city lights for miles. Leonard pulled me around in front of him, in a very gentle way. I snuggled my butt against him, rested my backside against his front. I wiggled to get comfortable. Felt part of him swell. I loved that I could arouse him like that. And that raising awakened slumbering parts of me. I shared his warmth while he enjoyed mine. I relaxed my neck, let my head rest against his chest. He pulled my hair back and put his face next to mine, his mouth on my ear. I felt his warm breath on my cool face. He seemed so at peace with himself. So quiet. I was at peace with him.

I asked, "What are you thinking?"

He whispered, "Reading poetry. Kite-flying. Story-telling."

His words trickled through me, gave me so much ease. It felt like we were in a place where nothing mattered but us. And of all the things in life that had bothered me, I couldn't think of one negative thing. At least none that mattered. Having him in my life made me feel lighter, gave me the freedom to walk with an obvious sway of happiness. Had me glowing so brilliantly I had sister after sister smiling at me with an I'm-so-happy-for-you grin. And it had brother after brother drawn to me, trying to find out why I was so exhilarated. Leonard had ignited me. I was on fire. I was the fire. Deep inside of me, I felt the heat of life. And I knew what all of those feelings added up to. I was losing the control I had struggled to keep in my life.

I said, "What do you want from me, Leonard?"

"I want you."

"That's a bit much."

"You can cover it, no problem."

"Been in love before?"

"Not like this. You?"

"Not like this. What makes this so special?"

"The makings of you."

"What do you mean?"

"If I knew what I loved about you, if it was your smile, or your walk, or your voice, or whatever, then that could change or be taken away, and I wouldn't love you anymore. I just love the makings of you. Everything you represent."

"Makings of you. That's an old Gladys Knight song."

"Yep. I play it and think about you."

"Really?"

"Yeah."

"Love the makings of you too."

"Cold?"

"Just on the outside."

"Want to go?"

"No. I want to stay right here in your arms."

"How do you like it up here in the hills?"

"I like it."

"Would you live up here?"

"Yeah. I would."

"Which house?"

"Stop all the questions."

"In a minute. Which house?"

My eyes went up Don Diego, perused over the different, beautiful Spanish-style homes, from single-level to the two-story stucco houses. Then my heart settled on the yellow stucco house right next to us. The one that offered a view of Los Angeles from on high, almost like we were on Mount Olympus. It looked like the most important spot on the block to me. Not to mention the safest. It looked almost as safe as I felt in the arms I was being sheltered by right now.

I said, "This one with all of the greenery around it."

"Let's take a look at it."

"We could get in trouble."

"Then let's get in trouble."

Leonard took my hand and we went toward the yellow house with all the greenery. A Red Carpet real estate sign was posted in the yard. It was a four-bedroom home with a den.

We went around back to the two-car garage. Peeped at the swimming pool and Jacuzzi. The yard was large enough to throw a nice gathering in. Room for friends and family, and friends of family. Plenty of yard, which was unusual for the city. Orange and lemon trees that lit up the air with a beautiful fragrance.

Leonard peeped in the backdoor. He said, "Kitchen looks nice. Marble counters. Has an island. The works."

I wiped dirt off part of the window and peeped inside too. I said, "That kitchen is nice. Plenty of cabinets. Plenty of room to move around. Three or four people could be in there at the same time and not be in each other's way."

"You make it sound like a restaurant."

"Might as well be." I turned the doorknob. "It's open."

"Serious?"

"Yeah. Want to go in?"

"I don't know. We're already trespassing."

"Come on, scaredy. Let's be nosy."

The place was hollow, echoed a little. Sounded the way a house did before it became a home. We went room to room. Held hands and went in every chamber and mental-shopped and imagined what furniture we would put inside if it was his house or my house. From foyer to bedroom to den we talked about everything from chandeliers to ceiling fans to Oriental rugs. Even in an empty house, going into a bedroom with a man seemed inappropriate.

Somewhere along the tour we switched from hand-holding, to hugging, to rubbing our hands over each other, then shared kisses in the dark. Walked the arabesque carpeting. Reciprocated touches. Shared tongues underneath the Bohemian crystal chandelier, from the French doors to the floor-to-ceiling windows. Room to room. In an empty house we filled it, kiss by kiss, with emotion. We were intense. So intense. And he gave me a look that scared me. Underneath the skylight the moon showed all.

What was revealed on his face scared me.

He was focused. His breathing sang that he wanted me. The way his mouth was almost open. The way he looked into me. I knew what he saw. What I couldn't hide. How I felt about him. I wanted him in so many ways. And in one particular way. *Now.*

I was scared of the weakness brought on by what I felt. I wasn't ashamed to let him see the drops of fear. Because now the line, that line seemed so obvious, where it had been thick and wide, now it felt so thin and narrow. Easy to cross. Too easy to cross. We were standing on top of it, waiting to fall one way or the other.

What I felt was so basic. Couldn't be intellectualized. It was too primitive. Too much of what we were made of. Too much of what I wanted but was afraid to allow. A tingling in my stomach was so severe it felt like my abdominal muscles and extremities were out of control. I was about to rip in half or burst into flames. I felt all the things I had taught myself to control. Things that if I wanted to control, it would be too late.

First my back was to the wall. Then I was on the floor. On the carpet. On my back. Kisses on my neck and his hands feeling my breasts. His mouth on my nipples. This wild courtship and foreplay lasted until I was stimulated to the right pitch. I felt savage, like I was in the middle of a mating ritual.

Then I slipped into a zone, a sweet zone, and I was no longer a person. Every nerve on my body came to life and made me an emotion. He slipped his hand under my jean skirt and touched me there and it felt good, but I was embarrassed because I was so wet, too wet. I didn't want Leonard to know he had this effect on me. But now he did know. Especially when I unzipped his jeans. Set him free. I stroked him like he fingered me, and I knew I had the same effect on him. Extreme, intense. He moaned with the movement of my hand.

What terrified me was that I didn't have condoms and I didn't care and I didn't think he had one single condom or Saran Wrap or a sandwich bag and I know I know better, but I'm weak and I didn't care, and I'm hoping he'll be strong enough for the both of us because right now I'd submit to whatever he wished to do, no matter how wrong I felt about it because I didn't care and I'm not in the mood to be the voice of reason. I didn't care about anything but the damn passion that had me shivering and aching in between my heavy breathing and sweating out my mushrooming desire that felt like it was about to become reality.

Then his hand is under my jean skirt. His finger slips inside my panties. He plays with me. Then his finger tries to open the skin. Part of me wants to push it away. A bigger part of me doesn't. Skin opens. Slides inside me like a whisper. Inside of me. I sigh. Moving on the sensitive spot that swells. Circles. Playing a tune. First one. Then two. I purr with pain at three. Murmur a tender sound of contentment that sounded like nothing but love.

I started off fighting what I felt, putting my hand over my own mouth to muffle my pleasures, then releasing soft sounds that matched his depth. We both had passion, but it felt like we were being polite lovers. Loving the way people did at first before they let it all hang out. I was trying to subdue moans that would not be subdued. I was being devoured—the kisses, the way his free hand touched me here and there and everywhere he could reach—and when his fingers crossed my face, when they touched my lips, I was starving and I relished his fingers one by one, over and over. He did the same for me.

The better I felt, the less I moved him up and down. A sound came from me. A panting like I was in so much pleasure and labor. When I thought it couldn't feel any better, it swelled inside of me. And he slowed his slow hand, slowed to tease and I wished him not to be slow, struggled with him to not be slow, not be so gentle, to take me there. All the way. Now.

He did.

And I was so wet it was a shame.

After I crossed that threshold, I found the part of him

I'd released before my release, squeezed him, moved him, teased him, found a rhythm of rise and fall, and took him to that same place.

Then we sat in the quiet. Part of me was ashamed because he saw me orgasm. That was very personal for me. And since we'd just had some kind of digital sex, some outercourse, I wasn't sure if he'd respect me anymore. Men do change their minds after they've conquered. And part of me felt defeated. I knew better than to do what I just did. But I have to pretend that it was business as usual.

Leonard kissed me. He asked, "You okay?"

"Yeah. We're messy. Your children are all over the floor."

We both laughed. That made me feel better. But my laugh was a forced relief.

He asked, "How do you feel?"

I knew a difference in my attitude showed. That feeling of uncertainty and insecurity that came after the fact had arrived. That what-now? sensation. I was stunned by what I had done in an empty house on a cul de sac on Don Diego in Baldwin Hills.

Leonard held me. Tight. But not too tight. I was glad I didn't have to ask to be held after the fact. Couldn't remember if I ever didn't have to ask to be held after the fact. My emotions felt like they were overflowing from my seat of passion. I loved that. And I resented it too. I felt frustrated and powerless. Where did we go from here?

I said, "Aren't you supposed to tell a joke or something?"

He kissed my forehead. "Nope."

I didn't want to waste my emotions. I knew too many women who had wasted their emotions over the years. I didn't like what they had evolved into. They were some mean black women. Disillusioned. Frustrated. Powerless in their own lives. Settling for another woman's husband or another woman's boyfriend or their teenage son's best friend. Exhausted to the point of being emotionally indifferent. Jaded to the point of being numb. Living with wounded souls. And most of them were under thirty.

I wanted to talk to him about it, but I didn't want him to devalue what I said. Make what I feel seem like less.

"Leonard? Does anybody ever see this serious side of you?"

"Few people."

"Would you share this side with a man?"

"With Tyrel. He's real. We have real conversations. Talk about how we feel. That's why he's my ace."

"Can we talk about how we feel for a while?"

"Okay."

"I mean about us. Not Tyrel or Shelby or your family or my family or anything else."

"Okay."

I sat us face-to-face so I could see his Asian eyes in the light we had. I needed to see his reaction to what I said.

"Leonard, just listen to me."

"As long as you need."

"I hope my words have a point."

"Okay."

"I need to define what we're doing so we can call it what it is. If it's nothing, we'll call it that. If it's this week, we'll call it that. That way I'll know how much of me to invest in this, whatever we're doing. I mean, I don't know if I'm supposed to just be dating you, or seeing other people, or what. I don't know if I have the right to think about you as much as I do. I think about you, it feels good, and that bothers me because I don't know if I have the right to think about you."

"I love you."

I said, "Saying it doesn't make it true."

"Where would you like to see this go?"

"You're sounding frustrated."

"Well, yeah. If I tell you how I feel, and you doubt it, that tells me what I say ain't being taken seriously."

"I want to believe you. Okay, I do. Just with reservations. I've brought some baggage into this, so it's hard."

"Once more again, where would you like this to go?"

I hesitated. Barricaded my feelings. "I'm afraid to say."

"Do you know?"

"Yeah," my voice lowered, "I know."

"Say it. I'm here for you."

"I'd like to get married one day. Eventually."

He didn't say anything. Left me hanging out there by myself.

I said, "I'm not saying that because— Well, I don't want you to think I'm trying to back you into that corner. But I've been thinking about you and wondering and imagining it. I think it's a natural process. Part of the evolution of a relationship. Maybe more for a woman than a man. Where do you go after intimacy? Either the relationship dissolves or moves to a higher plateau."

He smiled. "You're sounding intellectual."

I laughed. "Guess I listen to too much Dr. Laura."

We sat in silence for a moment. I smelled the sex we had left in the air. Wished I could wake up to that fragrance every morning. Then I wished I didn't wish what I just wished.

Leonard said, "I would too."

"Would what?"

"Like to get married. Actually, I was thinking about it. But it scares me, so I've been sitting on it."

"So what are you saying?"

"Maybe we should think about it. Be open with what each of us wants. Talk about it. We could make an appointment with a minister and talk it over. Find some direction."

"You're scaring me."

"Serious. I'm gonna need somebody to share this house with."

"What house?"

"This house."

"This house?"

"I'm gonna buy it."

"One more time, what house are you talking about?"

"The house we're trespassing in."

I laughed. "You're going to buy this house? This house has to cost at least a quarter million."

"Damn right. You said you would live here."

"Yeah. I did. But that was hypothetical. Stop talking about stuff like that. We hardly know each other."

As soon as I said that I felt stupid. The kind of stupid that made me feel twelve years old. Made me realize how little people knew about each other, even after sex. Knowing isn't a qualification for intimacy.

He said, "Then let's know each other. Tell me something."

"What?"

"Tell me all about your boyfriends. Tell me about what they've done to you."

I shifted. "That's an eerie request. Why you want to know my personal business?"

"That's the only way I'll know you, so far as relationships are concerned. If I know what you've been through, what brothers have put you through, I can make sure I don't go there with you."

And I became more afraid of this man than I was before I let him touch my private parts and see me make faces I couldn't hold back. I said, "Brothers don't like to hear all that."

"You don't think you're worth listening to?"

His voice was smooth, trusting. Nothing like the man I'd seen on stage or with Tyrel and Shelby. And I was nothing like the woman he had seen with Tyrel and Shelby. Nothing like the woman he had met at Denny's. We were beyond that. Only a few could say they had ever seen me this exposed.

I scooted up to him, put my back to his chest, pulled his arms around me so he couldn't see my face while I contemplated.

And I told him. Without names, I told him about those who left without a good-bye, told him about something I thought was real but ended up a one-night stand, about one who hit me, about being date-raped, about one who left because I felt uncomfortable with premarital sex. Another thought I went to church too much; one said I worked out too much, studied too much. About a couple who didn't listen to what I needed, so I left them. I didn't talk long, just five minutes or so. Long enough to bring up bad memories. Enough to make me wonder if there was a pattern.

Shelby had experienced much of the same. Different faces, different times, still the same. And I hoped she didn't earn any more pain from Tyrel. He came across nice, but sometimes those were the worst kind. But I didn't tell Leonard any of that paragraph of thought. I'd never tell my friend's personal business. Never. That's why we're buddies for life.

I asked, "Are you ready because you lost somebody?"

"What do you mean?"

"I mean, did you get busted and now you're trying to straighten up the way men do after they've lost their true love?"

Leonard said, "Nope. Not at all. I broke up with a few people because my priorities were wrong."

"What do you mean?"

"I had put entertainment in front of relationship."

"Typical entertainer."

"Yeah. At times when I should've been cultivating what

I had, I assumed what I had would be there when I got offstage."

"But it wasn't. She wasn't."

"Nope. After a while you end up with nothing but a script in your hand and a bagful of jokes. That's not what life is about."

"What's life all about?"

"Friends and family."

I smiled. "Sounds like an MCI commercial."

Leonard laughed. "Cracking jokes, huh? I'm the comedian."

"And I'm the butterfly. I'm sorry"—I laughed—"I didn't mean to cut you off. Go ahead, baby."

I surprised myself when I called him *baby*. Surprised because I didn't know if I had the right to use that term of endearment.

Then he said, "My oldest brother is forty and still out there playing the dating game. Forty is kind of old to be chasing twenty-year-old women and keeping up with the latest dances. Running three or four women."

"Kind of disrespectful too. Very disrespectful."

"That's all he knows. He acts like he's happy running women, but he's lonely as hell. He's the first one to get to the club, the last one to leave. I don't want to end up like him."

"Does he have any kids?"

"A handful."

"Same woman?"

He shook his head. "A handful."

I was quiet. Thinking about the frustrated women I knew.

Leonard's voice softened and he said, "I don't want to end up an old man, living alone, sitting on a porch, watching other people's kids walking home from school."

I dropped what he said about wanting to marry me. I

let his words and promises be just that—words and promises. I devalued it in order to keep my expectations from
changing.

Leonard said, "I've got a friend in a dilemma. Help me
out."

"What?"

"My friend's in love with this dream woman."

"Uh-huh."

"If the brother was going to ask the dream sister to
marry him, to be with him until three days after forever,
how would you recommend he did it?"

I swallowed. Tried to be cool about it. I said, "He could
always take her out to a nice restaurant. Over a candlelit
dinner. Just the two of them."

"Would he have to have the ring then?"

"It would help. That's usually the way it goes."

"What if he wanted to shop for it with her?"

"That would work too. He could be ceremonious and
ask after. But I guess he could always ask before. Depends
on the couple."

He kissed the side of my face. Again I was on fire, but
I made my mind subdue the flames.

He said, "What're you doing tomorrow after work?"

"Nothing." My voice was softer than it had ever been.
I'd never heard myself sound so sweet. So scared. "Why?"

"I want to take you out to dinner. Candles. Flowers.
Maybe we could go shopping after I get back from Arizona."

I paused. "Shopping for?"

"Just for a little something to keep your finger warm."

My eyes watered up. And my throat tightened.

He said, "Can you make it?"

I couldn't even talk, couldn't find a simple word. Overwhelmed is what I was. Head to toe I was stupefied, in a

good way. All I could do was nod my head a couple of times.

I said, "Let me check my day planner. I might be free."

Leonard kissed my face again. "If not, I'll understand."

I said, "About your friend who wants to marry this girl."

"Yeah?"

"He could just ask her. The restaurant thing is old. If he loved her, and he meant his words, and she loved him, and she wanted him too, that would be enough. More than enough."

"Maybe at sunrise on the beach. Watch a dark yesterday become a bright today. Sunrise could represent the start of something new. Leaving old pains behind."

"That would be beautiful. Most women never get asked to marry by the man they'd love to marry. I'm sure."

He held me for a while. Rocked us side to side in warmth.

"Debra?"

"Yeah?"

"Will you go watch the sunrise with me in the morning?"

"Yeah. I'd love to."

More tears rolled down my face. I didn't touch them. Contentment had never been as kind to me as it was that moment.

Neither of us mentioned it anymore. We talked about everything else, about other people, about Tyrel and Shelby, about his family, about my family. We talked about everything but what was on our minds before we cleaned ourselves and left.

At home I'd shower. Be restless. Avoid sleep. Wait. Be so afraid. Bounce back and forth between the words *yes* and *no*.

At sunrise Leonard would be with me on the beach.

Just as the darkness faded and the sunshine eased over the top of the mountains, when the coal-black morning sky turned to gold, Leonard would kiss me. He would bow, lower himself to one knee just as the brightness lit up his face. Just as it lit up my face. He'd tell me how much he loved me. And he'd have a ring in his pocket. A ring he'd bought weeks before.

Before he could get the whole question out of his mouth, I'd kiss his trembling lips and say the word *yes* so many times, in so many ways it would become funny. We'd both laugh with more tears of joy. Then we'd go to Denny's. The place we met. Tyrel and Shelby would already be there, with Faith and other friends.

SHELBY

13

I was on the back row of a 767 with Chiquita. She's an attendant, but she wasn't working. Outside was pitch-black and it was raining like crazy. Lightning was flashing all around the plane. The night reminded me of that *Twilight Zone* episode when the man looked out a window and saw a crazy gremlin on the wings, ripping up the engine.

I was working a late-night flight back into L.A. from D.C. with a quickie layover in Atlanta. Georgia was where my flight attendant friend Chiquita hopped on, dressed in violet slacks and a colorful jacket, bow earrings, double golden bracelets. She was off work, in civvies. She was bumped off her direct flight from Atlanta to San Diego and had to fly into LAX and catch a hop down to San Diego so she could be on time for work tomorrow. Just because we flew for damn near free didn't mean it was convenient.

Turbulence was no joke, and we had everybody strapped down to their seats. Me and Chiquita were seated in the last row, closest to the tail of the plane. I was reading a *Black Hair* magazine, asking Chiquita what she thought about this style or that style because I was tired of my bun and had been seriously thinking about redoing my do, maybe something short, maybe tresses.

Chiquita was looking at my pictures of Leonard and Debra's wedding. I'd brought two rolls to show off. Other attendants were on the opposite side, riding out the storm too. Chiquita was smiling, oohing, and sighing like she was longing for that broom-jumping day to roll into her life.

Debra's wedding was the bomb. That miracle worker pulled the whole thing off in less than six weeks. And I know why she rushed too. If I had've been waiting that long to make love, as soon as he asked, me and my man would've been on the freeway zooming at warp speed to Vegas, with a mattress tied to one of our backs.

You know I was maid of honor, because I've got it like that, and Tyrel was the best-looking best man I'd ever seen. Those bowlegs and dimples looked damn good in a tuxedo.

Chiquita said, "This was beautiful."

Chiquita's a sister in her mid-twenties, slim and trim, has Mexican brown skin and short, texturized hair. She spoke in her soft, sexy Southern accent and said, "Sister, sister. These pictures are *too* nice. Real nice."

"Cost a grip," I said. I put on another coat of wine-colored lipstick—deep shades looked good with my skin tone. Chiquita wore dark rose, pretty much the same hue Debra always wore. Lavenders and berries looked good on their medium and light skin.

She asked, "Who's the cute brother with the dread-locks?"

"Debra's cousin. He's the photographer."

"So she had the hook-up."

"If you wanna call what Bobby gave a hook-up."

I told her that Debra and Leonard didn't sleep together until they were married. That was why they broke out running for the nearest hotel as soon as they said the I-do's.

Chiquita said, "For real?"

I nodded.

Chiquita said, "No fingerprints on her window."

I said, "What was that?"

"I read this book, it said a woman should think of her virginity like it's a window. And every time you sleep with a guy, it's like letting him put his fingerprints on your window. Staining your glass." She was at the window seat and started dabbing her fingers on the glass, made it look nastier than before. "The way you talk about Tyrel, I know you're getting your window smudged on a regular basis."

We laughed. Soft, cute, professional, sisterly laughs.

Chiquita said, "You should come down to San Diego next week and hang out."

"No can do. Tyrel bought us tickets to the BWL."

"What's that?"

"Black Women Lawyers. It's one of those black-tie social events that bring out the black bourgeois. Single sisters and browsing brothers. A night of mingling and macking."

"Sounds like where I need to be."

"Ask your man to take you."

"If it's gonna be a room filled with single black lawyers, why would I bring Raymond? Don't take sand to the beach."

Chiquita looked at a picture of me and Tyrel. Best man and maid of honor. She said, "And this is Tyrel?"

I scratched my breast. My nipple hurt. I said, "That's my boo. Look at that dimple. I call it Shelby's Cavern."

"That's cute." She twisted her lips and said, "*Mmmmm*."

I laughed. I said, "What was that *mmmmm* all about?"

She flipped through a few more pictures. "Now, Shelby—"

I sang, "Uh-huh."

"You said all y'all met at the same time."

I smiled. "Uh-huh."

"And Leonard and your friend Debra are married already?"

I hesitated and said a curt, "Uh-huh."

"And you're playing house and shacking."

I checked to see if anybody could hear Miss Mouth telling all of my business. If anybody did hear, either they didn't care or they were pretending not to hear. My hand drifted up to my mouth, slid to my pearl earrings, twisted the hair at the nape of my neck, pulled at that part of my bun. Pulling tension like you wouldn't believe.

I did a silent countdown before I said, "Me and Tyrel have been living together for three months."

"Well, if you're good enough to sleep with, you should be good enough to marry. He ever talk about it?"

I stopped smiling. "Chiquita, you want me to go off on you?"

She said, "Well, sounds like you should've hooked up with Leonard instead of with Tyrel."

Now, I'll have to be honest, that "A man won't buy the cow when he can get the milk for free" phrase my momma used to say has popped into my head one, maybe two *million* times since I canceled my lease, let my emotions be my guide, gave up my freedom, and moved in with him. But thinking about it hadn't made me feel the least unhappy. Until now. I glanced at Chiquita and shook my head. Some sisters hate to see another sister happy.

Who in the hell said I wanted to get married any-damn-way? What me and Tyrel have works. We're in love. We've got a whole lot of lust, but the love is magnified by the lust. And the eroticism is increased by the feeling. I love everything about him. The way he sits around and reads, the way he dresses when he leaves for work, the way he smells, the way his sweat tastes after we've worked out. I felt stronger about him when I watched him speak at the youth center in Watts. Listening to how much he cared about the future of people he didn't know took my emotions over the edge. I love everything about that man. Everything. Inside and out, head to toe and in between.

I was just about to ask Chiquita why was she in my personal life, ask her if she knew where in the hell her man was, that Raymond she always complained about and could *never* catch up with for more than two minutes at a time. But I didn't go there.

One of us was saved from my thoughts when the call button dinged two times. That gave me a reason to get up and take my fake-ass smile for a stroll. A few people were sneezing, coughing. Germs for days. Then somebody's two-year-old rug rat had a temper tantrum and flung a Teenage Mutant Ninja Turtle doll across the aisle. It smacked me upside my damn head. I stopped walking for a second. Long enough for the brat's parents to see I wasn't in the mood. I thought about calling the FAA on his preschool ass, but I kept moving toward whoever had beeped me.

It was a caramel-coated brother in a dark green business suit. Short hair, faded on the sides. The way his knees were crammed into the seat in front of him, he looked tall. Needed to shave. It was his third time beeping. The first time was for a pillow and a blanket. The second time he just stared at me and said he forgot why he'd had me walk down the aisle.

He said, "I was hoping you'd be the one to come."

I smiled that fake smile. It might've been his cologne,

some Drakkar or Hugo or something, that had made me sick from the get-go. The closer I got to him, the worse I felt.

I held my distance from what he reeked, tried to bend without sticking my butt in anybody's face, breathed through my mouth and said, "And what can I do for you?"

"My name is Richard Vaughn."

He held a business card out toward me. I didn't take it. I'd been through this routine too many times to care.

He said, "I live in San Diego."

"Good for you."

"I own a flower shop. Have you heard of Flowers by Richard?"

"Good for you, no I haven't, and what did you need?"

He stared with his mouth open. Either his tongue was tied or he was trying to show me he had teeth.

I said, "Did you need something?"

"I was wondering if we could meet for drinks."

I sighed out some worthless air. I said, "Mr. Vaughn?"

"Call me Richard."

"Mr. Vaughn, please stay in your seat, keep your seat belt fastened, don't buzz unless it's urgent. We'll be serving you shortly, as soon as the plane settles. Have a nice flight."

I headed back to my seat. My shoes were killing.

Then I was rocked by another shot of turbulence. I'd been on gentler roller coasters at Six Flags. Felt queasy beyond belief. Somebody had on Chanel No. 5, and it was turning the hell out of my stomach. I belched and felt my insides bubble and rise. A little nasty stuff came up to my throat, but I'd be damned if I'd toss my cookies and embarrass myself.

It felt like the wings were about to get ripped off the plane. A quick image of crashed airplanes flashed through my mind. I pretended I wasn't scared, so the passengers who had stayed awake for this midnight run would remain calm, then held on to the seats to keep from getting my butt tossed into a fat man's lap. A woman on my left was hold-ing a Star of David close to her leather skin and praying. An Iranian passenger on my right couldn't find the barf bag in time and tossed his cookies all over the Mexican woman next to him. Her face scrunched, she gagged, then did the same right back at him. They'd bonded through misery. With the plane's recirculated air, we'd be inhaling and smelling puke for the next hour and a half.

When everybody was settled, I headed to the back to get ready to serve the cardboard-tasting food.

Chiquita had her Walkman's headphones on and was still looking at the pictures. She touched my hand when I passed by.

She took the earphones off and said, "You okay?"

I shrugged, rubbed my breasts. My bra, or the East Coast water I'd bathed with, or the different kind of lotion I was using, something was irritating the heck out of my damn breasts. I was having a sensitive day and the material was rubbing my nipples raw.

Chiquita repeated, "Shelby, you okay?"

"Nauseated."

She raised a brow, "Nauseated?"

I made a face and said, "Not that."

She tilted her head, made a silly expression of doubt.

I said, "I had some airline food. Sick as hell all last night. Spent half the night in the bathroom reading *Good Hair*."

She gave me a few antacids. She said, "Try drinking a 7UP. Or get some crackers and bread."

"Another one of your Southern remedies?"

"It works."

I grabbed my purse and went into the lavatory.

I sat there and felt damn dizzy. Woozy and winded. Felt the plane dip and rise. Damn air pockets. Thought I heard somebody cough and sneeze. Maybe I was catching an international germ the contagious passengers had lugged aboard. I wouldn't doubt it because day before yesterday I barely ran four miles at the hotel before I was exhausted. I thought I wasn't motivated. By mile two I was breathing like a heathen, sweating buckets, and it felt like I'd run a marathon. I'd been taking echinacea, valerian, kyloic, double doses of 500mg vitamin C, but I guess the viruses had been taking their vitamins too.

I opened my purse, shifted through panty shields, bills, and birth control pills—I call them poppa-stoppas—and took out my menstrual calendar. Looked at the no-fun and tampon-filled days I had circled. Counted. My last period was twenty days ago. No big deal. I might not get a visit from the cramp man for a while. My cycle was so irregular, had ranged from thirty to fifty days between my periods. The last time Miss Flow showed up was forty days, before that my "friend" didn't come around for forty-five days. Five of the last eight months I've barely spotted.

My head did feel a little warm. The glands in my throat felt swollen. I thought I had a touch of the flu. A stomach virus. I felt my body rejecting some kind of poison, probably the vegetarian airline food I'd swiped for myself yesterday had been laced with pork. I gagged and threw up a little, but it didn't help. I ended up choking and dry-heaving so hard I thought I was about to lose a lung. Somebody shook the handle on the door. A big-ass sign said OCCUPIED, but somebody didn't get the point. Then another one of the flight attendants called my name and asked if I was all right. I fanned my face and told her I'd be out in a minute. My Band-Aid kit was in the bottom of my bag. I took out four, put two in the shape of an X over each nipple. That felt better already. I dabbed the sweat from my forehead and neck, brushed my teeth, rinsed, but I still smelled those passengers' vomit floating around in my nostrils.

I reached in my pocket to get my lipstick and felt a folded-up piece of paper. I took it out and unfolded it.

Shelby
if you ever need
comfort love warmth conversation handshake
hug an ear safe-feeling shelter kisses loving me
I'm right here
                                        Ty

It was a handwritten note from Tyrel. He always slipped notes in my pocket and purse. A dose of his sweetness made me feel better.

Then another wave of queasiness rolled in. My nose held the wrong aromas too long. Just like some days I still smelled Nancy's cheap perfume from way back when, it wouldn't go away.

The flight leveled out.

After the soda and crackers, my insides settled a little.

I smiled and pushed that food 'n' drink cart up and down the walkway, fed the strangers who were still awake, watched Richard Vaughn watch me work. Then collected trash and served more drinks. Trust me, this job ain't all that. I passed by the evil screaming child who was throwing toys every whichaway. The rug rat's parents held the monster when they saw me coming.

Before I knew it, the time had come to prepare for landing.

When I made it back to my seat, Chiquita had her head back, blanket in her lap, Walkman on, eyes closed.

Her perfume came across loud and clear. I hadn't smelled it all flight, but now it reeked like hell. It was the same rose and mimosa scent I had on, but it suddenly smelled harsh.

I glanced at the window next to her. It was smeared and scratched. I wondered how many men had touched it, left their fingerprints, and moved on. Then I thought about that foul comment Debra had made about my coochie being worn down like Pico Boulevard. She was joking, probably wouldn't remember it if I threw it in her face, but I'll never forget that. Now I can't even drive near Pico Boulevard without getting upset.

Minutes later, our limousine in the sky descended. The landing gear clanked and whirred open. I was still beat, felt tore up from the floor up, but most of my illness was almost gone. Chiquita was redoing her makeup and slightly bobbing to someone's beat. My hand drifted down and massaged my belly. Think I felt a cramp coming on. Either that or gas. I couldn't remember the last time I felt so weak. Needed some serious sleep. To top it off, when I relaxed, my head started to throb from where I'd gotten hit by the rug rat's Teenage Mutant Ninja Turtle toy. I wondered if that pain was supposed to be some sort of a tap from reality.

TYREL

14

Shelby called me late Monday night from Miami. After I grumbled, "Hello," it took her a couple of seconds to say anything. Her voice was grainy, the words choppy; she sniffled.

"What's wrong?"

She cleared her throat and paused. "I might be pregnant."

That made me wake right up. Felt like I'd stuck my finger into a light socket. Partly because of the pregnancy, partly due to the angry way she said it. There was a fistful of hate, hurt, grief, and despair in her tone. It had the flavor of subdued fear. She was too far from home to be tripping out by herself. The distance made me feel helpless and useless.

"You sure?" I asked over my yawn. I clicked the three-way light to its softest setting and sat up. I put my bare feet into the powder-blue carpet and gripped it with my toes. Ripped up as many fibers as I could. The clock said it was twelve-thirty a.m.

She said, "I think so."

"You been to the doctor?"

"Nope." Shelby took a wealth of short breaths, another weighty pause, then trembled out, "Took an EPT test."

"When?"

"Hour ago."

"And?"

"Bugs Bunny died."

"You sure?"

"What the hell do you mean, am I sure?"

"I mean are you sure?"

"Unless I'm color-blind, I'd barely dropped two drops of piss on the strip before it changed colors."

"Why're you so upset?"

"Why did I call you?" She moaned. "You are such a man."

"Be such a woman and tell me what I'm missing."

"I'm upset because I messed around and got knocked up. And I know better. This ain't the order this was supposed to happen in my life. I've got bills up the ying-yang. I'm still not where I want to be with my career. I mean I've bounced from teaching, to taking the test for LAPD, to the test for the sheriff's department, to being a damn flight attendant."

"Don't focus on where you are, focus on where you want to be."

"Where I wanna be ain't pregnant."

"I was just trying to help."

"Did I ask for a solution?"

"No you didn't."

"Then don't give me one."

"All right."

"Why in the hell did I call you?"

"I was about to ask you that my-damn-self."

"I didn't need my degree to get the job I have. I can't keep working because they won't let me fly and be sick like this. What if I get dizzy? If something happened to me or a passenger, they'd be held responsible. I'm so damn miserable and weak and—"

"Shelby?"

"Don't cut me off like that—"

"Calm down. You're jumping ahead. Today before tomorrow."

"First you tell me to focus on tomorrow." She chewed and swallowed. "Then you say don't worry about tomorrow."

"You're tripping."

Sounded like she yawned. Sounded like her mood had switched again. She said a weak "Blow me a kiss, baby."

I did. "You get it?"

"Yeah." She giggled. "Thanks."

I pictured her with child. Her tummy and attitude growing, nose spreading around her high cheekbones. Me rubbing her belly, feeling the first kicks of a new life. Her pregnant, looking fine as hell, wobbling with her hands at her waist for back support. Me rushing us to the hospital. Her breathing harshly and sweating. Me holding her hands while she dug her fingernails into my skin. Her cursing me out and telling me I did this to her. A beautiful baby with her complexion. Me putting something on my fingernail cuts and smiling while I drove my family home.

Shelby let out a sad laugh and said, "Ready to give up your free Friday nights and trade your briefcase for a diaper bag?"

I didn't answer. I collapsed back across the bed. Exhaled.

She said, "What are you thinking?"

"I was wondering what kind of dad I would be. My family wasn't exactly functional."

"So what? At least you had some kind of a family."

"The only masculine role model I had was my dad, and I don't know. He's not exactly up for a reward on fatherhood."

"My mother wasn't—" Shelby started. "Never mind." She paused. I think I heard her tapping a spoon on a bowl. Tapping with a hard rhythm. She said, "Are you seeing somebody else?"

"Nope. You're too much to handle. No time for two."

"You're not like your daddy. Why should he matter anyway?"

"He doesn't." But he did. I said, "I was just saying."

She quieted.

Shelby said, "What do you think I should do if I am?"

I said, "We'll have to move into a larger place. Maybe it's time to buy a house, review our finances. It'll be hard, but—"

She snapped, "Tyrel, no."

"What?"

"Damn."

"What?"

"That's not the right answer."

"I think you just made a left and I made a right."

"I don't want to have a child. Not right now, anyway. Not under these circumstances."

"So what are you saying?"

"I have a career and this is not a good time. I don't have the same kind of job you have. I don't have the privilege."

"What privilege do I have?"

"I can't take my shoes off and kick my feet up on my desk and throw darts at pictures and play solitaire on the computer and bullshit around like that while I wait for a check."

"Bullshit? You think I bullshit all day?"

"I mean, Tyrel, you know what I mean."

"Let's talk about it first, all right?"

"It's not about us. This is about me."

"It's about us."

"It's about what I let happen."

"Calm down."

"Don't tell me to calm down. I hate it when you talk to me like I'm a child. You're not my damn daddy."

"Never said I was."

"You're not the one throwing up from coast to coast. It's my body that'll have to go through all those changes, and get fat and shit. Stretch marks crawling all up my ass. I see women up in the gym who have had children, and no matter how many sit-ups they do they can't get rid of their pooches, and don't get me started talking about saggy breasts and stomachs messed—"

"Shelby."

"What?"

"Calm down."

From my side of the phone, I heard Shelby rustle around; hotel drawers opened and closed, bathroom water turned on and off. She coughed, gagged, spat. She was as restless as I was. I was telling her to calm down and I was stressed my-damn-self, thinking about the same life-changing concerns she was talking about—money, change of status, us not being married, things being done in the wrong order. Order was for people of tradition. My voice was easy, as easy could be, I was still opening and closing my toes, had gripped up some of the Berber carpet.

Shelby's breathing was erratic.

I said, "You okay?"

"Hell the fuck no. Frustrated. Aggravated."

"Are you eating?"

"Yeah. Butter pecan ice cream and Oreos."

I ran my hand around the back of my neck and visualized her sitting up in the dark in her panties and no bra, running her fingers through her hair, twisting and yanking it at the roots.

"Shelby?"

She mumbled, "What?"

"Stop pulling on your hair before you go bald, baby. Pull all your hair out and you'll have to get a weave, and Leonard will be talking about you night and day, onstage and off."

She giggled, "Okay."

I said, "Can you see the moon from your room?"

"Hold on. Let me open the curtains. Yeah. Why?"

"I can see it from the patio. Look at it while we talk."

"What's that gonna do?"

"Make it seem like we're closer than we are."

"You are so silly."

Moments passed with us holding the phone, saying nothing.

She calmed and said, "Thanks for making me laugh."

"That's okay. Can't laugh and be mad at the same time."

"I'm sorry. I just don't feel good."

"Outside of the nausea, how do you feel?"

"Hungry. Stressed. Can't think. Don't wanna be at work."

"Fever?"

"I think I'm warm. I want to be at home with you."

I nodded at the moon. I said, "Wish you were here."

"Jet lag has me irritated." Her voice softened, started to sound more relaxed. She sounded worn, but the pitch was normal.

I said, "That's okay. Just stop stressing, all right?"

She whined, "All right, *daddy*."

"I'm not your daddy."

"Then do me a favor and don't patronize me when I get upset."

"If I was, if I did, it was an accident."

"You have a tendency to sound condescending. Like you're talking down and trying to call me stupid on the sly."

"Never."

"When you made those comments about me not picking up my shoes and clothes, then you left a note on the front door, what was that all about? How was that supposed to make me feel?"

I said, "You need to clean up behind yourself."

"You need to learn how to wash a dish or two."

"I'm trying."

She had attitude when she said, "So am I."

"Let's stay focused. We're getting off the issue."

"See," she said, "that's what I mean."

"Do I ride your back over nothing?"

"Tyrel Anthony Williams." She swallowed and chewed, talked with her mouth full. "I called you because I needed a friend, not a lover or whatever, just a friend."

"You call Debra?"

"Why the hell would I call her? This ain't got nothing to do with her. This ain't the kind of thing I want to broadcast."

"What's the problem?"

"You are such a man. I called you because I need you."

"I know. Just thought you might want to talk to her."

"What, you're not my friend?"

"Yeah, I'm your friend. I just meant to talk about whatever women talk about when you're talking about stuff like this."

"She's married. I can't just pick up the phone and call her or stop by her house whenever. It ain't that kind of party. Do you still call Leonard all times of the night?"

"No, I don't. But I would if it was an emergency. Plus Leonard is up late most of the time."

"It's not like that anymore. Debra's not single and living by herself anymore. She's probably getting her freak on and wouldn't let him answer anyway."

She laughed. I laughed. Two lovers' stress dwindled a touch.

"Tyrel?"

"Yeah."

"This is our business. Nobody else's."

"All right."

"Not Leonard's or Debra's or anybody."

"All right."

"Swear."

"I promise."

"Good enough." Shelby yawned and said, "I'm tired. I've got to be alert and on a plane at nine and it's after four a.m."

My clock said it was about twenty after one here.

She said, "I'm going to take another test. Just in case I screwed up and got a false reading. Let's talk about it when I get back home on Wednesday. I need sleep, baby."

"Call me if you can't sleep."

"Okay."

SHELBY

15

My eyes were the color of ketchup by the time I finished talking to Tyrel. After I peed for the tenth time in the last hour, I blew my nose, and then picked up the phone to call Debra back, but stopped when I saw my empty left hand. I put the phone back down and thought about Momma. She'd died with a teenage child and a ringless left hand. Left behind a hope chest filled with broken promises.

Then I saw my silhouette in the mirror. For a few seconds my mind wandered away, back to a time when I had ponytails, ashy elbows, dressed in secondhand tight jeans and a T-shirt. One day in particular always stood out. Crozier Middle School had a short day and I went home early, walked out of the sunshine and inside my darkened house. We didn't have an air conditioner, so the house was dark to keep it from getting too hot.

Momma's bedroom door was cracked open. I heard noises. Sounded like change jingling. My nose led the way, and I peeped through the door and became nauseated. A heavyset rust-colored man was on top of Momma, his blue work pants at his ankles, her flowered skirt hiked up to her waist, no emotion in her face, too much emotion in his. His janitor keys were jingling while he moved, made it sound like a bad Christmas song. Momma turned her head to the side and saw me in the door with my hand clamped over my mouth. She put a finger to her lips and waved me away like she was telling me to go play.

I went into the kitchen, dropped my books on the floor, and sat at the table. Shaking my head, trembling, rocking, twisting my greasy hair, and gritting my teeth while I bounced my leg up and down. Momma had taken out chicken wings and potatoes. That was for me to cook. I killed a roach or two before I started my chore.

Keys jingled on their way out of our front door. Saw that man cross Market Street and go inside of his peach stucco house. He was moving fast. Jingling a new song. I guess he didn't know the school had a half-day either. I went to school with one of his children. His wife worked the cafeteria. She was a cook. Just like Momma used to be before she got sick.

When he deserted, Momma came into the kitchen. She smelled like that man. Like car grease and unwashed sweat, unclean body parts, the way fat people did. Momma was a stout woman with four moles on her left cheek. We had the same eyes, mouth, and high cheekbones, so I guess everything else came from my MIA daddy. Momma was brown-skinned and always wore a brown wig. People at school would tease me about her size. They'd joke about the way her stockings went *swish-swish* when she walked. She used to be thin, like Dorothy Dandridge, but after she had me, she never lost the weight. They would taunt me about my dark complexion and tease me about Momma's weight. Momma lit her Salem on the gas stove and leaned against the doorframe. Momma inhaled, then coughed. She coughed hard; it sounded like her insides were coming loose. We didn't know it, but they had already come loose.

She said, "What the hell you doing home this time of day?"

"School let out early."

Her arms folded under her breasts. "You get suspended?"

"Call 'em if you don't believe me. You see everybody else passing by. You think everybody got suspended?"

"Stop rolling your eyes, and watch your mouth before I knock the taste out of it. Your sassy ass." She inhaled and coughed again. She said, "What you just did was stupid."

"What I do wrong this time?"

"Your fast ass. What you doing coming to my room?"

"I heard noises. Somebody coulda been breaking in."

"Told you about coming in without knocking."

"It wasn't nighttime. I didn't know you had company." She inhaled again. "What's that in your hand?"

"My report card. I got four A's and a B."

"What that fast-ass yellow gal get?"

"She's not yellow. And she's not red. I hate it when people call her that. She's the same as us."

"You wish. Keep on talking crazy. What she get?"

"Debra got three A's, a B, and a C."

Momma tightened her lips and said, "I used to make straight A's. You're stupid, Shelby. Just plain old stupid."

I started peeling a potato and pretended I couldn't hear.

She said, "Your fast ass gonna end up pregnant before you get out of high school. Your ass'll be on the county by graduation."

She'd said that so much, it didn't hurt. I said, "Momma?"

"What you want now?"

"What make you think I want something?"

" 'Cause you yanking at your hair. What you want?"

"Can I get one of those hideaway beds for my birthday? I saw one at the swap meet on La Brea."

"I ain't got no swap-meet hideaway-bed money to be giving them Orientals. You see them bills on my dresser?"

"I'll get my own bed."

She laughed. "How?"

My hands were busy peeling the potato. I stopped long enough to look across the street and saw that man's wife and kids getting out of their light blue Chevrolet. Laughing and shit.

Momma gazed across Market, watched him hug his wife and help her with the groceries. Momma looked at me.

I turned away, but her reflection was in a silver part of the O'Keefe stove. She chewed her bottom lip for a moment, then said my name, said it the way a momma filled with shame would. She held her arms out to me. I went over. She hugged me. I hugged her tighter.

"I'm sorry, Shelby. Sometimes Momma does and says thangs to drive you away, but you know you the only friend I got."

"Why you messing with him?"

"We gotta eat." She rubbed my back and kissed my face. "Momma gotta feed her baby so she can get all A's next time."

"Maybe I can get a fake I.D. and get a job at Boy's Market."

Momma said, "No, you're not. You're gonna go to school and work on them straight A's so you can get a scholarship and go to somebody's college. Say it."

"I'm gonna go to college."

"A four-year college."

"A four-year college."

"You better. Say that ten times a day. You understand?"

I nodded.

She said, "There's some good men in college. Get one of them high yellow boys. Or get one smart like Martin Luther King."

"Momma?"

"Yeah, baby?"

"Can I go over to Debra's and spend the night?"

"Can?"

"May I."

"What I done told you about sounding stupid. Men don't like stupid women. If you stop being trifling and don't end up lazy, fat, and stupid, you might get smart enough to get you a white man. They likes and treats dark women better than our own men do. Now, your prissy friend Debra don't have to be smart. She high yellow, they got their own special place in the world."

"If she so special, why does everybody treat her so bad?"

"How they treat her bad?"

"All the girls always wanna fight her over nothing."

"That's her problem. Stop playing with her so much."

Momma rambled on about that for a while. If I had've had a remote control back then, I would've pointed it at her and changed the channel. Maybe just pushed the mute button. Everything she said was a rerun.

She stopped planning my life and picking my friends long enough to rifle through the kitchen cabinet and find the rest of her carton of cigarettes. She sat back down, opened a new pack, tapped the life-taker on the table three times before she lit it. I used to hide her Salem 100's, but she would rant and yell and damn near tear the house up trying to find them, so I gave up. Especially after she grabbed my arm so hard it hurt for three days.

"Momma, please, may I go over to Debra's when I finish?"

"Why do you always wanna go over there?"

I shrugged. "So we can do homework together. Talk."

She said, "Why don't she ever come over here?"

"We got roaches. One fell in her hair the last time."

"Like they don't have roaches."

"They don't."

"Why you always have to run down there? This your home."

I shrugged. "Ain't you gonna have company again tonight?"

Momma didn't say anything. She went back to staring across Market. I went back to cooking, back to sweating like I had a fever and making french fries and fried chicken.

An ocean of grease splattered from the cast-iron skillet to the gas stove. The orange wall already had permanent Crisco spots. Oil spots that looked like tears. Like the whole house was crying.

Momma sat in the heat of the kitchen looking mad and hurt. Her head drooped. She bounced her right leg, hummed a church song, and picked at her cuticles. She hummed when she was upset.

"Momma, chicken'll be done in a li'l bit. We got hot sauce?"

She didn't raise her head.

"Momma." I put on my best laugh. "We eat chicken all the time. Fried chicken, baked chicken, thick chicken soup, chicken hamburgers, peanut butter and chicken sandwiches. Debra said that's why I've got chicken legs."

Momma raised her head and looked across the street again.

I giggled and touched my flat chest. "Guess I should eat a whole lotta chicken breasts, huh, Momma?"

She shifted and kept her eyes in that man's business. That man hadn't glanced her way one time since he'd raced out of our front door and stumbled across Market Street.

I stopped trying to be so damn cheerful. And I didn't look at her again while I started making the strawberry Kool-Aid.

Even with the backdoor open so the inside heat could go play with the outside heat, I sweated hard enough for my hot-combed hair to go back to a nappy afro. Usually I bitched about how nappy it would be the next day, but I didn't care. Didn't care about how her cigarette smoke had clouded up the room in a smoggy kinda way. Don't think I cared about much. Momma smoked the rest of her cigarettes, back to back, down to the filter. She smoked and coughed and smoked and coughed. I didn't mean to hurt her feelings when I slipped in my little dig about her having company. I did want to give her some pain, but after I did, it didn't feel that good. Sometimes a sister can lose through a victory.

Debra answered like she knew it was me calling back: "Well?"

I don't think I'd ever felt so down. I said, "I told him."

"What did you tell him?"

"I told him I took an EPT and the rabbit croaked."

"You didn't tell me you took an EPT."

"I didn't. I wanted to see what he would say."

She made a disagreeable sound. Debra said, "And?"

"Well, he didn't say what I thought he would."

"What did you expect him to say?"

"He talked about moving into a bigger place, reviewing some fucking finances, shit like that."

"What did you want him to say, Shelby? You call the man in the middle of the night and lie to him, what was on your agenda?"

"I didn't have an agenda."

"Sounds like it to me. What did he do wrong?"

I looked at my naked left hand again. Momma never had a ring on that hand. My last name is Momma's maiden name. On my birth certificate the places where the information about the father should be written in are blank. As blank as I felt right now.

I said, "He got all logical and shit."

"Hold on."

"What's that loud-ass noise?"

"House alarm."

"What's wrong? Debra, what's up? Hang up and dial 9-1—"

"It's just Leonard." She let out a hard sigh. "He keeps pushing the wrong button when he comes in."

"Oh."

"This house is too big when Leonard's gone."

She yelled, said she was in the den, then asked him how was his day. He'd been out in Pasadena filming some comedy movie. She put the phone down and I heard hugs, giggles, and kisses. I didn't pay attention to them. Just kept staring at the moon.

"Shelby?"

"I'm still here."

"When do you get back home?"

"Wednesday afternoon."

"Come to the clinic." She sounded hurt. Like I had disappointed her again. "I'll test you."

"You don't have to."

"Shelby."

"All right, all right."

"What're you and Tyrel going to do if you are?"

"Debra, not now please."

I thought about that little girl Debra had met a few months ago. Remembered "You fuck you get pregnant."

"What are you getting ready to do?"

"Leonard is getting ready to shower."

"And?"

"I'm going to get in with him."

I closed my eyes for a second. Opened them and understood Debra's priorities. Saw where me and my crisis didn't fit in.

I simply said, "Okay."

"Then I'm going to heat up his dinner and talk to him."

"No problem. Well, tell your husband I said hello."

"Him and Tyrel are going to Drew Medical tomorrow afternoon."

"I didn't know. What are they going to Watts for?"

"One of those all-day teenager-motivation things put on by the mayor. Last year they said Chaka Khan, Dawnn

Lewis, the sister who plays the mom on *The Parent Hood*, all of them participated."

That was so unimportant. My wet eyes were still on the moon. Half of my mind was on the past; the other half was pondering my future with Tyrel. So much of my damn life has been spent suffering consequences from crappy decisions and bad actions.

"Shelby?"

"Yeah."

"Get some sleep."

"Sure thing, Mrs. DuBois. Kiss the hubby for me."

"Shelby."

"What?"

"Don't do that."

"What?"

"Don't act like you're okay. It's me and you."

"Okay."

"You haven't taken an EPT, right?"

"Right."

"Then you don't know you're pregnant for sure."

"Right."

"Don't panic."

"Okay."

I let Debra go. Felt like I had to let everybody go.

16

Wednesday came.

When I got home from work, the living room had been cleaned top to bottom. Shelby had been home, changed, and left three pair of shoes scattered in the bedroom. Her work clothes were draped across the golden wingback chair. Workout clothes were in the bathroom—spandex over the shower rod, panties on the door knob, sports bra and tank top across the top of the door. *Life's Little Instruction Book* was on the back of the toilet along with a basket of potpourri. She left a scribbled note taped to the fridge. It said she'd gone to Debra's job to pick her up, then they were going mall-hopping, starting at the Westside Pavilion, then down on Melrose to Spike's Joint. Which was no big deal, because she spent quality time with Debra whenever they got the chance. Going to the mall was their social event. Department stores were their recreation field.

I paged her twice. She didn't call back.

Shelby was gone until midnight. She came home empty-handed. I was asleep when she crept in. Since I'd gotten home from Dan L. Steel, I'd spent the dimming of the day in the second bedroom working like a slave on a spreadsheet for a presentation tomorrow afternoon, changing the frequency of the graph to make the company look better than it really was. Sales weren't bad, but they were down a few percent. By nine I was asleep with that monk's chanting CD playing. That dry music always sent me into a coma.

I heard Shelby at the foot of the bed, slipping out of her jeans, black oversize man's jacket, and a baseball cap—my blue Nike cap with the swoosh on the front. She was in tomboy mode. Her eight or nine silver bracelets clattered and clanged when she slipped them off her wrist. Her earrings made the same sounds. That noise woke me.

She said, "You want me to turn the computer off?"

I cleared my throat, then licked the leftover tuna taste that had funked up my breath. "Yeah."

She yawned. "You save your files?"

"Yeah."

She was naked. Her figure was looking a little fuller, her thighs heavier. Did her justice. Her breasts were small, but stood firm like chocolate-covered pharaoh's mountains; a swatch of her ebony skin was more valuable than the Temple of Artemis. She always looked like one of the Seven Wonders to me. I could make an overnight fortune if I could find and bottle an ounce of the cultural mud she was made from.

I said, "I paged you twice."

She didn't respond. Shelby went down the hallway and into the second bedroom. The computer beeped three times; the screen-saver illumination that lit up the hallway faded. The bathroom door opened and closed. The shower turned on.

I fell asleep waiting for her to come back.

I don't know how much time had gone by before I heard her over at the chest of drawers, gulping a glass of orange juice. She threw a pill in her mouth and swallowed hard. After another swig of her juice, she belched a little, then stood with a downcast face, one hand deep in her mane, and stared at the wall.

I said, "What are you taking?"

She jumped. Almost dropped her juice.

I repeated the question.

Shelby said, "I went to the doctor."

She told me she had body aches, a touch of the flu, and she'd picked up antibiotics to knock the bug out of her system.

Shelby put the o.j. on the stand and tugged on a beat up brown T-shirt. It had white letters that read STILL GUILTY.

She said, "I'm going to sleep in the other room so I don't give you my germs."

"Lay down with me until I doze off. Come here."

Shelby pulled on a pair of my plaid boxers, a pair of my thick white socks, then tied a silk scarf around her hair. A minute or two later she pulled back our Aztec patterned comforter and eased into the bed.

I said, "Did you put your glass on a coaster?"

"No. Sorry."

I touched her; she shuddered like I had offended her.

"Shelby, you okay?"

"Yeah."

I patted her stomach and kissed her cheek. She moved my hand from her belly. I tried to make my eyes stay open.

I asked, "What's wrong?"

She said, "Get some sleep."

Her body was hot. Words not. I dozed when she kissed the side of my face and put her head on my chest. She was restless. Humming a church song. Shelby slowly danced her fingers through the hair on the back of my neck. That was how I fell asleep.

The next morning I trimmed my goatee, picked out a suit, then stared out my window at the park. Birds sang in the pine trees. Cars zoomed through the high-rent neighborhood and raced to participate in the bumper-to-bumper smog factory on the freeway.

Shelby was in the kitchen making herbal tea. Moving like her feet were made of iron. She'd been quiet all morning.

I asked her about going to see Faith.

She smiled under melancholy eyes, then said, "Don't have to. I got my period. Cramp man stopped by and hooked me up."

She said her cycle was off because of stress, her unpredictable sleeping schedule, and other things. She yawned, turned away from me, started unloading the dishwasher.

"I'm on the pill, remember?"

Her tone was matter-of-fact. Housed disappointment.

She changed the subject and asked me about the event that me and Leonard participated in at Drew Medical. While I sipped hazelnut coffee and ate a banana nut muffin, I told her it was an open carnival for preteen kids, impressionable youngsters they wanted to encourage toward the positive before they made it to gang-joining age. They had pony rides and games all afternoon. I'd spoken for about ten quick minutes before Leonard stole the show, had them doing positive chants and singing kids songs.

Shelby beamed, "That's good. 'Cause by the time those rug rats get to be twelve, most of 'em are wearing hundred-thirty-dollar Air Jordans and packing a .45."

"Not most, just some."

We debated about that for a minute or two before I steered her back to the real issue. Something changed inside me. I felt a hardness coming on. Not sexual. I was far from that. A hardness in my stomach, that same rigidness of mixed-up love and hate and sadness and resentment I had when I sat across the table from Lisa at our last supper. But I sat on top of what was rising, held it down with calmness and shallow sips of coffee.

I said, "So, when did you get your period?"

"Right before the plane took off day before yesterday morning."

I'd just emptied the bathroom's small trash can into a larger one and taken the refuse down the hall to the garbage chute. There weren't any tampon wrappers or whatever in the trash can.

I nodded. "Thought the test was positive?"

"What test?"

"The EPT."

"Aw." She hesitated, twisted her lips. "I made a mistake."

"How?"

"Ty, Faith said a man could piss on one of those cheap-ass things and it'll say he's pregnant."

"So you talked to Faith?"

"Not really. Not recently."

"Thought you went by the clinic to pick Debra up yesterday?"

"I did. I mean I saw Faith, but we didn't have a conversation. Women know EPTs can give whacked readings like that."

"I doubt that."

"You don't know everything."

"Didn't say I did."

Shelby put some wheat bread in the toaster.

I said, "What did you do all day yesterday?"

"Shopping. You read the note."

"You were too weak to stand up for five minutes, and you went to the doctor, bought flu stuff, then shopped all day?"

"Being sick ain't never stopped a sister from getting thirty percent off."

"Why didn't you call me at the job and tell me you started?"

She drummed her fingers on the fridge and scowled at me like I was Scrooge on Christmas Eve. Each of her words sliced like a deep cut from a rusty stiletto: "What the fuck you want me to do, send you a postcard when I get my fucking period? Why are you asking all these stupid questions?"

"You ever think I might be worried too?"

"What the hell do you have to worry about?"

I let silence buffer what was happening between us.

Tried to let it soften what hostility was growing and burning in my gut. She saw I didn't appreciate the way she was talking to me.

I said, "You weren't too busy to send up smoke signals when you took the test."

"Overreacted. My period wasn't due anyway. Told you that."

"I can work with, deal with, and understand that. But what about the EPT?"

"What about it?"

"Did you get an abortion?"

She paused long enough to tilt her head sideways. "I don't believe you could accuse me of doing some shit like that."

I said, "That was a yes or no question."

She spoke with venom. "Why can't you get it, huh?"

Shit changed real quick. We were both ready for an all-out, no-holds-barred fight.

I demanded, "Show me the pills you took last night."

"What?"

"Let me see the pills."

"I'm not showing you my medicine."

"You were damn sure you were pregnant two days ago, right?"

"Dammit, I made a damn mistake. I said I *thought* I was pregnant. Now I don't think I am. All right? That okay with you?"

"What about the pregnancy test?"

"The test was wrong." She shook her head like she was confused and shrugged. "Shit. I told you in plain English what happened. Now would you please get the hell out of my face and get off my damn back?"

I touched her shoulder to get her to look at me. I had to see her eyes. She repeated what she had told me, then jerked free and stormed off.

I said, "I want to believe in you, Shelby."

She stopped in her tracks and slowly walked back. She said, "You trying to say that you don't believe in me?"

"I'm questioning a lot of things right now."

"Like?"

"Your character and integrity."

Tears were in her eyes, but none fell. She whispered, "Then why are we together?"

I said, "You tell me."

"Guess you just needed a bed warmer, huh?"

"Guess so."

Curses. Screams. Heated things were said. Just half of the stupid, irrational, immature, ignorant things that we said had a tone that could damage the best relationship.

"And if I was pregnant, what the hell would I look like walking around with a baby in my belly and I'm not married. Or is that your kind of character and integrity?"

Her words were blistering. Sometime during the emotional fire, she snatched the closet open, damn near pulled it off the tracks, and started throwing her wardrobe on the bed.

"What're you doing?"

"What does it look like I'm doing? I'm leaving."

"Then pack your shit and go."

She stopped and glowered at me. That look would've sent most brothers running for the hills. But I didn't move. Shelby's eyes widened over her quivering lip. She frowned at me for a moment before she exhaled, took short pants, softened her shoulders, adjusted her stance, twisted her hair. Her head bobbed a few times. Her eyes watered up, but she held on to the tears like they were the last thing she had in the world.

"I meant I was going to work. I have a flight." Her voice dropped to a low tone, cracked. Saliva hung from her top teeth to her bottom lip. It didn't break when she talked.

She said, "I've got another two-day trip. But if that is how you feel, then hey, fuck this shacking up shit, and fuck you."

"Shelby . . ."

"When I get back, I'll pack my shit and go."

"That's not what I meant."

"Get your motherfucking hand off me."

"Watch your language."

"Don't touch me."

"Neighbors don't need to hear."

"Do I look like I give a shit?"

"Shelby—"

"Move out of my way."

I sidestepped her ire, lowered my tone in proportion to the amount she'd raised hers, hoped she'd do the same. I took a breath or two, then said, "I didn't mean for it to sound—"

"That's what you said, so I guess that must be what's on your mind, what you really want. I don't believe you disrespected me and said something like that to me."

"I'm not gonna let you turn this around."

"I never should've moved in here in the first place. You want me to get out, I'll leave."

"No, Shelby. I thought that's what you meant."

"No, you wished that was what I meant."

It was sounding too much like a riot, so I raised my palms to the sky and tried to stop the argument from ballooning. The condo had become too small, so I went and stood out on the patio.

My daddy did it to my family. Lisa did it to my hopes. People always made decisions that affected the remainder of my life and didn't ask me how I felt about it until *after* the fact. And that was *if* they asked. I was part of the equation but always left out of the loop.

Now maybe Shelby had done the same bullshit.

Or maybe I was just paranoid.

I tried to cool off before I hopped into my blue suit and Italian tie and landed in the middle of corporate America. I ran my fingers through my hair, over my goatee and reminded myself, Always leave personal problems at home and arrive to work with a smile and positive words. That would be hard to do today.

I didn't turn around when I heard Shelby walk into the living room. Hard, angry steps that dented the carpet. Her perfume came over and irritated my senses, tickled the hairs in my nose. Her heels went back and forth across the room. Sounded like her luggage-on-wheels was in tow behind her. The dead bolt clicked. The front door opened. Maybe she was standing there waiting to speak her mind, but she didn't. She might've been waiting for me to say something, maybe thought I'd fall into that *PleaseBabyPleaseBabyPleaseBabyBabyPlease* routine. Didn't happen. I kept my back to her.

She said softly, "You need to learn to talk what you know."

The door closed. Soft and gentle.

My gut sank like I'd been kicked over the side of a sky-high waterfall. Falling, falling. I sighed out my animosity.

I moved across the carpet, made a couple of steps in her direction, wanted to go after her and not let this argument be an open wound, but when my fingers touched the doorknob, I changed my mind. I wasn't about to chase what shouldn't be running.

SHELBY

17

Then pack your shit and go.

A moment or two passed before I realized the stoplight had changed to green. I probably would've cried through another green-yellow-red cycle, but a car behind me was blaring its horn. I was too busy staring at my reflection in the glass. Saw how nasty and smudged it was. Saw fingerprints from yesterdays. Everywhere, on every car on Sepulveda, fingerprints.

That was why I burned rubber getting to the clinic.

The Bugs Bunny test Debra gave me showed up positive. I shook my head and told Debra I wasn't gonna keep it. Debra led me from the examination room into the back office, made two cups of herbal tea, and tried to talk me out of it. Maybe not talk me out of it, just tried to get me to talk about it, because I had clasped my lips. Trepidation was the glue that shut me up. I was hardly speaking to myself, let alone anybody else.

Debra moaned. "Shelby, you know how I feel about this."

"Well, obviously we don't feel the same way."

I waved my hand and told her that if I couldn't get it taken care of with people I trusted, I'd drive across the street from USC, step over the crack pipes and syringes, and take a number.

"Debra, I'm afraid."

"I know. I can tell you are."

"I need you to be my best friend."

"Don't be selfish this time."

"Just be there with your favorite selfish bitch, from paperwork to dismissal. Can you please do that?"

Debra closed her eyes, like she did when she was praying, patted my hand over and over, asked, "Are you sure?"

"Debra?"

"Yeah?" Her tone rang like she knew I'd changed my mind.

I picked my cuticles and said, "Since I'm your patient, this means you'll have to exercise patient-client confidentiality."

Her posture weakened. She nodded and spoke in little more than a whisper, "Thanks for putting me in this position, Shelby."

"What about my position? Everything ain't always about you."

"Never said it was."

"Then stop trying to make me feel guilty."

"Guilt is internal. I can't *make* you feel anything."

I was two seconds from going off on her trying-to-be-psychological ass, but Debra held my hand the way my momma used to do after she knew she'd said the wrong thing.

"We're family, Shelby. What you, or any of us do for that matter, affects us all."

"You and Leonard are family. Me and Tyrel are two people living together. We haven't made any promises. We have separate checking accounts and separate charge cards." I stood up.

Debra said, "Where are you going?"

"Outside. I need some air. How long will I have to wait?"

"Not long."

I went back out to the lobby, stalled next to the two quarter candy machines and became mesmerized by the picture on the wall: a photo of a shirtless brother in jeans, holding his newborn daughter in his dark arms, smiling down on his baby while his baby smiled up at him. *L'Enfant.* I'd looked at that tri-matted picture a thousand times, but that was my first time *seeing* it.

I sat down. A chill ran through me and I started having second thoughts for the tenth time. I was about to call it off, leave, go trade my Z for a Saturn, then drive by Kids "R" Us and see how much this was going to set me back. All I wanted to do was crawl into a crack-and-crevice and suffer the consequences.

Then I remembered Tyrel was a bonafide twin. I'd met his sister's twin sons, and those loud-ass bad-ass rug rats could put Bebe's kids to shame. Tyrel's grandfather was a twin. And there were probably a thousand sets of twins weighing down his family tree before them. Damn. The brothers in his bloodline must've had some sort of super ninja Shaka Zulu sperm that sliced a sister's egg down the middle then impregnated both halves.

I tried to see me with two little bowlegged, dimple-faced children. After a couple of groans, I sat down and did a little bit of a prayer. Then I thought about how people always waited until it was too late to pray. What was done was done. As far as I knew, the angels had turned their back on me a long time ago. Had done to me what they had done to my momma.

So many thoughts.

I wondered if I could live up to the lifelong expectations of Tyrel, plus a baby. When a sister gets pregnant, she has to think about what she would do *if* the baby's daddy didn't stay around until its high school graduation.

That's the quicksand my thoughts were sinking in when Lisa came into the clinic. I heard that bitch cackling before the glass door swung open. That bitch walked in like a bad memory, both of her crumb-snatchers on her heels. She stood in front of me, smiling and toying with her brace-let. Her makeup was done to the tee. I felt fat and ugly as hell. I needed to rub ice over my puffy face and eyes to make me look close to normal.

I heard Lisa say, "Shelby?"

"What?"

"In for a checkup?"

"Well, this ain't Jiffy Lube."

She laughed. "Don't you look haggard."

"How's your daddy doing, Lisa?"

She stopped laughing then. "He's fine."

Lisa led her family away, found herself a ringside seat two chairs down. The other side of the room was empty, but she had parked her family next to me. The heifer found herself a seat where she could watch me like a chicken hawk.

Her little girl had braids and sat in Lisa's lap. The little boy had Coke-bottle glasses, looked like a black Mr. Peabody.

The door to the back opened and a white girl in her early twenties walked out, on the verge of tears. She brushed her blond hair from her face, breezed through the lobby and out into the sunlight without raising her head.

I would've sprinted and caught the door and gone into the back of the clinic and waited for Debra to un-impregnate me, but the door to the hallway and examination rooms closed too fast and automatically locked when the girl rushed out.

Lisa stared at me. I didn't see her, but I knew she was watching. I turned my body away from her, opened my purse and fiddled around with my checkbook, raised my head long enough to put on lipstick and see *L'Enfant*, then chewed a stick of gum and made my shaky hands count the cotton balls and Q-tips in my purse. Next I'd be counting lint.

Faith came into the lobby. Debra was at her side, holding a clipboard with charts. Lisa spoke. Lisa's kids spoke too.

Debra's smile was flat; her eyes were heavy.

I stood up, pushed my lips up like it was the best of my

birthdays, and moved my downcast limbs toward Faith and Debra.

Lisa said, "Hey, Shelby?"

I shifted my eyes toward her. She pointed toward the chair. I'd left my purse behind.

As I picked it up, Lisa spoke just loud enough for me to hear her say, "Congratulations. I'm sure your momma would be proud."

———

When the procedure was a done deal and I was recuperating, I felt a sense of loss, like I had when I was at Inglewood Cemetery, dressed in a black dress, holding a blossoming rose in my left hand, holding Debra's hand with my right, watching them toss dirt on my mother's peach-colored coffin.

Faith came in and held my hand for a while. She finally said, "Women are strong. Black women are the strongest. We always make it through."

I said, "Faith?"

"Yes, sweetheart?"

Other than asking if I was paying by Visa, Master Card, or American Express, that was the first human thing she'd said to me in my life. I was ready to fly off in a rage and scream f-you, but I sealed my eyes and whispered, "Close the door on your way out."

TYREL

18

A baritone voice rang out: "Tyrel Williams?"

Joshua Cooper was in my office doorway. Dark suit. Bright tie. Huge smile like he'd won the lottery. Paper-thin moustache on dark skin. Chubby and dapper. I gave him that same exaggerated business smile and reminded myself to lock and barricade my office door from this day forward. It was 3:17 P.M.

I said, "Afternoon, Mr. Cooper."

He extended his hand with the golden bracelet on his arm. "Mister Williams, your presentation was brilliant."

"Thanks."

He looked curiously at the eight-by-ten of me and Shelby resting on my desk. I hadn't heard from her for twenty-four hours. Her image was next to Leonard and Debra's wedding portrait. I had a photo of Twin, her husband, and the Dynamic Duo. Everybody in every photo looked like they owned tranquillity.

I asked Joshua, "How long have you been married?"

He said, "Since I was seventeen. Married right out of high school. Had a diploma in one hand, marriage license in the other. I've been married most of my life. Over forty years."

"Same woman?"

"Same woman. We have nine children. Fourteen grandchildren. None of them have ever been to jail. None are on drugs."

"You're blessed."

"Truly."

Joshua checked his Rolex. I checked him out and wondered how many designers we were keeping in business. Saw how neither of us settled for second best. I never bought lower-end in clothes or cars, but I always ended up in swap-meet relationships.

He gazed deeper into the City of Impatient Angels.

He said, "The view from the office windows up in San Francisco puts this to shame. Imagine the Golden Gate being so close you could reach out and touch it. There are no fish better than those at Fisherman's Warf. Chinatown. Theater. The Opera."

I wished he would *poof* and go away.

He smiled. "How does it sound?"

"Take away the Golden Gate and it sounds like L.A."

He laughed. Joshua unfolded the *Times* on my desk and flipped to an article about the school systems getting federal funding for Ebonics.

He said, "When did broken English and pure laziness become a language? Is this what all the marching for equality and getting beaten and chewed by dogs and sprayed with hoses has come to?"

I didn't want to debate, didn't want to be rude, didn't want company. I'd give him fifteen minutes tops, then one of us would have to leave.

A softer voice sang, "Tyrel?"

Lisa Nichols was in my door. In her purple suit and golden blouse. She looked like success waiting for an invitation. Her hair was short. It's strange seeing a woman after you've fallen out of love with her. It made me wonder what made her so damn special in the first place.

I said, "What can I do for you, Miss Nichols?"

Lisa was upbeat when she said, "I was seeing a client on your floor, and I didn't want to be rude and pass by without speaking."

I'd seen her in the hallway from time to time. We'd made eye contact, shared a cordial nod, but never said a word. Her company had moved from the MCI building to the third floor.

Joshua smiled like he was thirty years younger.

I was about to introduce them, but they introduced themselves. Joshua shook her hand long enough to make Lisa look irritated; it showed in the corner of her eye and on her mouth. But when he told her who he was, spoke of his high position in Dan L. Steel, her eyes opened up and a real smile blossomed.

I wanted to puke.

Lisa whipped out her dawn-tinted business card so fast her wrist popped. She told him they must do lunch and talk.

His card cracked like Zorro's whip when he snapped it out.

The conversation changed. We talked about tax shelters, had a short conversation about investment properties.

He said, "So, what's your financial plan, Tyrel?"

I said, "To live off my interest. I want to make sure me, whoever I marry, and my kids have something. More eighteen-year-olds have one hundred dollars in the bank than sixty-five-year-olds."

Lisa's grin was phonier than a smile at the wax museum, but Joshua was eating it up. That was my first reaction to her too.

I introduced reality and said, "How're the husband and kids?"

Lisa bumbled, said, "What was that?"

I repeated myself, crisp and clear.

At first she looked like she didn't have a clue, then Lisa smiled like she remembered she had a mate and offsprings out there somewhere. She said, "The family's fine. Their father took them out to San Bernardino to visit his parents. Their grandparents."

"Mr. Cooper was just talking about his nine children and his grandchildren. He's been happily married for forty years."

He chuckled.

Lisa said, "Really?"

Joshua peeped at his watch one more time, then excused himself. He had to make it to LAX and shuttle back to the Bay. Joshua closed my door on his way out. Did that on his own.

Lisa stopped smiling and massaged her hand.

Me and Lisa were alone. We made generous eye contact.

She said, "You look tense."

"Tired. Didn't sleep much last night, that's all."

"Too tired for a game?"

I checked my watch before I said, "Sure."

She opened the top drawer on my desk and took out my darts. Lisa handed me the black ones and kept the red ones.

She said, "Want to flip a coin to see who goes first?"

"Ladies first."

She stood behind the trash can, aimed. Her first toss was a bull's-eye; it thumped right in the middle of Bill Gates' mouth.

I said, "I see you've been practicing."

"A few things. Other things I'm getting out of practice on."

I let her comment go without response. My first toss barely made it on the board.

She said, "Seems like you could use some practice."

That remark went unanswered too.

She made a curious sound and said, "You know me and Shelby have the same OB-GYN."

"I heard." I threw a dart, hit Bill Gates in the right ear.

"I've been going to Faith ever since I was in high school."

"Uh-huh."

She threw a dart. "I was there yesterday afternoon.

Around the same time Shelby was going in for her appointment."

Her chase-me tone had my attention.

A beat later, I asked, "What time yesterday afternoon?"

"Around noon. Shelby was back there for quite some time."

I said, "What did she say to you?"

"We hardly spoke. I guess you don't know, huh? We went to Crozier Middle and Inglewood High together." She cleared some jealousy from her throat, then added, "Is Shelby doing okay?"

"What do you mean?"

"She was definitely upset yesterday. Whatever she was down there for, she was very unhappy."

I listened with burning ears. An ache was rising, made me want to loosen my tie, felt an urgency to race to the phone brewing in my soul, but I kept it all in check. I hadn't done anything wrong, so I'd be damned if I'd be the first to call.

Lisa continued instigating, "And right now you don't look satisfied."

"Is this why you've found your way to my office?"

She laughed. Then she shrugged and threw her last dart. Lisa picked up her attaché, checked her watch.

I said, "Leaving?"

"Meeting a new client over in Carlton Square. I'm doing a home presentation." She nodded. "But I could cancel."

I shook my head. "Remember, if you don't take care of the customer, somebody else will."

She sang, "My husband and the kids will be in San Bernardino for the next few days. Maybe we could meet somewhere real quiet like we used to. My treat for old times' sake."

"No, thank you."

Lisa laughed away the rejection and did one of those subtle, flirty moves with her hand. Ran the tips of her fingers through her hair, then slid hands over her backside.

She said, "Offer still stands. Redeemable on your demand. Some nights a man gets lonely for a change of venue. Sometimes a man needs a warm place to go where his troubles can't follow."

Lisa hopped on the elevator. It dinged, then the one-trick pony was gone. Yep, I'd have to remember to lock my office door.

I picked up the phone and tried to find out where Shelby was. Leonard would tell me, if he knew. We'd been friends forever, would be friends as old men, sitting in weather-worn rocking chairs, talking about days gone by, then we'd be buddies long after our spirits fled our flesh and our bones turned to dust.

With us, the truth was always a breath away.

He wasn't home. It didn't take much thinking for me to realize that I only had one other alternative. I had to go to the source. I called Faith's clinic. Asked for Debra.

After all the laughter, this was the first time Debra wasn't happy to talk to me. But I barreled through her distant attitude, made a beeline to the point, asked if Shelby was down there yesterday afternoon. And if she was, for what.

Silence.

Debra's words were low-spirited when she finally said, "You're my husband's friend. Shelby's my friend. I'm your friend. If I had some concern about my husband's whereabouts, or any other matter, I'd speak with him directly. I wouldn't come to you. I wouldn't run to Shelby. I'd ask my husband."

All of my interests felt second-class, if that high.

We said awkward, abrupt good-byes.

A rift widened between me and Debra. I stared out my office window, toward her job behind the Wyndam hotel, and reminded myself, that in reality, she was my buddy's wife. Not my friend.

SHELBY

19 | Tyrel had been blowing up my pager. Debra had been beeping me too, but I wasn't concerned about her. She could go hop her happy-go-lucky ass in the shower with Leonard for all I cared.

I finally called Tyrel, reluctantly. Soon as the brother said hello, well, I was gonna tell him I wanted to stop by so I could "pack my shit and go." But when I called his job and heard his voice this morning, it did something to me. Bad feelings were shoved aside. I went into a soft song and dance, told him how much I missed him, told him I loved him.

He didn't say anything.

I kept my attitude light, not too cheerful, kept yakking and asked him if he had a few minutes so we could get together, maybe meet on neutral grounds, maybe rendezvous for lunch at the Coffee Company in Westchester.

He said, "Sure."

Not a single emotion was in that word.

I ended up parking my Z behind the First Federal Bank on La Tijera and Sepulveda Eastway, then sitting under a ceiling fan, waiting for him in a place halfway filled with retired white people who hoped the heat from the tea didn't unglue their dentures.

I wore a cinnamon pink skirt and white blouse, friendly

colors, because I knew he'd show up in his suit, walking like he ruled the world. Tyrel saw me waiting in a booth, shifting around underneath an antique picture of an Italian coffee shop.

My heart dropped when our eyes met. I mean *dropped*.

After all the emotions I'd babbled to him over the phone, he didn't say a word then, and he walked in not saying a word now. He sat in front of me. When times were better we always sat next to each other, because he liked to rest his hand on my leg.

He stared at the picture over my head—"Internationale di Milano 1906"—for a moment before he cleared his throat, lowered his eyes to mine and said, "Your pager working?"

I nodded my head and sipped my tea.

"Nobody has known how to find you. Not even Debra."

"Haven't felt like talking to anybody."

"Where have you been staying?"

I didn't tell him that I'd been camping out in a cheap room with thin walls on Figueroa, some space that cost me one-twenty-five for the week, but with the kinds of people lingering the halls, and the noises that were creeping through the walls, I was more than ready to call this off and go home with him. I'd run away and was living in a stale room, on a hard mattress, shades drawn, trying to cope with who I was.

"Ty?"

"I hear you."

"I wanted you to know, there were a few others before you, but you're the first man I've ever loved like this."

I had to hurry up and get all of the words out, because in another minute I'd be blowing my nose and whimpering like an idiot, pouring out my heart. This was rough. Tyrel held his poker-faced attitude. I fought and held mine.

The bastard asked me if I'd gotten an abortion.

I could've gagged. I almost went off on him, but it was damn hard to un-lie a lie. My heart wanted to curse him until his ears bled, tell him that he was too naive and too stupid to understand how a woman's body worked, that he didn't have a clue about the things that threw it out of sync, played havoc with hormones, and kicked a sister's cycle off track.

I asked, "Do you ever give up?"

His blank expression didn't change.

I snapped in a low tone, "I'm not gonna sit here and be tormented by you."

Tyrel sipped his tea. "Why didn't you consult me?"

All of a sudden my makeup was frying. "First, kill the psychology, Tyrel. Second, stop making my business your business. Get a fucking life and stop trying to control my body."

Finally I hit a nerve and churned an emotional response out of his ass. I saw the vibration in his lower lip and the surprise in his eyes. That made him blink more than a few times. He had to regroup before he repeated, "Control?"

"What would you call it?"

"I thought this was a relationship."

"I guess we've both been misled."

He sipped his tea again, said, simply, "Did you?"

"If I ever decided to do something like that, hey, it's my body. End of story." I stayed just as cool as he was. I sipped my tea, smirked, then asked, "Any more false accusations?"

Tyrel was throwing down a glare that said he thought the police should come get me and make me pay my debt to society.

The brother switched gears, lost the cold-blooded tone, softened up his expression and said, "I ran into a friend of yours."

"What friend?"

"Lisa Nichols."

He told me what she'd seen. The things she said. I closed my eyes. Everything felt heavy. Too heavy. When I looked at him for what I hoped would be the last time in this lifetime, Tyrel treated me to a bushel of say-nothings.

He asked me the million-dollar question again.

I grabbed my purse, slapped on my shades, stormed away from the table, and left his ass.

TYREL

20

The next evening, by the time I made it home from work, Shelby had slipped in like a bandit and packed some of her clothing. Her toiletries were gone. Most of her *Essence*, novels, and *Runner's World* magazines were AWOL. Her feminine things-with-wings had taken flight.

Debra called me at work the next morning. Another voice I didn't want to hear. She wanted me to know that Shelby was crashing at their house, sleeping in one of the spare bedrooms.

Debra said, "This really makes me feel uncomfortable."

"Likewise."

"And it puts Leonard in a bad position too."

"I'm respecting what you said and I'm not pressing your husband for any answers, if that's what you're talking about."

She made a painful sound. I didn't pity her agony.

I said, "She ask you to call me?"

"I'm calling because I care."

I waited.

Debra said, "Shelby's transferring out of L.A."

"That's a pretty sudden change."

"She's emotional and impulsive."

I didn't grace her with a response.

She said, "It's not a done deal, not yet anyway. Come by tomorrow. You could pop by for dinner."

"No thank you."

"Don't be stubborn. You're the best thing that ever happened to Shelby. Leonard thinks Shelby is the best thing that ever happened to you."

I made a repulsive sound, then asked, "Where's Leonard?"

Debra said, "Leonard's out of town for a few days. He's polishing up his act for the HBO special he's doing next month."

"Have him call me when he gets a free minute."

Her tone had changed from strictly business into a soft plea when she said, "Come by and talk it out with Shelby. Please? The few moments that we have been here at the same time, she's been in the room with the door closed."

"Well, she's been closing plenty of doors."

A few days passed. I came home and everything Shelby owned was gone. Everything down to her stray pubic hairs were cleaned out. The three keys were scattered on the carpet. She left a pink note taped to the glass closet door.

> I've packed my shit
> I'm gone
> Your ex-whatever

At work I caught myself checking my messages every other minute, and when I was at home I jumped when the phone rang. I was home alone, sitting around waiting for a phone call, expecting like the ghetto child who stayed up to wait for Santa Claus.

There was no Santa.

No phone call.

No Shelby.

In between expensive eateries and sexual gadget shops, the Boulevard of Broken Dreams had people standing on corners selling maps to gone-but-not-forgotten stars' homes.

I parked in a lot behind the House of Blues, then went up the hill and dashed through traffic to the Comedy Emporium. African-Americans were filing into a stained glass door that had a caricature of Eddie Murphy. "Chocolate Comedy Night."

The terrace had a thirty-inch monitor showing footage of Richard Pryor live in concert. Pryor prior to the fire.

Two comics doubling as guards were at the back door. They sprung off the concrete rail, stood side by side.

I said, "I'm on Leonard DuBois's list."

Redhead crew cut took a sheet of paper out of his black satin Comedy Emporium jacket. He said, "Who you?"

I showed him my I.D. They flagged down a pale, Michael Jackson impersonator; he adjusted his Thriller jacket and moon-walked toward us. The bouncer with the purple Mohawk and the silver earrings in his eyebrows, nose, and tongue said, "This Leonard's homeboy."

The other one asked me, "You see his movie bill-board?"

"Where is it?"

"Up Sunset. In the curve at Fairfax. Can't miss it."

The Michael impersonator made a hurry-up motion. I passed by Madonna, a phony Sammy Davis Jr., and the Godfather of Soul.

Upstairs was crammed. Cigarette fumes were thick,

clinging to me like a sticky bugger. That was why I wore jeans and boots.

A chubby, countrified brother was on stage doing 7-Eleven jokes.

The fake Michael grabbed his crotch, moon-walked away.

A brother put his hand on my shoulder and said, "If my child ever did some shit like that, I'd shoot 'im dead."

We laughed.

It was Leonard. I knew his voice before I saw his face.

He was dressed all in black and had on a salmon jacket with three buttons. A little awkwardness was on his face.

I said, "Where'd you get the jacket?"

"Debra picked it up. How this color look?"

"Smooth."

"It don't make me look like a punk? If it do, let me know and I'll hit somebody in the face to make a point."

I laughed. "Look like you're ready for *GQ*."

He said, "Good."

He'd been dressing better since Debra started coordinating his wardrobe. Less trendy, more classy.

I said, "So what's up?"

"Shelby moved out."

Three sisters in skirts narrower than my belt came over with devilish smiles. One of them asked Leonard for his phone number.

Leonard raised his left hand and showed his wedding band.

The sister said, "What's that supposed to mean?"

Leonard said, "Means you're a day late and a dollar short."

"I paid to get up in here and meet you, and that's how you gonna treat me?" She pulled his arm. "Buy me a Long Island and get t'know me. You can buy some hot wings and zucchini too."

Leonard pulled his arm back. "You know you ain't right."

She dropped a hand to her hip. "You can't buy us a drink?"

Leonard said, "Us?"

"You don't expect my friends to drink some of mine, do you?"

He said, "I left my wallet in my wife's purse."

"You in all them movies and ain't got no money?"

Leonard raised his palms and shook his head.

Two of them did a wiggle-walk and hurried away. The third one stayed long enough to snake her neck at Leonard, "You ain't shit. Ain't nothing worse than a broke-ass nigga."

Leonard said, "If you didn't spend so much on that weave, you wouldn't be broke as a joke and walking 'round begging."

"I got money."

"Then why don't you buy us a drink?"

"Nigga, please."

She followed her friends.

I said, "Let's move away from your groupies."

We moved up the stairs, stood near the back of the room.

"What were you saying about Shelby?"

"She moved to San Diego. Debra said she's apartment hunting and camping out at Chiquita's crib."

An Elvis impersonator led a white couple over to Leonard. Another interruption. While they talked, Elvis left the building. The couple went up into the V.I.P. section.

Leonard said, "He's from HBO."

I clucked my tongue on the roof of my mouth.

Leonard touched my shoulder, "Yo."

"What?"

"Wake up."

"I'm here."

"You cool?"

I blew out some impatient air.

The crowd was laughing.

Leonard said, "Guess Chocolate didn't tell you."

"Who?"

"Shelby."

"Didn't think she would leave."

"She had Debra's cousin Bobby come down and help her put everything in a U-Haul. She call you before she left?"

I shook my head, coughed. I said, "When did she leave?"

"Couple of days ago. I didn't find out until this morning. I looked in the garage and saw she had moved all of her stuff."

He told me that him and Debra fell into an argument when he saw everything was gone. And he'd had a few words with Bobby too. Leonard sounded uncomfortable. Hurt was in his tone too. I knew what he was saying, but I understood what he didn't say. If he had've known what was going on, he would've called me.

I raised a hand and said, "I wish her nothing but the best."

The audience applauded. The chubby brother primped off stage. The M.C. went up and grabbed the microphone.

I hoped this bullshit hadn't caused too much strife in Leonard's new and improved life. I asked, "Why didn't Debra come out?"

"Smoke messes with her allergies. Plus she's studying."

"She's back in school?"

"Taking continuing-education classes."

Leonard took a card from his pocket and handed it to me.

I said, "What's this?"

"Shelby's number in Diego."

"She tell you to give it to me?"

"I borrowed it from Debra's day planner."

I folded the card, tapped it against my leg.

I said, "Let's step outside. I feel my lungs turning black."

"Can't. Show time."

The M.C. started Leonard's introduction. I checked my watch.

He said, "You staying to support a bro, right?"

"It's late. Gotta be at work in the morning."

"I know you didn't drive up here to go back home."

"I'll wait a few. I want to see what you've got."

"You upset?"

"Don't worry about me."

"Yeah, you're upset."

"It'll pass."

"Call her. Work it out."

I motioned toward the stage and said, "Break a leg."

Leonard lowered his head, folded his hands in front of himself, closed his eyes for a few seconds.

Then Leonard was on stage. He was good. He'd always been at the top of his game, but I hadn't seen his show in a few months and I saw growth. He had a new level of comfort.

For a brief moment, I wished his daddy could see him. Wished my daddy could see the things I've done on my own. Most of the time it felt like my daddy was as dead as Leonard's old man.

Those thoughts lasted a brief moment. Very brief.

I was aching about San Diego. Thinking about how my life felt like constant heartache with pockets of happiness tucked in between. I tore the number Leonard gave me into shreds. Dropped it where I stood. Starting over was nothing new.

Inside my car, I pulled out my c-phone. Called Joshua Cooper. Woke him up and asked how soon he could get me that corner office with a postcard view of the Golden Gate.

SHELBY

21

Chiquita said, "How do you like the band?"

I said, "They're nice. Me and Tyrel saw them a few months ago in L.A. on Melrose at Debbie Allen's restaurant."

A jazz sextet was under a chandelier playing Norman Brown–style melodies from a circular stage. A few of the brothers San Diego had to offer were by the door. Most of them were in suits. They held drinks and stopped talking long enough to check out every sister's backside when she strolled in.

Chiquita and I were at a marble table sitting in bar-stool-height seats, lollygagging, adding to the mild chatter.

Couples were slow dancing; the music and spirits gave the air of old romances being rekindled and new romances in the making.

This was the last place I wanted to be.

Chiquita said, "Told you it was the bomb."

"I should be at home unpacking."

"You can unpack anytime. Today's your birthday. You're the big thirty now."

Tyrel's birthday is on July the ninth. Day after tomorrow. I said, "Don't remind me."

"This is much better than being cooped up in an apartment all evening."

"If you say so."

I ran my fingers through my new lace braids, a style that was elegant and professional. My mud-cloth miniskirt was riding like it had a mind of its own. It looked better than it felt.

Chiquita said, "Next week we have to check out Humphrey's by the Bay, and there might be a TLC party."

"Sounds cool."

"If me and Raymond don't get together, I'll call you."

That flip-flop attitude let me know not to depend on her.

I'd been settled in San Diego—actually in Mission Valley—for three weeks. Long enough to get a new hairstyle, get my nails done, and jazz up my wardrobe with a few sparkling dresses and a couple of golden accessories. Long enough to get antsy.

Chiquita said, "So your friend Brenda—"

"Debra."

"So, Debra and her husband went to Europe?"

"For a couple of weeks."

"Must be nice being married to a celebrity. Hell, must be nice being married."

"I think that institution is overrated."

Chiquita had picked me up in her Miata and we were in a Radisson hotel located in the upper-middle-class area of San Diego called Mission Bay. The jazz band was supposed to play until ten thirty, then a DJ was going to take over and send it to another level. So the early crowd was classy, and it gradually changed to a sugar daddy and hoochie momma convention.

Chiquita didn't really know anybody down here. She was like me—motherless, fatherless, and friendless.

I put on another coat of blackberry lipstick, then looked over my new clothes, fresh hair, and hollow attitude. I had been eating healthy, so my weight was down a couple of pounds. I was stronger than ever. I'd run my best 10k in

Oceanside last weekend. I wasn't bloated. My breasts were back to normal.

I kept thinking about it. I'd be three months right now.

Chiquita danced with a couple of brothers, then came back to the table. She yawned. I did the same. It was before nine, but it felt like it was after midnight. The band was back from their break. People were partying. Other than making a potty run, I'd been glued to my leather high chair all evening.

Chiquita tapped my arm, "Somebody is staring. You know him?"

"You don't have to know a brother for him to stare at you."

I peeped toward the bandstand and accidently made eye contact with him. He had a smile of fascination.

He was six-foot, brown-skinned, with short hair that was faded on the sides. A full beard. His haircut was sort of like Tyrel's, only a little longer. Tyrel had curlier hair.

The stranger buttoned his suit coat, strutted through the crowd, came my way, but didn't walk his walk too fast.

He said, "Good evening."

"What's up?"

"You are what is up."

"Glad to hear I'm what is up."

Me and Chiquita exchanged subtle glances.

He said, "I didn't think I'd ever see you again."

"Am I supposed to know you?"

"You're a flight attendant. Right?"

I nodded.

He said, "I was on a flight with you a few months ago."

"And?"

"It was a rough flight from Atlanta."

"My life is a rough flight."

"Somebody's kid hit you in the head with a toy or something."

I definitely remembered that. I said, "Small world."

Me and Chiquita looked at each other. She knew the flight.

"My name is Richard Vaughn."

"Nice to meet you, Richard Vaughn."

Chiquita kept bouncing her leg to the beat.

I told him my name. Chiquita stopped swaying to the music long enough to do the same. Richard invited himself to a seat.

With giggling eyes, Chiquita crossed her legs and fixed her body in a way that said she wasn't including herself in the conversation.

Richard said, "Guess you really don't remember me."

"Sorry."

"Well, I didn't forget you."

He offered to buy us drinks. We let him spend his money.

The moment Richard treaded away to get us sodas, I leaned to Chiquita and said, "That's the brother who kept buzzing me the last time we flew together."

"When you were constipated and kept throwing up?"

"Ah, yeah. When I was coming down with the flu."

"Thought you didn't remember him."

"I don't forget much." I thought about bowlegs and dimples. Honey. A borrowed room in Obispo. I said, "Not much at all."

Chiquita ran her hands over her cute, short, texturized, reddish Afro. Her mane looked good on her gleaming brown skin. Maybe I should cut mine off too. Make a whole new me. I've got the body and the moves. If I could sing without making dogs howl, I'd give Toni Braxton a run for her money.

Chiquita stood and smoothed her hands over her narrow hips.

I said, "Where are you going?"

"To a pay phone."

"Calling Raymond again?"

"He should be home by now."

"You said that three hours and five phone calls ago. Anxious to get those windows smeared?"

"If you're not a virgin, you're not a virgin."

"Once you've stained your panes, you're never the same."

We laughed. It wasn't the same kind of laugh I shared with Debra, but it was a true laugh. It didn't have that kind of openness, didn't have a history. At the rate Debra was fading from my life, the way she was slipping into her new life, I'd give her a few months and I'd be lucky to get a returned phone call. Pretty soon we'd be having those "Girl, what have you been up to, I've been meaning to call you" conversations.

Chiquita didn't go to the phone. For a few moments, she stood and stared at her empty hands. Then she sat back down. The way she poked her lips out made her look like a pouting child.

I told Chiquita if a man hadn't made a date with her for a Saturday night before Saturday night, he didn't want to be bothered with her on a Saturday night. The same thing went for me.

Chiquita made her eyebrows dance. "Shelby, you got it going on. It's your night 360."

"What's '360'?"

Chiquita drew a circle in the air. "At 360 degrees. You got it going on all the way around. That handsome brother is on you like white on rice."

When Richard came back, Chiquita smoothed out her black, wide pant leg, adjusted her white silk blouse that showed hints of her seductive camisole, then thanked him with an accent that had sweet traces of Southern hospitality in every word.

I signaled for Chiquita to stay close, did the same batting-the-eyes signal me and Debra had shared since birth, but Chiquita either missed or misinterpreted the clue. She winked, grabbed her Coke, and did a sultry yes-I'm-single stroll through the crowd to the other side of the room.

Chiquita poured herself into an armchair facing the band and grinned with the beat. Every other second a different brother tried to get some play. She waved them all away, even the cute brothers sporting nice shoes, flattering ties, and coordinated belts. Tyrel was always coordinated head to toe.

Chiquita saw me, winked, then drew a circle in the air.

I damn near blushed.

Then she checked her watch and headed for the pay-phone.

I pretended I was listening while Richard small-talked by himself for a while, told me about this flower business, about how he was putting his sister and brother through school.

He said, "Are you married?"

"Nope. Not married."

"Why not?"

"I've never been asked. Never been engaged."

"Children?"

I sighed. "Nope."

He said, "Are you single?"

"Pretty much."

"Pretty much?"

"That's what I said."

"What does that mean?"

"I've got strong feelings for somebody."

"So, he brought you up here to San Diego?"

"He's still in Los Angeles."

"Is he moving here with you?"

I shook my head. "I'm here by myself."

"You love him?"

I tried to shake my head, sell myself a cup of denial, but I nodded. He smiled. That smile didn't do a damn thing for me.

He said, "Well, all I can say, from what I see, and from the way you carry yourself, it's definitely his loss."

I tasted my soda and glanced toward the people cha-chaing. The band was playing an old George Michael song, from way back when I thought he was fine and he had hit records.

Richard said, "Would you like to dance?"

"I don't dance. These big feet have got no rhythm."

He asked three more times. I said no three more times.

Richard said, "He must've really hurt you to make you leave."

"Yeah. He messed up and lost a good thing."

Chiquita was dancing with a brother who was so old I'd bet he used to baby-sit God. But he could cha-cha his dentures off.

Richard chuckled. "Can I change your mind?"

"Nope. I hate dancing."

"I meant about this brother that dogged you out."

The brother was redundant. I said, "It's been nice talking to you, Richard."

"Are you leaving?"

"Nope, but you are. Me and my girlfriend came together, and I don't want to be rude and leave her sitting by herself all evening."

"She looks like she's doing fine."

"It was nice meeting you. Take care."

Richard gave me his business card. He said, "Since you're new down here, let me take you to dinner."

"If I get hungry enough, I'll let you know."

"May I have your number?"

I patted his card. "I've got yours."

He cleared his throat, touched his beard, and said, "Okay."

"Thanks for the soda."

"Enjoy the night."

We shook hands. I knew he did that because he wanted to touch me. His hands were softer than mine, like he'd never had a hard day of life or a cruel moment of love since he'd been born.

He buttoned his jacket and went back to his side of the room.

Chiquita came back. She had two glasses of Chardonnay.

I took mine without complaining about the calories.

For a few songs, I was lost in the music. The band had a serious groove, played like a symphony. I sipped my wine, closed my eyes, and enjoyed the way one instrument talked to another in harmony, how all the sounds overlapped, how it made a melody.

That was how me and Tyrel used to kiss and make love.

I wondered how much time I would need to feel normal. To get over my shame and forget about Tyrel. The way I felt right now, I needed something stronger than the tick-tock of the clock to cauterize my back-to-back thoughts about Tyrel. I'd had too many daydreams. And the all-night dreams about him definitely had to go. Repetitive, intense, night dreams. The kind of hallucinations that came too often and in too much detail, felt too real, like he was loving me in thirty-one different flavors, ones that made me wake up touching myself, pretending my hands were his. I'd have to be honest, the leftover passion made me scared to take a nap, let alone go to sleep.

Off and on, me and Richard made brief eye contact.

TYREL

22

"May I speak to Vardaman Williams?"

"He ain't here. Who this?"

Outside my twenty-sixth-story window was an overcast Oakland. I was in my high-rise at 1200 Lakeshore, living a life so elevated that everybody below me looked like ants wandering to and fro. Not many brothers and sisters were jogging around Lake Merritt's three-mile course. Bodies of water gave me peace. Composure. I should've been across the lake at Gold's Gym, working off stress, but I didn't have to open my ivory linen curtains to see it was a drowsy morning made for being inside watching game after game.

I said, "Tyrel Anthony Williams."

"Uh-huh."

"I'm his son."

"Uh-huh."

I played the game and asked, "Who am I speaking with?"

"Yeah, this is Mrs. Williams."

I readjusted my mental barometer, set it to calm, clear, and smooth, before I asked Mrs. Williams, "How are you doing?"

"What you want?"

"Well, is my father coming back home soon?"

"I don't know what time Vardaman gonna be in."

"Is he at one of the stores?"

She made an irritated I-don't-know grumble. This fight was an upstream battle. Sounded like she put her hand over the phone and said a word or two to somebody. I glanced around my place. Wondered how long I'd have to be here before it felt like home.

Purple satin panties and a dark padded C-cup bra were on the back of my maroon wingback chair. Fresh cut sunflowers were in a purple vase on top of the whitewashed dresser. My entire place had bright colors—reds, yellows, greens. Almost everything was new; most of the furniture I'd owned in L.A. was sold.

Down the hall, my toilet flushed.

Then Mrs. Williams finally took her hand off the receiver.

She said, "Uh-huh. What was you saying?"

I said, "I left my new number on your answering machine, do you know if he got it?"

"I wouldn't know."

"Could you write it down and give it to him?"

"I ain't got nothing to scribble on."

I walked in the living room, stood near all the pictures of my family. "When will he be in?"

"I ain't sure."

"Well, if you turned the answering machine on, I could call right back and leave the information when it picked up."

A ticktock later she said, "The machine's broke."

"Okay."

"Uh-huh. Is that all?"

"Tell him I said, 'The cat's in the cradle.' "

"What's that?"

"It's a song."

"What's that supposed to mean?"

"Never mind. Tell him I called. I'll call back."

Mrs. Williams hung up.

Twin fumed, "See, that's why I don't call that bastard."

I'd had Twin on a three-way when I called Daddy.

She was in an uproar. "I'm not a psychic, not a prophet, but didn't I tell you that bitch was going to do that?"

"Don't curse in front of the kids."

"They're downstairs in the den."

Twin was at her home in Atlanta; I was in my leased condo in Oakland, cordless phone in hand, walking around like I woke up, butt-naked.

I said, "Twin, no matter how far he goes, he's our dad."

"Momma could've found a better sperm donor."

"Sounds like you want to kill the messenger."

Her anger kicked into overdrive. I sat on my queen-size black iron bed, shifted to avoid a wet spot on the rumpled green sheets, cut her rampage off and said, "Hey, no matter what, he's your dad."

"Unfortunately," Mye said. "Tyrel, if he wanted to be bothered with us, he would've called by now."

Mye had called me Tyrel; that meant she was upset.

I said, "He's just busy. He's got three stores out there."

"How many years has he been busy?"

"I'll call him back and leave the number."

"The bastard didn't even give me away at my wedding. Hasn't called his own grandchildren. What kind of shit is that?"

"Mye—"

She snapped, "Tyrel, get a fucking clue."

Me and my former womb mate let the hush settle between us.

Red pumps with a blemished heel and a dark scarf were jumbled in front of my television. A dark jacket with stripes on the sleeve rested underneath my newest piece of original artwork—an erotic scene from *Porgy and Bess*. I'd picked it up at a "starving artist" sale in San Francisco at the Exhibition Center.

My sister said, "Twin?"

"Yeah."

She blew her nose, then spoke in a low and controlled

tone. "You can't make him feel something he's incapable of feeling."

My shower was still running. A soft voice was behind the bathroom door, singing along with the shower radio.

I'd been on the phone with Twin for ten minutes; we started talking about Daddy, and I told her I'd call him on the three-way and leave it up to her to say anything, or nothing. She could either stay in the background and listen to his voice, or speak up and say whatever words her heart shoved out of her mouth.

Another wasted call.

Twin said, "You ever hear from Shelby?"

Bitterness grew in my mouth. "Nope."

"She still in San Diego?"

"I wouldn't know."

"So, who's over this time?"

"Tina."

"Tyrel, what does this Tina do?"

"I don't know."

"What's her last name?"

I made the same stupid I-don't-know sound.

Twin went off on me, dogged me out, talked about me in the same tone she had used for my father.

The Bay had a plethora of distractions to offer a brother with anesthetized spirits. Oakland was home of an abundance of cocoa-brown stones that were ready to be turned over and spanked from the rear.

Mye lectured, then said, "Look, be careful."

"I am."

"A tisket, a tasket, a condom or a casket."

"Trust me. No glove, no love."

We said a few more things, said we loved each other. I told her to kiss the Dynamic Duo, then we disconnected.

Tina was still in the bathroom, fixing herself up.

Leonard had asked me if San Francisco was my countermove to Shelby's sudden move. I told him that life wasn't a chess game where I was chasing the queen. I said that on a personal level L.A. wasn't working out. I'd given the dysfunctional sisters of Los Angeles thirty years, but they couldn't get it right.

After I had called Joshua Cooper in the middle of the night, within three days my job had sent a moving company to pack everything down to the last crumb. I gassed up my car, threw on my Ray-Bans, and took the scenic route up the 101.

My bathroom door finally opened. The radio turned off. Humidity drifted out and settled on the wall like a morning dew. The light went off; the motor to the fan stopped humming. I heard the *psst* from her deodorant. She was singing. Sounded good enough to make Mariah Carey beg for a lesson in soul.

Tina had an orange towel wrapped around her body. She stopped in the hallway and checked out the family pictures I had on the wall. She did a double take at the wedding pictures.

"You know this guy?"

"Leonard's my best friend."

"I saw his movie last month." She made an impressed sound. "We saw him at a comedy club in Walnut Creek last year. He's married?"

"Yep."

"His wife is pretty. Is she a model?"

"Nope. A nurse."

"Her maid of honor's beautiful too."

I almost said that that maid had no honor.

Tina's skin was the color of Folger's straight out of the can. She had a thin space between her front teeth, high-waisted, legs shaped like drumsticks from KFC. With her hair cut shorter than mine, and golden Africa-shaped earrings, she looked like a risqué centerfold for *National Geographic.*

She said, "Okay, sexy black man, do you have any lotion?"

"On the dresser."

She came into the bedroom. Blushing. Her sweet aroma spiced the cherry freshener in the room.

Tina made an untamed animal sound while she kissed me, then she tossed her wet towel on my clean white comforter and started searching through her yellow overnight bag.

My eyes were on her damp towel.

I waited until she had the lotion, then said, "Tina."

She stopped massaging the lotion on her breasts.

I said an easy, "Please don't put wet towels on my bed. White comforters stain easily."

Her eyes darkened.

Maybe my tonicity wasn't as agreeable as I intended.

The liveliness left her features.

I watched her.

Tina turned her back to me.

Eased into a pair of lime French-cut panties.

Squeezed into her jeans.

I said, "Tina?"

She pulled on her red and white sorority T-shirt.

"Tina?"

She was as mute as a mime. She shot me a look, then lowered her head, raised it, bit her bottom lip with her top teeth. She was probably mad because I didn't shower with her.

"Hey, Tina, did you still wanna go to breakfast?"

She picked up her red pumps, took a breath, shook her head a few times, calmly collected her clothes, and said, "Why don't you ask Tina?"

"What?"

"My name is Lillian."

She walked away in silence. Her shoes made soft thumps on the carpeted part of the hallway, then moved in a depressed stride when she got to the sand-colored hardwood floor. My front door opened slowly, then slammed hard enough to make the milky-white venetian blinds in the front room rock to and fro.

Purple panties and a dark padded bra were still drooping on the back of my maroon wingback chair.

SHELBY

23

Richard's momma, Mrs. Vaughn, was cool the first day I met her. Yep, we got along for about ten minutes. Richard talked me into going over there for dinner. His whole family was there. The problem was, nobody told me that many people were gonna be there, or that the Thanksgiving-sized dinner was for me. Because if they had, I would've told them from jump street that I didn't eat red meat or pork. There was a big ham, collard greens cooked in ham, beef, corn bread doused in fattening butter.

Mrs. Vaughn insisted I eat and slapped a mountain of food on my plate. One of us wasn't listening. I politely pushed the plate away from my face, let her know that me and the pig didn't see eye to eye. She humphed. Said she'd eaten the pig all her life, said her momma and her momma's momma ate the pig every day and both lived to be a hundred. I ignored her diatribe, sipped on a cup of 7UP, and called it a day.

What made it worse was when I went to church with

Richard the next week, his double-chinned momma acted like she didn't remember me. Richard introduced us again, and the heifer ignored me, raised one of her chins to the sky and huffed, "Why she wear pants in the house of the Lord? Ain't she been to church before? She sho ain't as pretty as that *light-skinded* girl you used to spend all your time with."

That was my first time being speechless since words were invented. Richard apologized for his momma, and I didn't hold what she'd said against him; just like I didn't expect anybody to hold what my momma did, or what my daddy didn't do, against me.

───

Another month dragged by, went on and on, felt like I was riding the back of a snail through Texas. I'd never been so happy to be able to change a calendar. I had a couple of days off and went where everybody knew my name.

While the plane was coming down into ocean air and smog, it felt good to see crowded freeways and surface streets that were familiar. I saw the towering MCI, Blue Cross, and Herbalife buildings. When the plane banked, I caught a glimpse of the Dan L. Steel structure standing tall too. That made me hold my breath for a moment. Guess me and that bowlegged tyrant would have to finally be in the same space for a few minutes.

Leonard had set it up for all of us to powwow with some teenage girls in Watts. I wasn't down with the program, because even though I'm a gabber, I'm not a public speaker, but Leonard had made a big deal about me growing up in a single-parent home.

Whatever. With perfume dabbed all over, I had my own agenda.

I left the plane with my luggage-on-wheels in tow, and Debra was at the gate waiting for me. She was holding her shades, had on a dark green business suit, with slim pants and a hip-length jacket. My brown miniskirt was the bomb, plus the matching jacket hugged my waist and drew attention to all the right spots, and I'd brought out the brown shade with a beige camisole.

Debra made a face of surprise and said, "Damn, you look good. Don't take that outfit off. I might borrow it forever."

"Thanks. You look good too. If I was like Nancy the Nympho, I'd be hounding you and trying to get your phone number."

We laughed.

She hugged me, told me how much she had missed me. She even had the nerve to shed a single tear. People from about twenty nationalities wrestled their carry-on luggage around us and gave up sideways stares. One Asian woman raised a brow.

I said, "Debra?"

"What?"

"Get a grip and let me go before people think we're funny."

"Hug me."

"Don't get your war paint on my new clothes."

"Hug me. *Now.*"

I showed her what a hug was and said, "How's that?"

"Ouch. You're so cynical."

"Am not."

"Are too."

"You act like you ain't seen me in years."

"You act like you see me every day."

"Debra, I can't breathe."

"Stop acting silly. Why have you stopped calling me?"

I said, "Sweetheart, you're married."

"All that to say?"

"You don't need to hang out with wild and single women."

"Shelby?"

"Uh-huh?"

"It's okay to make new friends, but cherish old ones."

"Hush before you make me upset."

We put on our shades and headed down the escalator toward the lower-level parking. If you asked me, we looked like one-half of En Vogue—two-thirds since one of the sistas flew the coop—and we were more supreme than the Supremes. I was so exhilarated I was ready to break out in song and dance.

Debra said the meeting was going to have thirty-five girls, ages thirteen to eighteen.

I said, "I wrote down a please-go-to-college bit."

"No, talk to them and tell them how you grew up. Be real."

"It was just me and a momma who cooked food at the school cafeteria and cleaned up after white-collared white people."

"And you made it through college on her blood, sweat, and tears. We went, we struggled, and we graduated."

"You're a bonafide nurse. I'm working for a funky airline."

"You have a dream job. I wish I had your freedom."

I'd never heard her say that before.

"Other than making my life of welfare and food stamps an open book to a room of strangers, what's on your agenda for this little town hall parley?"

"I'll tell them I grew up around the corner, then do a few minutes about teen pregnancy and sexually transmitted diseases."

"Doing a slide show?"

"Leonard found a twenty-minute video."

"Hope the girls don't eat before the movie."

She laughed.

It felt like old times. USC old times. When we were ready to kick the world in the seams of its jeans. My soft and sweet aroma was so vivacious it made roses bend in envy. I hadn't been this concerned with my looks since God knows when.

In Debra's Hyundai, I pulled down the mirror on my side, double-checked my new Matte Espresso lipstick. Some new Victoria was covering my rusting secrets. My suit was fresh off the rack.

Debra had the radio on AM talk; I turned the radio to FM and feasted on a helping of KJLH's musical soul food. Karen White and Babyface's old love duet dissipated; Maxwell crooned a snazzy solo about a little something-something. That was my exact mood.

Debra said, "Turn that up."

We sang along while she fought her way out of LAX's lunacy. We had to flirt with a couple of Buckwheat-looking brothers driving a dirty Fleetwood to get invited into traffic. They pulled up and begged for our phone number, pager number, cellular number, any number they could get. Just like old times. Debra raised her ring hand, shrugged, and wiggled her finger. I laughed at Stymie and Purina, and showed them the ring on my right hand. One I'd bought for myself at Mervyn's.

She floored the accelerator—which didn't make too much of a difference in an asthmatic Hyundai—whipped from lane to lane, and chugalugged out of the airport into the six lanes of insanity on Sepulveda, headed toward the 105 freeway.

I said, "What does Leonard and his friend have planned for the rugrats?"

"They won't be there."

"Just us?"

She nodded. "It's a closed-door girl and woman thing today."

"Why aren't Leonard and his friend speaking?"

"Leonard's in Hawaii." A slice of time went by. Debra said, "Tyrel's taken a promotion and moved. He left L.A."

Something in me throbbed. The world swayed out of focus.

I did my best to sound blasé when I asked, "Where?"

"Oakland. But he's working out of San Francisco."

"Good for him." I felt demoted. She told me he left while they were in Europe. Again I said, "Good for him."

It had taken me forty-five damn minutes to do my stupid makeup this morning. I'd run all over to find the right hose.

Debra was running her mouth. I tuned in when she said, "Tomorrow me and you are going out into the Inland Empire."

"Where?"

"Glen Ivy. We're getting mud baths and getting pampered and massaged by strange men from head to toe. My treat."

I faked a perky "All right, all right. Sounds good."

Debra said, "Bobby asked about you."

"How's his business doing?"

"Fine. He's on a photo shoot in Cabo for the next few days."

Debra was babbling about her cousin, my play brother, telling me he'd moved from Palmdale to Pasadena and opened a studio in Old Town—shit I already knew. Every now and then I threw in a soft "uh-huh" just to make her think I was so damn interested in hearing about weird-ass Bobby and his successes.

Tyrel had moved.

Without a thought I opened my purse and made sure I had the receipt for the new suit I had on. Nobody worth knowing was going to see it, so I might as well send it back to the rack.

In the bottom of my bag I found the receipt for the Hugo Buscati ankle-wrap pumps I was wearing. Then I fumbled across two three-week-old movie tickets from when I'd gone out with Richard.

I wouldn't have gone to a second movie at Horton Plaza with Richard, but after the first matinee he sent me two dozen long-stem roses. And on a rainy day, going to dinner was much better than sitting around playing with the lint in my navel.

My heart wasn't in it, and it felt like I was cheating. I wouldn't have gone out with him again, but little country-and-funky-ass Miss Chiquita got a booty call from Raymond and left me high and dry in the thick of the night. She's sprung, she's a flake, and will never be my friend. I deprogrammed her number from my phone. I'm thinking about blocking her number too.

But she did make me appreciate what me and Debra have cultivated and nourished. Until now. Debra knew Tyrel was gone before I came up here. Heifer could've told me long before now. Just because I'd asked her not to mention Tyrel's name around me *ever* again, didn't mean she had to do what I said.

Tyrel had moved. Call the fat lady and start the music. This party was definitely over.

TYREL

24

Leonard flew up to do a show in downtown Oak-town at Geoffrey's Inner Circle. I told him to cancel his room at the Carlton in San Francisco and have his limo driver bring him over the bridge to my place when his plane touched ground. From here I'd feed him, chauffeur him to the show and back to the airport.

At my door he said, "We've got some things to discuss."

We hadn't talked much since I'd moved. He was never at home, and when I was, I wasn't answering the phone. And I didn't call as much because he was married. After the way Debra had let me down, I avoided being in contact with her. Most of our correspondence had been messages sent back and forth over the Net.

It seemed like a lifetime since we'd hung out. I was damn happy to see him. Even for men among men, absence does make the heart grow fonder.

While I lit up a cherry incense to kill the smell from the fish I fried the night before, Leonard cursed me out, smacked me upside the head, then gave me a brother-to-brother hug.

He tossed his luggage in the bedroom, then checked out my new life, gazed from wall to ceiling with a grin of approval.

"This is dope. Who decorated for you?"

"This girl named Jodie."

"This place has more colors than a cartoon."

"I was trying to make it look friendly. Should I change it?"

"Your Melrose Avenue flair works."

"I brought some of L.A. to the Bay."

"Hey, you know what I wanna do?"

"You want to call Debra and check in."

"Besides that. Where's the phone?"

"It's on the sofa. What did you want to do?"

"Go to Frisco and ride the trolley."

"We can park and ride the trolley into Chinatown and eat."

"Bet."

This would be one of those days where we could act like the boys we kept locked inside, let out some of the juvenile delinquency we kept tucked beneath age and responsibility.

"Tell Debra I said hello."

"I just left her and Shelby."

Hearing her name made time stop. No matter how far I went, that damn name kept coming up. I shrugged away the bitter feeling and asked, "What were they up to?"

"Going to see a play."

"Which one?"

"*Talented Tenth*. I might understudy, so Debra's gonna tell me what she thinks about it, then we'll decide."

I noticed how much the word *we* was in his vocabulary.

He called home. No one answered. He left a flirty message. Leonard went to the pine bookcase that was filled with the same old pictures. I waited for him to see the new one.

Leonard's face lit up, he said, "Hey, that's us."

"Yep."

It was a photo of me, Mye, Leonard, and Daddy. Mye had mailed it to me as a housewarming gift. She'd come across it and was about to rip it to shreds. I'd had the original blown up poster size, matted, and framed. In the Kodak moment, we were in South Central, on the sidewalk of Vermont Avenue, posing in front of Daddy's first store. We'd captured that memory a couple of days before we walked in on him and that woman. Mye was on Daddy's lap, hugging his neck, smiling like Daddy was the man of her dreams.

Leonard cringed and said, "Look at our greasy shag haircuts. Man, what the hell were we thinking? Damn, your daddy looks young. With that black fedora and Elton John shades on, he looks like the Mack. Me, Mye, and you look like we were in the Sylvers. You talked to your old man?"

"I called and left a message."

Leonard moved on with the conversation, "Don't let me forget to leave you a copy of the pictures me and Debra took in Europe."

"All right."

Leonard kicked off his shoes, grabbed a handful of gourmet jelly beans out of the glass jar on the coffee table, moved from sofa to loveseat to bar stools, butt-tested everything.

He said, "You got all new furniture. And you got enough workout stuff in that room to start your own gym."

Leonard strolled into the guest room, came back with my new photo album under his arm. It was a photographic journey of my delirium, a gallery of the transitional team.

With each turn of the page, he bobbed his head, occasionally shot me a look, and griped, "Yep."

"What're you tripping off of?"

"I'll show you in a minute."

"Hope you don't see somebody *too* familiar."

"You know I don't live my life like that."

He moved my glass planter, the one filled with a rainbow of marbles, lined up about ten pictures on the coffee table, then made one comment as his finger tapped each one.

Leonard said, "They all look like Chocolate."

"Who?"

"Shelby. You know who I'm talking about. All of 'em look like her."

"Bullshit."

"They all got itty-bitty, cute, tiny little pug noses."

"They don't."

"Different skin tones, taller, shorter, but they're Chocolate. Damn. Look at the booty on this girl in the negligee."

"Which one?"

He pointed at a photo of Lorna. He said, "If that ain't a Shelby booty, I'm a white man with a day job."

We laughed.

"How did you get these sisters to pose damn near naked?"

"I asked."

He flipped through the album again.

He was serious. "All right. How would you feel if some guy had pictures like this, and it was Mye. Or your momma."

"Leonard—"

"Think about if you had a daughter, and some shit like this was going on. You've been in Oakland, ostracized from society, and nobody knows what you're doing. You don't have any accountability for your actions."

"Stop preaching."

"Not preaching, teaching."

I said, "You still go to Bible study?"

"Every chance I get. Damn right."

"You sound like you should be tutoring the preacher."

He stood and grabbed the business section of the newspaper.

I said, "Where you going?"

"Bathroom. You got incense?"

"Hall closet."

I flipped through the pictures while he was gone. Checked out the dark skin and different hairstyles. Photos catch the person in the moment, but can't capture the real personality.

I felt bad. Some of my enthusiasm for passing on the heartbreak was gone. Nobody on the pictures meant a thing. If none of them ever called again, I wouldn't miss a single voice.

Leonard joked ninety percent of the time, but the other ten percent was too deep for most to handle. Especially when it dealt with family matters. Like me, he knew when things were worthy enough to be important. I was part of his extended family, so right now I was important enough for him to be serious. His tone always told me I mattered.

Thirty minutes later, we were playing Super Nintendo on the big screen. I'd been sucked into some sort of therapy session.

Leonard said, "Mye told me to give you a message too."

"What is it?"

He opened his overnight bag and handed me a Thrifty bag. Inside was an over-the-counter home HIV test. I didn't think it was funny. Not at all.

"Hey, don't look at me like that. Your sister told me to buy it for you." Leonard laughed. "She said, 'A tisket, a tasket.' "

"You two have launched a conspiracy."

"C'mon. Enough of the bullshit. Let's talk."

I rested my bare feet up on the glass coffee table, rubbed the back of my neck, and admitted the anger I had for Shelby. Anger for Lisa. Anger for a few others. Running amok was the only way I knew how to respond to the animosity that had germinated in L.A.

"If you asked me, I'd say you're trying to solve your problems through geographical distance and physical duplication."

"Don't get anal."

"Work with me. Now where was I?"

"In the middle of intellectual masturbation."

"Shut up. Listen. You and Shelby broke up."

"She clocked out and walked. That goes without saying."

"Right. *We* didn't break up. Not you and me, or you and Debra. My wife is pulling her hair out over this shit."

"I hear your diagnosis, so what's your prescription, black man?"

"Choose between one of these babes or call Shelby. Ask her to meet you and talk. Find out where you stand. It's on you. But three out of four doctors recommend Shelby."

I made that stupid I-don't-know sound.

He said, "I can try to get her phone number or address, and you can contact her yourself, or I'll tell her to call you."

I shrugged.

"I know you ain't scared. Don't turn into a punk on me."

"You know better. I never cross the same river twice."

"But you don't have to burn the bridge either. At least, you know, be cordial. You don't have to be her friend and send Christmas cards, but clear the air. Put some closure to it and go on. I don't want it to get to the point that if I was gonna have a pool party or something at the house, I'd have to decide who *not* to invite because of friction."

"What you trying to say?"

"I think I said it."

A few moments went wherever unnoticed moments go. Moments I lost because I was staring at the gallery of photos Leonard had left spread out. Staring at the transition team.

I said, "Get me Shelby's number. I'll call her to say hi."

He reached into his shirt pocket and took out a card.

After Leonard finished his show and I dropped him off at the airport, I sat on Shelby's number. Sat and thought.

Lorna came over for a Friday night dinner. We caught a movie down on Lakeshore. It started to rain like rain was never going to end. She ended up spending the night.

By ten p.m. she was asleep, and I was restless. Earlier in the evening a plane had crashed and killed everybody on board. Until I heard it wasn't Shelby's airline I was high-strung, and most of that feeling of dread hadn't fled. It was an old feeling I used to get most of the days Shelby went to work, sort of the same feeling a police officer's spouse lived with as soon as their mate went to work. Thought I was over her. Not yet.

I was standing around in my pajamas, thinking about my life. I'd done that every night I'd been home alone. Every morning like clockwork, I'd wake up at one thirty and four a.m.; wake up, pace for a while, straighten up the place, then walk across the room, stare out at the lake, check out the Big Dipper and Orion.

And the moon.

The wind was so hard it looked like the rain was falling sideways. The sky rumbled its storm warning. Sounded like the heavens had an ulcer. Lightning flashed across East Oakland.

Lorna twitched. Stirred. Didn't wake up. I stood over my bed, stared at her. Felt like a stalker in my own home. An hour ago she was climbing the walls, making noises that could deafen a thunderstorm. Now she glowed like a cocoa angel on break.

On my dresser was one of those "Love Is" cartoons she had clipped out. She'd dropped it off in the lobby of my job along with a book she'd picked up at Marcus Book Stores, *Think and Grow Rich*, that and a personal, sexy note of invitation that had a red-inked devil's horn on the top of a yellow smiley face.

Lorna is a petite sister with an everlasting smile that brought pleasant feelings into any room. She could replace Shelby. And if Lorna didn't, she could diminish my psychological net worth for that shrew. Could lighten the baggage with a kiss and a smile.

I went to the bathroom, stared at myself in the mirror for as long as I could stand to see me, then headed to the kitchen and poured a glass of bottled water. Moved around like a man gone blind, did everything in the dark.

The phone rang.

Lorna woke and said, "Tyrel, you here?"

I'd hoped that by the time I'd reached thirty, I'd own a house filled with music, maybe overlapping and contradicting radio, television, and phone conversations, home-cooked dinner, children fighting over the remote, maybe sprawled out on the floor doing homework. I hadn't prepared for relationship after relationship, always starting the fuck over.

She repeated, "Tyrel?"

I stopped sipping the water and said, "Yeah."

"Your phone is ringing."

There was a phone on the wall, singing in front of my face. I reached for it, then I thought about Lorna. She was a PK—preacher's kid—raised on character and integrity. Had a Ph.D. Good job. Good conversation. Good catch.

So as far as everybody else was concerned, good riddance.

The phone rang again. The chiming sounded like my conscience coming to life. Since John Donne didn't live in this condo, the two a.m. bell must've been tolling for little old me.

I said, "Answer it for me."

She sounded startled, "Answer it?"

"Yeah. Catch it before the machine clicks on."

She cleared her throat, then said, "Hello."

She said hello a couple more times.

Then she put the receiver back in its cradle.

I said, "Who was it?"

"They hung up."

I crawled back in bed, slid in between the sheets with Lorna. For a second or two, I thought that phone call might've been Lillian, calling to reclaim her majestic drawers. Then this feeling of exemption from death, the one that shielded me day and night, that feeling left my soul. I felt so weak. So human.

I wondered if that phone call was Leonard. It was his time of the night. I wish I had known that the moments we spent riding the trolley cars and having serious conversation would be one of the last times I saw him.

PART THREE

HOME-GOING: EVERYTHING MUST CHANGE

25

TWO police officers were at my door. I saw them through the peephole, then spied through the venetian blinds to make sure there was a real LAPD patrol car out front. Any actor or psycho—sometimes there wasn't a difference—could rent a police uniform from anywhere on Melrose or Hollywood Boulevard.

It was three a.m. Police were at my door. Leonard was late.

I reached for the door and jumped when our phone line—the business line—started ringing. That was the phone line we gave anybody who wasn't a true friend. Leonard always checked the messages when he came home. I had hoped that it was the other line, because I had been thinking about Shelby a lot lately. Over the past seven or eight months, I hadn't seen her too often. She used to call every day, now she hardly called at all. Her life had taken a life of its own; she was always too busy.

I pulled my red-hooded housecoat around my pajamas, pulled the coat tight, then tied it loosely, and stood barefoot in front of the door. Had a sudden feeling of dread.

Radios were squawking, destroying peace and quiet.

The doorbell rang again.

I prayed that nothing bad had happened to Shelby. Prayed that another plane hadn't crashed.

A long second went by before I wiped my damp hand on my housecoat and touched the doorknob. I tried to let the chill pass through me. I'd felt that same chill around midnight. That was what had woken me up. What had made me turn the burglar alarms off so I could peep out the windows and wait and wait.

It was three a.m.

A news van was coming down Don Diego, toward our cul de sac.

I wished my husband was here to open the door to these strangers. Leonard was later than normal. We had a rule: If he was going to be more than fifteen minutes late, he had to call so I'd know not to wait up.

The doorbell rang again.

I freed the dead bolt and opened the double door.

The police officers identified themselves.

Sounded as if they were saying an awkward speech.

Maybe just following procedure.

The female officer asked if I was Mrs. DuBois.

I said I was.

The officer's faces were solemn.

I made mine smile, tried to smile the fear away.

Wanted to let them know that it was okay to say what they had to say. That what had to be done, had to be done.

The taller officer said he was sorry to tell me that there had been an accident. On Crenshaw near Venice. Where the street curves.

I nodded.

He told me my husband was dead.

My body wanted to swoon, but I wouldn't allow it to. I took a deep breath, held my right hand out and gently touched the doorframe. My left hand stopped opening and closing. Then I wiped the new dampness on my pajamas and put both hands on my stomach.

I asked if he had suffered. They said it was instant.

I wanted to laugh, to tell them that their joke wasn't working. I'd just made love to my husband this morning; we'd showered; he'd rubbed lotion on my body; asked me to rub some on his back. He'd told me I was gaining a few pounds; I'd thrown my towel at him and made him apologize. He wouldn't apologize because he said he loved the way I looked with the weight. We laughed our way into a lovers' argument about that, he started teasing and messing with me, tickling me here and there, then tried to get frisky again.

The officer said something about the coroner, spoke about identifying and claiming my husband's body, asked me if I was all right. Before his words finished their flow, his face changed, made an expression that said he regretted the question.

I nodded, blinked a few times, said I would be fine. Then I asked them if they would like to come in for some herbal tea.

I don't know why I asked them that.

They said no.

Again, they asked if I was okay.

I told them I needed to notify friends, call family. Funeral homes would be calling soon. That's what I had to do.

My words told the officers to be safe as I closed the door.

Then the doorbell rang again. It was somebody from the news van. An independent channel. I didn't answer the door.

When I was walking down the hall, it felt more like I was anchored and the room was moving by me. The room quit moving and left me on the spot where I'd first made love to Leonard.

A moment passed and I realized the cordless phone to our private line was in my hand. And I was sitting on my bed. On the dresser were the three keys Leonard gave me when we were dating.

The other line was ringing; I heard the noise floating up the hallway from the den. As soon as it rolled over to the answering service, it would start ringing again.

Who'll be on the program? Casket. Funeral home.

I had to call somebody; I had to call my mother in Montana. Had to call out to Palmdale and talk to my cousin Bobby.

No. Bobby moved to Pasadena. Didn't he?

My mind led my fingers, dialed Shelby's number.

A man answered. I didn't know she was seeing anyone. He was wide awake with the television loud in the background.

In front of me, on the dresser were wedding pictures. Me, her, Tyrel. And Leonard. In the album near the foot of the bed were pictures from Europe, photos taken in Africa.

The man said hello for the second time.

I asked for Shelby.

He repeated, Shelby?

Words rolled from my tongue, very stiff, pained words. I told him my husband had been killed. That I needed her to help me make preparations. I wanted to know how soon she could get over here to take me to view the body. I needed to go now.

He said my name.

I stopped explaining, made a sound, a noise that came when words were weighed down by grief.

I asked with whom I was speaking.

He told me he was Bryce.

I apologized for calling them so late.

He told me I'd dialed the wrong number, had dialed a number from way back when, back before I met my husband.

I felt like I'd lost time. Maybe not lost time. Everything that constituted then and now was jumbled.

Bryce said he hadn't seen Shelby since she'd walked out, then told me he was sorry about what had happened.

Then he hung up. I hung up.

Dropped the phone, let it thud into the carpet.

My hands roved back and forth over my belly.

I tried to think through the tears that wouldn't appear.

My husband was dead.

TYREL

26

My car became an eagle and flew me toward familiar ground. My neck was tight, like I was being strangled by a rope. A hundred toads were in my stomach, leaping around a rising fire.

I don't remember seeing anything on the 101. Didn't remember crossing the Golden Gate bridge. Didn't see the windmills in Solvang. Didn't notice the sign welcoming me to L.A. I know I did, but I don't remember when I stopped to refuel.

I checked into the Red Lion in Culver City, right across from my old office at the Steel building. Near my old condo. After I showered, I took out my cellular and let my job pay for my call to my mother in Chicago. She was enjoying her first few months with her new husband. She told me to send her condolences to Debra, asked me to send her a program from the funeral.

When I hung up, the phone rang.

It was my sister. My Twin.

She said, "It's all over the news."

A baritone voice said, "Young buck, how you holding up?"

"Daddy?"

Twin had Daddy on the three way. He'd seen the news too, then called his daughter. We talked about Leonard, about the situation, had a conversation like time had never derailed us.

For moments we were three adults. Then we were children talking to their father. A father who was consoling his children.

In the middle of a feeling of bad, it felt good.

I said, "I'll call my travel agent and make reservations for everybody. The tickets should be ready in a couple of hours."

Twin said, "I've already made reservations."

"Daddy?" I asked. "You coming out to the home-going?"

Twin said, "I'm bringing your grandchildren. We can get together. This, what's happened, puts things in perspective for me. I couldn't imagine losing my husband. Or you, Daddy."

He made a sound that said he was afraid. He said, "Thangs are pretty tight back here."

Mye said, "I'll pay for it. I'll take care of everything. Hotel, food."

Daddy paused. "I ain't been back that way since I left."

"Old man?"

"Yeah, son?"

"Cat's in the cradle."

Time slipped a moment into the future.

Daddy perked up and said, "Who gonna pick me up from the airport?"

I said, "I am."

We sealed the deal with Daddy; he hung up. Part of me already knew he'd come back to see Leonard.

Twin said, "He surprised me."

"Me too."

"I don't know how I'm going to take seeing him."

"Why're you paying his way if you feel like that?"

"Because I don't know how I'd take seeing him dead. I don't want my kids looking at their grandfather in a coffin. It's not for me. Believe me, I feel the same way I've always felt."

Me and my sister talked a little longer. She changed the subject, talked about friendship, talked about Leonard's wife, discussed Shelby.

Twin asked, "Is she there?"

"Don't know."

"Three keys."

I let her statement go unanswered. I said, "Kiss the dynamic duo for me. See you when you get here day after tomorrow."

"Tyrel, call me if you need to talk. No matter how late."

"Will do."

"Love you, Twin."

"Love you, Twin."

Debra was in a purple dress, worn rabbit houseshoes, thick white socks. The first thing she did was lick her fingertips and rub underneath my eyes where salt had dried.

She saw my car parked in the cul de sac. About ten other cars were parked there too.

"Tyrel, you should've flown."

"I know."

"Anything could've happened on the road."

There were about ten people in the house. Flowers and telegrams were in the living room; the house smelled like I supposed people wish paradise does. I spoke to grieving people from church, show business, and politics. Debra's eyes were dried out, puffy. A plastic smile and a paralyzed expression.

One of the church people led a prayer. Then, one by one, everybody left. Went back to continue living.

Debra closed the door and asked, "You all right, Tyrel?"

"Cool."

"Sure? Don't lie to me. It's just us."

"Yeah. For now."

Her stomach was starting to round out, but not too much. She was barely showing. Even at six months, it looked like she was hiding a small ball under her clothes.

I asked, "Anything I can do for you?"

We hugged and rocked side to side. Her body was tight and rigid. Fragile. If I held her too tight, she'd snap in two.

She said, "Not right now. I'm just glad you're here."

"Just let me know what you need me to do, okay?"

"Your being here is enough."

Debra's expression changed. Pretentiousness had been removed. She weakened enough to show what was inside. Water dripped from her face, splattered on her blouse. She didn't wipe it away. I held her tighter.

"I'm here, Debra. It's okay."

"I'm so scared, Tyrel. I don't believe this shit is happening to us." The phone rang. "Damn reporters keep calling back to back. Those insensitive bastards were here with microphones stuck in my face before the sun came up."

"Shh. It'll be all right."

Debra wiped her eyes; made circular scratches on her stomach.

The phone rang again.

I said, "I'll get it. Sit down. Rest."

Debra shook her head, ran her fingers through her hair, took her time about walking into the sunken den. I watched her reflection in the black glass on the refrigerator door until she went to the far side by the fireplace. She was telling the same story she'd have to tell over and over as she headed toward the back of the house. I heard her say something about head and chest injuries, died at the scene wearing a seat belt.

My friend who had this nice house had died on oil-stained pavement.

The doorbell rang two times. I went to the front to handle it. It was another delivery of flowers. I put them with the rest and went back to the kitchen.

A few seconds later, she drifted back into the kitchen, cordless phone in hand, and stood by the cooking island. She put the phone down and pulled out a chair on my right side. She was calm. I was drinking a glass of grape juice.

She said, "Where's your stuff?"

"I checked into the Red Lion."

"*No.* You're not staying at a stupid-ass hotel. Go get your clothes and get back here before you piss me off. Pick a bedroom and stay as long as you want. This is your home too." Debra let out a wounded sound that stopped as fast as it started. "And I can't stand to be here by myself. I need to be surrounded by my friends."

"What about your family?"

"You're family too. They'll be here day after tomorrow."

I said, "Okay."

"Just want to see my close friends. Leonard's best friends."

I gave Debra another long hug, rocked from side to side, tried to absorb her hurt. Her body trembled along with mine.

She pulled back and looked at me. "I'm so happy to see you."

"Me too." I kissed her forehead.

"Leonard loved you so much. Talked about you all the time. Said you guys were blood brothers with different parents. I always wished you hadn't moved so far away."

I never liked the Bay. Not because the Bay was the Bay, but because it wasn't L.A. If I had stayed in Los Angeles, had never moved, this wouldn't have happened.

She picked up her cordless phone and walked me to my car.

Debra said, "Shelby should be here tomorrow."

SHELBY

27

"Ouch! Richard, no. *Stop*. No, that hurts. *I said stop*."

"Why can't I suck on your neck?"

"Quit!"

"What is up, Shelby?"

"You've never sucked on my neck, why now?"

"Because I want to make you feel good."

"Gnawing on my damn neck don't feel good."

"We're getting married and you're my woman, right? I should be able to suck on your neck if I want to, right?"

"You're trying to put a damn passion mark on my neck. *Stop*. Move! Richard"—I tried to twist my wrists out of his hands—"get the hell off of me. All right? I'm serious. *Move, dammit*."

He wouldn't let go. I tried to buck him off me; his

weight had me pinned down. He was trying to sneak himself inside me.

"Stop, please. Get off me. Richard, you're raping me."

"What? I'm not and you know it."

I knew why he was tripping out and trying to chew marks high on my neck. It didn't take but a tick of the clock for his attitude to change when I told him about what happened to Leonard.

"Dammit! Get the fuck off me."

"What's the problem?"

"You've got the *damn* problem. You know I can't go to work with that shit all over my damn neck. You know it. Now *move!*"

"But you're not going to work."

"I'm not gonna walk around L.A. looking like a ho. Get up."

"I'm not through."

"I'm *through! Now, get off of me, Richard.*" Yelling wasn't working, so I went the other way. I said, "Please, stop." Okay, being nice and *asking* wasn't working, so I went back to yelling. *"Bastard, get off me."*

Richard's face cringed like he couldn't believe me. It wasn't like I was hiding my feelings. Right about now my glower was the definition of disdain and eyes felt hot enough to glow and let him see me through the darkness. He had a nervous tremble when he eased his grip. I scowled and waited. Didn't blink one time. He tilted his head like that confused RCA Victor dog.

Richard exhaled and said something that sounded like it might've been an apology, then scooted to the far side of my bed. Damn, I hate this sorry-ass waterbed. Anyway, I was relieved, sad, mad as hell, but not as pissed off as I wanted to be.

We'd been tussling like we were the opening match for Hulk Hogan for about five minutes. My back ached like a big dog because I had bucked my hips too hard and too fast. Sweat had dampened both my down pillows and humidified my earth-tone sheets. My red and gold comforter had been kicked off the bed.

My waterbed surged when he jumped up. For a sec, I thought the wave was gonna toss me overboard and make me land on the oak nightstand. Richard's feet slapped the floor when he marched across the room, sounded like the soles of his feet and the tips of his toes were sweating and sticking to the hardwood.

Six a.m. and I was marinating in puddles of my own sweat. Then the bedroom door slammed so hard it sounded like a gunshot. I tried to play it off, but I still twitched and squeezed my eyes. My jewelry box rattled. Photos on the dresser danced.

My compact kitchen was a few feet away, but I heard my glasses clinking. Time and time again, I've asked him to be careful and not bump my damn glasses. Last week, I'd found two chipped, which messed up the entire set I'd bought from IKEA. I'd gone out of my way and left paper cups in plain view, right on top of the marble counter.

When he came back into the bedroom, I slit my eyes enough to peep out. The room was dim, the venetian blinds were closed, but it wasn't all the way dark because the hall light was shining down.

First Richard ran his fingers through his beard, then stooped close enough for me to smell the Merlot fermenting his breath. He whispered my name. Said it real sweet. Get real. His knees popped when he stood up and walked away, rubbing his face and gaping back like he was trying to figure out what to do or say, like he still didn't know what he'd done to piss me off.

Coins in his pants jingled that irritating song when he pulled his jeans up over his thighs. His belt buckle clanged. He was making noise after noise. When it got quiet, I rolled over to see what was going on behind my back. Richard had leaned against my dresser with his fists pressed hard against the wood.

He saw my expression, rubbed his neck, lowered his head, then put his eyes into the oval mirror and watched my reflection.

Richard said, "I'm sorry. Maybe we had too much to drink."

We? Somehow, I don't think so. I turned away. He zipped his pants, grabbed his shirt, and a beat later the door slammed. My jewelry box rattled again. The pictures of me and Debra, the photo of my momma, and the one of me in my blue and gray uniform, wobbled. Richard's photo didn't move.

Richard's voice came through my door, "I'll try to be back in time for your flight. I want to see you off. Okay?"

I didn't breathe until his car started and pulled away from the visitors' parking under my window. Another one of my senses defrosted and I smelled his liquor and cologne.

The day didn't start off like this. Hell, the year didn't start off like this. In the early part of yesterday evening we'd talked. I'd just made it in from work, got the message about Leonard, called Richard, he picked me up, and took me to eat.

Damn, I shouldn't have called him. But you're hurting and baffled and your emotions are shooting every whicha-way, you have to pick up the phone and vent to somebody. And in San Diego my friends were few and my options were thin. Chiquita was all I had, which wasn't much, and she was on a two-day trip and unavailable for hand-holding conversation over a box of Kleenex.

What had pissed me off was that after I told Richard that Leonard had been killed and I wanted to leave to be with Debra, all he wanted to know was if Tyrel was gonna be there.

He never asked how Debra was doing. Now he didn't know Debra or Leonard, because that was the way I wanted it. But he knew I knew Leonard. I'd played enough of his comedy tapes and bragged on his movies enough for everybody in a two-hundred-mile radius to think they knew him like a brother. To me it shouldn't matter that Richard hadn't met my best friend or her husband. They were my friends, and that's all that should've mattered to him.

Before I knew it, I was saying, "I don't know. I didn't ask about Tyrel. He should be there."

"I see."

"Richard, it's a funeral, not a date. All right?"

I swapped soggy linen for fresh sheets, then showered a long time with the water hotter than usual. This couldn't be real.

When Debra had called, I almost grabbed my tissue, hopped in my car, and drove up the 5 freeway right then, but she didn't want me on the road while I was as upset as I was. Guess I was a bit on the hysterical side. I'd never had a friend die before. A few people in high school had clocked out, but they'd been living in the fast lane.

Anyway, Debra calmed me down, made me put my keys back in my purse, told me one tragedy was enough, then asked me to get a grip and stop being impulsive and irrational. Debra wanted me to come tomorrow because she wanted time to settle herself. Somebody from her family was going to be there with her, so she was fine.

That was just like her. But I'd be there today whether she loved me or not. I understand how she felt because I was the same way when I had to bury my momma. And this brought all of that back. That sense of loss that I'd experienced two times too many already. Debra needs me. I'm gonna be there from beginning to end, from January to December. And the sooner I leave here, the less attitude I'll carry into the altitudes.

After Debra told me what had happened, we cried and tried to make sense of it all. Right before she hung up, Debra told me, "Tyrel is flying down tomorrow."

My throat tightened. Felt like somebody snatched a rug from under my feet and time shifted. He'd been out of sight, out of mind, but I couldn't help but wonder what the brother looked like now. Wondered if he still had that boyish face and soft laugh. *Shelby's Cavern.* Bowlegs and dimples. Perfect imperfections. I have to admit that all of his tokens of affection meant more after we broke up—the African dolls, the notes had more value when they stopped coming.

Richard wanted me to trash and burn everything that Tyrel had given me. He said he'd dumped all of his, bought kerosene and a book of matches, and put a flame to his old flames.

I had gathered my pictures, my eight Dan L. Steel T-shirts, the boxer shorts from Tyrel, the cards, the African dolls, and headed for the big green Dumpster around back. But I changed my mind. Somebody was tripping and I was following their program. These were my memories. I put *my* memories in the back of *my* closet, stored the rest in a corner in the back of my mind.

It felt kinda creepy that I'll have to cross paths with Tyrel the Tyrant. Regardless of how fucked up his attitude is, or mine, I'll chew my lip and be cordial. For Debra's sake. For Leonard's sake. I'll keep my distance and try to curl my lips inward. But I know how overreactive I am when I get pissed off.

After all of this is over, I'll tell Debra I've been engaged a couple of months. As far as she knew, I hadn't had a decent date since I moved. Every time I went up there, the engagement ring came off on the plane. She'd only been down here twice; both times Richard was out of town. I'd planned it that way.

Richard is a businessman who takes care of his family. That's rare. A brother who takes care of his momma, puts his siblings through college, and comes out ahead in the game of economics. I should be happy for myself. Hell, I am. He's the kind of brother that sisters dream of getting their Lee Press-on Nails into day in and day out. He's my husband-to-be. Now I don't have to worry about any more fingerprints getting on my window. I can jump the broom, grab a bottle of Windex and a roll of paper towels, and wipe the stains away. Scrub my window clean.

I mean, it wasn't like I didn't call Tyrel. His number was on Debra's refrigerator, so I copied it. Some bitch answered his number when I called at two a.m. End of story. Life goes on.

It'll take a little longer, but I'll open my heart, take down my wall and love Richard the way I deserve to be loved.

But right now, love don't live here anymore.

I went to the medicine cabinet and stood close to the mirror. Sighed so hard I sounded like something off of *Wild Kingdom.*

Looked like somebody had been munching on the chocolate. My dark skin couldn't hide the bruises. I forgot about the towel I was holding up in front of my naked body; it slipped and dropped on my feet. I moved back to see how far I had to go before the hideous bites weren't so noticeable. When my back bumped into the wall, the three bruises were humming, pouting up on my neck.

I cursed like I'd *never* cursed before, held my breasts and bumbled and stumbled into the bedroom, spread out newspapers and dumped the contents of my makeup box on the floor and tried to find a shade to camouflage my jacked-up neck. What didn't match was flung to the side.

Then I glanced up and saw me looking at me. My expression was so innocent, it scared me. For a moment I was a child.

It felt like I'd never seen me before in my life.

I didn't know who I was.

I said forget the dumb stuff. All I had to do was dress in something that accentuated my figure and covered my neck. Make 'em watch the butt when I strutted my stuff. Use one personal asset to drag attention away from the other.

When I went into the closet, I thought about Debra and Leonard. Thought about all the things we did, all the movies, and dinners, and evenings we sat around playing Jenga. How we played dominoes and talked about each other like we were crazy. Thought about all the fun that felt better than sunshine on a cloudy day. Thought about all the things my girlfriend and her husband wouldn't be able to do now.

My friend's soul mate had died, and here I was standing around, worrying about how my ass looked. I'm such a fool. Such a selfish bitch. Forget the stupid monkey bites too. The reality of the trivial things that I was tripping out over rushed over my nerves and slapped some sense into my scatterbrain.

Then I couldn't move. Couldn't breathe.

My arms numbed from my shoulders to the tips of my fingers. My knees started to bend. Legs began to wobble. Lip trembled uncontrollably. Dizzy. If I found the strength to hold on, there was nothing to grab for support that wouldn't drop on me.

Garments slid from my hands. I reached for something to keep me up. Everything—boxes of shoes, hats, magazines—rained down on me, hit me over and over. Buried me. My soul was so heavy, had always been too heavy, but now I couldn't hold it up. I collapsed, hit the floor, and cried. Moaned my tears.

TYREL

28

Shelby will be here tomorrow.

Debra's words were stuck in my head.

Lorna almost replaced Shelby. Almost. And she would've, if the lies hadn't risen to the surface. It's hard to forget. I'd been seeing Lorna for almost two months. It was a Saturday meant for riding the Great Highway into Golden Gate Park and visiting the riding stables.

That morning I went to the bathroom to take a leak, and it burned like I was being cauterized. The sudden pain knocked me and my scream down to my goddam knees. Found myself on the floor, grabbing the edge of the toilet. I panted, panted, panted. While I lay there sweating and cursing, what scared me the most was that I'd only let out a small squirt and my damn bladder was full. So, like it or not, the rest had to go, and that meant the pain and fire had to come. I was dank, gobs of sweat popped up from my hairline down to my toenails. My teeth clenched so hard I saw sparks.

When I finished and the pain eased up, I washed my face, cleaned myself up, then limped to the phone and called Lorna. I told her how bad I was hurting, and she dropped the phone and cackled like it was some kind of a joke.

Calmness fled and my temper came through. She realized my four-letter words were real, then denied everything and hung up.

About three hours later, I was walking out of the doctor's office with a bottle of 500mg antibiotics in my hand. All afternoon and all evening, I dialed Lorna's number; she didn't answer. Paged her. No calls returned. Her cellular phone was turned off, so the calls I made all rolled to the message center.

I went by her town house in Pacific Heights. Her BMW was there, but she wouldn't open the gate. First thing Monday morning I rang her office, all I got was her voice mail.

Since she was a PK, I knew where to find her early on a Sunday morning. The same place she was every Sunday morning, rain or shine. I waited until church service started, drove around the parking lot and mixed with the late crowd. Hung out in the lobby until the golden-robed choir danced their praises down the aisle. I waited for a song to end, the one where everybody was singing because they were happy, chanting because they were free, then strutted in while their eyes were on the sparrow. That was right before Lorna's father started his second sermon of the day.

I eased down the red carpet, moved toward the pulpit in front of a beautiful mural of a black John the Baptist baptizing a black Jesus, and found myself an end seat close to the front.

Lorna came through the side door by her daddy's office, spry and all smiles, happy-walked to the podium on the right side of the pulpit, stood before the congregation, prepared to do the announcements. She adjusted the microphone, raised her palms to the sky, and spoke a very uplifting "Praise the Lord!"

The room brightened up and the congregation spoke the same spirited phrase back to her in unison. Lorna was up there in an angelic cream suit, spreading a bucket of grins, a mask for her sins. I waited until the room had fallen quiet, played the quiescent role until Lorna was about to open her mouth, then I shouted a very spirited "Praise the Lord."

I unbuttoned my coat, stood, stomped my foot, waved my hand like an old black minister at a late night summer revival. Everybody clapped and co-signed with a healthy *Amen*. The organist kicked in. All around, hands waved side to side. Even her daddy hopped up long enough to cut

the rug with a sanctified dance. Lorna choked on the spirit.
A bucket of holy water couldn't wash down the lump in her
throat.

I sat down and nodded at her. She swayed, fanned herself.

Lorna bumbled her words and sped through her
speech, sped through the announcements, then skipped
three out of four steps and dashed through the side door
without raising her face.

She'd grabbed her Bible, but had fled without her
purse. By the time I took her bag from the usher and casually strolled out the side door, Lorna was at her car. Patting
her pockets.

I said, "Hard to get in without keys."

She turned around. The sun was warm, but the air was
brisk and breezy. It could've been the wind, might've been
my stone-face, but something made her shudder when she
saw me walking toward her. I raised her purse.

"You can either talk now," I held up a bottle of penicil-
lin I'd pulled out of her bag, shook it side to side like a
tambourine, "or we can go inside and when it's time for
people to confess, we can take a number. Might make your
daddy proud to see his daughter tell the truth. He might
even change his sermon."

Her lip twitched, "You wouldn't dare say anything in
front of my father's congregation."

"Try me."

She wilted. "I think we should take this somewhere
else."

"Off sacred grounds?"

She nodded.

Lorna drove the streets of Oakland and ended up near
my place on Lakeshore, across from Lake Merritt. Jogger
after jogger toured around the tranquil water. She pulled
down the visor to block the sun, wiped her eyes, told me

about the baseball player whom she didn't know how she got involved with.

Lorna said, "It just happened."

"Just happened."

"Given the right conditions, things just happen."

"We agreed, both of us said we were going to be one-on-one."

"Tyrel." Her page boy bounced. "Tell me something."

"What?"

"Are you in love with somebody else?"

"Why you ask me something like that?"

"You're always distracted. Always. When we're together you get real quiet for no reason and start to stare off into space. I ask what's on your mind and you always claim you're just a little tired, not thinking about anything. Sometimes you look at me like you're seeing somebody else. You never say anything, but I get a feeling that you're comparing me to somebody. Who?"

"*Nobody.*"

"Sounds like I hit a nerve."

"I've been stressed over the last few weeks."

"A few times I called and you didn't sound as happy to hear from me. Not like you used to. A couple of times you told me you'd call me back and I didn't hear from you for two days."

She was quiet for a long while. So was I. When she spoke again, her voice was more bitter. She said, "Outside of us just fucking, I have to squeeze quality time out of you."

I stared out the window at the rows of one-level bookstores and coffeehouses. Watched crowds come and go. Saw nothing worth seeing. If what I was searching was just physical, Lorna would've fit the bill. My needs were way beyond that. So deep-seated that they might not be realistic.

She touched my leg in an unkind way, said, "You want to hear more?"

"Regardless, I didn't sleep with anybody else."

"You might as well have," she said wistfully. "I've never been your woman. Just an escape."

I chuckled, wondered if anybody ever could. "Escape?"

"Call it want you want. Escape. Relief. Am I wrong?"

I wanted to disagree. "You're right."

The bitterness left her voice and it went back to a feathery tone, "Is our business finished?"

I didn't say anything else. Neither did she.

Lorna dropped me off at my car, gave me a loving hug and said, "I love you. Probably will for a while."

She said that like heartbreak was nothing new for her either.

She bobbed her head, said, "But I'm a big girl. I can handle this feeling until it's gone. I don't have a problem dealing with reality. I'm just sorry about what happened to us. You know if I had've known about, you know, I would've told you."

In my rearview mirror, I saw her wipe her eyes and wave a strong good-bye. She straightened her clothes, held her head high, floated back inside her daddy's sanctuary.

SHELBY

29 **Whitney** Houston was grooving on the radio while I rushed and watered the pothos, English ivy, and Boston fern plants that filled my apartment. I was breaking my neck so I could get out of my cave in the next five minutes. I hurried, bumped into the dresser and hurt my hip, limped and double-checked that I'd crammed everything I'd need to survive the next week inside my luggage-on-wheels and garment bag.

I had on a beige blouse, and a brown vest the color of my slacks, then put on a studded baseball cap and pulled my ponytail through the back.

The doorbell rang.

Damn.

I looked through the blinds and was pissed twice. Richard had come back. *And* he'd brought his momma. Something had told me to let my plants rot and leave ten minutes ago. After I counted down from ten, I went back into the bedroom, took the ring case from the bottom of my underwear drawer, and slid my engagement ring back on. Then I counted down from twenty before I opened the door and painted a phony look of welcome on my face.

I said, "Good morning, Mrs. Vaughn."

"Good morning, Shelly."

Last week I was Sheila. The week before Shirley. She can remember every word in the Bible, but she can't get my name right. She adjusted her sky-blue hat, which was filled with rainbow-colored fruit. The sight of her Fruit Loop-looking hat made my stomach growl. The woman was five feet tall, just as wide, and weighed in at about one-eighty; she'd weigh about one-ten if she scraped some of her makeup off. Her eyebrows were sketched in like the arches at McDonald's.

"How're you feeling?" Richard asked me.

He strolled by and kissed my cheek like nothing negative had happened between us a few hours ago. Ignored my feelings.

He said, "Love you, Shelby."

I wiped his kiss from my face, then ran my fingers across the crack of my butt.

Mrs. Vaughn scrunched down on my queen-size black futon. She had a foul-scowl on her face that made me think she'd just inhaled a fart.

"How've you been, Mrs. Vaughn?" I said and kept moving toward the bedroom. Like I really cared.

"Just fine. I've been just—"

"Would you like something to drink?" I was talking, not listening. "I've got water and juice."

"No, thank you, Shirley." Mrs. Vaughn cleared nothing from her throat, then whispered louder than necessary, "Why she always dress like a tomboy? Got on a man's vest and carrying on. Don't have no decent dresses. At least I ain't seen her in none since your daddy's funeral. You ought to tell her to fix her hair up like that pretty girl you used to go with."

I leaned against the dresser, folded my arms, unfolded them, then made my hands busy stacking and restacking my James Baldwin and BeBe Moore Campbell novels. I did a silent countdown from fifty. Did it twice. I mumbled, "Stinky, ugly, smelly, decrepit, hideous ho. Your daddy should've used a condom."

"Need some help?" That was Richard yelling down the hall.

"Nope, I got it."

I closed my bedroom door and sat on my dresser, took a last inspection of my neck. People would think I'd had an interview with a vampire. I wrapped a paisley scarf around my neck.

When I huffed and puffed and dragged my stuff into the living room, I caught Mrs. Vaughn running her f-u finger through the thin layer of dust resting on my table.

She said, "Umph. Trifling."

"I'm sorry, were you talking to me?"

She moved side to side but didn't have the decency to give a sister some eye contact when she said, "I ain't said nothing, Sheila."

I smiled over clenched teeth and said, "Shelby."

"What was that?"

"My name is Shelby."

"Ain't that the truth."

Richard was in the kitchen. The cabinet clicked open, my glasses clacked together. He was pouring something to drink.

I said, "Paper cups are on the counter."

Richard swallowed and belched. "What's that?"

Mrs. Vaughn stared at my cap like it was heinous. I gave the same look, double-or-nothing, at her curly brown wig. Then she spread her glare toward my disorganized entertainment center. I'd picked up so many trips that I hadn't had time to clean or reorganize my CDs or videotapes.

"What do you and Richard have planned today, Mrs. Vaughn?"

"Me and Richard?" Mrs. Vaughn shifted around like she was scratching the crack of her butt. "After I drop y'all off, I'm going right back home and cook me something t' eat."

"Oh," Richard called out. "I was just about to tell you. I'm flying down to L.A. with you. I booked a ticket for the flight you're on. I'm checking in with you so we can sit together."

I know I didn't hear what I just heard. Something percolated inside my body and tried to erupt out of my head. I had to use every ounce of strength not to drop my bags.

"You all right?" Mrs. Vaughn asked.

I made a noise like a Gregorian chant. I said, "I'm fine."

"You needs to eat."

I know we didn't discuss going together because I'd avoided bringing that up as an option. It wasn't an option. The most I'd ever said was that he could take me to the airport. And I was gonna bail out curbside. He hadn't planned on going, I know he hadn't, and I had the marks on my neck to prove it.

Mrs. Vaughn had a crooked grin. I knew why Richard had dragged her blubber along. Not to take us to the airport, but because he knew I wouldn't start any shit in front of her.

Richard called out, "Momma asked when we're going to sit down and set a date for the wedding."

"Eventually."

She said, "What kinna answer is that? A woman is 'pose to obey her husband."

"Dogs obey. People collaborate."

My mind kicked into overdrive. I struggled to think of a legitimate argument for Richard not to go.

"What about your business, Richard?"

Mrs. Vaughn acted like I was talking to her, "The flower shop will be fine."

I wanted to scream my way back into my bedroom and slam the door. If I had've known it was gonna be like this, I would've zoomed north up the 5 freeway with the rising of the sun.

That bastard was slick. He was staying in the kitchen sucking up the last of my juice, keeping out of sight.

Richard put his glass in the dishwasher. That pissed me off because I'd already cleaned up the kitchen, and he knew he could've washed that one glass out. He strutted into the living room and smoothed his hands over his polo shirt.

We stared at each other. His eyes were on the scarf around my neck. I waited for him to say something.

He said, "Ready?"

"Yep. As ready as I'm ever gonna be."

After I locked up, I moved right by them, made it to parking first, then hurled my luggage into the trunk of Richard's SAAB. Mrs. Vaughn was ten yards back, wobbling like a Weeble; Richard was snailing along too. Before they caught up I had crawled in the backseat and had sucked my bottom lip hard enough to smear blackberry lipstick across all my teeth.

Richard's work papers were on the seat. I yanked the mess from under my butt and tossed everything on the floor. The next thing I did was let out a fake yawn and pretend I was so sleepy I couldn't stand it, even threw in a soft snore and a fake nod or two. My plan was to have a bogus siesta from airport to airport, so the sooner I inaugurated the charade, the better.

Richard and his mother chattered about what needed to be done at his business down on the harbor, about which one of his brothers was going to help his sister. Their conversation was a damn shame. My best friend's husband, my friend, had died, and they were stuck on irrelevant crap.

I peeped at my engagement ring. Saw how it sparkled like a star in a night of gloom. All the other attendants thought it was the bomb. They thought Richard was the bomb. Maybe I was a fool to not do a quick wedding. At thirty years of life and strife, being single and living alone in a one-bedroom apartment wasn't exactly where I had pictured myself. This wasn't my plan.

But I was comfortable. No complaints. No regrets.

My mind started to wander. Wandered and wondered. I wondered when things had changed between me and Richard. Things used to be damn pleasant, and I used to look forward to seeing him every now and then. Sometimes I'd called from a layover. It gets damn lonely on trips. Yep, I missed him. But that was when I didn't see him as much.

Three months ago, Richard had taken me back over to his parents' house. It was the day his daddy, Papa Ray, had gotten out of the hospital. He was around eighty and spending more time with doctors and nurses than he did with his family. So, everybody was there, and before I realized what was really going on, the relatives had circled me the way the Indians surrounded Custer. Scared the hell out of me. I guess when you start to accumulate secrets, every little *boo* rattles your nerves.

Richard got down on his right knee and clicked open a maroon case, stuck a ring under my nose. I was the only one surprised.

"Will you marry me?" he asked, smiling ear to ear.

It wasn't exactly a sunrise on the beach proposal, but that wasn't the point. We had never, ever talked about marriage. Broom-jumping wasn't on my mind at the time. I didn't even consider him my boyfriend because it wasn't that kind of party. He sent me flowers every Friday, had told me he loved me, but that emotional confession was on him. I made him call before he came over, never talked to him long, always ended the conversation first, never let him lounge two nights in a row. And I hadn't done all the sensuous, creative things with him that I'd shared with Tyrel. Either I was like a stick in the mud, or he didn't have the spark to ignite this powder keg.

When he proposed, the room was full of anxious cousins, aunts, uncles, Richard's brothers and his sister. A whole family tree with broad, smiling faces filled with expectations. And my panties itched in a personal spot. I hated pressure.

My first mind wanted to know why he didn't take me to a nice romantic place so I could laugh my ass off and reject his butt.

Then there was his momma. Mrs. Vaughn lurked in the door, fat under her arms swaying like a child on a swing, foot tapping. When I saw her, a nightmare kicked in and I imagined my crumb-snatchers being the image of that, rug rats with sagging skin and dingy rollers. I almost jumped out of my seat and screeched *"Hell no."*

But then I saw Papa Ray. Richard's father was alive back then, but he had died in his sleep a month back. He was a princely, peaceful man. Tall, thin, white hair, walked with a cane. He always hugged me, always got my name right. A time or two he'd called my apartment and we'd talked for a couple of hours. I loved that man and wished he had've married my mother. I would've loved to have been his child for a while. Papa Ray smiled at me. I smiled at him.

Maybe the real reason I went with the program was because the night before I had called Tyrel. I'd stolen his phone number off Debra's refrigerator, called him in the middle of the night and a woman answered. I know I had the right number because I had dialed it earlier and got his answering machine, but I didn't leave a message because I wanted to hear the first reaction to my voice. So I guess somebody else was sleeping on the right side of his bed. Resting at his kitchen table on Sunday mornings.

Richard smiled at me, offered a lifetime of love, and while he was humbling himself, I felt like a fool. Like I said, my momma died without ever having been offered a ring.

Eventually, my eyes went to Richard and said, "Yeah."

Richard screamed and scared the hell out of me. He jumped around like he'd caught the winning pass at the Super Bowl. All of the Vaughns were laughing and hugging me. Papa Ray smiled at me; I smiled a little. Mrs. Vaughn left the room and headed toward her kitchen and that pork smell.

The ring hadn't cooled off on my finger before Richard

grabbed a calendar, a Bic pen, and wanted to mark a date.
Every damn day, every time he asked, I said I wasn't ready,
told the brother we had plenty of time. He started making
funky comments about me going to Los Angeles so much.
Then, out of the blue, he started asking if Tyrel called,
would I go back.

I said, "Hell no. I don't do reruns. That's extinct."

Richard asked, "If he wanted to get with you, would
you?"

"I don't do shit like that."

"Have you been talking to Tyrel?"

He was asking more questions than Perry Mason when
I marched out of his place and drove home. Before I stuck
my keys in my door, Richard was there, apologizing. We
couldn't have a two-minute conversation without him asking about the wedding, or making some funky insinuation
about Tyrel. Richard made me so damn mad I changed my
answer.

I snapped, "You know what? Anything's possible."

His voice softened, "So now you don't know?"

I thought Richard was gonna take his ring back, and I
was ready to give it up, but he's been trying harder ever
since. Calling, calling, hanging up, then calling. And when
I blocked his number, fifteen minutes didn't go by before I
thought I heard his car driving by my bedroom window.
Money was tight, so I picked up extra flights, bidded for as
many trips as I could stand, and boosted my work time
from seventy to damn near ninety hours a month. I needed
breathing room; no matter where I went, he called the hotel
before I could get out of my damn uniform.

Richard said, "What I do wrong?"

"You haven't done nothing wrong."

"You love me?"

"You're working my damn nerves."

"You love him?"

"Him who?"

"Him."

"I'm hanging up. Look, I'll see you when I get back. I'll call you, don't call me. Don't leave all those sad-ass messages on my machine, and please, no more flowers. Okay?"

He exhaled. "All right."

"I'm sorry." I sighed. "You just get too intense and a little bit too pushy. I like to breathe my own air sometimes."

"So do I. Don't I give you space?"

"Your version of space."

" 'Bye, Shelby."

I hung up, then gazed at the marquis on my finger. It wasn't a token from the swap meet, had clarity and quality, and I had the certificate of authenticity to prove its flawlessness. My hand tilted side to side and I remembered how it sparkled a happy song of always and forever in the sunlight. Yep, diamonds are a girl's best friend. Chiquita the Confused said I should be happy; good brothers were hard to find. And she ought to know.

SHELBY

30

Richard said, "Are you hot?"

"Nope."

"You're sweating."

"I sweat easily."

Our yellow taxi stopped in front of Debra's crib. A few neighbors were outside. I spoke and made a break for the trunk. Two things happened: Richard went to pay the driver, and Debra opened the front door. They saw each other. She put her hand up to her eyes and stepped out into the sunshine. Damn. She was baffled, but I read her new pain from the distance. She waved. I waved. Richard waved. Debra hesitated, then waved at him.

In the meantime, my luggage was trapped. His Samsonite was laying on top of my garment bag, holding it down. By the time I had yanked out my gear, Richard was following me like he was the LAPD chasing O.J. down the 405 freeway.

I told Richard, "Keep off the grass."

"Why?"

"Sprinklers."

What made it worse was that Debra came down the walkway and met us halfway. Debra's breasts and hips were filling out; her face was fuller, nose was spreading, had that fruitful mommy-to-be glow.

Debra pointed at my head, "Boss hat, girl. Don't take it off. I might borrow it forever."

"Then I'll leave it for you forever."

She said, "You're a day early."

"Shut up and hug me." I put my bags down and kissed her cheek. "How're you holding up?"

She rubbed my back with both hands and whispered, "I'm so glad you're here. I need you, girl. About ten people and a reporter from the *Sentinel* just left." Debra slowly let me go and wiped away her dark rose lipstick. Then her attention went toward Richard.

I said, "Richard, this is Debra."

He said, "I'm Shelby's fiancé."

Debra rubbed small circles in her stomach and said, "Nice to finally meet you. Shelby has told me so much about you."

The lawn sprinklers kicked on. That killed the conversation and snatched our attention. Richard was acting like he'd never seen wet grass before, and Debra was glancing at my ring finger.

I was saved again when one of the phone lines rang. Debra headed back toward the crib and told us to come in from the heat. I picked up my bags and followed the trail of her Bijan scent.

It was a weird feeling stepping inside the house. I expected Leonard to come out of the back room, smiling, saying "What's up, Chocolate?" It didn't happen. Wouldn't happen again.

Richard was riding my heels when we went through the arched foyer and headed toward the den.

Richard said, "House smells like pasta."

"Yeah. Neighbors have probably been bringing food over."

Richard chivied too close for comfort, so I made a pain noise, shifted and accidently-on-purpose dropped my garment bag at his feet. He stumbled. My timing was off. If I'd've dropped it a second later I could've tripped him up.

I said, "Ouch. Shit, it slipped off and pulled my shoulder."

"I asked you to let me carry it."

Richard left the bags and moved over by the glass cabinet full of African artifacts. He saw me watching him.

He asked, "These are her wedding pictures?"

"Yep. Her cousin Bobby did the photos."

"You look nice." He didn't sound thrilled.

"Thanks." Neither did I.

Forever ticked by before he went down toward the civic awards in the glass casing, stood like a tourist in front of Leonard's pictures and certificates.

Richard asked, "Isn't this the mayor and the chief of police in this picture with you and your friends?"

I nodded. Somebody did a catcall. My nerves twitched, and I almost pissed all over myself.

That familiar voice said, "Shelby Janine Daniels."

My heart did cartwheels. His look was fresh, vogue

enough to make a sister rub her eyes. He smirked. We hurried toward each other, kissed each other's face, hugged, rocked side to side.

He said, "Damn, you look good."

"Thank you."

"How're you doing?"

"Fine, considering the circumstances."

Behind me, Richard made a few funny sounds, then his luggage dropped hard to the floor. He cleared a lump of nothing from his throat, then moved right up on us, stood closer than a shadow.

He put his hand out and said, "My name is Richard Vaughn."

"I'm Bobby Davis. Are you the shuttle driver?"

"I'm with Shelby."

"With—*Oh*. You're Shelby's friend?"

"Not exactly. I'm her fiancé."

"Oh. Congratulations."

Richard said, "You didn't know?"

Bobby said, "I haven't been in touch for a while."

I didn't waste a second before I interrupted the jacked-up conversation. "What you done did to your hair, Bobby?"

Bobby raked his fingers through his wild dreadlocks. "You like?"

Before he could get his laugh on, a Hispanic woman with full red lips stepped down from the kitchen. She was darker than Debra, but lighter than me. Her light brown hair hung down to her bra strap.

She asked, "Are you Shelby?"

"Yeah."

She came over and hugged me.

She said, "Nice to finally meet you. My name is Alejandria."

"Nice to meet you too."

"I'm Bobby's wife."

I echoed, "Wife?"

That rocked me. I was glad I didn't say what I was thinking, because I'd thought she was a new housekeeper.

Bobby said, "We got hitched in Vegas two weeks ago."

"Two and a half," Alejandria corrected. "We came over to help Debra take care of things so she can rest."

All the tee-heeing and lollygagging was nice, but the reason all of us were showing up was undercutting every word. People would've thought we were crazy. We were laughing, smiling like smiles were two-for-one, but the humor wasn't exactly funny.

I said, "Alejandria, anything I can do to help?"

Alejandria shook her head. "Relax. Make Debra relax too."

"I heard that," Debra yelled. As soon as she came into the living room, the phone rang again. Debra threw her hands up and said, "Let the machine earn its keep. Bobby, forward the calls to the service. Check it every hour, if you can."

The second phone line rang. The doorbell ding-donged.

Debra said, "This is ridiculous. I don't feel like being bothered every other minute."

Debra had a touch of frustration in her stride and continued moving on toward the kitchen. She stopped in the doorway. Richard was in his own world, checking out all of her artifacts.

He pointed at a statue. "Where did you get this African sculpture? Senegal?"

"Crenshaw swap meet," Debra said.

Everybody laughed. Richard too. All those veins in Richard's face took a powder. I smiled at Richard. And I meant it.

I said, "Debra, Bobby, and me all went to college together."

Richard said, "USC?"

"Yeah, USC."

"I'm Debra's cousin," Bobby interjected. "Shelby and me are kinda like brother and sister."

I asked Debra, "Which bedroom should we put our junk in?"

The room got quiet as hell. I could've kicked myself, because I know I should've asked that question when I was alone with Debra instead of spreading my business.

"Richard," Debra said politely. "Why don't you put your bags in the back room, on the left? Shelby, come here, dear child."

"What's up?"

"I need you to run me somewhere."

Richard walked over to me. I surprised myself when I gave him a genuine embrace. He lowered his voice and whispered in my ear, "Was that Tyrel in the wedding picture with you, Leonard, and Debra? I assume he was the best man, right?"

Shit. I lost the laugh I had and walked. Richard picked up our luggage and followed Alejandria. As soon as they rounded the corner and their footsteps faded, Bobby took a step closer.

I raised my hand to Bobby. I said, "Don't say it. If you do I'll slap the shit out of you."

"I ain't said nothing," Bobby whispered. "Engaged, huh?"

I snapped, "Married, huh?"

When I marched into the kitchen, Debra was outside, holding the door and waiting. Once again, I was in trouble. I slowed down and chewed the inside of my lip. Debra shook her head.

Debra said, "Stop dragging and come on."

When we got into the garage, my eyes roamed every which-a-way, went to and fro across all the tools along the far wall. Hammers and saws and oil and filters. Leonard's manly stuff was waiting for him, inside a two-car garage with only one car. Leonard's Celica would never come back home. The thought seemed so freaking absolute that it made me shudder.

Debra went to the passenger side of her new Benz and got in. The Hyundai had been stolen a month or so ago. If I didn't know better, I'd think she'd avoided stepping into Leonard's space.

When I opened my door, she said, "Drive."

I got behind the wheel, did my usual routine and drove the Dons—Don Diego to Don Carlos to Don Felipe to Don Miguel to Don Lorenzo. We crossed Stocker, breezed through Angeles Vista and went to another middle-class section, called View Park. By the time the tires hit Slauson, Debra still hadn't moved or said a word. Debra always used silence and attitude to make me uncomfortable. Shit worked too.

We were heading toward the ocean when Debra sighed, then said, "When did you get engaged?"

My neck was warm. I loosened my paisley scarf a little and said, "Couple of months ago."

She patted her Bible. "How long have you known him?"

"About five months."

"Selfish bitch. You know what you are?"

"I'm pretty sure you're about to tell me."

"A wild ass used to the wilderness. And you can save that sorry face you're wearing." She was talking matter-of-factly. It hurt like hell. Debra said, "How long have we been so-called best friends?"

I tried to sound like it didn't matter, "Since we were eggs waiting for sperms."

"Guess we're not friends anymore."

That really hurt because she meant it. "Don't say that."

"It's true."

I just barely said, "I'm sorry."

"Had me standing out there looking stupid."

"Sorry, but—"

"Kill it and save the story."

She let her seat back so far it looked like I was riding by myself. Debra inhaled and released a shaking exhale. Tears were seeping down her face.

"I can't believe he's gone," she whispered like she was in conversation with herself. "I keep thinking I'll wake up and this shit will be a dream. Or he'll call laughing and say it was some stupid publicity bullshit thing they thought up."

I let a little time go by before I said, "How do you feel?"

"Numb. I don't feel shit. It's too sudden. Going through the motions. Afraid. Unsure about the future."

It sounded like I was listening to a mirror. Numb. Don't feel shit. Not a damn thing. Unsure about the future.

Debra said, "The funeral will be closed casket."

My eyes shut themselves and a few moans trickled out of me.

She said, "Because I want everybody to remember him big and strong like he was. The way he looked when people saw him riding down the Dons smiling and waving and being silly. Not the way the accident messed him up."

"What happened to the other driver?"

"It's out of my hands. But you know how the system is."

"Black?"

"Japanese," Debra said and stared off into a vast nothingness. "*Times* said the kid was nineteen years old."

"Damn. Japanese."

"Leonard was taking care of everything. I'll have to sell

a couple of the houses, probably. Maybe dump the condo in Vegas. Because of a stupid nineteen-year-old drunk bitch."

"Don't talk like that."

"Bet they own a chain of liquor stores down Manchester."

She stopped babbling when I reached over and held her hand. She trembled like she was going through detoxification.

I said, "That attitude ain't you."

"Everything's going to be different."

"I know."

Debra's voice dipped and cracked, chilled me when she said, "Everything's going to be so damn different."

"I'm here for you."

"Thanks, Shelby."

Tears fell from Debra's puffy, bloodshot eyes. I wished I could steal all of the pain. It didn't take long before I was trying to stop my own lip from quivering.

I parked out near Venice Beach in a not-too-busy area facing the ocean, near a row of condos, but we didn't get out of the car. On the way back home, I wasted some more time so Debra could pull herself together, and drove by the upper-class homes sitting high on Mount Vernon Drive. A sky-high spot where we could stand under the eucalyptus trees and see the rolling mountains on the other side of downtown.

I said, "Let's walk."

Debra didn't look my way, but she nodded.

She held my right hand, we went through the turnstile, over the grass separator, held hands like we were still in grade school, stood near the bent fence. Down the hill, in the cool air, traffic zoomed up and down Stocker. Debra came to life, put some pep in her step, and led me around the trail. We held hands but didn't hold back the tears. And even then my girl was cool. At her worst, she was her best.

She cried but she wasn't hysterical and flapping around like sisters in a Baptist church on Sunday morning. She cried a bit, wiped it away, and went on with her life. I was supposed to be helping her, but she spent most of the time trying to calm me.

An elderly black couple was on the pathway too. The lady reached up and ran her hand across the man's receding hair line; he held her hand. We slowed down and watched them flirt.

I was busy watching the old people who thought they were still young when Debra eased over and put her hand up to the scarf around my neck. I put my hand up to stop her, but she slapped both of my hands hard enough to get sued.

"Move your hands, Shelby."

I gave her a have-you-lost-your-fucking-mind? glower for a second or two before I said forget it and lowered my palms. My eyes closed, my head dropped. The scarf was gently pulled away. Two warm and gentle fingers tilted my head backward, then side to side. Over and over, Debra's fingers touched the spots where the territorial marks were still breathing and scowling.

She said, "I was wondering why you were choking yourself in that scarf."

"Ouch. You're hurting my neck."

"Jealous?"

I nodded. Guess that's what I get for telling him all about me and Tyrel. Brothers ask questions, you're honest, and they sharpen the truth and hold it against your neck.

She walked away, moved closer to the fence. When she stood on the edge, she shuddered and scared the hell out of me. I put a hand on her shoulder, told her not to get too close to the edge, but she didn't budge.

Ten times I said a tender, "Debra."

She said, "Where did I fuck up?"

"Watch your language." I put my arms around her. "You didn't."

Thirty minutes flew by before Debra led me back to the car. Her stride had its original gentle stroll. Her game face was on. But a false face can't cover a false feeling. This time she eased in on the driver's side. I wiped my face with my palms, then saw that Debra was doing the exact same thing.

I said, "Debra?"

"Shhh."

We reached out and hugged each other. We were sharing a mood that we'd never shared before.

"Debra, we look like raccoons."

"You're the ugly one."

"Never as ugly as you. Want me to drive?"

"Do I look like Miss Daisy?"

I flipped down the vanity mirror on my side, craned my neck so I could see the damage from all angles.

I said, "How does it look?"

"Like some pretty tacky shit."

That pretty much answered that. It wouldn't have been so bad if there was some pleasure and orgasms to go along with the passionless marks. I'd have to wear a scarf for at least three days.

I said, casually, "When is Tyrel going to get here?"

"Shelby, don't play me like that."

"What?"

"That question has been burning to get out your mouth."

"I'm asking because I need to make sure I have the right information in the program."

"I'm his wife. Whatever you need to know, I know."

"Oh. Well, that was the only reason."

"Why didn't you call Tyrel?"

"What are you talking about?"

"You stole his phone number off our refrigerator."

Next thing I knew, I was digging up my nose. I said, "What you talking about?"

"It was Leonard's idea. You always ate as soon as you got in the door, so he figured if I put the number on the refrigerator it wouldn't take you two seconds to see it. And I know you tampered with it because you never put things back how you found them."

"Think you know me so well."

"We set you up and you played yourself."

"Whatever. Either way, things have changed since then. I could've done without ever meeting Tyrel. He was just something to do until something better came along. A one-night stand that went on for a few months."

Debra said, "You love Richard?"

I stared at my ring.

"Shelby? It's a yes or no question."

"Yeah. He's good to me. He's good for me too."

"You're happy?"

"Yeah. Couldn't be better."

"Then why haven't you mentioned him before?"

Debra started the car. That meant she was finished with that part of the discussion. If I had've answered her, I would've been talking to my damn self. I put the scarf back on, adjusted it, let my black hair hang so I could cover up as much wounded flesh as I could. On the radio, KJLH was playing that controversial bisexual song about some brother named Bill. Guess it always created a controversy when people told the truth. Debra changed to a jazz station, then to an oldies station, then she pushed a button and an old Chanté Moore CD came on.

I said, "Wanna go get some ice cream?"

"Praline pecan?"

"Yeah."

Debra grinned a little and said, "Thrifty?"

"Yeah, Thrifty."

"Waffle cone?"

"Double scoops?"

"My treat."

"Your treat."

TYREL

31 MY top was down while I rode Crenshaw Boulevard from Manchester to where the street ended at pothole-filled Wilshire.

The ride was different. Superficial. Nobody was in the car lollygagging, cracking jokes about the creatures on the Strip, philosophizing, and flipping the radio from KJLH to KACE to KKBT every other second. I switched from my Enya CD to a Blackstreet CD and tried to give the ride a pulse, but the pulse just wasn't there. Wasn't happening no matter how hard I tried.

Mexicans were in the streets selling fruit and nuts at the freeway ramps. Bow-tied Muslim brothers hustled bean pies and the *Final Call*. A brother dressed in a green dashiki peddled five-dollar pictures.

Another hustled Malcom X, Martin Luther King, Bob Marley, and Tupac T-shirts. The dead were making a living for the living. The old, worn-down brother scurried through traffic, begged people to buy the T-shirts. I did a double-take when I saw the struggling brother was wearing a faded Tommy Hilfiger T-shirt and scuffed Kani boots, a dark scarf on his head. It was Jackson.

After I slowed down long enough to get my hair trimmed at Magic Shears, I rode through South Central and passed by the spots where my daddy's stores used to be. One place was boarded up and had graffiti on every brick; another had been turned into a storefront church; another looked like a crack dealership.

While I rode under sunshine, streets lined with palm trees, and chased memories, I took out my c-phone and called Daddy. He said he'd picked up his tickets and he was through packing. I called Twin. She was packed and waiting for Momma to call her back so they could arrange a connecting flight together.

Everybody would be here in hours. It's a damn shame what it took to get some families together again.

I went to La Brea near Venice. People had made a shrine and put flowers on the spot where Leonard took his last breath. Chipped glass had been swept away from the oil-stained concrete.

Part of me wanted to drive to West Angelus funeral home. I didn't have the strength. Not yet. Not alone. I couldn't bear to see my buddy's shell with his spirit removed. But I wanted to be close enough to send my feelings.

Love you, Buddy. I'm gonna miss you. Thanks.

I talked to him like he was sitting in the car with me. Leonard understood. He felt and knew the rest.

———

It was getting dark when I rolled up the concrete mountains rising from the jungle into Baldwin Hills. In Los Angeles every evening, darkness chased away heat and brought a chill. I parked close to the garage, right behind Debra's Mercedes, turned off my thumping music, pushed the button to make my top ride up.

When I bumped my overnight bag and suitcase up the walkway, by the pool, and into the kitchen, lots of voices were coming from the other side of the door that led to the den and front room. Enough noise to know the house was cluttered with people.

Bobby came in the kitchen and tossed a Snapple bottle in the overflowing trash. He sounded exhausted. "What's up, Tyrel?"

I said, "Hey, Bobby."

He had on ripped jeans, no shoes, no shirt. We both stopped by the marble-top island, in front of mountains of food.

A bearded brother stuck his head into the kitchen, watched me for a second, I nodded at him, then he vanished.

I asked Bobby, "When did you get here?"

"Right after you pulled off."

"Who's here?"

"A few comics, some actors, people ain't nobody ever heard of in their life are stopping by."

"Make sure you watch Leonard's people."

"They just left. His momma and Debra weren't seeing eye to eye on the arrangements."

"Pretty much like the wedding."

"Worse."

Bobby's wife walked around the corner. Alejandria is Mexican with skin the color of sunrise. She has the body of a woman and the soft voice of a child. She had a novel in her hand.

She said, "E-mail is coming on the computer."

Bobby said, "And I need to check the service again."

We talked a few minutes while I snacked. Spoke our concerns about Debra. Nobody had seen her cry, so we were on guard.

I mingled my way into the living room; several of Leonard and Debra's friends were sitting on the tan sectional sofa and the ivory carpeted floor, talking and sipping on sodas.

A few people I recognized stepped up from the den, Emil Johnson and Edwonda White. They were making conversations with a black actress off of a soap opera I never watched, either *General Hospital* or *The Young and the Restless*.

The CD player was on random, alternating from Coltrane to Natalie Cole to Rachelle Ferrell.

"Hello everybody," I said, and gave a generic wave.

I turned around and the same brother who had peeped in the kitchen was stroking his beard, easing my way. I thought he was checking out the women, but he was watching me.

"Are you Tyrel Williams?"

"Yeah." I dropped my luggage to shake his hand. His grip was strong and sudden, felt like we were arm-wrestling.

"Richard Vaughn."

I repeated, "Richard Vaughn. I've heard your name before."

"I know. So, what is up?"

The way he gazed deep into my eyes, I hoped I hadn't tripped into a homosexual moment.

I said, "Nothing much. Same old same old."

I was about to ask him where we had met, if he was a frustrated comic, or nonworking actor, or something, when somebody dropped a tray of drinks. When one of the glasses broke, the comics didn't miss a beat and cracked a joke or two.

Richard didn't laugh with the crowd. He stood over me when I picked up my luggage, watched me while I strolled toward the bedrooms. I glanced over my shoulder and he was still watching, bobbing his head and masturbating the hair on his face. I hoped he wasn't butt-wishing because I'd hate for us to have a misunderstanding.

I opened the middle bedroom door and saw four pieces

of luggage by the dresser. The bed had been sat on. That room must've been taken by Bobby and Alejandria.

Debra's giggles came from the back bedroom. Hearing her lighter mood made me feel better. Before I claimed what was left, I'd checked with Debra and made sure none of the family was going to show up tonight and need a place to rest.

Actually, I still hadn't checked out of my hotel, because with the amount of traffic that would be coming through here for the next few days, I might need a place with some space. Might need to get away from the pain.

When I put my bags down to the side, Richard Vaughn was still watching me. Somebody started talking to him and stole his attention. The moment I knocked on the bedroom door, the chatter inside the room stopped. I knocked again.

Debra said, "Come in."

I smelled banana and coconut incense before the door opened.

Debra was sitting on the bed. Next to Shelby.

My eyes locked on Shelby. Stuck on a memory gone by. I finally said, "Hello."

Shelby answered with a dry, "Hello."

She didn't smile. Didn't look at me. Didn't matter.

I'd be a liar if I said that Shelby didn't look good. Much better than she did the last time I saw her. The entire Transitional Team couldn't come close to being a Shelby.

Debra's bedroom was the size of an apartment. There was a loveseat, a couple of valets, a circular shower with two shower heads, and a bathtub. Around the corner was a dressing room that looked like a makeup room on a movie set. Debra and her friend had kicked their shoes off.

Shelby squirmed around then got up off the queen-size bed. After she turned her back to me and straightened out the section of gray and peach comforter she'd rested her butt on, she meandered toward the black lacquer dresser.

She moved, fidgeted with her neck, adjusted the red-yellow-gold scarf around it, shoved her hands in the pockets of her slacks.

Debra was peaceful. Her breathing was calmer than when I first showed up.

I said, "Debra?"

She raised her head.

"Which bed should I sleep in?"

Debra pointed next door. "Sleep in the middle room."

Shelby said, "My stuff is in the middle room."

Shelby glanced at Debra in the mirror. Then at me. When our eyes collided, she made herself busy adjusting her vest and blouse. Something about her irked the hell out of me. I'd have to pretend that being in the same world as she didn't bother me.

Debra scratched her nose. "Then take the end room."

"Okay."

I'd be a wall away from Shelby.

Debra said, "There's plenty of food in the kitchen."

"I know. I ate some."

Leonard's day planner and golden bracelet rested under Shelby's nose. Comedy tapes were on top of the television, next to copies of the movies he was in.

I picked up my luggage. "Anything you need me to do?"

Debra said, "I'm fine."

I left.

My room had plain white walls. A regular size bed with peach sheets and a green heavy comforter. Quilts and extra pillows were at the foot of the bed. I clicked on the ceiling fan and cracked a window to get the air moving.

I had just put my suitcase on the foot of the bed when I saw Richard Vaughn was in the door, steady-bobbing his head like one of those children's toys from the zoo. Maybe his beard was new and that was why I couldn't place his face. His hands were too rough for him to be gay, but in L.A., you never knew.

I deepened my tone, "What's up, my brother?"

"I was just about to ask you the same."

"Have we met before?"

"Not face-to-face. I'm Richard Vaughn."

I shrugged, said, "Okay."

"I'm with Shelby."

I paused for a second, then let out a stiff "Oh."

Now I understood. I kept my cool, played it off, and continued unpacking. Used my busy hands to hide my surprise.

"We're getting married." He let loose a sardonic grin. "I'm her fiancé."

"Fiancé?" I parroted.

"So, you're telling me you didn't know?"

"Didn't watch CNN this morning."

I almost closed my suitcase and chopped off my fingers. He was standing in my space like he was waiting for something.

My voice lowered and I said, "Well, congratulations."

"I wanted you to know that."

"Thanks for the update."

He didn't move. Kept on bobbing his head like there was some offbeat music between his ears. That repetitive move was getting on my nerves. We stared at each other for an endless second. Felt like he was taunting me.

I went back to unpacking like it was no big deal.

Shelby called out from the hallway: "Richard. Come here, sweetheart. I want to show you something."

Her voice had changed from the lifeless pitch she'd had with me, had livened up to a cup of sweetness with two cubes of tenderness. Richard gave his beard a break and put his hand on the tip of his nose. Again we looked at each other for a moment. Glared man to man. He closed the door on his way out, left me standing holding a pair of green drawers.

Shelby had brought her fiancé to my friend's house.

They were sleeping together in the bedroom next to me.

What bothered me was that I could see who she'd picked after she'd walked out. But if she's already engaged, she might've picked him before. It shouldn't matter. More important things were on my agenda.

After I stood and looked myself over in the mirror, I decided to head back into the living room and see who was still out there lingering. Maybe make myself busy with irrelevant conversation and a strong drink. Better yet, I could throw on a jacket, let the top to my car down, drive around a while, find some old watering holes down on Rodeo by Dorsey High, blow some time tracking down some old friends of Leonard's and mine.

Just as I opened the door, Shelby and Richard were holding hands, flirting their way back down the hall. The corridor was wide enough, but the space closed in and crammed us together. I felt awkward, wanted to stare, but didn't want to glare.

Shelby gave a rude smile and then turned her head away. Richard kept his eyes on me. Smirked like he'd won a battle.

"Shelby, Richard?" I said that when they got right up on me. We were face-to-face, close enough to taste each other's breath.

Shelby slowed down, let Richard's hand go. A set of lines sprinted in her forehead when her eyes met mine.

Richard's attention went to her, then to me.

Shelby's hand went up to her head, twisted her hair.

He said, "What is up?"

"Congratulations," I said. "You two look good together."

It hurt to say it, and I didn't mean it, but it was time to

bring some order and reality into my life. To show I was a bigger man than the other man. And I had to respect my friend's home. I tried to keep my heart from flavoring my words and hoped I didn't sound too contrived or too disappointed. Didn't want to come across as petty or jealous.

Shelby didn't smile. "Thank you, Tyrel."

"Yeah, thanks." Richard continued walking into the living room. Shelby followed like the loyal women of a Middle Eastern culture who stayed a few steps behind their men. After he turned the corner and headed toward a crowd of people who were standing near the door, she glimpsed back toward me before moving on.

Shelby waved good-bye.

"Tyrel?" That came from behind me.

Debra was standing in her door, leaning against the frame with a hand on her belly, smiling. Shelby wasn't waving at me, she was waving at Debra. I'd deceived myself once again.

I went into Debra's room.

I asked, "How're you feeling?"

"Fine." She sighed. "Best as I can under the circumstances."

Debra sat on her bed and rubbed one of her feet. She told me that the obituary was done, but she wanted me to look it over before it was taken to the copier. She didn't want anyone wearing dark colors to the funeral. That was a point of tension between her and Leonard's mother. That and the fact that Leonard's mom wanted a wake and a funeral.

Debra said, "I've never understood the wake process."

"It's an old Southern tradition."

"Well, we're not old, and we're not in the South."

"I'm with you."

"She wanted to talk to me about insurance papers."

"They're after the money already?"

"Already."

I sat on the floor and scooted close to her. I reached up and massaged her foot. Debra jerked away.

She said, "I'm ticklish."

"Forgot."

We sat for a couple of minutes and listened to the buoyant music floating from the living room. Rachelle Ferrell was singing a duet with Will Downing. I told her Twin and Momma were coming. Told her my daddy was coming too.

"Want to go back out to the front room?" I asked. "I just saw some people from the businesses in Leimert Park out front. The guy who owns the black museum and the Lena Horne–looking lady who has the bookstore and card shop were walking in."

"I should," Debra said and made half a motion to get up. She sat back down. "But not right now."

"You okay?"

"I don't want to be sad. Leonard wasn't a depressed person, so I don't want to cry—in front of them, anyhow."

"People understand. You don't have to be strong. We're here for you. Your holding everything inside worries me."

"Let me be me." She rubbed the top of my head. "When I'm ready, you'll be the first person I call."

"Promise?"

She kissed her hand and touched my face. "Promise."

Debra said she was throwing a celebration of life at the house, before the home-going. Leonard loved jazz and blues, so she'd hired a band Leonard used to drag her to go watch at 5th Street Dick's. My eyes roamed across the pictures of them that flooded their dresser. Pictures from South Africa to South Central. Wedding pictures were on her nightstand—me standing next to Leonard, Shelby next to Debra. She saw me looking, then leaned back, picked it up, and handed it to me.

"Tyrel, that reminds me—could you please try to get the garage door opened?"

"Stuck again?"

Debra tsked, rolled her eyes, nodded. "Yep. I couldn't get it up and Shelby was no help. I wasted my ice cream on my blouse struggling with the remote. If you can get it open, please pull my car in. You can park your car in Leonard's space."

I took another look at the picture before I put it back.

Debra said, "You are staying, I hope."

"Yeah. Why wouldn't I?"

"Well, I don't want you to feel uncomfortable with Shelby and her friend being here."

"Why would I be uncomfortable?"

Debra paused, "She's engaged, and you still care for her."

I went over to the dresser and picked up her car keys.

Debra's face was reading a question in mine. She said a soft, "I didn't know."

We traded weak smile for weak smile.

SHELBY

32

I snapped, "What's up, *Richard?*"

I'd dragged his six feet of attitude out back, close to the garage where we'd be camouflaged by the hedges, but the sensor activated the lights. They couldn't see us from the backdoor, so I was in a good spot to let my hair down and have space to clown my best clown.

Richard leaned against Debra's car and yanked at his

beard. He heard what I had said. He was taking his time, pissing me off. My temples hurt. I stopped, blew out the negative and sucked in the positive, found an ounce of focus.

"They have a pool," Richard said. "Too bad I can't swim."

"Don't ignore me."

"What?"

My hand was on my hip, I'd let my backbone slip, and my damn neck was snaking. I was almost a motherless child gone wild, but I found the switch to cut that ghetto mode off, then found a mature USC tone, and whispered, "Why are you tripping?"

"You're the one tripping."

"Richard, I heard you. Debra heard you. Why in the hell did you walk up in Tyrel's room and try to start some shit?"

Richard opened his hands, held his palms up to me like he was surrendering. "Maybe if you took the time to introduce me to your so-called friends, it wouldn't come across like I'm tripping. When we walked in the door you ran off—"

"I didn't run off. Debra had some business to take care of."

"You left me standing around with my hands in my pockets. I don't know anybody, and I'm just being friendly by introducing myself. Is there a problem with me knowing who you know? These will be my friends after we get married. Right?"

I almost dropped down on all fours and shrilled like a bitch at the half moon, but I caught myself. Tried to practice a little self-control before I lost control. My neck was sweating. Embarrassment was draining down my back. Right about now, I didn't need to add to my humiliation by letting my wicked tongue carry all the crap that had been stirred up.

From where I was sitting, I saw everybody leaving in droves, like it was last call at Joseph's and the lights had been clicked on. A few people got in cars waiting in the mouth of the cul de sac, some strolled up the Dons to their houses. I stewed in my pisstivity until the front of the house was pretty vacant.

Richard finally said, "What is up with you and him?"

"Him who? *Him* have a name?"

"Don't act stupid."

Stupid? He'd straight-up said the wrong word. I doubled up and swung as hard as I could. It wasn't exactly a Holyfield punch. I missed, pirouetted, lost my balance, fell on my butt, groaned. Damn, I wished I could fight as good as I ran my mouth.

Richard said, "You all right?"

I pouted and reached my hand up to him. "Help me up, baby."

When I got up, I whined, dusted my butt, and swung again. He fell for a sucker move. I hit his shoulder. Hurt my damn hand. That was the first time I'd ever hit somebody when I was mad.

"Hey!" Richard jumped back. He held his palms up and made a move toward me, but backed away when I got ready to swing again. I caught my breath. Then we got into a nowhere argument. Richard came closer, but left plenty of space.

"All right, Shelby. I'll be straight."

"Good."

"Which is more than you have been with me."

"Yeah, right. Anyway."

Richard exhaled. "So, what is up?"

I slapped my head along with each of my words, "Not

a damn thing is up. I told you. Richard, you knew he was gonna come."

"You didn't tell me that you were going to be staying in the same house. You were probably going to be in the same bedroom."

"It's not that kind of party."

Richard lowered his voice, "Why didn't you want me to come?"

"I didn't say I didn't want you to come. You didn't ask."

"I'm your fiancé, so I shouldn't have to ask."

"Yes, you do."

"Why should I?"

"Being engaged doesn't mean you own me."

"Have you been seeing Tyrel?"

My throat tightened. His question was stiff and rang out more like a statement. *Seeing* sounded like *sexing*. He was trying to play me; I wasn't in the mood. As far as I knew, neither of us had done anything that could be a good reason for breaking up. Nope. I hadn't done a thing I had thought of doing. Hell, I regretted having no regrets.

Richard said, "You've been flying down here very often."

"L.A. is up from San Diego, not down."

"Don't get flippant."

I was gonna leave his ass and go inside, but stopped because I had to finish this. No way I wanted to have a domestic dispute in front of Debra. Definitely not in front of Tyrel.

Richard leaned on the hood of the Benz. I avoided him and tried to sit on the trunk, but the car was waxed and each time I hopped on, I slid off like I was being thrown, and stumbled, like I was intoxicated with anger.

Richard moved toward me. "He hasn't called you?"

"What part of this conversation don't you understand?"

This was jacked up. I came out here to dog him and put him in check, so how in the hell did I let him turn this around?

He said, "You're a liar, Shelby."

That rocked me. Richard stuck his hand in his pocket, then spun around like he was leaving. But he came right back.

He said, "The phone I bought you has last-number redial."

His voice was chilly, but I was still the Ice Queen. "And?"

We stopped our ping-ponging conversation because somebody was talking in the dark. Over by the backdoor. Then the backdoor closed. We straightened up. I corrected my posture, took a half step closer to Richard.

Tyrel tramped out of the shadows like a dark cloud ready to rain on somebody, frowning like somebody had puked in his Kool-Aid. He marched his attitude our way. When he brought his bowlegs deeper into the light, came close enough for the depths of his dimple to show, his eyes were glazed and his mouth was fixed.

He shot me a look so intense it felt like his eyes slapped me. That scowl made the fine hairs on my arms stand up, skin bumped like I had the chicken pox.

Tyrel stared at me. Then at Richard. That's where his eyes locked. They didn't say anything for a second or two.

Tyrel said, "Nice to talk to you again, Richard Vaughn."

Richard nodded. "So, you decided to stop playing naive?"

33

"I'm not playing a damn thing."

Richard replied, "Nigga, please."

I spat on the ground and moved toward Shelby. When I got too close, she twitched and stutter-stepped out of my way.

"Excuse me." I opened the car door, leaned in, reached up to the visor. When I touched the remote, there were a series of clicks. The garage door opened, smooth and agreeable. The way life was supposed to be for a brother like me. Shelby was propped against my friend's Benz.

I jingled the keys and said a rude and rugged, "Shelby, if you don't mind, Debra wants me to pull their car in the garage."

While her perfume was waltzing in the breeze, Richard Vaughn was opening and closing his hands, like he was checking himself for arthritis, eyeballing me when I slid inside Debra's car. I checked the remote control again. It didn't work this time. I got out, opened the trunk, reached into a bag Leonard had bought from Sav-On drugstore, took out a pack of Duracells.

"Tyrel." That was Debra's voice. It startled me the way my momma's voice used to when she called for me after the streetlights had come on. The way Shelby and Richard flinched, they were knocked out of their thoughts. Debra stepped into the light. She had her red-hooded house coat over her clothes and was holding a glass of orange juice. Her eyes were bloodshot.

I asked, "You okay, Debra?"

Shelby jumped to attention. "Everything all right?"

"Just checking on everybody before I went to sleep." Debra paused, looked at each one of us, then took a swallow of her juice. She cleared her throat, wiped her face and pointed toward the garage. "It's late and my neighbors are sleeping. Move the car, Tyrel. Then come on back into the house, please."

I nodded. She'd been waiting in the shadows for a while.

Debra went on, "Shelby, we've got things to do in the morning."

Shelby said, "Okay."

Debra walked away, went up the two brick steps, closed the backdoor a little too hard. Not intentionally. Sometimes the door slammed because it needed some minor adjustments.

Richard was facing me, but his eyes were on his woman.

I inhaled some of the cool night air and exhaled the heat of a dragon. Since I remembered his voice, it was hard to pretend I didn't know. When I was pissed, the first thing on my tongue rolled out of my mouth, uncut and uncensored.

Shelby said, "Richard, let's go inside."

She headed across the grass. Her pace turned into a jog.

I opened the pack of Duracells, popped the back of the remote off so I could replace the weak ones. His energy was too close, I didn't feel him move, so I glanced his way again. His hands had stopped opening and closing. His passion was toward the house, sending his woman a meaningless gaze. A soft, weak stare. Then his mad-doggin' glare shot my way.

He was two inches taller, twenty pounds heavier. That didn't matter. One blow to the throat and he'd be wheezing and crying. It was a good thing Debra came out when she did. Seeing her put things in perspective, reminded me why I was here, and kept me from testing the waters. I spat on the ground and moved my anger toward the car.

He spat on the ground and held his position.

My expression said I wished he would. When he didn't take a step toward me, I blew him off, went about my business and started changing the weak battery in the flaky remote.

He made a grizzly sound, "I'll fuck you up."

I said, "You're a long way from home to be talking shit."

His fist doubled up. He took a short step.

I eased into the light. Six horizontal feet of mother earth lived between us. The face he gave, I gave back to him in harder granite. His eyes softened up like overcooked spaghetti. He flexed. Just as he opened his mouth to say something, Shelby yelled, "Richard!"

I whispered, "Your bitch is calling you."

"What?"

"Your best bet is to go on after your ho."

He swallowed, gritted his teeth. Richard moved backward a few steps, like he was reluctant to turn around.

Richard frowned. "Watch your back."

"Richard!" Shelby called again.

Richard double-timed and followed her into the house.

I mimicked·Shelby's fiancé: "What is up."

When I had first come out a few minutes ago, I'd stood like a soldier in the cut, lingered at the backdoor and heard snatches of their argument. I didn't mean to eavesdrop on purpose, but I did. From where I was, their conversation was low and fast, so I couldn't make out much anyway. They didn't hear me come outside because the backdoor didn't make any real noise that time. Debra had eased up behind me and caught me listening. She was lending an ear herself. Worry had piled on top of her worry. I hung out on the top step long enough to remember the cadence of Richard's speech. Long enough to realize he was trying to punk me in my friend's house.

Months ago, some fool had called my condo in Oak-town every hour on the hour. I'd answer, they'd hang up.

Once I answered and the brother said, "I'm going to be straight, *Mister* Williams. What's between you and my woman? I know she's been sneaking down to see you. So, what is up?"

"What is up?" I mocked and laughed. I was seeing Lorna, had broken off with the Transitional Team, and didn't know or care who he was talking about. He was try-ing to start a battle when the war was over, long after the smoldering ashes from the dying flames had been blown away. I was in a mood, so I played along.

"Coming down? No, she's going down."

He couldn't take a joke. "I'll find you and mess you up."

That threat hit a nerve.

"What's your name again? Dick John?"

"Richard Vaughn."

"First off, if she was with me, she must've been my woman. Might've been yours that morning, but that night—mine."

"Nigga—"

"Okay, Tricky Dick. Me and your girl had it going on, but I'm through with her now, so *chill*."

Richard started screaming obscenities; I moved the phone from my ear before he yelled me deaf. I put my TV on mute and got quiet. He quit yapping when he thought I'd hung up.

"You still there? Hello? Tyrel Williams? Hello?"

"Did I tell you she likes it doggie-style? Arf, *arf!* Bow wow-wow-wow, yippie-yo, yippie-yay!"

I hung up. The next couple of weeks he thought I was worth at least one hang-up a day. I did a *69, but his num-ber was outside the range. Eventually the calls tapered off. I had figured the lunatic phone call was about Lorna. I thought it was her jock with an itch trying to track her down for a rendezvous.

Richard didn't call back.

But he showed up here.

SHELBY

34

I left those fools outside and went into a house that was empty and quiet. Men are so confrontational, especially when there was nothing to be confrontational about. If you asked most brothers why they fought in a war, they couldn't tell you. Fought just to be fighting. Always trying to start some shit or ready to hop in some shit that somebody else started.

Anyway, most of the lights were off, and the only things that broke the darkness were the night-lights in the halls and the snippets of moonlight coming through the blue curtains in the kitchen window. That was a nice welcome quiet that made me glad that everybody had jetted off the property for the day.

I could've made it to the bedroom without another incident, but Alejandria called me. She was trying to get comfortable on a bar stool in front of the island. If she hadn't called my name, I wouldn't have slowed down enough to notice how different the kitchen looked. Top to bottom, it was spotless. That was enough to let me know I'd been outside too damn long. Dishes were stacked; garbage bags were tied. Everybody else had helped, and I was outside being public nuisance number one.

Bobby's wife was surrounded by pictures. I thought she had a few shots from her and Bobby getting hitched at the

White Chapel drive-thru in Vegas. I peeped over her shoulder right when I heard Richard coming up the back steps.

Alejandria asked, "Is this one you?"

It was a snapshot of me and Tyrel, one we'd taken at the L.A. Zoo. His leg was wrapped around me like he was climbing on me, and my tongue was stuck out while I laughed and crossed my eyes. That photo was old news, and I didn't care for the sight of it.

Before that bitch started answering his phone, I used to imagine that the first thing I'd do if I ever ran into Tyrel was speak, smile, shake his hand. If he welcomed that, then I'd give him a friendly hug. Something nice that started off as a sister hug and became a back-rubbing, ex-girlfriend embrace. And if he didn't pull away, I'd slip in a kiss on the cheek. If he was smiling by then, a soft kiss on his lips, maybe a slight of the tongue. I'd whisper "Obispo" and gracefully and sexily drift away without a peek back, leaving the ball in his court.

All of that noise was extinct.

"Yep, that was me." I said that so fast my words overlapped. In my next breath I was twisting my hair. "That was me."

"You look so pretty."

"Thank you."

The red numbers on the face of the coffeemaker said it was one a.m. I didn't think it was a second after ten. Without a word, I left her midsentence and sped toward the bedroom that me and my fiancé were gonna be sharing tonight. The back door shut kind of hard. When I peeped back, Richard had made it into the house and was peeping over Alejandria's shoulder. Looking down at my past. Staring at what used to be. Drooping his head.

As soon as I made it to the bedroom, I flopped at the foot of the queen-size bed. Lowered my head and hugged the back of my neck with the palms of my hand. Rubbed,

rubbed, rubbed. Richard closed the door when he came in, then sat near me.

"I'm sorry," Richard said. He was pleasant. Each syllable was filled with apology. "But I love you. And I want you."

I was so deep inside my own head that, well, I knew he was there, but I didn't realize he was that close to me until he started talking. He'd snuck up on me the same way Nancy the Nympho had done that time I was butt-naked in the sauna.

"I don't know what," he said, and ran his fingers up and down my leg, "but I know something's been going on between you two."

"Stop." I moved his hand. "Nothing's been going on."

I hopped up and went to the mirror so I could put some space between us. The scarf had loosened on my neck, showing me that the marks were just as bad as they were at sunrise. When I began combing my hair, Richard sighed and lay across the bed.

"One night I came over your place," Richard started, "and when I walked in, you were hanging up the phone. You hung up real quick. In fact, you slammed the phone down. You said you were surprised to see me so soon. You thought I was coming by later, and you said you were calling me to make sure."

Richard's reflection was in my face while he babbled. Whatever he was saying felt as interesting as listening to a six-year-old prattle. What he was saying was not new news. Richard usually came by my place late at night. As soon as we got engaged, he started popping up without calling, ringing my doorbell right after he closed up his shop. He did that so much, no particular night stuck out in my mind.

Richard laid on his back and closed his eyes. Guess he was tired of me studying him.

"At first I didn't think much about it," he continued.

"The next morning, you hopped in the shower. And I decided to check my answering machine. Since I was the last person you said you called, I pushed the redial button."

His circle dance was getting old. "Does this have a point?"

"It dialed more than my seven digits."

"And?"

"Tyrel answered the phone."

Something in me numbed, felt like I was having a stroke. The brush slipped from my hand. It fell on top of my foot, hardly made a sound. I know I called Tyrel, but only remembered one time for sure. When that bitch answered. That was a moment that changed everything. If she hadn't answered, I wouldn't have gone to Palm Springs with Richard a week later. I remembered being jealous, but I didn't remember slamming down the phone.

Richard was like the Energizer bunny, he kept on going. "I guess I walked in on you. I didn't mean to. And I wasn't snooping. Your door was unlocked. You knew I was coming over."

I tried to think of something to say, but nothing came out. He sat up, opened his eyes, and watched me. I looked away.

If Richard did redial Tyrel's number, that same heifer could've answered. Maybe Richard heard numbers and *assumed* I'd called Tyrel. It could've just as easily been Debra's number, because Richard never spoke to Leonard and wouldn't have recognized his voice. I'm not talking about the comical strong voice he used on stage, but the mild-mannered tone he had when he was kicking it at home and with his friends.

Yeah, Leonard could've answered the phone. It could've even been Bobby. Hell, Tyrel could've been here for all I know. It didn't take but a second to come to a conclusion;

he was bluffing. Either way, I was offended because he'd rummaged through my life and violated my privacy.

I said, "Richard, why are you lying?"

He shook his head. "That's the best you can do?"

Tyrel's bedroom door clicked open. Then it closed. I stopped doing whatever I was doing and looked in that direction. When my attention came back, Richard was smirking at my reflection. His eyes were still on top of mine, and I did my best to push them off.

Richard said, "Shelby, why're you looking so paranoid?"

"Why're you doing this?"

"If you don't believe me, run over there and ask him," Richard said. "But *you* already knew. *He* already knew. Both of you are just playing it off."

"There's nothing to play off. Since you claim to have talked to him, you'd know I haven't talked to him."

Richard raised his voice a little. "That's not what he said."

I said, "Why would he lie?"

"Why would he?"

"One of you is lying, and both of you are tripping."

"You're wrong. Both of *you* were lying. He just admitted it right in front of your face and you still won't be straight."

"What did he admit?"

Richard said, "That you two have been talking."

"No, he said it was nice to talk to *you* again, not me."

"Well, if you had never talked to him, then he would have never talked to me."

"I never talked to him."

"Maybe I'm wording the question wrong. Did he talk to you?"

Enough was enough. I opened my suitcase and jerked out a pair of pajamas, toothbrush, and toothpaste.

Richard asked, "You going to answer me or what?"

I threw my pajamas over my shoulder, then snatched out a container of Noxema to clean the hostile emotions from my face. My head throbbed with each heartbeat. Richard sounded muffled, like he was moons away from my life.

After I slammed my suitcase shut and threw it back into the closet, I headed for the door.

Richard asked, "Where are you going this time?"

I didn't answer.

I left the door open so he could see that I didn't stray in the direction of the tyrant's chamber. When I made it to Debra's door, I gave one last glower back to see if Tyrel was in the hall. He wasn't. And for a moment I hated both of those bastards. Then in the next beat, my face softened. I was relieved and disappointed.

Debra was snoring. Not much and not loud. I went around the bed and kneeled by her face, wondered what she was dreaming about. I used to always dream about my momma. Used to dream I was on the plane, working first class, and she was right there, on row one in seat A. Sitting and smiling at me. Whispering that she was proud of what I'd done with myself. She'd ask me for a hug, and I'd tell her I had to serve the other passengers first. I'd turn around and somebody like Blair Underwood or Robin Givens or Whitney Houston would be waiting for a refill on their champagne. And when I turned back around, Momma would be gone. I'd wake up so sad.

I wished I could get inside of my girlfriend's dream.

Debra smelled freshly showered; her skin was lit by the night-light on her side of the double sink inside the bathroom. My knees popped when I stooped. Debra didn't flinch. I watched my best friend for a couple of minutes. And I smiled. Then I pushed Debra's hair back and kissed her cheek. When I sat back on the floor, I heard a clock ticking on Leonard's side of the bed. I eased over and took the batteries out.

I whispered, "Peace."

After I showered, I threw Debra's paper plate with the half-eaten lasagna into the small plastic trash container inside the bathroom door, then slipped into the bed. I shifted around a bit, found comfort on a decent mattress, moved closer to Debra's warmth. I wanted to be alone, but didn't want to be by myself.

I always felt stronger when I was with Debra. More in control. It was a good thing Debra was asleep so I didn't have to blunder my words trying to explain or rationalize. But on the other hand, I hated that I was awake in the middle of the quiet because I was so absorbed in thought. Too many thoughts were rolling in too fast. Galloping in so fast it felt like each old one was being trampled by the new one.

For a long time I tried not to keep moving around too much and ended up on my back staring at the ceiling, marveling at how jacked up one life could be.

All of this madness would start again tomorrow.

Tonight I'm not gonna cry. And I'm gonna make myself sleep.

TYREL

35

I was with Leonard.

We were driving someplace I had never been before. A narrow road with blooming greenery on both sides. We were moving swiftly, but I didn't feel a breeze. There wasn't even a slight bumpiness in the pavement. A smooth ride. I couldn't tell who was driving or even if the car had a steering wheel.

Leonard was laughing hysterically as he recited some of his new material to me. I couldn't hear what he said, but I knew it had to be funny because I couldn't stop laughing.

Then it became bright.

Leonard smiled. "It's time for me to go back."

"Back where?" I shielded my eyes from the brightness.

Leonard gazed directly into the light. "To work. I'll save you and Debra and Shelby a table. Kiss Debra for me, all right?"

"Leonard?"

"And rub that belly too."

The light became brighter. Too brilliant for me to see. Then, just as quick as the light appeared, it vanished. It disappeared. When I moved my hands from my eyes, Leonard was gone. I tried to call his name. No sound came from my mouth.

———

I woke and glanced at the digital clock: 3:43 A.M. I knew I'd just dreamed something, but I couldn't remember what.

Debra was on my mind, and I had the urge to check and see how she was doing. See if she could sleep. If she was up crying. Maybe up pacing the floors. I went down the hallway to her room and put my ear to the door, didn't hear anything, then I pushed it open enough for me to stick my face in.

The thin beam from the hall night light fell across Shelby's face. She still slept on her back. She'd kicked the covers off her. Her legs were twisted and her hair tangled in her face. Paisley pajamas. I walked over to Shelby and looked in her face.

Without her makeup on she looked young and innocent. And I knew she was everything but virtuous. I put my finger on her bottom lip and gently pulled it down. It made a subtle popping sound when I let it go. I froze when she reached up and scratched her nose. Just as I started to back away, I wondered what it would be like to touch her lips again with mine. Wondered if she still tasted the same.

My lips touched hers, and I smiled through my sleepy eyes. Chocolate always tastes sweet. I kissed my fingertips, then lightly touched her face and ran them across her lips. Her mouth was open a little bit, so I put my finger inside and stole more of her nectar. Chocolate always tastes sweet. I looked down at her thighs and thought of repeating the ritual.

I went around to Debra's side and kissed her on the cheek. When I stood up to leave, Debra sat up and said, "Night, Tyrel."

Her voice was clear. She wasn't asleep.

I asked, "You okay?"

She made an unsure sound.

I scratched my butt and went back over and sat next to her. Rubbed her belly. She put her hand on my hand. Again, I asked her if she was all right.

"Yeah." She didn't open her eyes. "I keep waking up. You?"

I yawned. "Woke up a minute ago."

"I'm sorry." She patted my hand. "I must've woke you up when I checked up on you. Thought I heard you talking, and I clicked the light on for a second. I was worried."

"That's okay. Get some sleep."

"You, too. Night, baby."

When I opened the door, Richard Vaughn was standing in the dark, right outside his room.

I yawned, went back to my room. Fell asleep trying to remember my dream.

SHELBY

36

"You asleep?" Debra said.

Debra had been up since the crack of dawn. When her alarm-radio blasted on at five a.m., KJLH's *Front Page* kicked into my dreams. I woke up, tried to hold a conversation, but I dozed off before Cliff and Janine What's-her-face took over at six a.m.

"I'm up, I'm up."

Somebody else said, "Good morning, Shelby."

My vision cleared up a bit, then I wiped the slobber from my mouth and said, "Oh. Morning, Alejandria."

Bobby's wife was dressed up in a golden pantsuit and heels, mascara done *early* in the morning. Both smelled fresh.

Slobber slipped out of the corner of my mouth and spotted the pillow. I only did that when I was tired as hell. Stress was a burden to be reckoned with. They'd seen the circle of dampness, so I didn't deny it or try to hide it.

I stretched and yawned out, "What time is it?"

Alejandria said, "Almost eight."

Alejandria kissed Debra's cheek, then went out the door. Debra had on an oversized sweat suit; her hair was combed back. I guess everybody and their momma had been up for a while.

Debra kicked off her flat shoes. "Get up, sleepy head. The news people are coming by to interview me."

"Which news people?"

"*Entertainment Weekly.*" Debra's voice softened, "They're doing a thing on Leonard. I want to make sure it's done right. I don't want them to make it a black-being-wronged-by-an-Asian thing. I don't want to be exploited."

Her tone had more anger than I'd heard from her since I don't know when. It hit me like I was IV'ed to caffeine.

I said, "You gonna be okay with it?"

"I thought about it. Prayed on it. I hate the media."

"Why?"

"Can't trust them. They distort, hyperbolize, misquote, selectively print misleading information."

"That's their j-o-b."

"That's why I'm doing the interview."

"You're camera shy."

"That's why I want you guys there."

I didn't ask who *you guys* were. Before the tick made it to the tock, I saw some of that leftover attitude from the old days coming through. Looked like she was about ready to flip the script from being a diva and digress to a rug rat from Market Street. Then she went back to acting like the diva she was born to be.

The sun peeped through the vertical blinds. Debra was talking about getting her hair done, asking me how she should wear it for the interview while she browsed through her walk-in closet for something to wear. Then she stopped. Her heavy sigh made me get goose pimples. She was motionless, staring at Leonard's suits. I held my breath and tensed. Debra ran her fingers back and forth over each piece of clothing, touched the shoulders like he was still in them. Her fingertips grazed his belts. She sucked her lip in. Her shoulders slumped.

I went to her, moved her hands. I said, "Let me do that."

After I eased Debra back to the bed and sat her down, I brought out dresses, one by one. Debra shook her head if she liked what I had grabbed, did a serious sneer if she didn't. My mouth tried to fill the room with a sound other than the radio, but she was quiet. I talked as I yawned, said, "How long you been up?"

"Cover your mouth when you do that, please."

I yawned again. "Hush."

She covered her own yawn. "I've been up long enough for Alejandria to take me down to the funeral home. I had to drop off"—Debra swallowed—"drop off a suit."

"Why didn't you wake me?"

"I wanted to do it by myself," Debra said. "That blue dress is fine. You know how Leonard hates dark colors."

Once again, the cat had a serious grip on my tongue. I tried to be lively. "Yep. Bright colors and light women."

"I know that's right."

She was staring at her wedding ring. It became real awkward when silence took over the room. Then Debra was gazing at nothing. From where I was standing, her eyes were out of focus with the world.

"Debra?"

She jumped up and hurried into the bathroom. My heart thumped. I was thinking the worst, having visions of stress and miscarriage and all kinds of crap like that. I said, "You okay?"

Debra laughed. "I had to pee and didn't feel like moving."

She left the door open. I heard the sound of water breaking water. She started humming something. I exhaled, twisted my hair at the roots. Wondered and worried and worried and wondered about my best girlfriend. Tried to smile, but didn't own one at the moment.

I wondered why Debra didn't ask me why I had slept here. Why with a jealous fiancé and an arrogant ex-boyfriend so close, I'd crawled between her sheets and cuddled with her. But then again, she never asked me why I did much of anything. I guess I'd done that move so many times, had crashed at her side so many a night and kept her up talking while we watched videos, ate fattening microwave popcorn, chowed down pounds of Tolberone if either of us was on the PMS train. Kicking back in our undies doing the girl-bonding thing.

I stood at the closet door, leaned forward, peeped in-side. This time, with her out of the room, I was too scared to really commit to a long look. I took a breath, then made easy steps back into the closet, went to the side filled with things that belonged to a man. Gave myself time to take another breath before I held my hands out and touched Leonard's suits. Ran my fingers across his leather belts.

All of my memories were in the way back part of me, stuck on that night we met Leonard at Denny's. There was a light knock on the door. I jumped and moved away from the memories.

"Yeah," I said. "We're up."

I knew it had to be Richard, but it was Bobby. He had on blue gym shorts over his black biker shorts and a ma-roon Morehouse College T-shirt.

He said, "Where's Debra?"

"Pissing."

"You are so crass."

"It's a crass world."

"Debra!" Bobby yelled.

Debra yelled, "Can I have a minute to myself, please?"

Bobby told her the *Entertainment* crew would be here to set up at eleven. They wanted to finish by twelve-thirty.

Debra said, "Okay."

I asked Bobby, "Where are you going?"

"Running."

"How far?"

"Maybe five."

"Where?"

"Down at Dorsey High School."

"Let me get my stuff."

When I went into the bedroom, the curtains were drawn. The room was dark. Richard was sound asleep, which meant he'd been up late. Probably waiting for me. I grabbed my running shoes, borrowed some of Debra's biker shorts and an oversized white T-shirt. By the time I rushed into the living room, Bobby was on the floor, stretching.

"Let's roll," I said.

The doorbell rang just as Bobby put his hand on the doorknob. Bobby looked through the peephole.

I asked, "Who is it?"

He shrugged and pulled back one of his loose dreads.

When Bobby opened the right side of the double doors, an Asian girl was smoothing one hand over her jeans and black midriff shirt, like she was trying to make herself look decent. The girl looked middle-school young, and she jumped and dropped a book. Her leg wobbled a touch and she almost fell off the porch. She bent over and picked up her Thomas Guide.

"Good morning." That was Bobby.

I asked, "Are you with the news people?"

She wiped her face, put her eyes on the welcome mat. She opened and closed her mouth over and over, but nothing came out.

I said, "What can I do for you?"

She choked, cooed, covered her face. It was getting ridiculous. Before I knew it, I was shaken up and had bumped by Bobby and put my arms around the girl. Her shoulders were shaking like jelly. Shit. Pain was contagious. My throat felt snug and when I blinked, tears splurged out of my own eyes.

I kept saying, "Shhh. Don't cry. It's all right."

"I didn't m-m-mean to. Pleeease forgive me."

The girl whimpered and stuck her head deep into my chest. Held on so tight I got winded. I tried to ease her away from me. That didn't work. So I pushed her away from me. When I broke free, I stumbled back into Bobby. She almost collapsed before I found my footing. She was still wailing for us to forgive her.

I asked, "Mean to do what?"

"It . . . it was . . . an accident. I d-didn't mean . . ."

That was when I glanced at Bobby, then peeped out the door. An older Japanese couple were waiting in front of a sedan at the foot of the driveway. The old lady's hands were clamped over her mouth. The man was wearing a suit with no tie, and from what I could tell, was wiping his eyes, just like the girl.

Damn. A big fat wave of emotion tried to numb me, but I shrugged it to the side. Then it came back, rushed and chilled me from the top of my head down to my toes.

I held the girl at arm's length.

"Go get Debra, Bobby. Tell her to come here."

By then the girl had cemented her hands over her mouth. It didn't drown out all of her cries. Sounded like the regret was oozing out of her eyes and ears, echoing from her throat.

TYREL

37

There was a stampede outside my door. A set of hoofs raced down the hall yelling Debra's name. I grabbed my jeans from the foot of the bed and stopped putting the finishing touches on the obituary. I'd been up awhile, had gotten up when Alejandria and Debra were leaving.

A second later, Debra shouted, "In my house?!"

A calvary of feet raced toward the front of the house. When I stepped into the hall, shrills loud enough to break glass and shouts harsh enough to rock the house met me. Richard was to my right. He'd stepped out into the corridor and blocked my view. I moved right by him without a word, rushed toward the foyer.

Everybody was in front of the glass case filled with awards, facing pictures of Leonard and Debra that had been taken last month at Bobby's studio.

Debra screamed again, "Why?"

Shelby yelled, "Debra, no!"

Bobby was behind Debra, holding her back, begging her to calm down. Bobby's only about five-seven, so for him, holding Debra was like wrestling with a mule. Shelby was crying, protecting a teenage girl who was balled up like she was trying to make herself smaller than an ant. Debra tried to yank free from Bobby with each of her words. Each time she jerked, the girl flinched, blinked, yelped. The girl raised her palms to cover her face, then she dropped her hands like she wanted Debra to attack her.

"Answer me!" Debra's chest was rising and falling.

When the girl eased her hands to her side, sweat had waterfalled from her pale skin down over her eyes. She had the same tight eyes Leonard had. Only hers could open. Her black hair fell over her eyes, like it was giving her a hiding place.

"I'm sorry," the girl said. She became fixed on the pictures on the wall, then lowered her head. She wailed, "Forgive me . . ."

"Look at all the people you hurt," Debra snapped and wrestled away from Bobby. When she slipped free, I made a quick move and jumped between her and the girl, leaped at the same moment Shelby did. We collided, tripped. Shelby grabbed my arm for balance, then pushed my chest so I wouldn't knock her down. I twisted my ankle, and Bobby caught me. While we were off balance, Debra pushed Shelby to the side and Bogarded her way to the girl. Shelby dashed in between them again. Debra stopped and glared at the child. The heat from her eyes could have melted metal.

Debra held her hand out to the girl and said, "Come here."

Shelby looked at Debra, Bobby, me, then at Debra again.

Shelby pleaded, "Debra, no."

"*Move,* Shelby. I want her to come here."

Bobby nodded. Shelby stepped to the side. I moved too. The girl trembled like she'd been abandoned. Up the hallway, Richard was watching like he wanted no part of the scene.

The girl took baby steps toward Debra. Everyone had quieted. I was afraid of what Debra might do. I'd never seen Debra this vicious. But this was the first time she'd been in this situation. The first time any of us had had to face something like this. None of us had adjusted to the reality of the tragedy.

Debra took the girl's hand and slowly raised it.

"I want you to feel something," she said. Debra's body was peaceful, but her voice was disturbed.

She placed the girl's hand on the curve of her stomach.

The girl whimpered, dropped her head.

Debra said a turbulent "Look at me when I talk to you."

The girl raised her head fast enough to snap her neck.

Debra took the girl's other hand and gently placed it on her stomach and moved them around in a circle.

She said, "Feel that?"

The girl looked confused, then nodded.

"That's a baby inside of me. Leonard's child."

The girl was still nodding. Shoulders slumped. Head heavy.

Debra took her hand and led her to the pictures of Leonard, his friends and family. She put her hand under the girl's chin and brought her eyes to each photo. Calmly told her where they were taken, when. Debra took the girl's moist hand and put it back on her stomach, held it for a few seconds before her voice calmed.

"My husband will never be able to feel that again. *Never*."

The girl stopped twitching her head. She was rigid.

Debra said, "This baby will never, ever see his daddy. You know why? Because of you. You and nobody but you. Your stupidity has changed my life in a way that can't ever be fixed by your sorry-ass tears telling me how sorry you are. My husband was here with me a few days ago. Right here. Now he's dead. Little girl, you killed my husband. Messed up my life. Messed up my baby's. What do you think my future is now? Huh? Look at our friends."

Her eyes moved in fear when she gaped around at us. First back to Shelby. Then to Bobby. When she looked at me, I stared and her body rocked from my vibes. I'd never seen a murderer before, up close in person. Never wanted to. I had imagined that the person driving would look like the stereotypical Manson. This was somebody's pock-faced child.

Death had a face, and it looked like one of us.

I asked, "What's your name?" My voice sounded strange, felt strained. My face was wet.

She said, "Nikki Yamamoto, sir."

Debra moved Nikki's hands from her belly, "You're only nineteen."

"Yes, ma'am. I was celebrating my birthday, and my friends kept buying me drinks—"

Debra cut her off, "I don't want to hear. I don't care."

Nikki lowered her head, but jerked it back up and looked at Debra. Shelby moved over and eased her arms around Debra.

Shelby said, "Go sit down. The baby."

Nikki wobbled a little bit, then caught her balance. She said, "I want to apologize to everybody." Each word sounded awkward. Made me think she'd been up all night, practicing each word or pause. "I am so sorry. I know that there is nothing—"

"I'll never forgive you," Debra sliced into Nikki's dialect.

Shelby was wiping her face. Bobby too. So was I.

Debra said, "There is nothing you can say to me to make me feel better, so don't even go there. There's not a damn thing you can say to make me understand why you did what you did. Your crying won't make me feel sorry for you. When your tears dry, nothing will have changed."

Debra looked at each of us, straightened her posture and ran her hand across her auburn hair. She eased Shelby's hands off her shoulders, then stepped to Nikki.

This time Debra's voice was more political. "At eleven, news reporters will be here. If you want to do something, if you are sincere and are not here for show, be back here and talk to them. Tell them how you feel about what you've done."

She stammered and her eyes bucked. "Yes, ma'am."

"And after that, don't ever step foot on my husband's property again. Understand?"

Before the girl could answer, Debra put her hands to her own face and hurried toward her bedroom. Shelby followed. Richard was gone from the hall. Bobby opened the front door. Nikki bumbled out of the foyer with her head hung low enough to drag on the ground.

Me and Bobby stepped outside into the light. Nikki had made it down the stairs, into the mouth of the cul de sac, and was being comforted by an elderly Asian couple who looked like they needed comforting themselves.

"Tyrel! Bobby!" That came from behind us.

Shelby was in the French doors, her head sticking out.

"Debra said come inside and close the door. Now."

She let the door go and went back inside.

We headed back up the stairs. Nikki and her family walked back toward their car. Bobby put his hand on my shoulder and led me back into the house. I put my hand on his shoulder.

He asked, "You all right, Ty?"

I shook my head. "What about you?"

Bobby shook his head. Wiped his eyes.

SHELBY

38

I was on mile seven in the eighty-degree heat. I didn't slow down when Bobby had cramped up and faded, and that was almost three miles ago. My pace and pain were a bit too much for him. When his breathing had slowed and became controllable, he headed toward the bleachers and stretched.

Mile seven and a half.

I was passing runners left and right, but it didn't feel like I was moving. Everybody was less than a blur. I couldn't hear. I'd run a couple off the track on my last lap. The sweat on my back made my shirt stick to my skin and show off the outline of my sports bra. My shirt was clinging to my bubble butt. Stares were coming from brothers and Mexicans. I ran by lusty comments. That was the last I heard for a while.

I was gone. Spiraling deep inside my head. I wiped my face on the front of my shirt, kept on having a talk with myself.

Mile eight.

A damn bug flew in my nose. I coughed it out and sped up.

After Nikki left us shattered, I had sat on the bed and comforted Debra the best I could. She ranted and screamed about the nerve of that bitch. But even then, while Debra was going off, my thoughts were being dragged in a different direction.

Nikki was barely nineteen and had stepped up to the plate and confronted her troubles. She had looked at her problem, had been honest with her mistake, and had done it as soon as she could, didn't let it linger, did it face-to-face. If that girl had the address, she could've been a coward and just mailed a letter or an anonymous sympathy card. Or come in the middle of the night and left a note on the door. She took control, made a decision. Hell, by stepping inside Debra's house alone, Nikki had put her life on the line. And she didn't run when she felt the heat.

I was mad as hell, wanted to strangle the rug rat myself, but jealousy was brewing and bubbling over my bereavement. Resentfulness because of Nikki's character, the way she'd handled herself in a crisis. That made me disgusted with my own damn self. Nikki was honest. Couldn't help but respect that.

We thought she'd flake out and vanish until it was time for her to go to court, but she showed up with her shoulders slumped and a pack of tissues in her hands. When they interviewed Nikki, she didn't offer any excuses. Not a one. We all wanted to know how the hell she made it from the jail to the streets before Leonard's heart had barely taken its final beat. Her folks had some cash and had bailed her out before the blood had been rinsed away from the sidewalks. That girl sat by herself, aimed her bloodshot eyes right into the camera and said she was willing to accept her punishment. She said that on a tape that would air on national television before the sun had set.

Nikki had wiped her eyes. "I was wrong. I let my friends talk me into doing something that I already knew was wrong. I let my grandparents down and hurt a family. Forever. And I want to do whatever it takes."

The sister reporter asked, "Would you go to jail, or do you think it would be the proper punishment to do community service?"

"Whatever I deserve," she cried, "and more. There are no excuses for what I did. I will not make any. It was my fault."

Nikki said all of that in front of a crew of black people, in front of her family, in front of Leonard's family and friends. The *Sentinel* had sent a reporter and a photographer. So had the *Times*. Now, before another sunrise had dipped into an orange-colored sunset, everybody and their momma would recognize Nikki. She'd stepped up to the plate and created her own scarlet letter.

Mile eight and three quarters.

Every time my shoes met the ground, I asked myself about last night. Why couldn't I just tell Richard, "Yeah, I called Tyrel."

That wouldn't've killed anybody.

Part of my pisstivity was coming from the fact that it seemed like I was wading in the pool of life instead of swimming through. Just treading in the same old comfortable spot and avoiding any ripples. I'd had the same job for the last few years. The same safe position that kept me zooming from place to place and didn't leave enough mental space for me to stop and think about me. Debra said Tyrel had changed positions, had been promoted, and he'd moved into a different place. Debra'd jumped the broom and taken her existence to another level. Now my friend was widowed, but she was standing in the face of heartache and disaster with her head high and her shoulders back. This situation was another transition that would redefine my friend and our friendship. So much has happened. Everybody had changed.

Here I was being the same old Shelby. Still confused and making bad decisions every chance I got. Waking up smiling like life was fine. Not being honest with myself or anybody else.

I picked up the pace. Punished myself a little more.

I was on a mission, running away from dark parts of me and chasing the things I'd never brought into the light. For a second I thought somebody was slapping my booty. It was the heels of my Reeboks hitting my backside with my hard strides.

Another lap. The pain was deep. I wanted to scream like a slave being branded.

After the interview, Debra pulled Nikki to the side and had a talk with her off camera. Debra apologized for her harshness. She thanked the kid for doing the right thing. Told her that Leonard would smile on her for that. Then she told her again not to step on her property.

I've never known what made Debra so strong. I had strength, but mine didn't feel like it had that kind of depth.

After the camera crew cleared, Debra changed and left with Tyrel. It didn't take much talking to convince Debra to go by the clinic and have Faith check on the baby. When I told Richard I was going running, he had an attitude furrowing in his brow, but I blew him off and told him to hang out with Alejandria. She had to go downtown, then into Watts to pick up a picture that Debra wanted on the obituary. Richard got dressed and tagged along so he could see some of the inner city.

After they left, I ran out of the house. Bobby followed.

Two more laps of pain and suffering.

I refused to allow thoughts of any man—or woman—invade my mind. Refused to allow anybody to drive what I needed into my life.

Mile nine and some change.

I stopped. Didn't slow down. I just did a Forrest Gump and stopped. My body had been begging me to give it up, turn it loose, because I'd run far enough from whatever I was leaving behind and had almost caught up with whatever the hell I was chasing. The numbness in my head faded when I walked around the track once. People were in the stands, applauding and whistling. I looked around to see what the hell was going on, then I realized that I'd been the show. Bobby was in the stands leading the woof, woof, woof thing. Nothing could make me smile. I wiped my face, dropped my head, put my hands on my hips, then walked on by with my thoughts, soggy T-shirt, and drenched spandex. Kept moving around the track. Kept going in circles.

"You one bad sister," a brother huffed as he went by.

Weak-minded brothers always felt obligated to say something when nothing needed to be said. I stayed in the slow lane, kept my eyes on my feet, and let the slowpokes jog on with their lives.

Somebody whacked me on my butt. That felt like a man's hand. Did the same crap that Bryce used to do. I jumped around with my fists doubled up, arm cocked, ready to throw down.

"Whoa!" Bobby said and jumped back. A few people in the stands laughed. I flipped him off and kept on trucking.

"Looks like you're ready for a wet T-shirt contest." Bobby tried to make eye contact. "Feel better?"

"Don't ever do that again."

I was in the middle of enduring pain and numbness. Felt like my legs were swollen. Feet ached. My lower back throbbed. I put my right hand on my waist for support. Obliques cramped. Throat was dry as Bobby's conversation. I licked my lips and tried to spit. My insides were so dehydrated, dust came out. All my lotion had been sweated away, so I had to be ashy as hell.

Bobby said, "You're limping."

"Legs hurt."

He took my hand, led me over to the grass, and made me stretch my calves and hamstrings. Bobby was running his mouth. I stayed in my world and let him have that conversation by himself. I wasn't ignoring him. I just wasn't with him.

Bobby's mouth was dried around the edges. He scratched the top of his scalp, dug under his dreadlocks and asked me, "Wanna talk about it?"

I whispered, "No."

We walked forty minutes back to Leonard's house in silence. By the time we made it up the hills, soreness and stiffness were taking control. All of it was a new pain, and I made myself welcome it under my backache and grimace.

I limped into Debra's room, closed the door. After I stripped to my skin, I filled the master bathtub with hot water and Epsom salts. Soaked and listened to some Marvin Gaye.

Mercy, mercy, me. Thangs ain't what they used to be.

TYREL

39

From the Christopher Columbus International Freeway—the 10—smog was thick enough to make both the Griffith Park Observatory and the Hollywood sign disappear.

We were riding eastward and sweating in the sixty-five m.p.h. breeze. Debra cranked up my Brand New Heavies

CD and let the ear candy lead us around the southbound exchange to the Harbor Freeway. Traffic was thick and Mr. Heat wasn't a joke, so I jumped off at Manchester, slowed down long enough to pull into the car wash and get the road stains and streaky smudges washed away.

Back on the road, Debra tapped my arm. "Thirsty."

Graffiti-tagged trees, monikers etched in street poles. Debra pointed at a Boys Market up the street. I headed that way. In the store's lot, Debra looked at the armed security guards, craned her neck toward the wrought-iron fences around the parking area. Every store had armed-and-dangerous foot security patrolling behind fifteen-foot gates. Some lots had barbed wire.

Debra said, "Paint must be a good thing to invest in."

"Why do you say that?"

"Stores sell the kids paint to spray the graffiti, then sell the businesses paint to take it down."

After we got the bottled water, I hopped back into the car and said, "You've got an hour before your appointment."

Debra's eyes were glued to my dash. "Head down to 107th."

Minutes later, we were parked outside of the Watts Tower of Simon Rodia. Debra was still staring at my dash. Her eyes went to my steering wheel, then her attention went back to the dash.

I asked, "What's wrong?"

She sniffled and shook her head.

Her hand reached out and felt the grooves where my passenger-side air bag was installed. She'd been staring at the one on my side too. She massaged the dash, patted it, eased her hand away, then did her best to smile while she turned off the music.

We were on a narrow street lined with stucco bungalows. I let the top up, kept the engine running, and tuned the air conditioner to sixty-five degrees. Traces of water left over from the car wash rolled down the window like tears.

The African-American center was down a narrow street in an area that was damn near all Hispanic. A crowd of brothers were standing around talking, sipping drinks from containers hidden in paper bags. I pushed a button and made sure all the doors were locked. Then I thought about what I'd just done. I shook my head at the irony of how, when we stopped around a crowd of my own people, my guard went up. But like the man said, stupid is as stupid does. If a brother had jacked Rosa Parks, then nothing and nobody was sacred. Everybody was up for grabs.

I asked, "What are you thinking about?"

Debra smiled, rapped her fingers on her leg and said a wispy, "Poetry readings. Kite-flying. Storytelling."

"Nice." A second later she sighed. I asked, "You okay?"

"I was thinking about how most of our neighborhoods have turned Mexican, that's all. There're no real black areas."

Debra wore a something's-on-my-mind expression. I waited for her to get to the point she was creeping up on.

She put her hand on my hand. "Be honest with me."

I said, "Okay."

"Did I sound prejudiced today? When they were talking to me about what I felt, did I sound prejudiced?"

I shook my head and held her hand. "No. You sounded like somebody who was hurt. Sounded real. That's all."

We sat and held onto each other.

Debra nodded, bit her top lip with her bottom teeth. She said, "Good. I'd hate to send the wrong message. It was Nikki that fucked up. If people thought I was mad at her people, it would make everything be in vain."

A couple of people were in Faith's office. Soft jazz played over the intercom. Peaceful, soothing. No security prowling.

On the way over, Debra didn't say much. But she didn't look like she wanted to cry either. I knew she was troubled because she wasn't changing the radio from station to station like she always does. Like Leonard always did.

Faith peeped over the counter and rushed to greet us.

"Come on in," Faith said, then hurried over and shook my hand. "Hello, Tyrel. Nice to see you again."

"Hi, Faith."

"I thought you wanted me to come by the house," Faith said as she ran her hand over a gray spot in her short Afro. "Are you all right? I was just about to drive up to your place, since I hadn't heard from you."

"I needed to get some air," Debra said and handed me her purse. "Hell had broken loose."

Faith said, "Something wrong?"

"I'll tell you what happened. Make sure my baby's okay."

Faith asked, "How's the family holding up?"

"Everybody's fine. The rest of my family is driving in tomorrow. Leonard's family got in this morning, and they called right after I finished the interview."

Faith looked at me. "When's Shelby coming?"

My head tried to lower with the weight of resentment, but I held on to a blank face, sent my eyes to Debra.

Debra saved the day and said, "She's already here."

I waited for Debra to tell Faith that Shelby was here, at my best friend's house, shacking in a bedroom with her fiancé.

"Good," Faith replied. "Alejandria was in for a checkup this morning."

I headed toward the lounge room that had a small

radio/television. Faith took Debra into an examination room.

Fifteen minutes later, we were on the road again. I drove her over to Hyde Park to see the rest of Leonard's family, the ones they hadn't heard from since they'd loaned them some money. We got there just as they were on their way to see Debra. She told them she had some more errands to run and would meet them later. They wanted to help, but Debra told them everything was under control and wanted them to relax as much as they could. The looks on their faces said they didn't understand why Debra was doing so much, but they didn't force the issue.

We were heading back to the house when Debra said, "I'm not ready to go back."

I still had the passkey to the hotel in my glove compartment.

When we got in the room, Debra went to the bathroom. She came out with a wet towel over her face and lay across one of the beds. I took my shoes off and relaxed across the other. She'd pulled the thick curtains back just enough to leave a streak of day lying across the room. The window was closed, so the noise rising from Sepulveda Boulevard and the 405 was shut out.

"Tyrel?"

"I'm here."

"Your feet stink."

I laughed.

She giggled. "I'm joking."

"Good."

She clucked her tongue. "What do you think about Richard?"

My chest expanded. I said, "What?"

"*Don't* do that. Shelby always does that same shit."

"Sorry about that."

A second later she said, "Well?"

"I guess that he's what she wants. They make a good couple."

"Nice general answer, but not to the specific question I asked." Debra sang, "Well?"

"I don't know what to say."

"Say what you feel, and stop being such a man."

I rested on the bed in silence for a few moments, thinking.

She said, "What's the first word that came to your mind when I said his name?"

I eventually said, "Jealous."

We held on to the peace and quiet for a while.

She said, "There were so many things I wanted to say to Leonard. And I did. He knew exactly how I felt, and I knew how he felt. We weren't afraid to tell each other how we felt. Mad, we'd say it, talk about it, and get over it. Knowing that is part of what keeps me going. I have no loose ends so far as that's concerned. When I cry, it won't be because of some coulda, woulda, shoulda bull. It'll be because I miss and love him."

Debra didn't move or say anything for the next thirty minutes. She fell asleep. I did too. When I woke up, Debra was on the phone.

"Who else?" she asked. "Okay. Yeah, I want Stevie to sing. When did he call? His people called? Why couldn't he call? One song will be fine. Keep it simple and short. I don't want it to turn into a circus. What time did the insurance company call? Set an appointment for next Saturday. Put Shelby on the phone."

Debra saw I was awake, smiled, then went back to talking.

"Hey, selfish. What's wrong? You sound funny. You sure? I'm at a hotel with Tyrel. Call the funeral home and tell them to pick up all the flowers that were delivered. No, don't take them down. And confirm the jazz band. Make sure we have everything we're going to need for the celebration at the house tomorrow afternoon. Tell them don't start CP time either. Who's in the house? Lock my bedroom door, and make sure they don't steal shit."

Debra pointed at the television. I wandered over, turned it on. She whispered, "No, the radio. Jazz."

Debra hung up the phone and lay back on the bed. "Bobby and Shelby are returning all my phone calls. People have been in and out all day. Leonard's folks are there but are about to leave and go visit some more people."

I opened the curtains and gazed across the 405 freeway. Glanced toward Dan L. Steel, then toward the condo I used to lease. Sometimes it felt like I still lived there. All of the dreams I had while I was in San Francisco were about L.A.

Debra let out a long scream. When I turned around she was stretching, with a sunny grin on her face.

"You're going to be the baby's godfather. Shelby's going to be the godmother," Debra said matter-of-factly, like she'd just made a critical decision. "I want this family to stay together."

"Okay."

Debra rubbed her hands over her stomach like she was soothing the itching from her stretching skin. She straightened her clothes then played patty-cake on her belly.

She said, "Let's go before somebody starts some rumors."

SHELBY

40 **After** the funeral home had picked up the flowers, I loosened the scarf around my neck and
headed toward Leonard and Debra's bedroom.
Richard called my name over the music when I
left the den, but I let my sashay lead me away. Walked
through the wafting flower smell, closed and locked the
bedroom door while my name was being called again. I
popped a mint, grabbed my clippers, polish remover, sat on
the bed, pretended I didn't hear him when he knocked.

I caught a cramp when I tried to fold my legs under me.
It hurt like hell, and when I snatched my feet from under
my butt, I kicked the purse off the bed. It bounced across
the floor and my stuff went every which-a-way: cosmetics,
perfume, a sewing kit, and six dollars in change. That was
my laundry money. When you lived the apartment life, a
bag of quarters was a necessity.

Richard called my name over and over like it was the
word of the day. He was wearing it out. He did a few more
soft knocks.

A minute after that, his footsteps faded back down the
hallway. By then I was topless in front of the full length
mirror, unbuttoning my Levi's, stopping to touch my neck
three or four times. The scarf I'd been wearing was on the
dresser.

I put a little thought into it, then draped the paisley
scarf around my neck again. Practiced smiling just to see
how silly I'd been looking all day. Then I let go of the scarf,
let it fall in the trash can, and went to the window. No smile
on my face, just a bunch of thoughts rattling inside my
head. Heard them clinking like a pocketful of change.

When I got down to my birthday suit, I slipped into my

dark green unitard. No shoes. No bra. No makeup. No scarf. Hair barely combed. I didn't give a—. I was tired of this game.

By the time I made it back to the den, the music had stopped. Maybe it screeched to a halt when I walked into the room. It was a little on the quiet side, so I stooped in front of the Panasonic and put on a Sade CD, let it flow through the Bose speakers anchored to the walls. It was the one room in the crib that was never clean for too long, mainly because it was the kind of room that wasn't meant to be too clean. It wasn't dirty, just looked comfortable and lived in. Like a home.

The den was my favorite part of the house because it reeked of intelligence. Wall to wall, it was filled with Leonard's and Debra's books. New books that smelled of fresh knowledge; old books with the scent of wisdom. Debra's bookcase reached from the floor to the ceiling, lined from end to end with small plants. Magazines were on the bottom shelf, and the other rows were filled with everything from Morrison to Mosley to Shakespeare to Ice Berg Slim to Cummings to Dickinson.

Anyway, when I bent over to find some uplifting music Richard shot me a hard look. He was on the sofa watching TV. A few people were here a while ago, but now the only loiterers were a couple of the not-too-funny comedians, Kwamaine and Perry. They'd dropped by to leave word for Debra that they had set up a tribute to Leonard at the Color of Comedy. That part of the celebration was happening later on tonight. The brothers had stopped chewing their food and started gawking at me the moment I'd sashayed back into the room.

Richard's mouth was tighter than a mummy. One look at the brothers lounging in the room should've let him know they would never be my type. Perry was five feet tall and dressed in oversized designer everything, so he looked like a walking billboard from head to toe. Kwamaine was a beanpole, about six-two, and barely had enough meat on his bones to hold up his baggy jeans.

"All right, Kwamaine. I told you about staring at me like that. If you can't respect me, get out."

"Aw, Miss Thang." Kwamaine shook his head and took another bite of his turkey sandwich. "I wasn't looking at nothing."

Perry cackled, "If that's nothing, I hate to see something."

Grunting and throat-clearing sounds came across the room, loud and clear. Richard moved over enough to block Perry's view, then glared at me and once again cleared nothing from his throat. Instead of counting my mistakes, I should've been counting the times Richard had done that since we'd been together.

I went to Richard, stood toe-to-toe and tilted my head. "Richard, is something in your throat?"

Richard grunted, "No."

"Then stop doing that. It irritates the hell out of me."

When I turned to sashay away, he put his hand on my shoulder. He lowered his voice. "Why're you dressed like that?"

"Problem?"

Richard dropped his shoulders and ran his fingers through his beard. "Shelby, you shouldn't be half-naked in front of these kind of brothers."

"What kind of brothers are you talking about, Richard?"

He tsked and had the nerve to sharpen his tone, like he was talking to somebody's child. "I can see your nipples. Your outfit is hugging your crotch kind of tight too."

Well, I guess my clothes did fit like a glove and made my coochie look like a fist. A nice-sized one too. Never noticed that. Cooch must've been mad and ready to hit somebody.

Richard gave me an aren't-you-gonna-change? frown. You know what I did? Said forget the dumb stuff, grabbed my bosom, fell into a bodacious you-want-summa-this? stance, turned and looked at everybody: "Does anybody have a problem with what I'm wearing?"

Perry's eyes bucked out and the brother choked on his soda. "Lawd help us all, you go, girl!"

"Naw, babe!" Kwamaine smiled. "You straight."

"You all that and a bucket of hot wings," Perry added as he straightened up and high-fived Kwamaine.

"Babe, you all that and ain't nothing left for nobody."

I playfully raised a hand. "Thank you for the competitive vernacular, my brothers. Now keep your eyes off me."

Everybody except Richard laughed.

I skipped like a preschooler back over to Leonard's desk and sat down in front of the computer. E-mail was coming in left and right. Before I could see if it was anything Debra should know about, a sharp pain woke up my calves. Time for some ibuprofen.

I must've looked too happy and had too much space, because Richard dragged a small chair across the carpet, parked in my real estate, and sat next to me. I picked up the phone, made sure the limo and band and whatever and whoever were confirmed.

For a minute I was back at Momma's grave site, wishing she could've been sent off with a celebration, instead of sad songs and dark colors and a handful of people surrounding what was starting to turn back into dirt.

Those thoughts went away when Richard touched my elbow. I didn't pull away. He leaned over and kissed my cheek.

He was glaring at my neck like he was a carpenter who'd just finished building the house of his dreams. My emotions switched gears. What was on my mind now was that struggle. That battle for control yesterday, early in the a.m. If I could've kicked myself for letting him do that to me, I would've. Better yet, I should've been kicking him.

He touched my neck. Rubbed all three spots like he was making a wish. I moved his hand away.

"Don't worry," I said. "All of it's still there."

Alejandria walked Perry and Kwamaine out. Richard exhaled and rubbed his neck. Alejandria came back, took out two novels, and relaxed against Bobby. They kissed, whispered a few words to each other, then kissed again before she opened one of her books.

"We haven't kissed since we got here," Richard said. Now he'd eased his hand on my leg. Started massaging. He winked and dropped his voice an octave. "I hope you're not going to sleep with Debra tonight. I want my wife-to-be in my arms."

He was trying to get his mack on, and I was thinking about how he kissed. All tongue. No technique. No emotion. Never kissed just to kiss; only kissed if he was trying to get some. Another one of those brothers who tried to seduce without romanticizing. It hadn't really mattered before today, but that was another thing I'd tolerated and settled for. Which goes to show that sometimes the things you hoped would get better with time never changed because they were already at their best.

Tyrel kissed slow and deliberate. Used to anyway. Sucked on my neck just because. Made my breasts feel like the best thing on my body. And when his wicked tongue found its way and dropped me off in a land called ecstasy, it was always like he was talking to me. And it wasn't a hit-it-and-quit-it thang. His tongue had a rhythm that took me deep into the night. Shit, I was getting the shudders just thinking about it.

Richard leaned closer. "You'll be with me tonight, right?"

"Why?"

"You're my fiancée. Do I need a reason?"

"Depends. Something wrong?"

"I need some attention."

"Oh? So what you're saying is you're horny."

Richard said, "Yeah. I want you with me tonight."

"Anything else?"

He leaned over and whispered, "I feel out of place. You haven't spent any time with me since we've been here. I understand the situation, but don't leave me stranded."

I used to really like that selfishness about him. How he wanted me. That greed for me showed up at a time I was indifferent about everything and didn't feel wanted by anybody. The truth be told, I couldn't get my shadow to show up on a sunny day. So I needed and deserved that kind of attention. What's jacked up is, well, it's odd how the things that attracted me to somebody could be the exact things that pushed me away.

I opened a manila folder and said, "I'm here for Debra."

"I know, I know." Richard lowered his voice, sent his eyes and wonderment toward Alejandria and Bobby, then eased toward me. If I didn't know any better, I'd think he was trying to mimic the passion they were sharing.

The phone rang and Alejandria went out to get it. Richard said, "And I don't feel comfortable being here with your ex in the next bedroom. I told you the shit he said about you. He called you a bitch, said you were a ho. And now you're walking the halls half-dressed."

I said, "Tyrel's already seen me butt-naked on payday."

His tone sparked. "Why'd you say something like that?"

I did one of his numbers: cleared nothing from my throat.

Richard groaned and gave me a harsh look. Then his face softened, became almost childlike.

He said, "We shouldn't be here, not with him here."

"You're right. We shouldn't be here."

Richard's eyes were calling me, but my emotions were off the hook. He gave up a devilish grin, and that was when I saw how much he favored his Nutty Professor–looking momma. He was lurching the same way she did the day he asked me to be his forever.

Richard ran his fingers through my hair.

I said, "Why you so touchy-feely all of a sudden?"

He shrugged, "I was worried about you when you didn't open the bedroom door. What was up with that?"

"I was busy." I moved his hand away. "And I'm busy now."

Alejandria came back yakking in Spanish on the cordless phone. She was barefoot, had on black biker shorts and an oversized T-shirt. No bra, and she had C-cup breasts.

Richard gave me a break just long enough to watch Alejandria. She went to Bobby. They looked happy. I felt it too.

Richard asked, "Why are you smiling so hard?"

"Better than me frowning. Does my happy face bother you?"

"What is up with you?"

I laughed. Laughed damn hard too.

Richard's eyebrows furrowed. The brother was confused. Especially when I turned my chair and faced him so fast he jumped. I gave him my sexiest smile, cruised my brown eyes from his head to his feet. Ran my fingers over his beard. It used to feel good against my skin, but now all I could think of was that it always scratched the hell out of my face.

I asked, "What do you see in me?"

Richard twisted his expression. "What do you mean?"

"Why do you want to be with me the rest of your life?"

Richard made seven bewildered faces. "I love you."

"That's it?"

"*That's it?*" His eyes moved closer together. "What's more important than my love for you?"

"All right, fine. You love me. But who am I?"

"What?" Richard strained his face like he was trying to improve his hearing.

I put my face so close our noses touched. I repeated, "Who am I?"

Richard whispered, "What's wrong with you?"

I jumped back when Debra stuck her face inside the room. Tyrel was behind her. Richard's hand was slipping back and forth over my leg. I backed away from Richard and made his hand fall free. He put it back. Debra was at the top of the three stairs, rubbing her belly. Her skin was clearer, and my girl came across as being focused, almost as if she was coming to terms with all of the feelings I'd been avoiding.

Debra said a perky "Hello, everybody."

Tyrel's dull expression fell across me and Richard. My fiancé squeezed my leg. Tyrel turned around, moved away from the door. What made me feel more bad than bad was that after all the friendship we shared, I hadn't really seen Tyrel without gazing through my own neurotic eyes. I hadn't respectfully looked into his face while I was calm enough to shake his hand and give him a kind word. We shared the same pain but we hadn't shared condolences. No matter how much he despised me, part of me wanted to gossip with him and see how he was doing, ask how he'd been, regardless of what Richard thought.

Those thoughts dried up when Richard scooted closer and ran his palm up and down my thigh.

"Tyrel?" I called his name over a lump in my throat. Richard's hand stopped moving. He didn't let go, he just eased off, acting like a squatter with no rights.

Tyrel stuck his head back into the doorway. First he looked down toward Alejandria. Debra had already waddled down into the den and was hugging everybody, reassuring us that she was fine. Richard tried to ease his hand closer to my crotch.

I spoke my gentlest. "Richard, don't do that."

When I moved his claw, he said, "Why?"

I hissed out, "Because Shelby said don't do that."

I was damn nervous, but I made it to my feet and sauntered toward the bottom of the steps. My head lowered a touch so I could mark a spot to stop in front of Tyrel. With each step, with every forward movement of my hips, I slid my agitated hands over my hair, then twisted my neck until it popped twice. Before I knew it, I was under the breath of an ex-lover. Standing beneath a fresh pair of designer jeans, hiking boots, pullover shirt. Had stumbled into the zone occupied by Tyrel's manly-sweet aroma. Tyrel used to wear body lotions with soft fragrances. He'd switched from colognes after I'd bought him some Red Musk lotion. I'd pick out light fragrances, beautiful scents that we'd have to be intimately close to appreciate.

I stared at his dimple and didn't know what to say. I asked, "How are you holding up?"

Tyrel's barren gaze went to Richard. Behind me, the room was quiet as hell, like they were waiting for a bomb to blow us all away. Then I heard the creases in Richard's jean shirt snapping, but I refused to look back. Wouldn't be turned around this time.

"Tyrel," I spoke with a soft, professional voice. "I asked you a question."

Tyrel's focus came back to me. His eyes made me nervous as hell, and I shifted my weight a time or two.

Dropped my head a little, just enough to steal a view of his bowlegs.

"Okay," Tyrel responded. "I took Debra to the doctor."

"That was sweet of you."

"What are you doing?"

"Returning phone calls."

"Want me to do that? You and Richard can take a break."

"No, but thanks." I barely moved my lips, hardly opened my mouth wide enough for the words to slip out, "How do you like it up in San Francisco?"

The small talk felt so big. Thought the words would be impossible, more difficult than they were, or what I had to say would wither away before I'd traveled this far.

Tyrel was staring at me, strange and strong.

I said, "What're you looking at?"

"Your neck."

Damn. I forgot. My hand came up so fast, I slapped the spot like I was swatting a mosquito. Added damage to the damage. I would've turned purple, but by then Richard had moved next to me, and was touching the small of my back with his hand. The little smile I had ran away, but my cool stayed behind.

I turned to Richard and released an easy "What's up?"

"What is going on?" Richard asked. His eyes were moving like he was watching a tennis match at the French Open, darting from me to Tyrel. Then Richard said, "What happened this morning?"

I said, "We did an interview. You saw us."

He turned to Tyrel, "What happened?"

Tyrel paused for a second, then moved his worn gaze from Richard and said, "Debra, I'll be back in a little while."

"No, you're not going," I said. "Tyrel, we were talking."

Tyrel made some disgusted sound. Richard kept bumping up against me. The world wasn't big enough, so I stepped to the side to gain some space.

"Richard." I said his name with my eyes on his fists. Richard's eyes followed mine. He opened his hands. My head was heavy. Nerves tingled. I blew air and frowned at Richard.

"What's going on?" Richard's tone was getting a bit too demanding. Damn loud. A bit too strong.

"Don't raise your voice to Shelby," Debra snapped. "Not in my house."

Debra had hopped her beach-ball belly up and was over there with her arms resting on the top of her stomach. Tapping her foot to the beat of her anger.

"Debra, chill," I said. "All right?"

Even Alejandria had a vicious glower in her eyes. Things were getting trippy, so I eased my hand in a downward motion, like I was a choir director. Alejandria sucked her lips in and cradled back into her man's arms.

"I apologize," Richard said while he kept running his hands over his hair. "This is an awkward situation. I don't want to say anything, but it's hard when everything is right in your face."

"Shelby—" Bobby said.

"Everybody, I'm okay. It's okay," I reassured. And damn, I was surprised at how calm I was. I hadn't raised my voice once.

"You okay?" Debra asked. She came to me. "What's wrong?"

We held hands. I had a hard time finding my voice. "I'm *really* sorry for being such a problem. I'm sorry for bringing all of this shit to your house."

"It's okay." Debra squeezed my hand. "That's your style."

"No, it ain't."

Richard stuck one hand in his pocket; the other was on his chin. His momma wasn't here, so he couldn't control the situation. Even if Mrs. Vaughn was here, it wouldn't matter. I had things to say, only I didn't know how or where to begin, how to drop the four-letter words and phrase what was brewing and boiling in my heart in a reasonable way.

I used my sweetest Shelby voice and sang, "Richard?"

"Yeah?" He stopped pinching his flesh. "You all right?"

"Come with me, sweetheart."

I sprang up the stairs and bumped by Tyrel without raising my eyes. All I left behind was a weak, "Excuse me."

Richard followed my swift pace, and we headed through the kitchen and straight outside. I'd crossed the grass by the time Richard came through the back door.

I yelled back, "Pull the door up behind you, please."

My feet led me to the pool area, through the gate. The deck smelled like chlorine, fresh-cut grass, and a hint of smog. The concrete felt cool under my bare feet. It wasn't until then that I slowed long enough to dip each foot into the pool. Then I pressed each into the concrete and left my footprints behind. My eyes checked out my chest; my nipples were sticking out like two happy raisins.

Richard snapped, "What's this all about?"

There was always a little something about his voice that made me feel like I was being challenged. I don't know how he did it, but he had a way of making me soften my words or change my mind about what I wanted to say. That shit wasn't gonna happen today.

After he closed the gate, I moved closer, looked him in

the face, and got ready to let my mind flow out over my tongue.

There wasn't much of a breeze now, and cumulus clouds were dawdling in the sky. It wasn't dark yet, but the moon was in full bloom. The moon was facing the sun. I wondered what that meant. A DC-10 breaking through the clouds and heading toward LAX could barely be heard. And a helicopter was flying close by, probably hounding somebody down in the Jungle.

I cut to the chase. "I lied to you, but I didn't lie to you."

He paused for a second, jerked like he was jarred, then asked, "What do you mean?"

"I mean I lied to you. I called Tyrel."

"When?"

"Oh, I dunno." My voice had no real feeling. Numb. I shrugged, "I called him. Maybe twenty, thirty times. Fifty times. Like I said, I dunno. I lost count. Sometimes I'd call from home. I used my calling card and called him from your house a time or two—sorry 'bout that. Sometimes I'd get the urge and call when I was on a trip. But I *never* talked to him."

"You called him, but you didn't talk to him."

"I'd listen to his voice on his answering machine—"

"From my house?"

"—or if he picked up, I'd get scared and hang up."

"You called him." Richard rocked side to side. Everything about him—his posture, his voice, all of it weakened. His face started to shine, glowing with the sweat that was collecting on his forehead. His voice was rigid, but it didn't faze me. He said, "I already knew. I looked over your phone bills."

"Hold up. You read my phone bills? You were rummaging through my stuff."

"I had to know. Something wasn't right, and I did what I felt like I needed to do. And when I did, I saw your calls to San Francisco. Plus you still had all of the stuff he gave you, all of that bullshit you lied and said you'd thrown away is tucked in the back of your closet. You ran up here every chance you got, never gave me a number where I could reach you. So, it's not like I didn't have a reason to be suspicious."

Right about now my mouth was open like I had lock-jaw. A fresh wave of heated anger was on the way. My chest burned, rose and fell like a lung was ready to pop. If he'd gone through my bills, that probably wasn't the only thing he'd rummaged through.

I said, "Thought you pushed redial?"

He shrugged. "I made that up. Wanted to see what you were going to say."

"So you thought this was some sort of a game?"

"This isn't a game."

It all came back. Every time I thought I heard him driving by my bedroom window. Then of the nights I'd get late-night hang-ups. But I wasn't gonna let my resentment slow me down. This buffet was already on the table. It was time to feast before the food got cold.

I said, "Yeah, I called. But we never talked."

Richard's voice cracked. "Why didn't you?"

"I was afraid."

Richard opened his arms and stepped toward me. "Shelby."

I snapped my hand up with my arm extended. The place was serene, but I felt like thunder and lightning. He kept his distance. Richard slid his hands over his butt, then looked around as if he was trying to see if anybody else was outside. My arm stayed out until he took a step back and softened his posture.

"Are your friends trying to get you and him back to-gether?"

"This ain't their business."

He was drumming his fist into the side of his leg. "Why?"

"Why what?"

"Why did you call him?"

"I missed him."

"Missed?" Richard kicked his heel into the concrete several times, each time saying, "Shit."

He took quick steps over to me, was up in my face before I could raise my hand again. He sucked his teeth, bobbed his head.

"You fucked him, didn't you?"

"What? No."

"I saw him coming out of your bedroom last night."

"You what? Please, quit."

"Shelby, if you're going to tell the truth, go all the way."

"I didn't have to tell you that much."

Richard held his glower, shook his head, let out a groan.

He said, "I woke up and saw him sneak out of your bedroom."

"You wish. Don't even try that."

"Why the hell was he tiptoeing out of your room at four o'clock this morning?"

"Is that what you were asking about this morning?"

"And you were all up in his face. With that shit on. It's funny how you didn't put it on until right before he came back."

I snapped the creeping spandex out of my butt. "Tyrel was not in my bedroom. I was with Debra and you know that."

"I don't know where Debra was. Yesterday you had an attitude with him. Now you're ignoring me and chasing the nigga. Something happened last night. I can put two and two together."

"If you thought you saw something, why didn't you walk down, say something, then?"

"Because."

"Because you're lying."

"Because I love you, dammit. Don't you get it?"

Richard sat on one of the deck chairs. He was doing it again. Taking control. Pushing me to get what he wanted. This time I love you was his weapon of choice.

"If I hadn't come down, would you be with him?"

I sat on a deck chair facing Richard. For a few moments, my eyes went back at the house and contemplated. I'd never know how different things would've been if I'd flown alone. Maybe me and Tyrel wouldn't't've said a damn thing to each other. Maybe we'd've had a conversation about Leonard, and the emotions would've bonded us, and we would've loved away the pain like wild rabbits. Or maybe we would've just chilled, had a few laughs about old times, and been friends for a few days, then drifted our separate ways. Regardless, my feelings for Richard would be the same.

Richard reiterated, "Well, would you?"

"Maybe."

"Would you want to be with him?"

"What do you mean?"

"Would you have fucked him?"

"A few days ago, yeah."

"While we were engaged?"

I nodded. "If you don't want to know, don't ask."

Richard shivered. His eyes misted. He gripped his beard and let out a long moan that chilled me more than the cool evening did. I was already cold enough, and my nipples were so hard they hurt. But this was jacked. Even when I tried to come correct, somebody always got hurt. And I was always at the top of the list.

"After what he did? After he mistreated you?"

"He never mistreated me." My voice went distant, like I was reminding myself what had happened back then. "Tyrel didn't kick me out. I dogged him and ran away because I was pregnant and I was too scared to think straight."

"Pregnant?"

"Yep. Pregnant."

"By him?"

"Yep."

"You never told me that you two had a baby—"

"I didn't have it. Keep wishing I had. Then me and Debra would be popping out rug rats close to the same age. Our children could play together, like we did. But I didn't. So like Momma used to say, don't cry over spilled milk."

Richard didn't make a sound. If he was gray, he could've passed for a statue. When I wiped my eyes, the tips of my fingers came back wet and salty. I straightened my back, cleared my throat. Gazed out over the hill and saw the city was lit up like a million candles.

I said, "I'm sorry. Seems like everybody gets hurt because of me."

Richard grunted like he was constipated with pain. I held on to mine. Tried to puff some air, but my wind was short.

He said, "I don't understand you."

"I'm the only one who has to understand why I do what I do. Half of the time I don't."

He laid back and closed his eyes. After we shared an ungraceful moment of silence, his body calmed.

He asked, "Do you love me?"

"Nope. I've tried, but it's just not gonna happen."

"So you got engaged to me, but you won't marry me?"

"Well, I guess you could put it that way."

"You accepted my ring in front of my entire family."

"Yep, I sure did."

He let out a sad chuckle. "We just need some more time."

"Time isn't the problem. It's compatibility."

"What about him?"

"*Him* who? Why can't you say his name?"

"Do you love—?" he coughed. "How do you feel about Tyrel?"

"What does that have to do with the cost of coffee in Jamaica? I'm talking about me and you."

"Shelby." His voice was so pained that it made me want to hold him, but I didn't. As far as I was concerned, I'd resigned from the job I never wanted. He said, "Do you love him?"

"Think so."

"In love with him?"

"Used to be. Think so. Yeah."

Richard withered, shrank to half his size. "Fuck."

He shut up and sat motionless for a long time. Gave me time to think. Time to rub and feel the diamond on my finger. Maybe it wasn't such a bad thing that Momma didn't have a ring on her finger when I gave her back to the earth. Just when I got used to the quiet, just when I thought I heard Momma talking to me in the winds, Richard sat up. Opened his eyes. He picked up his hand real slow, like it was made of lead, and wiped his face. Then he popped up like he'd stuck his finger in a light socket.

"I'm leaving." He sounded revived. "Going back home to San Diego."

I didn't argue. Didn't question.

We took short steps and roamed back to the house together. I even let him hold my hand. His touch didn't feel so bad now.

Leonard's voice came in loud and clear when the door opened. Debra was laughing and screaming.

When we passed by the den, Alejandria was resting on

the sofa with her eyes closed, bouncing her foot. Bobby was on the floor, remote in hand, playing a VHS tape of Leonard and Debra. I'd recorded it, so I heard myself laughing in the background. Bobby was preparing some footage to be shown at the home-going.

Bobby sat up when I stepped in the den. Richard kept going toward the bedroom. When Richard was out of earshot, Bobby came to me, frowning. Alejandria stood, but didn't cross the room.

Bobby asked, "You okay?"

"I'm okay."

The lines in his cinnamon face smoothed out. Alejandria gave me a golden smile. I sent a thank-you smile, finger-waved back.

Bobby said, "You're sweating."

"I know. Where's Debra?"

Alejandria said, "She walked to a neighbor's house."

I lowered my voice and asked, "Tyrel?"

"He left when you and Richard walked out," Bobby said. "I think he was heading down to the comedy club. You guys going?"

"Nope. I'm in for the night. No more drama for the kid."

Richard had closed the bedroom door. I slowed, reached for the doorknob, but didn't touch it. Stood there and listened. Snooped on him like he had been snooping on me. Dresser drawers were opening and closing. I did a slow walk down the hall.

Tyrel's door was partway open. I peeped inside. Suitcases were on the bed. After I pulled my hair back, I went into Debra's room. Closed the door. Looked over myself in the mirror, showered again, put on Debra's wrinkled, white Malcolm X T-shirt and plaid USC sweat pants. Pulled on a pair of ragged Thorlo hiking socks. There was a gentle knock on the door.

I paused, counted backward from ten, then sighed, "Come in."

The door opened and Richard stood in the doorway. Bloodshot eyes. Skin puffed out, bags underneath. I felt bad for him. Actually, I felt bad for us. Once again, I'd wasted my time.

He said, "I wanted to apologize."

"You didn't do anything."

"I knew you cared about him. But I love you and I'm not used to this. I don't know what to do or how to make you love me."

I didn't answer, but that plea bargain wasn't a real question. He was old enough to know you can't make people love you. But I suppose when you're wounded, logic ain't logical. I let loose my empathy and kept my words soft. Tried to let him down easy. He was so unlike the intoxicated man who had pinned me down and gnawed my neck.

But it was hard to do the opposite of what you really felt. So much bullshit had happened so fast. Maybe it had been happening all along. Everything was different for everybody. Leonard was gone. Three days ago he was the dog who ran this yard. Now he was gone. Made me wonder where I'd be three days from now. This relationship was dead. It just needed to be buried.

He asked, "We'll get together and talk when you get back."

"No."

"Just like that, no?"

"No."

"Should I wait to hear from you?"

"No."

"Will I hear from you?"

"Maybe."

"Maybe?"

"Maybe. But I wouldn't count on it."

"Can I get something more definite?"

"I don't know."

Richard sighed.

I said, "Please don't push it, okay? You always do that. I need to make my own decision uninterrupted."

"Shelby—"

"Damn." My empathy went away. "Right now I don't know. All I can say is maybe. Maybe, all right? But that's not a promise."

Richard cleared his throat. "Sorry. Nervous habit."

"It's okay."

My engagement ring sparkled when I took it off.

"No," Richard's eyes widened when he said that. "Keep it until this blows over and we'll talk. I bought it for you."

"No. It doesn't work like that." My feelings were definite without room for doubt. "I don't want to owe you anything."

"What are you saying?"

"The bottom line?"

"Yeah."

"Let me break it down for you. You ain't the one, the two, the three, the four, or the five. So, don't expect anything."

He whispered an offended "Don't expect anything."

When he reached out and took the ring, his hand touching mine felt strange. Like it would be the last time I ever touched him. Final. And that hurt, in a way. I cared more than I thought I would, but I didn't mind the pain. I'd just pack it up and add that little hurt to my big hurts. It didn't make me happy, but the new pain wasn't unbearable. It was dull and fading.

I said, "I'll take you to LAX."

"Don't bother. I already made reservations and called a cab. It'll be here in a few minutes. I'll be back home in a

couple of hours. My sister is going to pick me up from the
airport. Soon as I get home, I'll call and let you know I
made it in safely."

"Don't."

He made a humph noise. "Well, at least tell Debra and
Bobby and Alejandria I said good-bye. Give Debra my condolences."

I shook my head. My voice wasn't soft. "I don't think
so."

"What?"

"You know what's really messed up more than anything between me and you?"

He was clueless.

"My best friend's husband died. You own a big-ass
flower shop. You did not bring or bother to send one single
flower."

My hard words made his jaw lock and his back
straighten.

I asked, "Don't you think that's just a little bit fucked
up?"

Richard stood for a moment, bobbing his head. His
eyes were still calling me. He said, "I'm hurting, Shelby.
You know you hurt me. You led me on."

Richard stared at the ring, shook it around in his hand,
bobbed his head, put his eyes back on me. I'd been nothing
but a big frown with hair since my last words. Richard
made a fuck-it sound, then turned and marched to the
doorway.

He wiped his face and said, "Remember, what goes
around, comes around."

"It already has."

The door made a soft clicking sound when it closed.

My hand was much lighter. Much.

Richard's footsteps faded to nothing as he trudged
down the hall toward the bedroom. Ten minutes later, a

horn blew out front. More soft footsteps left the room down the hall. The front door opened. Closed. A taxi pulled away.

I thought I'd be ready to break out the Korbel champagne, but some sort of hollowness took over. Damn, I was empty.

Things I've read ran through my mind. Stuff like "Speech is a mirror to the soul."—"Think a lot and talk very little."

The thought that felt the heaviest was "One is not born a woman, one becomes one."

I lay back on the mattress and watched the pearl-white ceiling fan spin. Going in circles. Just like my life. Sniffled a few times. Let the silent tears roll down the side of my face and wet Debra's pillow. Chewed my bottom lip, hummed a Luther Vandross song about a house not being a home, twisted my hair at the roots for a while, then leaned over to the nightstand to grab some tissues for my stuffy nose. Blew, then coughed, then blew again.

When I sat up, I faced myself in the closet mirror. I ambled over to the glass, stood nose to nose with my reflection. Reached out and put my hand up to my hand. Added a few stains to the already smeared glass. Dabbed my prints everywhere.

TYREL

41

I sat on the shower floor, warm water raining, eyes closed, seeing the bites on Shelby's neck. Imagined her and Richard in the throes of passion, expressing themselves in such a way that made my wildest fantasies bland. I've been here, holding back grief, and that bitch has been in my best friend's house fucking.

I didn't want to go to the tribute. Didn't want to go anyplace that might be surrounded by sadness and tears. The only reason I said I was going was because I needed an excuse to get away from the house. Bobby and Alejandria said they might go, so I'd have to go. At least make an appearance. Which would be the right thing to do anyway. My mood wasn't its best, and I had planned on going back to the hotel room and sitting around until about three, maybe four in the a.m., then slipping back after I thought Shelby and Richard had finished doing whatever and had gone to sleep.

I had to focus on the reason I was here. Didn't want to lose focus. Didn't want Debra upset. This was really hard on me. I was biting holes through my tongue.

Five minutes later I was in Girbaud jeans, black leather boots, collarless white shirt, Pierre Cardin blazer. Back in style because I knew how it was when my people had a function. Casual never meant casual. It meant be ready for a fashion show.

The parking lot next to the Color of Comedy was packed. Sisters sauntered and sexy-swayed from the lot and up the street, draped in everything from kente fashions and mud cloth dresses to jeans and short Lycra skirts. Everybody from the broke to the bourgeois was in line. Brothers sported *GQ* styles and African fashions. Nobody wore tennis shoes.

A comic was passing out black armbands with red L's embroidered on them. He handed me a satin band, told me I didn't have to pay the cover. I slid the band on, stepped around the crowd.

About three hundred people were in the club, listening to the DJ jam some old-school. I found some solitude up front at the reserved Robin Harris section. Ordered a 7UP, buffalo wings, and fries. The show started thirty minutes late.

Comic after comic celebrated the friendship they had shared with Leonard. Everyone laughed as each stood in line and told an anecdote. Straight-up lies mixed with the truth. Comedy.

One too-fine sister named A.J. told a hilarious lie about the time Leonard's car broke down on skid row, and when he got back three homeless people and a one-eyed cat had moved in, complaining about his eight-track messing up their Sly and the Family Stone tapes.

Everybody referred to him in the past tense. That didn't feel right. Especially when I felt him in the room. But I knew that in a few days one of these tables would be named after him. I just hoped they'd put it up front.

After a couple of hours, the tables were moved and the house DJ took over. I stepped to the bar while they were playing some Warren G and everybody started dancing.

Before I could wave down the bartender, somebody tapped my shoulder. It was Shelby, standing in my space, wearing a black body suit, white jacket, golden earrings, necklace, and bracelets. I saw her and wished I was blind.

She took off her armband, slipped the satin sadness in her pocket, then smiled at me. "Hello, Tyrel."

"Hello, Shelby."

"I saw you sitting over there when we came in. She pointed. "We sat in the Negro Baseball League section."

My eyes followed her fingers to the front. Bobby and Alejandria waved from the dance floor.

"Feel like dancing?" she asked.

I said, "Not in the mood for bullshit right now."

"Don't take that tone with me."

"Why don't you get out of my face."

"Sounds like you want me to 'pack my shit and go.' "

"That's what you do the best."

"You're an asshole. Some brothers never change."

"Why are you up in my face?"

"Dance with me," she asked me again, then poked out her bottom lip. "C'mon, pah-wheeze dance wiff me?"

"You think Richard would like that?"

"Do you feel like dancing?" she repeated. Her dark and lovely skin was still smiling. She crossed her eyes and hand signed her words. "Are you deaf? Will you dance with me?"

She laughed. I didn't. Her tone changed when she touched the spots and said, "Stop looking at my neck."

Her phony lightheartedness faded. We stood and stared at each other's emotionless faces like we were both in the other's way.

"Tyrel, the record will be over in a minute."

"And?"

She held her hand out. I didn't give her mine. She grabbed my arm and pulled me through the crowd, bumped around people without apology, and led me to the dance floor. Her soft hand slid down my arm, held my fingers.

Shelby had always been a great dancer. Smooth and elegant. She would take all the hip-hop dances and Shelby-cise them. Like Leonard, Debra was a hard-core rump shaker. They'd dance all night and sweat until they couldn't sweat any more.

Shelby was subtle. On the floor was the only time she

looked tame. While we grooved to Toni Braxton I had a hard time not watching her float with the music. We danced the cha-cha. Each time she grinned and invited me to follow her rhythm. Watching her threw me off a couple of times, but I grooved in place until I got back on track. She danced close, slid her hands on my hips, moved closer, and rocked with me.

I pushed her away.

I asked, "What's wrong with you?"

She tilted her head, mocked my tone. " 'What's wrong with you?' "

The music changed to a slow groove. I turned to walk away, but she took my hand and pulled me to her. I looked for Richard. Didn't see him in the room. Either way, I backed off.

She put her face close enough for me to feel the texture of her skin. Her perfume was magnetic. Her breath, pleasing. I inhaled when she exhaled and stole what she was leaving behind. The aroma of a sweet liqueur breezed over my lips. She slid her hand up and down my back. For a moment I was hexed, forgot we'd broken up. Expected to glance to my left and see Leonard and Debra sneaking in kisses while they danced. I closed my eyes so I couldn't see all the armbands in the room, sent myself back to a safe time. I pulled Shelby closer to me. She lured me closer, her hips slowly bouncing side to side, rocking. My groin tingled. I almost ran my hand down her back and across her butt. But I caught myself. Then I did it anyway. She jerked her face back from mine and frowned. I thought she was about to curse me out, but she eased her face back where it was at first. She ran her hand over my backside the same way I'd done hers.

Shelby whispered, "I need to talk to you about something."

"What?" I asked. She was curt and serious. "Debra okay?"

"Debra's doing okay. Something else."

"What kind of something?"

"Something something."

"Okay."

She held my hand and led me through the sweaty crowd, toward Alejandria and Bobby. Shelby's middle finger raked across my palm. I smiled at Bobby. "Nice suit."

"Thanks." Bobby had surprise living in his eyes.

"I bought it for him," Alejandria said. "I'm trying to get him out of those same old dirty blue jeans."

"Uh, Bobby," Shelby said, "I'm riding back with Tyrel."

My body shifted. I must've missed part of the conversation because I didn't remember offering to take anybody anywhere.

Alejandria smiled at Shelby, took her hand, then said, "We can all sit down and have breakfast together in the morning, no?"

"Sounds like a plan," Shelby said. "We'll see you back at the house."

She hugged Alejandria. Bobby and his wife headed for the dance floor. Shelby led me to the exit.

After we got in my car, she reached over and stopped me from starting the engine.

Shelby said, "Wait."

"What's wrong?"

She adjusted her body so she could stare me in my face. "Did you kiss me last night?"

It was foggy, but I remembered. "Yeah, I did. A little."

"A little?"

"Can't kiss a woman much when she's asleep."

"Debra told me. I thought she was lying."

"I'm sorry. I was— I guess I was, you know . . ."

"No, I don't know." She put her han[d]
made me look at her. "You always kiss sleepi[ng]

Before I could answer, she leaned over a[nd]
First her soft lips were on mine, barely touchi[ng]
over. Then her mouth parted a little; she eased
to mine. Pulled me a little closer, adjusted her rh[ythm,]
kissing me, slow, long, and deliberate. Kissed me[,]
breath roughened with passion. Her tongue tasted
blis and a peppermint stick.

When she finished, she sat back, blushed, and
more lipstick. The light from a streetlight fell throu[gh]
windshield and cast a soft shadow across her face do[wn]
her lips, gave her a sultry, Max Factor appearance. He[r]
was mysterious, serious, and sensuous. Arched eyebr[ows.]
Perfect makeup. Smelling like a rose, and built like an in[tel-]
ligent Nubian goddess. Arrogant enough to make her una[p-]
proachable. And she was sitting in my car. She had slipp[ed]
me the tongue.

Her voice was plain when she said, "You love me?"

"I'll always love you. Even after you're married."

"Tyrel. Damn. Why did you have to say it like that? A
simple yes would've been cool."

We both laughed. Then talked. Old times. Kept the
conversation light. What concerts I'd been to. What celebri-
ties she'd met on the plane. She reached over and took my
moist hand with her sweaty palm. I felt her trembling. Her
eyes widened. She took a couple of short breaths, then went
back to normal. She used her other hand to pull her hair
back.

"Tyrel, I want to know something."

"What?"

She clutched my hand, opened and closed hers. "Well,
actually I wanted to tell you something."

"Okay."

"I mean, I have to tell you something."

"All right."

"I want to get this out of the way today." She sighed. efore I lose my courage."

I nodded. "All right."

"I was going to wait until after the funeral, but I don't ink I can wait. And I didn't know how long you'd be round. We need to clear the air before we go our separate vays."

She quieted for a couple of minutes.

Bobby and Alejandria came out of the club holding hands and crossed the street into the parking lot by the BBQ place that was giving the area a cultural aroma. A moment later, Bobby's Paseo headed up MLK Boulevard.

Shelby was smoothing her right hand over her legs. I was holding her left hand and felt the trouble rising from inside her.

She said, "So many memories are inside that building."

"Yeah."

"He's really gone, huh?"

I paused. "Yeah. He's gone."

We held hands, but in a different kind of way.

I asked, "Are you gonna cry?"

"I don't know. Ignore it. Don't feel sorry for me."

I took my hand away from hers.

She said, "What's wrong?"

"Where's Richard?" I asked, and threw her rhythm. She jumped. My voice carried ill will. My tone startled even me.

"San Diego. He's gone back home."

"Back home?"

"Yep."

"Oh. So, he's coming back?"

She told me they had had it out, broke up. That he left in a cab a few hours ago. I didn't have any real reaction.

"So what about your wedding?"

She raised her left hand, wiggled her empty fingers.

I asked, "Is that why you're all in my face?"

"What do you mean?"

"Using me to get even or something?"

"Don't flatter yourself."

Shelby took my hand back, my questions were still coming, then she shushed me. Asked me to listen for a moment. She closed her eyes, puffed, then talked over her trembling lip.

"Tyrel, I lied to you. I got an abortion."

With slow and uneasy words, she told me the whole thing. I held her hand tighter.

She confessed, "I lied. I was afraid."

I didn't say anything, but I kept my eyes on her. Watched how humble she was. Yesterday was yesterday and what was done couldn't be undone. Everything else, except how she was doing right now, was irrelevant. How she felt in the present. The past seemed so trivial in comparison to what I supposed she was going through and had gone through. And since I would've never really known, just supposed, she didn't have to tell me.

"Well, Tyrel Anthony Williams, do you forgive me?"

"Yeah."

"Please be honest."

"What part of *yeah* don't you understand?"

"Why?"

"I love you."

"Who am I?"

"Shelby. The only woman I've ever wanted to be with, the only person I've ever wanted to share everything with."

"Who's Shelby?"

I grinned. "Don't do this to me, okay?"

"Stop stalling." She beamed and twisted her fist into my shoulder. "Who am I?"

"*S* is for Sexy. *H* is for Headstrong. *E* is for your Ebony skin. *L* is for the Love you give. *B* is for your firm Butt. *Y* is for You. You are all I need."

"You still remember that?" She cackled and blushed. "How do you do this to me?"

"You're the only one I've ever given three keys to."

Shelby wiped her face. "The key to your house."

I nodded, said, "Yep."

"The key to your car."

"Yep."

"And the key to your heart."

"Yep. I'm surprised you remember."

Shelby smiled. "I thought it was nice."

Shelby let her seat back and looked up at the stars that were guarding the night. "That night you gave them to me was nice. Beautiful. Different. But if somebody had've walked in, they would've thought we were about to sacrifice a goat."

"So what're you trying to say? You didn't like it?"

"I *loved* it." Shelby fanned her face like she was still there. "You lit *too* many candles. It was so hot in there."

"You were special."

"So, where are the three keys now?"

"I've got a different crib. The same car. The third key is still in my pocket."

"So, why didn't you bring your woman?"

"I'm not seeing anybody."

"Who was the girl who used to answer your phone?"

"What girl?"

"The one I used to call and hang up on."

I said, "Why didn't you say hello?"

"Thought you hated me. Didn't know what to say."

Shelby took off her flats and put her feet up on the dashboard. Pedicured feet. No hammertoes. No odor.

She said, "I've missed being around you."

"I've missed you too."

She slapped my shoulder. "You are full of it tonight."

"Why can you say you miss me and it's cool, but if I say it I'm full of it?"

"Because you're a brother and I know how brothers are. You'll lie to get what you want."

"Who said I wanted anything?"

"Tell me you don't."

"I guess you must be psychic."

"Some."

"What do I want?"

"You want to drive me to Obispo, then act like you don't know me tomorrow."

"Really?"

"Yes, really."

"What makes you think that?"

"Because your jimmy got hard when I kissed you."

"Really?"

She sang, "I'm not blind."

Everybody was filing out of the club. It was twelve thirty.

Shelby opened the car door. "I'll be back."

"Where you going? Bobby's already gone."

"I just gotta take a piss."

Five minutes later, she bumped through the crowd meandering the parking lot and eased her splendor back in my car. Shelby leaned over and kissed me before the door closed.

She had me simmering. I said, "We'd better get back."

"I'm not sleepy. You?"

"Nope."

"Hmmm. Everything's closed."

"Want to go to 5th Street Dick's and listen to some jazz?"

"Too cool to be sitting outside." She sounded nervous. "Debra said you had a hotel room."

"Yeah."

"I mean, you still have the room?"

"Yeah."

"Let's go there," she whispered. "I want to chitchat some more. That's if you're not too sleepy and don't mind."

"Okay."

"Just promise you won't try anything."

"The hotel has a lobby."

"Yeah. That would be nice. I don't want you to, you know, get the wrong idea." She stroked the palm of my hand. My throat tightened. I swallowed. Shelby whispered, "Do you buy CDs?"

"Yeah. Through BMG or at Blockbuster."

"Tower has an outlet off the 101 up in Sherman Oaks."

"Kind of like the Nordstrom's Rack out in Chino?"

"Yeah. Kind of like that."

I started the car and pulled out of the parking lot. It hit me that I was with Shelby. We'd talked. Touched. Kissed.

At the traffic light on MLK and Crenshaw, in front of M&M's soul food, we kissed again, savored each other like we were more fulfilling than red beans and rice. Kissed until a car behind us blew its horn and flashed its lights from low to high. Whoever it was whipped around us, threw us a few curses, went through the light, zoomed past the Baldwin Hills Crenshaw Plaza, headed into the depths of the Jungle.

We kept on kissing.

It was real.

SHELBY

42

I couldn't believe I'd been *that* bold. My nerves were so bad, I damn near peed on myself. I had the shakes. My insides quivered hard enough to make my silver bracelets rattle.

I had been up front. With a glass of help, of course. Okay, when I walked into the comedy club with Bobby and Alejandria, I did sit back, sip and savor a white wine. Stared at Tyrel for minutes on end, watched him smile and laugh at the comedians.

My eyes were on him when Alejandria leaned over and touched my shoulder: "Go over there and be with him."

"Am I that obvious?"

Alejandria winked, gave me a little nudge. "Go."

Before I made a move, I chilled and waited for Tyrel to go somewhere where I'd have a reason to be in his space. The bar had worked fine. It was a good spot where if I was rejected or he started going off and screaming like a madman, no one would really notice over the chitter-chatter. I could laugh like he'd just told me a joke, play it off by giving him the finger and walking away. Another swig of Alejandria's Chablis didn't match the effect that Tyrel had on me while we talked.

When we slow-danced, there was a serious swelling in the pit of my stomach, a romantic tension that could only be kissed away. It was a damn good thing that women don't get erections, because mine would've pushed Tyrel fifteen miles out to Santa Monica.

All the way to the hotel I'd put my feet up on his dash, let the window partway down, and allowed the cool night to blow over us. I closed my eyes and enjoyed the brisk air.

From Stocker to Slauson to Sepulveda, I held his hand

and repeated in my head, "We're only gonna talk. Just talk. I'm not going up to his hotel room. He can forget that shit. We're staying our asses in the lobby. Nothing but words about old times. If he's lucky, maybe another short kiss, then I'm outta there, back to Debra's and I'm crawling into the bed with me, myself, and I, snuggling with a pillow, and getting some z's."

We were on the elevator before I knew it.

When the hotel room door opened, the curtains were spread apart and the hall light cast a beacon across two beds. I said to myself, I don't think so. I took myself straight to a chair, plopped down at the table facing the freeway. Crossed my legs scissor tight.

Tyrel moved his bowlegs over to a chair facing me. Quiet. Neither one of us had said a word since the elevator. Hadn't really said much since we'd left the car. All we said was how crowded the hotel lot was. A few cars had been blocked in by others. How we hoped we wouldn't get blocked in. Then when somebody pulled out, he said how lucky we were to find a parking spot back in that corner. That wasn't a real conversation. All those words were just a bunch of silence breakers.

I said, "How're you holding up?"

"I'm holding up pretty good, thanks. What about you?"

"I'm okay. For now. I was the same way when my momma died. I was cool until the dirt hit the coffin."

We lost conversation after that. Emotions changed. I know mine did. Grief was rolling in. Made me sentimental. Made me wonder if dirt would be hitting my coffin three days from now.

I made my voice a little perky and said, "How's your family?"

He smiled like a kid when he said, "Daddy's coming out."

"Really?" My grin was so wide you could see my wisdom teeth. Damn, I sounded excited. That made me feel good. "That's great."

Tyrel had so much cheer in all of his words. Enough joy to make the little boy in him shine through. That made me a little bit jealous. Whenever he mentioned his daddy, he was as passionate as I was whenever I talked about my momma.

"Yeah." He smiled. "Tomorrow night all of us will be here."

"Your whole family. Wow. Well, count that as a blessing."

"I never did thank you."

"For what?"

"Encouraging me to call my daddy. When we were in Obispo."

My friendly eye contact fell to my lap. I bounced my legs and kept my face low when I asked him about his twin sister.

"Fine, happy as ever."

"The dynamic rug rats?"

"Fine, and growing like weeds."

Then I pretended I was interested in his new watch so I could touch his hand again. And he touched mine. It didn't take long for the hand touching to become hands stroking each other. The tingles made me chew my lip and I almost reached for that dimple I used to own. That desire and easy touching went on for a minute or two before I pretended my face itched so I could take my hand back. Then I looked at my watch and let out a fake yawn.

Tyrel moved across the lion's den he'd lured me into, went to the radio, tuned it to KACE. Late-night love songs were coming on strong. He stayed away and rocked to the music by himself. Smiled and watched me. I slid my chair back, went over to him.

Something in me percolated. I glanced at my watch again, felt nervous. I said, "Thought we were gonna stay in the lobby?"

He shrugged. "Let's go back down. The bar is still open."

"That's okay. Too much smoke down there. And the funk'll stay in my hair. I'm feeling tired." Which was true. Exhaustion from the run I'd done today in the eighty-degree sun was creeping up on me like a cheap pair of panties. I cleared my windpipe, swallowed, took out the extra keys to Debra's house, chimed them and said, "Time we headed back to the house."

"Sure."

The brother didn't move an inch. I watched him watch me watch him. Nobody moved. Then he turned off the lights.

This sound came out of my body. A sound of the truth. The keys dropped from my hand and I went to his open arms. We swayed with the Isley Brothers, then with Luther Vandross, then to Anita Baker with Chapter 8. He held me the same way I held him.

Tyrel rubbed his nose across my face. Kissed around my lips. Tongued my ear. That was *the* spot. I tiptoed and sucked on his neck, rubbed his back, and let my hands move across his butt. Then I put my pinky finger in his dimple and twisted it.

That was when he moved my hand.

I said, "Why're you looking at me like that?"

"Does it bother you?"

"No." But I took a step away from him, moved over to the door and opened it so the light in the hallway would show us the way out of here. The brother was staring at my femininity with sexy eyes. Love-filled eyes. When I opened my mouth, my voice had sunken to the wrong kind of tone. I said, "You want me?"

Tyrel nodded.

I didn't do or say a damn thing.

He waited.

Slowly, I closed the door. Leaned against the wood for a second. Kept my eyes on his while I slipped on the dead bolt. My hands went up over my head.

Tyrel's expression became softer. "Take your clothes off."

My voice had changed to a velvety flavor I hadn't had in a long time. A wanting tone I forgot I owned. But this wasn't gonna go down like that. "You want me, you take 'em off."

Pleasure took over and wouldn't let me remember him easing me out of my white jacket. He was kissing up and down my back. Did a sucky-sucky here, a licky-licky there. He hit a sensitive spot that made me tense and jiggle my hips like an erotic dancer. Short spasmodic twitches were coming from every which-a-way.

"This isn't right, Tyrel."

"Want me to stop?"

"Keep doing what you're doing till the cops come knocking."

My heart sped up when I thought my legs collapsed, but he'd picked me up, was carrying me to the bed. He sucked my fingers. Damn, I liked that. That freaky-deaky licky-licky made me squirm and give up all kinds of silly sounds of wanting. Made me want to say stupid stuff. He put me on my stomach, pulled my outfit down a little at a time. Kissed my skin again and again.

"Oooohh, Tyrel."

"Want me to quit?"

"Huh-ell no." He had me begging like I was one of those career panhandlers on Crenshaw. I let out a candy-coated "Please, don't stop. Baby, please, don't."

He rolled the bodysuit over my butt, did it real easy

like a drop of rain sliding down a smooth rock, nibbled and sucked my booty like it was today's special at Baskin-Robbins. He hit another nerve, fiery tingles rushed up into the back of my head. The heat made me push down deep into the bed and arch my back.

"How's it feel?"

"Slow down."

"Thought you had to get back to Debra's?"

"We do. Ten minutes, then we're leaving."

"Okay."

"Slow down. Don't rush."

Tyrel hit the right nerves, long and strong. Made me hum a song of pleasure and damn near chew off my lip. I was slapping a pillow, gripping the covers, and yanking sheets with the feeling.

"Tyrel?"

"Yeah."

"Can I tell you something?"

"Yeah."

I tilted my head and kissed him. "You hear me?"

He said, "You crying?"

"Maybe."

There I was. Naked and vulnerable. My legs were moving, rubbing each other, crossing and uncrossing, squeezing and releasing. When I opened my eyes, Tyrel's eyes were on me. He was so extreme. His eyes said he wanted me so much.

I said, "Take your clothes off."

"Not yet." He smiled. "Don't rush."

"You make me sick."

He licked my calves, outer thighs, knees, up my inner thighs. I closed my eyes, put one hand in my hair, pulled with pleasure. Tried to pretend it didn't feel as good as it did.

I said, "What do you think you're doing?"

"Should I stop?"

"No."

He eased my legs apart. Took his taste buds for a stroll around the block. Passed back and forth. Teased me crazy.

My shudders kicked in like a big dog when his tongue moved inside, swayed around like he was searching for something. He kept that same slow groove, held the same rhythm and made the feeling flowering in my belly spread and curl my toes. I wiggled with the wanting; he held my thighs and moved with my tempo.

"Ooooooohhhh, Tyrel."

I was still trying to pretend it was no big deal, act like the loving didn't feel as good as it did, tried to play the love game, but couldn't stop my hips from gyrating if I tried. Ecstasy had kicked in. The more I wiggled, the more he worked it. The more he worked it, the more I panted a song so sweet. Those surges built, I was about to peak, he slowed down, then let it build back up. I'd damn near yanked the white sheets off the bed. Covers were everywhere. It felt so good, if somebody asked me where I was the answer would've been *YesTyrelYes.*

"Tyrel, damn, baby," I said and slapped the top of his head. My eyes were starting to sting because of the sweat. Hair was tangled and sticking to my face.

"Want me to stop?"

"No," I murmured, licked my lips, then put my arms behind me and pushed up. I was trying to muffle my scream by biting my lips. It didn't work, started feeling *too* good, and I snapped my legs closed, clamped my thighs fast and hard into Tyrel's ears.

"Damn, Shelby."

I eased off a little, but not much. "You okay?"

"That shit hurt."

I laughed. "Oooops, upside your head."

"That's all right, I'll getcha back."

"Try me."

"Is that a dare?"

He was about to get his groove on, but I stopped him.

"I want you in me. Come hold me."

My body became too limp to do me any good. Tyrel undressed, then eased his naked body into the bed. My right hand was on my breasts. Had to make sure my heart was beating. Yep. I was still alive.

I tried to hold him, but I was still twinging, experiencing subtle aftershocks of enjoyment. Damn. And that was just the foreplay. Two orgasms and he hadn't even broken the skin.

"Shelby, why're you giggling?"

"Why you think?"

My hand took a tour down his chest and between his legs. Held on to a memory.

He said, "You sure?"

"Yes, yes." I whisper-moaned. "But hold on a second."

I reached over to my jacket and pulled out a condom. Didn't bother to check which one. When I'd run back into the Color of Comedy, I jetted into the crowded men's room, surprised a few brothers who were tinkling at the urinals when I tapped them on the shoulder and asked for change for a one-dollar bill, bought four condoms, just in case we ran out of words. One regular, one ribbed, one cherry flavored, one with kinky-kinky French ticklish things that glowed in the dark.

After I helped him roll on the latex poppa-stoppa, he put me back on my stomach, and a wicked smile came over my face. Another memory. We used to wake up like that in the morning. Most of the time I hated the a.m., but it wasn't so bad when I met the break of day with him sleeping behind me.

With high hopes, I got on my knees, put my hands against the front of the bed. Felt him wiggling at my door.

Then I was him and he was me. When his erection slid inside me, I shivered and made a sound like a newborn taking its first breath. Started gulping for air when he rubbed my butt and moved in and out with Mozart rhythms. Damn near pulled the headboard off when it became a slow, ambitious groove. We took the show on the road, to the floor, standing, then ended up on the other bed when I needed to feel a little more pressure.

I loved the way he listened to my body, how his movements complemented mine. It didn't feel like I had to race and try to find my satisfaction before he found his.

There was another long, low groan, but that time I couldn't tell if it was him or me. I was frenzied and reached down and pulled the condom off, took this to another level. Made my poppa-stoppa pills and diaphragm work O.T.

I wanted him to experience all I had to give. Wanted him to feel what my body had to say, listen to it say how much I'd missed him. Then I reached to the nightstand and turned on the light. Wanted him to see me, and I had to see him. Tyrel massaged my sweaty breasts, then licked his fingers. He moaned.

I sucked his neck. "You so nasty."

"You were a good teacher."

We were in the middle of the dance to end all dances, and I took his hand, sucked each finger, one by one.

"You love me?" His words were smooth as he exquisitely pulled out, then slowly eased his life back inside mine. Out. In. Again. Slow. Fast. Again. Slow.

"Yeah," I mumbled with a giggling moan. "Hell, yeah."

I forced Tyrel back down on the bed and sat on top of him. "I want to see your face when you come."

My quick and sassy moves chased him into a new gratification. I sexy-smiled when he tensed up, wailed like he was made of thunder and lightning, then firmed his grip on me. His face was so damn serious. He made a bunch of erotic noises for a long time. Growled like he was trying to break free from the spanking I was putting on him. Forced his hips upward. The stronger his expression, the harder I threw down. I was gonna turn him every which-a-way but loose. He reached at me, but I shoved his butt back down and held his wrists like I was the warden of this prison. Then I felt him jerking inside me.

"Look at me, Tyrel, I want to see you, baby."

When the buck in his hips eased up, I turned mine back on and rode my lover until I matched what he had just done. It wasn't as big an explosion as my last one, but it was strong enough to bring the shudders back to life. And I rode that wave, moved with that ripple of sensations until it was all gone.

I collapsed on top of him. We shared a few soft laughs while I wrote my name in the sweat and hairs on his chest.

I murmured, "Told you I wanted to talk."

He sounded hoarse, whipped. "I noticed."

"You hear me?"

"Every word."

Nothing in my life had ever felt so right. Where I was right now made me feel like I was the greatest gift to civilization. I gave up another long kiss. Some conversation.

After I went to the bathroom and soaped up some warm towels, I cleaned us, then we got in the other bed. Turned off the light and snuggled. Sleep was on me before I stopped sweating.

A few minutes later, Tyrel woke me up again.

———

The stupid phone rang before five in the a.m. Damn I hated that noise. Made me want to hurt somebody. I liked to gradually wake up, not be jarred back into somebody else's reality. If that phone was an alarm clock, I would've slammed it into the wall. It was a whole hour before the wake-up call was due to roll in. Since I was the closest, and Tyrel was KO'd, I bitched, moaned, rolled over, and snatched the receiver off the hook before the next ring.

I looked at Tyrel. Still asleep. Still here. I smiled, pulled my hair from my face, tried to sound bright eyed and bushy tailed, but all I managed was a coarse, "Morning."

Nobody said anything.

Maybe my voice scared them. I cleared my throat, "Yes?"

The fool hung up.

That was when I held the phone and frowned at Tyrel. My body felt like lead, but my mind was waking up. Maybe that was Tyrel's girlfriend. Who else would call him, at a hotel, this early in the morning, then hang up when I answered? Kind of made me wonder who else knew he was back in town and had a hotel room.

I'd asked him if he was single. He said he was available. But that didn't mean he was available for me. I know how some brothers are. They woo, then they walk. I had lied to him when telling the truth should've been easy. Why shouldn't he return the favor? A little late-night sex was always the best revenge.

Regardless, I'd do last night over and over again. I gazed at him for a while, leaned over and kissed his dimple, then held the phone across my chest and lay back. My body ached. I was sore from head to toe. Throbbing from running and Tyrel. If I ever have sex with him again, I'm popping a handful of ibuprofin first.

Just when I was about to relax, I saw something glowing on top of the covers. I smiled and kicked the covers, made it flip off the bed onto the carpet.

Some more of that sleepy feeling rushed in. Felt myself fading. So tired I couldn't remember why I was holding the stupid phone. I closed my eyes and held the receiver to my chest.

TYREL

43

I woke and jumped to a loud irritating sound. The noise was in my ear. The oscillating frequencies and high-pitched noises the damn phone made when it had been left off the hook.

Shelby jumped up and looked around. Her eyes were wild and on fire, like she didn't have any idea where she was. The phone dropped from her hand and rolled to the floor.

She put a hand across her breasts, leaned over, and scrambled to pick it up; I gripped her thigh to keep her from slipping out of the bed headfirst. She grabbed the phone, found her balance, slammed it down on the hook, then wiggled close to me.

"Were you on the phone?"

She put her head on my chest and mumbled something. The mumbles changed to snores and twitches. She was already asleep.

The phone rang again.

Shelby's arm went straight up in the air, "Tyrel, phone."

We changed sides of the bed and I answered, "Hello."

"Did you kidnap Shelby?"

"Yes, ma'am."

"Why the hell didn't you call somebody? I've got enough shit to worry about."

"Sorry, Debra. We were going to get back before you got up."

"For all I knew, you could've been in an accident."

"You doing okay?"

"I am now. I expect absentminded crap from Shelby, but not from you, Tyrel."

"You're right. It's not even five o'clock. What're you doing up so early?"

"Baby was kicking, and I had to pee." She yawned. "You enjoy yourself last night?"

"Yeah. It was nice."

"Good. Shelby asleep?"

I asked Shelby, "You sleep?"

Shelby kept her head under the pillow and reached for the phone. Whatever she said was muffled, she giggled, then handed me the phone and wrapped herself around me.

Debra sounded relieved. She said, "Alejandria is taking me to the funeral home later."

"Everything taken care of?"

"Yeah. The programs look nice. What you wrote is excellent. I'm going to go sit a little while with Leonard. By myself. I need to make my peace with him."

I said, "Okay."

She held onto the phone and sighed.

"Debra?"

She sighed. "I was so mad at Leonard last night. I kept going to the door every time I thought I heard a car pulling up."

I knew what she meant. Understood how she felt.

Debra said, "Bobby should still be here. He's fixing the backdoor before it drives me crazy. Everybody else in the family should be here around noon. Be on time."

"We'll be on time."

"Love you, Tyrel Anthony Williams." Debra yawned. "Please, take care of my girl."

"Love you too."

"I'm serious."

"I will."

"Be careful out there, okay?"

Debra hung up. She didn't know where we were until she called. So Shelby was on the phone, but she wasn't talking to Debra. I knew Shelby's situation before I brought her here. I thought I could work some magic. Use my wand and cast a spell.

Maybe she was making her last rounds as a single woman, getting her groove on, draining the lust out of her system before she made up with Richard and jumped the broom. Saying her good-byes in a freaky kind of way.

She said she loved me. Those three words and six dollars would get me a fresh bean pie on Imperial. I had to stick with what was real. She said she loved me before, and that didn't stop her from lying and leaving me then.

SHELBY

44

It was too early to be this early.

When the alarm clock buzzed, I did a Jackie Chan move and karate-chopped it until it shut up. The curtains were open. Sunrise was waking up the Saturn dealership, the cemetery on Slauson, and Pepperdine University. My hair and skin smelled like sweat, a blend of my Bijan and Tyrel's Giorgio body lotion. I groaned and cursed the sleep off me, licked around the insides of my mouth and tasted how stale and chalky turkey and wine could get overnight.

I closed my eyes for a second. When I opened them up

again, the sun was brighter and inside the room. I wiped my mouth and focused on the digital clock radio—8:14. Two hours had flown by in a wink and a slobber. Now I know how Rip Van Winkle must've felt. I tugged the heavy cover and blanket back up to my neck, spooned up to Tyrel, rubbed my breasts on his warm skin, started kissing him, ran my fingertips over his body. It was time to wake him so we could hit the road. I played with the hairs on his chest. He pulled me closer and kissed my lips.

Tyrel washed me and rubbed my shoulders while we showered. I told him my legs were sore; he lay me on the bed and massaged the pain while I moaned and yawned. I didn't have to touch my head to know my hair was tangled. There was nothing on the dresser but hotel brochures, a room service menu, and most of our wrinkled clothes.

I asked, "You have a comb or a brush?"

"Nope." Tyrel yawned. "Everything's at the house."

"Damn." I pushed myself up on my hands and tried to peep in the dresser mirror. "I don't have a damn thing to comb my hair with or makeup or lotion or nothing. We're both tore-up from the floor up."

"Speak for yourself."

"You look broke-down too. We gonna walk out of here looking like two rusty, crusty, nappy-headed, dried-up African-Americans."

"But we'll be smiling. At least I will."

"I will too. Hell, I bet I won't be able to stop smiling all day. Glowing, crying, giggling. Emotions gonna be all over the place. Leonard and Debra's folks are gonna think I'm crazy."

"So?"

"Everybody is gonna look at us and know."

"Know what?"

"*Know.*"

"Shamefaced?"

"No." I blushed and put my hands over my face. "Well, maybe just a little."

Agony and ecstasy lived in me while Tyrel kneaded my calves. I still felt him within me. His imprint was definitely there.

Tyrel said, "You know what I miss the most?"

"What?"

"Us being friends. I don't know how good of a friend I was to you, but you were a great friend to me. Leonard was my boy, but you were my best friend in a different kind of way. I've missed that. Maybe that's what makes you so special to me."

"Maybe that's why I can't forget you, either. I wonder what things would be like now between us if we—I mean, if I hadn't left. If I hadn't done what I did."

"Oh, you'd probably hate me by now."

"Probably." I laughed through my yawn. I was beat and tired as hell. My body was getting heavier by the second, but I wasn't so exhausted that sleep and rest couldn't wait another day.

The funeral is day after tomorrow, I thought.

Tyrel rubbed my other leg. I arched my back and twisted my neck from side to side. He hadn't said a word about my jacked-up neck. Had kissed all over what Richard the Rummager had left behind. I bit my dried-up lip and wondered what would happen when I went back home to San Diego.

I was surprised at the nothing I felt for Richard. No guilt for sleeping with Tyrel. No remorse from telling Richard off and kicking him to the curb. No regrets for waking with Tyrel and having a quickie before we hit the shower this morning. And if I wasn't so worn out, I'd try to love him again before we left. Not because of lustful hormones, but because I didn't know what kinda reality would exist between us when we raised up out of here. Wanted to seize the moment and make it last.

A room service cart rattled by the door and I imagined a tray full of scrambled eggs and fruit and croissants and butter and jams. My stomach growled.

Tyrel asked, "Hungry?"

"Starvin' like Marvin in Nickerson Gardens. Let's hurry. If they've eaten up all of Alejandria's cooking, I'll make you breakfast."

I had to hold my belly and laugh after I said that. That was so typical, the stereotypical response to a good brother who had dished out some good loving, a sister offering to cook breakfast to refuel his empty tank. I envisioned my standing over a hot old-fashioned cast-iron stove with an apron on and a checkered scarf wrapped around my head, sweat dripping while I grinned and tap-danced and sang.

I dressed, didn't even bother straightening my hair. It was a perfect match for my wrinkled outfit. So I let it be.

"I look homeless," I whined with my lip poked out. I felt so juvenile. "And your clothes don't even have wrinkles."

He said, "I'll have to change before I go pick Daddy up."

"What time is he coming in?"

"His flight's due in a little over two hours."

"Can I ride with you?"

He smiled. "Sure."

No way I was gonna go through the hotel's lobby looking this jacked up, so I talked Tyrel into taking the musty stairwell down the five flights so only a few people would see us. Last night, the palm tree–lined parking lot facing Centinela was packed because some social organization was having a black-tie gala to close off a weeklong conference in one of the ballrooms, so we had to park in the lower-level underground parking.

As soon as we stepped out of the stairwell, we saw a towtruck pulling away a four-door rental car. Tyrel cursed. His 240ZX was blocked in by a white Corsica with a Hertz sticker on the window, pretty much the same way a few of the other cars next to us had been blocked in last night.

I looked at my watch and sang, "Oooohh. Debra gon' be mad. I'm already feeling bad for not being there last night."

Tyrel went over to the stupid rental car. The Corsica was parked horizontally. Tyrel's car was stuck between it and the wall. Half a foot and there would've been enough room to maneuver out without ripping off the bumper.

I should've been mad, but I smiled. Maybe somebody had done like we'd done, reunited because it felt so good, rushed their emotions to a warm room, undressed, and slipped into a moment of passion and pleasure and sympathy that went past daybreak.

"Damn." Tyrel shook his head.

He pointed his remote at his car. The alarm chirped, his power doors clicked open. Tyrel walked over to the Corsica and peeped inside before he tried to open its doors.

He said, "Locked."

"Keys inside?"

"In L.A.? You must be joking, right?"

"Not joking, just hoping." I rubbed his shoulders to keep him from getting anxious. "Guess we're trapped together."

Several people got off the elevator, yawning and too tired to smile, but they walked to other parts of the structure. Tyrel put his hands on the rental's hood. He said, "Engine's cold."

"They must've been here all night too."

"Let's hope they're registered and wrote down the plates on the registration form." Tyrel pointed inside at an empty Jack Daniel's bottle and Twinkie wrappers. "They came in loaded."

Tyrel raised a brow and licked his lips. "If we didn't have to go, I'd kidnap you a little longer and wait it out."

"Mmmmm, sounds tempting." My eyebrows wiggled. "If we didn't have to go, I'd let you."

"Maybe another day?"

I blushed, felt relieved that this might turn out to be more than a one-night stand with an old flame. "Maybe. If you're a good boy and be nice to me, you might get lucky a time or two."

We grinned at each other for a moment.

Tyrel said, "Let's go tell the front desk we're blocked in."

I shook my head at my wrinkled clothes. No comb, no brush, no mascara, no Listerine. Not a single luxury. "You go. I look like a Heidi Fleiss reject. I'll be fine waiting right here."

After we shared tart tongues and funky breath, Tyrel handed me his keys and trotted toward the hotel.

I licked around my mouth and shouted, "Tyrel, get some gum."

He waved and kept on trotting. I loved the way his bowlegs moved with a smooth athletic rhythm and thought about the times we'd jogged the beaches from Venice to Santa Monica.

He hopped on the elevator. I leaned against the car and tried to push some of the stubborn wrinkles out of my jacket, just in case we ended up having to go straight to LAX to get his daddy. This first impression would be unforgivable. Trying to hand-iron my clothes was a lost cause.

I sighed and smiled. The air in this penitentiary wasn't really circulating, but it was cool enough to keep it from smelling too old. It was dusty, but not enough to bother me.

Every time the elevator opened, people went to other

cards. More cars pulled in. One parked by me. It was an older white lady in a powder-blue leisure suit. When she saw me, the hag pursed her lips and gave up a sideways glower. I spoke. She didn't. The blue-haired prune gripped her shoulder bag and scurried toward the elevator. I flipped her off.

I looked myself over again, in a Catwoman suit and a wrinkled jacket, hair out of control. I didn't want anybody else to think the wrong thing, so I got inside the car, let my seat back, closed my eyes, and decided it was time to doze off. I got comfortable, started grinning and thinking about all the love I gave last night, thought about how I had worked Tyrel like he was going out of style and gave myself a buncha mental high fives. I was the one, the two, the three, the four, and the five.

I dozed into euphoria and dreamed I was a queen of queens, riding down the Nile while caramel-coated servants fed me ripe grapes and fanned my face with big, colorful peacock feathers.

Gentle taps on the car window woke me up.

He said, "Want some gum?"

I yawned out, "That was quick, baby."

I giggled, sat up, gave a broad smile, then opened my eyes. It wasn't Tyrel. Our eyes met. Definitely wasn't Tyrel.

He was close enough for his breath to fog the glass. I shrieked. The brother had on clothes so wrinkled and dirty they made the homeless look decent. Hair was too nappy to be happy.

I twisted my body so fast I thought my rib snapped. My eyes searched for help. Not another soul was in the garage. I tried to swallow, but I ended up choking on my own saliva.

Richard the Rummager's eyes were the color of old ketchup. He told me to open the door. I shook my head and leaned away. He banged on the window, yanked the handle, scowled down at me.

My heart rose to my throat when the car rocked like a seesaw. Cigarette smoke oozed out of his greasy face like he was a dragon getting ready to burn me to a crisp.

I yelled, "What's wrong with you?"

"Morning, Shelby." Richard stopped tugging on the car door long enough to drop his cancer stick and stomp it. "You have a good night last night?"

I swallowed a mouthful of disbelief, jerked around, looked behind me, then out the driver's side, then behind me again. Not a single soul was in the garage but me and the Rummager.

I didn't know where he came from or what the hell to do. Richard took a step back, smiled, and threw his arms open.

"Come here, Shelby. *Now*."

Over and over, he told me to get out of the car and come to him. *Think, Shelby, think*. With his hate-mug grimacing down on me, I was trapped, so when he backed up a few feet, I jumped out and slammed the car door. That hullabaloo the door made rang like steel snare closing. I took a step his way with a serious don't-start-no-shit-won't-be-no-shit look, and my body language backed me up.

Richard came toward me. I went toward the end of the car. This was unreal. I blinked a few times, pinched myself, but when I opened my eyes, he was in front of me.

"Don't look like you got much sleep." Richard sucked his teeth. From where I was, his breath smelled more putrid than rotten fruit. He said, "Neither did I. You know why?"

It was time to run to the elevator like I was Gail Devers, my mind screamed *go, heifer, go,* but my limbs had locked up with shock. I didn't have control of my body. Plus I didn't know where to run, toward the hotel or up to the streets. I could run farther than Richard, but in flat shoes with smooth bottoms, I wasn't sure I'd outsprint him up the ramp, around the building, and into the lobby. If I did outrun him, I wasn't so sure I wanted to break into a four-star lobby of white people and Asians, looking the way I did, with an indignant black man staggering on my heels.

"What do you want, Richard?"

"What is up?" He spat and the slobber dangled from the corner of his face. He jammed his hands into his pockets. My heart did a boom-boom. Richard snatched out a wrinkled pack of Camels, popped the last one in his mouth, then yanked out a green disposable lighter. Tobacco burned to life when he inhaled.

"You know"—he coughed—"I used to be able to smoke these without choking. But that was before I met you. You didn't know it, but I quit smoking for you. The day I met you, you asked me if I smoked. I said no, that I had been around a bunch of people smoking. By the way you asked I could tell you didn't like men who smoke, so I quit"—he snapped his finger—"just like that. Proud of me, baby? I did it all for you."

He balled up the empty pack and slung it into my face. I tried to swat it away, but it came too fast. Felt like it had cut me right over my eye.

Every second made the space between us smaller, helped the distance between me and freedom stretch out. The sounds of cars rolling by on the streets were loud. But nobody came down.

"Did you have fun?" He was sneering and inhaling and coughing and spitting. "Did that punk-ass have a good time with you? You rock his world?"

I said, "What're you doing here?"

"You mean, what are *you* doing here?" Richard's upper lip clung to his teeth. "Why do you think I'm here? I followed you."

"Why?"

He blew smoke out of the corner of his mouth and his

nose at the same time. "You're intelligent. Why do you think?"

"Why're you doing this to yourself?"

"Why're YOU doing this to ME?"

A yuppie couple in Bermuda shorts and tank tops got off the elevator before the echo faded. They turned their heads and walked away so fast all I heard was sandals flapping against their soles. Their car started and screeched away.

Richard grabbed my arm. "You coming back to me?"

I jerked away and growled, "Richard, will you please leave?"

He grabbed at me again.

I jerked away again.

He snapped, "Are you begging me to go?"

"Yeah, whatever it takes to get your monkey ass out of my face. Now, please, leave me alone."

I started imagining Tyrel finding me laid out on the cold concrete, blood dripping everywhere. Then being laid up in Daniel Freedman's ER, hooked to an IV, trying to talk over my swollen lips and explain to a frantic Debra what happened.

He snapped, "Look at me."

I got up in his face. *"What the hell do you want?"*

"How was it?"

"Richard, don't clown."

"How was it?"

"Why?"

"Because I want to know, dammit. Was he better than me?"

"None of your damn business. Now leave me alone, will you? Please go the fuck away and stop harassing me."

"You just couldn't wait for me to leave, huh? At least you could've waited for me to get on the plane. You know, this shit hurts real fucking bad." Richard kicked the ground, dropped his cigarette. "You know what I ought to do?"

He slammed his fist into the hood of the Corsica. I moved away. He moved and cut me off. The brother was more psycho than Norman Bates. He picked up his cigarette and took a long pull. My eyes were darting from wall to wall, searching for security cameras so I could jump up and down and do a help-me dance.

Richard was standing like a bull and growling like a bear. "Look, even with all the bullshit you are putting me through, I still love you, and I will still marry you. I mean, I want to marry you, and we can work our way through this. Maybe we'll have to get some professional counseling, and— and— I can forgive you for this because I-I understand that you just had something you had to get out of your system, and even though I don't like it, this is the only way you knew how."

"Richard, stop. Please! It's over. Ain't no me and you."

"Don't let that nigga come between us."

"It's not because of Tyrel."

"I understand. Don't be ashamed. I forgive you."

"What?"

Richard leaned against his car. "Baby—"

"You ain't the one, two, three, four, or the five."

"What?"

"Hold a mirror up and check yourself. Look at how you're acting. You think I would wanna be with you?"

"You did this to me." He spat at me. "You!"

"You're doing it to yourself."

"So are you dumping me for him?"

"This ain't about him or you. This is about me."

"You trying to tell me he makes you happy?"

"Fuck. You don't listen."

"I listen. That's why I'm here. I know what is up. I

knew about you calling him. I knew about last night. I listen."

He smiled and reached to touch my face. I slapped his hand as hard as I could and pushed him so hard he stumbled. His eyes bucked. Right then I knew that was the wrong move. He ran at me and shoved me hard into Tyrel's car. Threw me so hard my side slammed into the hood and my leg walloped into the grill. I stumbled, but I refused to fall. Then he pushed me again and I tumbled into the side of the car. I shrieked and the next thing the rough asphalt was catching my body.

He roared, "See what you made me do?"

I scooted away and screamed, "You're a punk, Richard."

This was a brother I'd never met before. This wasn't the businessman who sent flowers and begged to take me everywhere. Hold on, maybe this was the real Richard, with the mask off. If I'd married him, this was how I would've been living.

When I made it to my feet, I wanted to kick his dick so hard it would come out of his throat, but he was sideways, like he knew I wanted a shot at the million-dollar mark.

The hotel seemed so far away. If I screamed my loudest, he could be choking the air out of me before my scream became significant. I moved again. He cut me off again. The bastard pushed me, cursed me out, and shoved me. He bulldozed me so hard I toppled against the car harder than I did the first time.

When I hit the ground, Tyrel's keys jingled in my pocket. Made that Jingle Bell sound. When I stuck my hand in my pocket and fished around the three condoms, I fingered the remote. Yeah, I could use the keys as a weapon. Charge at him and poke his eyes and scratch his face. But that meant I'd have to get too close. If I was close enough to touch him, then he would be close enough to hit me.

"Leave me alone. Richard, stop."

"No. Nobody fucks me over, especially a bitch."

"Richard, you can find somebody else."

"*I am meant for you.*"

"*Grow up.*"

"Grow up? It's not me. You got around your— your so-called *friends* and changed. All of a sudden, I'm not shit. You didn't even tell Debra that we were getting married— and don't lie, I saw it in her face. I wasn't nothing but nice and friendly to your cold-ass niggas. You can't run over people and walk off like shit didn't happen. All you give a damn about is what Shelby wants, screw everybody else. What goes around comes around, and I'm bringing it back to your damn face, special delivery."

"Please, stop. I'm sorry and I'm begging you, all right? You're right. I'm wrong. Now stop."

"You're sorry?"

"Yes, I'm sorry this happened."

"*Then make it right.*"

"How?"

Richard went to his Corsica and opened the passenger door.

"Get in the car, Shelby. We're leaving."

"What?"

"We're going to Vegas and we're getting married right now."

"I'm not leaving with you."

"Get in or I'll knock your ass out and drag you in. *Now.*"

He staggered back toward me, grimacing like he was an overseer trying to reclaim a runaway slave. I scurried to the opposite side of Tyrel's car, pulled out the keys and almost lost my mind trying to figure out which gray button to push.

Richard jumped when the alarm chirped and the doors

locked. Then it chirped again and the trunk locked or unlocked. Then the alarm kicked on—loud, vibrating, and irritating. That's what I was trying to do, hit the panic button and make the ruckus echo out into the streets. At first I felt some victory. Then I realized that was a false feeling of hope. I was in L.A. Nobody cared about a fucking car alarm. Nowhere to run, nowhere to hide, and Richard was coming my way like a steamroller.

The elevator dinged open and three brothers stepped out. One of the brothers was bald, had a goatee, and no neck. He moved like an oxen and looked like a football player hunting for steroids.

A fear dance took over my body and I squealed for help.

The brothers slowed down.

"Hey, my sistah," the oxen said, and lowered his purple gym bag. "Everythang ah'right?"

His thick friends said, "What's up over there?"

Richard said, "Everything's fine."

"Like hell it is. Don't y'all know what *help* means? *Help* means *help*." I was shouting so loud I think the concrete pillars cracked. "This bastard has been stalking me. He ambushed me, and now he's trying to rape me. He hit me. He knocked me down."

The brothers looked at each other, mumbled something, then expanded their chests and made slow steps in my direction.

Richard gave me a damn angry glare, stroked the part of his beard that still had spit hanging on the edge, then quit moving.

"Lying bitch," Richard murmured, then stumbled and hurried to his car. "You ain't about shit."

After they took a step or two, the brothers stopped and watched Richard change direction and stagger toward his car. All of the brothers were shaking their heads. After

Richard whisked into his rental, I pushed the buttons until I found the right combination to deactivate Tyrel's car alarm.

Richard rolled down his window. He wasn't that close, but he was too close and too threatening for me to even think about relaxing. He gritted his teeth. A vein popped up in his neck.

"Bitch. Tell your nigga he can have his stank ho back."

"*What?*"

"My momma kept telling me you weren't about shit. Said she saw the deceitfulness in your eyes. If I ever see you again—" Richard bobbed his head and sucked his teeth. The bastard craned his neck and spat at my face. The spit landed on my jacket.

I was cursing when his car screeched off and fishtailed. He barely missed a concrete column. First the echoes from his car faded, then I heard all four of his tires' rubber burning a hole in the concrete all the way to Centinela. Toward LAX. The screams of the rubber against concrete finally faded.

"Everythang cool?"

That was one of the brothers calling out. I blinked. I felt alone and thought they were gone. I broke out of my trance.

It was the oxen. He said, "You straight?"

"Uh," I said, "thank you. I'm okay now."

"You wanna call the po'lease?"

"Poor what?"

"Po'lease. Y'know, the cops."

"Oh, police. Yeah. I mean, no. I can handle it. Thanks."

"Want me to stay down here with you, sweet thang? Want me to look out for ya?" The oxen smiled and made me feel naked.

"We'll protect you, honeybunch."

"No, thank you. I can manage. But thank you for your help."

I tried to sturdy myself, wake up that firm, flight-attendant tone. Hoped I hadn't jumped out of the frying pan into the fire.

I said, "My husband is on the way down."

They were still coming my way. Smiling. That drowning sensation came back, felt like I was chained to the bottom of a pool, gurgling for a cup of air. My knees bent a little, I dipped in sprinter's position. If they made two more steps in my direction, I was gonna start screaming and run toward the lobby.

Then the elevator opened. First two waif blond women in flossing bikinis, sandals, and thin T-shirts sashayed out. Then Tyrel appeared. I started tiptoeing and waving like I was marooned on a desert island and he was the Love Boat passing by.

He smiled. Laughed.

"Hey, baby!" I called and focused on him like he was the only one in the garage. The only person in my world. My voice cracked while I wiped my face. "What took you so long?"

While Tyrel grinned and held up a shopping bag, Mr. No-Neck-Oxen had the nerve to wink and wiggle his tongue at me. Bastard. The brothers picked up their bags and followed and flirted with the skinny Caucasian women. That was the first time I was ever glad to see brothers chase a Barbie doll.

I took a deep breath, then let my air out in short pants while I twisted my hair. The moment I touched my mane, Tyrel's expression darkened and his body stiffened.

He sped up and yelled, "What's wrong?"

I couldn't move and could hardly say, "Hurry."

He ran to me.

TYREL

45

The crowd was rumbling in ten different languages. Everything from DC-10s to L1011s roared out on the concrete field. Planes floated in one by one. Below us, blue-uniformed workers in steel-toe boots and earplugs loaded, unloaded, and directed planes to their destination.

Shelby handed me the red roses, then adjusted her sundress. She pulled her cap back, made a sound of pain and touched the Band-Aid on her two broken nails, frowned at the scratches on her palm, then dabbed a few drops of sweat from her face with a tissue. She'd showered again and changed before I checked out of the room and we headed toward LAX. The sleeve to her jacket had almost been ripped off. She'd trashed it at the hotel.

We had been standing at the United Airlines terminal for about thirty minutes. The monitor said Daddy's plane was ON TIME, due to touch down in ten minutes.

I'd been gone from the parking lot so long because the front desk said the Corsica wasn't registered and it might take an hour for another tow truck to show up. Busy morning for AAA. That would've cut our time close, so I gave Debra a call to let her know what was up, then went by the gift shop and charged Shelby a bright paisley sundress to pull on over her body suit. Picked up dental kits, a comb and a brush, some lotion so we wouldn't stroll around looking crusty. Found her a mud-cloth baseball cap, just in case she wanted to cover her head. Had wasted time and bought everything but the pack of Juicy Fruit I was sent to get.

The intercom called for final boarding of a plane heading to D.C. A sister was behind us, crying because her man was about to go back to Howard. We scooted down, let them have their moment.

"I'm sorry." Shelby took my hand, held on tight, squeezed it, then released it over and over.

"What he did wasn't your fault."

"I know. I mean, I don't want to mess up your moment. I want you nothing but smiles when your daddy gets off the plane."

She leaned close to me.

"Tyrel? Any regrets?"

"Other than wishing I was with you when he showed up at the car, no regrets." I pulled her closer to me. "You all right?"

"I can fake the funk."

I asked, "What kind of a brother would do that to you?"

Shelby stood in the sunshine that was heating up the glass, one hand covering her face, shaking her head, "A low-down, trifling brother who doesn't have an ounce of character or integrity. I used to think he was so nice."

"Has he always treated you like that?"

"Like that, no."

The more Shelby talked, the choppier her breathing became, and the harder she wrung her hands. We were waiting off to the side of the international, multicultural crowd that was jabbering in a hundred languages.

We'd driven from the hotel to LAX, hit damn near every terminal that flew to San Diego, looking for Richard. It wasn't until then that I noticed how many Corsicas polluted the roads of L.A. Twice I had followed and tried to run down the wrong car. Twice I'd scared the hell out of a carload of Asians.

People were being paged to the white courtesy phone. A young brother next to me had on a Walkman. The music was so loud I heard Tony Toni Toné grooving over the call for boarding.

I asked Shelby, "You want to file a police report?"

"Right now, I'm just glad he's gone. We've got more important things to do. Debra needs us."

"Just let me know what you want to do and it's done."

I made a fist, then let it loose when I felt a chill across my chest. Felt a brotherly hand patting my shoulder, telling me to let it go and stay focused. That must've been Leonard's vibe.

And I was feeling young, like back when me and Leonard would be at the store and my daddy would be in the back balancing the ledger. Leonard and I would be cleaning up, sweeping the floors, straightening up the canned goods. Back then, Daddy gave Leonard pocket change when he stopped by and worked. But our version of working was cracking jokes on everybody from ages eight to eighty, half-blind, crippled, or crazy.

Shelby nudged me. She was fidgety like she had to pee. I smiled and put my hand in the small of her back. Shelby was still intact. At my side.

I said, "I'm just glad those brothers walked out."

"Yeah, I guess."

I said, "What about a restraining order?"

"I don't want to think about it right now, okay? Your daddy's plane is coming into the gate."

Daddy's plane was being directed to the gate. The ground crew was ready and the bridge from here to there was set to be connected. Separation was about to become a memory.

She said, "Nervous?"

I swallowed and nodded once.

Shelby pulled my hand to her face and kissed my fingers, then picked up the roses and card we'd bought on the way. Straightened out her clothes again, put on some more lipstick.

She was talking fast, "Should I lose the hat?"

I spoke slower, "It looks nice."

She adjusted my shirt, picked some lint out of my hair. After she licked her finger and rubbed something off my face, Shelby found her reflection in the glass, picked her teeth and modeled. She said, "I don't look like a homeboy, do I?"

"You'd be the finest homeboy I'd ever seen."

"Damn. Oh, no."

"What?"

"No perfume. I don't smell sweet."

"You're fine."

"Should I call him Vardaman or Mr. Willliams?"

"Shelby, calm down."

"You should be anxious too."

"Why?"

"Because you have a daddy, that's why. You're such a booty."

We watched the flight come in, moving slowly like it was the tease of all teases. Nashville had finally come to L.A.

I held on to Shelby's hand, and we bumped through the crowd and shuffled closer to the gate, found a better position so we could watch the people leave the plane and come up the tunnel.

They came out in droves. Laughing. Yawning. Rushing.

We waited. Waited until no more people were heading our way.

Shelby's eyes were misty. She lowered her roses.

Then the old crew left. A new crew boarded. The plane took to the skies. Vanished in the clouds.

I looked at the piece of paper with the flight information. Checked the gate. The time. Double-checked the airline.

I went to the pay phone and called Daddy's home number. It had been changed. To a nonpublished. Had changed.

Shelby was rubbing my back and asking, "You okay?"

I'd dialed most of the digits to one of the stores, the main one, but I stopped before I made it to the last number.

My hand opened and let the phone fall. Did the same with the flight information. Shelby held the roses to her chest, let out a harsh sigh, then stared at me like she was trying to read my feelings. Her eyes asked me if I was okay. I kissed her, hugged her awhile, took her hand, and we moved on. We walked away without a word or a tear.

Behind us, the phone screamed, letting me know it was off the hook. Disconnected.

SHELBY

46 **When** we left LAX, I asked Tyrel to drive by the Great Western Forum and take me to Inglewood Park Cemetery. I hadn't been there in a couple of years. We stood over my momma's grave for a few, shared some memories. Tyrel stepped to the side and I stood alone and smiled down on one beautiful woman. I did a little prayer thing. It was awkward, but it was the best and came from my heart. The roses that Tyrel had bought for his daddy, we left those leaning against Momma's resting place.

We made it back to the house on Don Diego right around three, and *damn*. By then the cul de sac was crowded with everything from Pintos to Rolls-Royces, had more rides than the L.A. auto auction, and there was hardly anywhere to park on the narrow street. Most of the neighbors had come down early in the morning and helped with the decorations, beautified the place and made it look like the gateway to an African village, so most of the day Debra's house had been crowded.

Leonard's mother and stepfather showed up right after we made it back, along with a van crammed with relatives. Leonard's mom saw what was going on and hopped out of the van with *mucho* attitude, talking about she wanted something more solemn.

My girl Debra stepped up to their faces, in a polite way, and stood firm.

"I know he was your son, that goes without saying," Debra spoke up in that soft tone that let you know she was a force to be reckoned with, "but he was my husband. We knew him in the same way, but I knew him in a special way too. Believe me, this is what he would want."

I stood next to her and agreed, co-signed every thing Debra said. Tyrel stepped up and told them that the music should play strong and long with nothing but Leonard's favorites—hip-hop, rap, reggae, and R&B. I rose to the occasion, put in my two cents and told them if it would make them feel better, we could toss in a few up-tempo gospel songs by Yolanda Adams and Kirk Whalum. But if they were gonna to hang out up here after dark, they'd better be in the mood for nothing but hot jazz.

Even after we said all that, they missed the point and still thought that Debra should be grieving "in a mo' traditional manner"—whatever the hell that meant. Now you know we had spread the word from the desert to the sea, from the mountains to the valleys, and everybody else respected Debra's wishes for the home-going, but Leonard's parents were both wearing dark colors. Leonard's stepdad had on a jet-black polyester suit; his mom's face was sulking behind a thick, midnight-colored veil.

Somebody always has to put a nasty cup in the Kool-Aid.

Leonard's mother's attitude, the way she shook her

head at everything *positive*, how she made face after face at all the people in vibrant colors, the way she slumped her shoulders and shook her head, implied that she thought Debra had lost her mind and was giving her son a speedy send-off to hell.

"I am grieving," Debra stressed as she put her right palm on her stomach. "This isn't easy for me to do, but this is what Leonard Junior would want. It's about him, not us. I don't want to bury his memory; I want to keep it alive. We have all our lives to mourn. Today I want to celebrate the fact that God gave him to us. I love both of you and will do anything for you, and I do want you here with the rest of our friends, my family and extended family. But if you get back in your van and leave, I won't be offended."

They stayed.

—————

By four p.m. the sun was smiling down on our world and the backyard was filled with people from both sides of the family and the neighborhood. A couple of politicians showed up for a photo opportunity. Friends. Old lovers. Comics. Actors. Fifty, maybe sixty people. Some played dominoes. A chess game or two. Bid whist over by the pool. A serious block party. Debra's two older sisters had made it in from Seattle and Minnesota and both drove down the hill to the Shabazz bakery to get cakes and pies. Her baby brother wouldn't get in from NYU until late night, about the same time that Tyrel's mother and sister would be getting here.

So a full-scale pool party/fish fry/dance/barbecue was in full bloom by five. The gate to the pool and the trees and bushes around it were decorated with bright colored balloons and streamers.

It was so beautiful. That's the way things should be.

A lot of people brought food. Bobby barbecued chicken

and turkey dogs. Alejandria fried the fish. Alejandria had a secret Mexican recipe she used to season the fish that made just about everybody forget about Bobby's prizewinning barbecue.

Some of us slipped inside and huddled around the big-screen TV. The den had standing room only while we kicked back and played Leonard's concerts and movies. "The DuBois Marathon." There was a lot of laughter. Very few people cried. And when they did, it wasn't long. Debra looked around at everybody, smiling as she sat on the sofa next to me and Tyrel.

"Of all the things I have, I would gladly give it up to kiss my husband one more time and hear his voice. I'm not saying that to make anybody sad, 'cause if you cry I'm putting your ass outside until you through." Everybody laughed. "I just don't want you guys to take each other for granted. Ever."

I squeezed Tyrel's hand, then kissed him on the cheek. He held on to me. I wanted to kiss him every morning. Every night.

Tyrel walked me around to the front of the house and we sat on his car just as the sun lowered itself enough to give the city that orange glow. For the first time in a long time, I relaxed. And I checked out how fast the sun goes down, even when you're paying attention.

I smiled and told Tyrel, "Chiquita will be here later on. I want you to meet her. She's a flake, but she's kinda cool."

The second she saw me and Tyrel, I bet she'd grin and draw sweet circles in the air. Already I heard her Southern-fried voice boasting, "Grrl, you got it going on at 360 degrees."

Rap music kicked in and thumped in the back of the house, and all the children were screaming, chanting along with the lyrics as they danced into the night. My thoughts pulled me, made me quiet for a long time. Tyrel was quiet most of the time too.

I nudged him and asked, "What's on your mind?"

Tyrel said, "Billie Holiday songs. Pear-apples. Soft kisses in the dark. What about you?"

"Beaches in Rio. Sultry music at sunset. Candlelit dinners."

We held hands and slipped back inside our thoughts. I had so many, and they all were clear for a change. I was the first one to speak up when I whispered, "That's what I'm gonna do."

"Want to share?"

"Promise not to laugh?"

Tyrel made a Boy Scout sign. "Promise."

I cleared my throat, took a breath, let it seep out before I spoke my soft words, "When I get back to San Diego, I'm gonna pack and move my things up here to Debra's garage. I was thinking about leaving a nasty note for Richard's momma, but that would be a waste of ink because the Nutty Professor don't know my name. Nothing for Richard because I don't care enough about him to waste the paper. I'm moving in with Debra. She needs me. I'm not running away from anything this time. Just coming back to the place I never should have left."

"Older and wiser?"

"A little wiser. I'll never, ever get old."

"Whatever."

"Anyway." I nudged him. "I'll transfer back up here, but I don't know how long that'll take because everybody and their grandmomma wants to be based in Los Angeles. But it shouldn't take long. I'll shuttle back and forth in the meantime."

Tyrel chuckled. "Anything else?"

"I'm gonna ask you if you still want to see me. And if

you say yes, I'm gonna ask you to move back too. You could stay here with me and Debra. And since there's going to be a baby pretty soon, you'll have to sleep in the room with me so the rug rat can have its own room. And I'm gonna trade my Z in for something with four seats, maybe a Jeep, because those are so cute. Then we can all ride together. You say you love me, and I know I love you. Well, I might as well do the right thing. I figure if you're good enough to sleep with, you're good enough to marry. But not until after I see how well we get along together, because it has been a long time. And if we do still want each other, and I hope we will, I'll promise to never run out on you and to always talk about what's wrong. Well, at least try to because sometimes I can't help it. Nature sneaks up on me and I PMS real bad. But if you say no, at least I tried."

Tyrel said, "You make it sound so easy."

"Hey, you're the one who asked." He put his arms around me, gingerly. Made me feel like a schoolgirl on a first date. I loved that sensation.

He said, "Anything else?"

"I want two girls and a boy. Twins and a single."

"Finished?"

"Give me a minute. I'll think of something."

Tyrel teased, "Need help?"

I purred along with a righteous sensation. Closed my eyes for a moment. Smiled and enjoyed the night air dancing on my skin. All over my body, I was captured by the crush I had on him. "Let me feel as young as I look and relish my high school daydream. You know how sentimental I am."

"Pretty extensive for a simple fantasy."

"It's just a romantic notion, that's all. My little fairy tale. Life doesn't ever work out like that."

"Stay hopeful. It's sweet."

"You know what I really would like? No joke?"

"What?"

"I'd like you to call me up to ask me out on a date. Maybe pick me up and take me to a matinee. Buy me some popcorn and chocolate-covered raisins. Maybe we could drive down to that place on PCH in the Long Beach Marina."

"The yogurt shop downstairs by the movie theater?"

"Yeah. With your top down and my feet up on the dash."

Tyrel chuckled. "What about everything else?"

"Sorry, but you know I ain't selling my Z for nobody. My insurance just dropped, and I have only two more payments left. A movie and a bucket of popcorn will be just fine. For now."

We laughed.

Tyrel whispered in my ear, "Can I have your phone number?"

"Sure. I've already memorized yours."

We shared a smile.

"If you've got time on your social calendar," I said, "I want to earn *my* three keys back." I stuck my finger in that dimple and twisted. "I want my cavern back, too. That's my real estate."

"Consider yourself in escrow."

We kissed.

Debra walked out, rubbing her belly and eating. "I was looking all over for you two. You guys okay?"

Tyrel smiled and nodded.

"What are you two doing out here all by yourselves?"

I smiled and batted my eyelashes real fast.

Debra brightened up and said, "Good."

She stood next to Tyrel, then sent a warm and wide don't-mess-it-up-this-time expression back to me. From the house to the cul de sac, Debra hadn't stopped licking her fingers.

I asked, "Dang. Is it that good?"

Debra said a naughty "You tell me?"

"What?" I blushed. "No, you didn't."

"But y'all did last night." Debra took a step back and looked out over LaBrea, then up into the sky, toward the stars. "I wish he was here to see this. You two talking. Leonard would get a kick out of this. And a good joke. But mostly, he'd be so happy to see you two together. He really would."

Debra held that same pleasant facial cast, but tears ran out of her eyes. I moved to hug her, and when I did, a spot of my sorrow came out of my eyes too.

"Stop," I said. Damn. So much for being the strong one this time. I was wiping my face before I could help her dry hers. "You gonna mess around and choke on a chicken bone."

"I'm eating fish, knucklehead."

"Whatever," I said and held Debra's hand. We stood for a couple of minutes and helped each other not cry too much.

Tyrel said, "Shelby?"

I stopped dabbing tears and said, "Uh-huh?"

"How would you like to go on a date with me? To a movie, and maybe if you have the time, we could go get some yogurt. I know this nice little place on PCH. We could ride by the ocean with the top down, your feet on my dash."

I blushed and wiped his misty eyes. "I'd love to. As long as you don't try to pull an Obispo on me."

Debra used a paper towel to mop her face and said a lighthearted "Don't you two look tame."

Tyrel moved in between us, held onto us, and we all swayed for a little while. Every now and then I wiped Debra's eyes. Her eyeliner was running, just like mine. The shivers crept in and my tears got a little out of hand. She dabbed my face, held my chin until our eyes met, deepened her voice. "I'm not an airline stewardess. I'm a flight attendant. Airline stewardess sounds too much like a waitress."

I laughed. "And I ain't nobody's waitress."

Tyrel added, "What flavor is that?"

I giggled, "Strawberry."

Debra told one of Leonard's jokes.

I told another.

Tyrell messed one up. But we laughed anyway.

We stood out front and gazed over the city, watched planes floating in, saw headlights chase each other down below. It cooled and we cuddled in the light winds.

"We're going to bury Leonard tomorrow," Debra said, then paused like she was thinking. "I want everyone in bright colors. Everybody. I want it to look like a sea of happiness."

I was massaging Debra's belly. Touching, feeling the warmth.

Debra smiled over her tender words, "And me and Leonard the third are going to need you godparents for a long time."

Tyrel said, "I know."

"Now my priority is to be a good mother and let my child know what his father stood for."

I was still drying Debra's face. I said a motherly "We're gonna need each other."

Debra sighed. "Let's party before we get melodramatic."

"Okay," I said. I kissed my girlfriend on the cheek.

"Shelby," Debra said. "You look like a raccoon."

"You're the ugly one."

Tyrel held our hands, and we walked back to the house.